SHAPE OF MY HEART

Gráinne has moved back to Dublin to get her life straightened out. She dreams of college and a better life. She's working for her brother, Kieran, in the Blues Tavern, but the money isn't enough to support herself and pay tuition. Moonlighting at The Klub! as an exotic dancer seems to be her answer. John 'JD' Desmond is a detective working undercover in the Blues Tavern. The Klub!, owned by Jimmy Malloy, is being used as a drug front, headed by notorious Taylor Wade. JD had intended to get Gráinne to snitch for him, but when he falls in love with her things get complicated.

SHAPE OF MY HEART

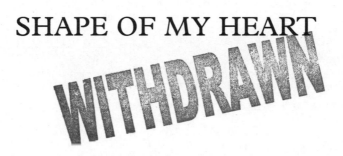

SHAPE OF MY HEART

by

Kemberlee Shortland

Magna Large Print Books
Long Preston, North Yorkshire,
BD23 4ND, England.

British Library Cataloguing in Publication Data.

Shortland, Kemberlee
    Shape of my heart.

    A catalogue record of this book is
    available from the British Library

    ISBN   978-0-7505-4062-9

First published in Great Britain in 2014 by Tirgearr Publishing

Copyright © 2014 Kemberlee Shortland

Cover illustration by arrangement with Tirgearr Publishing

The moral right of the author has been asserted

Published in Large Print 2015 by arrangement with
Tirgearr Publishing

Magna Large Print is an imprint of Library Magna Books Ltd.

Printed and bound in Great Britain by
T.J. (International) Ltd., Cornwall, PL28 8RW

ACKNOWLEDGEMENTS

I don't know an author who doesn't struggle with giving acknowledgements. There are always so many people to thank, and we don't want to miss anyone. My family has always been instrumental in my writing – my mother for teaching me to read early, my father for my love of music, my brother and sister for being generous in their own ways. I love you all!

My friends have been wonderful about prodding me when I need it, and those who I also critique with, they've been wonderful to have plot parties with, or pity parties when the plot just won't go the way I want it to. Thank you!

My readers deserve a massive thanks, as well. Without them, I'd still be writing for myself. That's not entirely a bad thing, as I write for myself first. But I love when others enjoy what I write, and 'get' it too. Your enthusiasm also helps drive me forward.

I want to thank my editor, Christine, for her un-wavering dedication to this series. Her advice is always sound, and her gentle nature through the process helps keep me grounded.

Special thanks goes out to Mairead Sherry for her help with my Irish. A native gaelgoir from the magical isle of Inis Oirr, Mairead is always generous with her time and advice as I continue struggling with my cúpla focal.

And finally, a huge thanks to Kim Killion of the Killion Group – http:///thekilliongroupinc.com – for her amazing cover designs on the whole Irish Pride series. She captured the essence of each book amazingly well. She's a magical rock goddess!

DEDICATION

Always for Peter
My own Irishman

Chapter One

The Klub!, Dublin City
October, Halloween Night

Standing in the darkened backstage, Jett waited for Mystique to finish dancing. Just visible through the curtains, her friend spun on the pole at the end of the stage. Bright flashing lights winked off the chrome pole and drinks glasses on stage-side tables.

As she spun, Mystique's pink feather boa swirled behind her. Her black stilettos accentuated her already long legs. The high-cut matching pink thong, with its small triangle of bright pink feathers in the back, was the only other garment the woman wore. Men whooped and made cat-calls, egging her on to remove it as well.

Music pounded over the sound system, making the room vibrate. Jett felt it thrumming through her. She swallowed hard against the lump in her throat, pushing it down into her stomach where it lodged uncomfortably. She was up next.

This wasn't her first time on stage. She'd already danced twice tonight, but it always made her nervous. Not the actual dancing. She liked dancing. It was doing it here, in this place, that made her uncomfortable.

Worse, she was always anxious about being discovered.

When the music ended, Mystique slid off the pole and pranced toward Jett, blowing a kiss to the men behind her as the house lights came up.

She passed Jett on her way to the dressing room, winking as she flew by. A few pink feathers came loose from her boa and trailed along in the woman's wake.

'What are you supposed to be, anyway?' Jett called to Mystique.

'A flamingo. You?'

'Meow!' Jett clawed the air with her long nails.

'Go get 'em, pussy cat!'

Jett chuckled and turned her gaze back through the curtains.

The men out there were an unforgiving lot. They were already keyed up and knew she was up next.

Jett had quickly developed a following at The Klub! since she started a couple months ago, but she didn't think she'd ever get over pre-performance jitters. If it weren't for that, she would have pursued her musical interests sooner.

Dancing allowed her a certain amount of anonymity she couldn't achieve as herself. Here, she worked in disguise and no one was the wiser.

Taking a breath, she nodded to the house DJ. The instant the music started, she stepped onto the stage. She wore similar black stilettos as Mystique. With each high step she took, her hips swayed exaggeratedly to the distinctive saxophones and violins.

Etta James' powerful voice came up as Jett reached mid-stage, singing the infamous words from the Diet Coke commercial. She looked each man in the eye as she moved toward the pole. She picked out a few men sitting stage-side as she mouthed the lyrics to her theme song, the one she always played for her final performance.

Etta wailed out the first line as Jett pointed to a man on her right, who practically melted in his chair.

On the second line, she pointed to a man on her left whose hopes of being singled out were dashed as she passed him by.

Then she pointed to a third man, back to the right, who nodded vigorously that he would be true to her.

As she reached the end of the stage, she quickly looked to see who was sitting at the head table in front of the pole. She had, from the start, dubbed the man lucky enough to claim that seat as Mr. Tonight. Sometimes it was some aging business-man who looked like he could use some cheering up. Not tonight. Her gaze settled on a young ginger-haired man who she could see followed her every move.

She pointed to him, locking gazes, and mouthed the lyrics directly at him – *I just wanna make love to you.*

His gaze became so intense it was like he could see through her disguise – it seemed to strip her naked. Strip her of the black Lycra full-body cat suit and matching tail; remove the wig hanging waist-length in straight, shiny black strands, in-cluding the cat ears pinned in place; and wipe clean the Halloween make-up she wore tonight that included whiskers to complete the feline dance costume. It was as if he saw *her* and not her character, and it caught her off guard. She nearly forgot her next step.

Most dancers avoided looking men in the eye, but not her. It was part of the act. Making each man think she was dancing just for him was what got her big tips. By the time she'd step off the stage, her thong would be straining with money the men tucked into it.

There was something about this man, though. He unnerved her. Certainly, he was good looking, though not stunningly so. But his eyes were incredible. Even in the dim stage lights, the whiskey color of them was piercing, intent, smoldering – a lover's gaze.

She shivered at the thought as she rounded the pole again, flicking her tail at him. Her panic was unfounded. She didn't know the man so she shouldn't be assigning emotions to his gaze.

Mentally shaking herself, she got on with dancing, smiling seductively as Etta crooned. She pranced back up the stage away from him, continuing to tease him with her body. She cast him a glance over her shoulder before stopping in front of men waving their money at her. She let them slide the notes under the velvet strap of one of her black pumps.

One man tried to stroke her leg. She slapped his hand away, playfully wagging a clawed finger at him. The look she gave him told him he was a very bold boy. She winked then spun away.

After stopping at a couple others to accept their gratuities, she returned to the end of the stage to continue her dance for Mr. Tonight.

She gyrated to the music, her gaze locked with

his. It was time to shift gears in her performance.

She felt for the zipper at the back of her suit and slid it down. While holding the top of the suit over her breasts, she slid her arms free, first one and then the other.

She turned away from him to reveal her bare back as the suit parted. The other men around the stage whistled louder when she bent over to slip the material over her hips and down her legs, being careful not to break off the cat tail attached to her thong.

Jett continued moving to the music as she straightened and kicked the suit off the stage, out of her way, and turned back to Mr. Tonight. She flipped her hair over her shoulder to reveal the two-piece bra and thong set she'd been wearing under the cat suit. The black velvet was piped with orange cording, and the front of the thong was stitched with green sequined cat eyes.

Halloween at The Klub! was nothing if not festive. All the dancers were wearing a sexed-up version of traditional Halloween costumes tonight, and all around the room were black and orange streamers, jack o'lanterns, skeletons, black cats, and everything else representing traditional modern-day Halloween.

This year Jimmy Molloy, The Klub!'s owner, had splurged by putting bowls of Smarties on the table beside the salted peanuts. Classy, Jett thought sarcastically when she saw them.

She leaned back on the pole and pulled the black velvet tail between her legs. She arched her back and closed her eyes in mock-arousal, rubbing the tail over her stomach.

When she opened her eyes again, Mr. Tonight's eyes burned with desire. She shouldn't have been surprised. Her dance was meant to entice. But this man's eyes sparked embers within her she'd fought so long to dampen, and she found that for the first time her dance was actually arousing her, too.

Focus, focus, she silently chanted, and turned back to the stage.

Judging from the lyrics, she knew the music would end soon, so she skipped to the top of the stage where she quickly unstrapped her pumps. The stagehand gathered up her cash and shoes as she concentrated on the pole on the opposite end of the stage. For this she would need total concentration or she'd end up sprawled embarrassingly across a few tables, or worse.

Waiting for the right moment in the music, she leapt into action. She skipped down the stage, grabbed the pole and swung her body out over Mr. Tonight. As her legs came around, she hooked the pole behind one knee and slid to the stage floor with the pole between her legs. Holding onto it with one hand, she bent over backwards, practically into the man's lap, as she rose and fell erotically against the pole. Her free hand waved in the air as if she rode a bucking bronco.

The crowd went wild.

Everyone except Mr. Tonight. He sat with his arms crossed, his gaze following her every move.

Blood rushed to her head when she flipped her body up and spun around the pole. She came around to the front and put her back to it. Bracing her legs slightly apart, she let her arms hang loose

16

at her sides, feigning exhaustion. Her head lolled forward while keeping her gaze on her prey. The metal pole was warm from the lights. She felt it hard and hot against her spine as her legs slowly slid her up and down against it.

It was time.

Jett came to stand in front of the ginger-haired man and pulsed her hips in his direction. She grasped the clasp at the front of her top. The velvet cups were soft against her palms as she pushed her breasts together in his direction, licking her lips invitingly.

When she released the clasp and her breasts fell free, the crowd was on their feet again, cheering, but Mr. Tonight only stared at her, his gaze smoldering. He looked like he was about to leap on the stage and take her right there.

Her heart flipped.

His gaze was very effective. Her job was to arouse the men. It was part of the act. That's all. It wouldn't do *her* any good to get turned on, too. Especially by a man who sat motionless. If it weren't for his fiery gaze she would have thought the man a statue, because he hadn't moved a muscle since she started dancing.

With a wink, she slid the bra-top off her shoulders and twirled it in the air before dropping it in his lap. Only then did he move. He brought the top to his nose and inhaled. He smiled in appreciation, amusement finally lighting his eyes. He had a killer smile, she noted.

She shot him an air kiss then rounded the pole once more, putting it between them.

Stretching her hands up the length of the pole,

she gripped it tightly and coiled her legs around it. She grasped the warm metal between her feet and slowly hauled herself up, stopping with each thrust to extend a long shapely leg, before grasping the pole again. She'd seen this stunt on TV once on a French circus program and had adapted it for the pole. She was sure it would go over well in The Klub!. And it had. Very well indeed.

The crowd howled and whistled, knowing what was coming. This stunt was her signature ending. No other dancer at The Klub! could do this move and, if Jett was honest with herself, she could only just manage it herself. But the more she practiced, the stronger she became.

At the top now, she clenched the pole between her legs, the warm metal at the juncture of her thighs. Straightening her legs, still gripping the pole with her hands, she leaned back as far as her arms allowed.

She pushed her legs over her head and wrapped her ankles tightly around the pole. Once she had a firm grip, she released one hand and then the other and bent all the way back until her back was against the pole and she was hanging upside-down.

The whistles were so loud they almost drowned out the music. Even upside down, she saw the bouncers moving in to keep the men off the stage. Her heart pounded, blood rushing to her head. She knew she must work quickly to stay in time with the music, but not so fast she'd end up falling and hurting herself.

She grasped the pole below her head for support, curled one leg around the pole then

18

stretched her other leg straight up along it toward the ceiling. Finally, releasing her hands from the pole, she brought them up to stroke her breasts, her ribcage and stomach, before loosening her foothold on the pole, letting her body slide slowly down.

Just before she reached the stage floor, she pulled herself up, grasped the pole with both hands, and swung her legs forward in a V then came down gently to land on her bottom. Wrapping her ankles around the pole, she leaned backwards off the stage, practically into Mr. Tonight's lap, and blew him a kiss before hauling herself up again.

The other patrons had to be appeased before the music ended, so she quickly trotted up the stage. She swiveled her hips seductively as she allowed the men to add a few more euro notes to her thong straps before the song ended.

And as it did, Jett looked back over her shoulder to Mr. Tonight, kissed the pads of her fingers as if to blow him a kiss, then, with a loud whack, slapped them on the fleshy curve of her bottom as she turned away. She winked once more over her shoulder then trotted up the stage and disappeared behind the heavy black curtain. Whoops and catcalls trailed after her, as she ran for the dressing room at the back of the building.

'You're a mad woman, Jett,' Mystique said as Jett entered the dressing room. She'd passed the other dancers on the way back, so the dressing room was empty now except for the two of them.

She went to her dressing table beside Mystique's

19

and set the money she'd retrieved from the stagehand on the table before pulling on her robe.

'What makes you say that?' she asked, removing
her thong and slipping into sensible panties. Once
she had the robe adjusted, she sat down at her
dressing table and started sorting through her tips.

Mystique glanced quickly at her. 'You tease
those guys mercilessly.' Mystique had finished
her costume change while Jett was on stage.

'They love it. They know it's part of the act.'

'Maybe so, but that guy you were playing with
looked serious to me. I'd be careful, if I were you.'

Jett thought about it and was sure Mystique was
right. He could be dangerous. He could cause her
to forget the promise she'd made to herself when
she moved to Dublin last year: No men allowed
until she learned how to appreciate a good relationship.

She'd never find Mr. Right if she kept settling
for Mr. Right Now. She was tired of being a
doormat and it was time she learned to stand on
her own feet. Mr. Tonight was no Mr. Right. The
kind of man she wanted wasn't the kind who frequented The Klub!.

Jett snickered to herself. No better way to learn
independence than to hide in a wig and dance
naked for strange men.

'I'll be careful,' she promised.

Muffled bar music came through the dressing
room door as they went about their tasks in companionable silence.

Mystique stubbed out her cigarette and turned
to change her make-up for her next dance, as Jett
touched-up hers. She wouldn't take the chance

of being recognized on the street, even by Mystique. The Halloween make-up gave Jett an added sense of safety tonight.

Mystique stopped mid-eyeliner application and turned back to Jett. 'Do you ever wonder?'

'Wonder what?'

'Do you ever wonder if you'll meet someone special enough you'll want to give up all this?' Mystique's voice sounded wistful. Jett put down her lip liner and turned to her friend. It sounded like Mystique wanted to say something and, as always, Jett had an open ear. She waited for her to continue.

'I mean, there's got to be a guy out there meant for each of us, right?'

'I'd like to think so,' Jett replied, 'but I don't hold out much hope I'll find the one I'm looking for in a place like this.' She gave Mystique a slanted grin.

'You don't think so?'

'No, I don't. Look at the losers out there tonight. If they had women, or women they appreciated, they certainly wouldn't be in a place like this. The stage is lined with homely, overworked, stressed-out, and bored men. I don't want someone else's baggage.'

'What about that guy you danced for tonight?' asked Mystique. 'His gaze nearly melted the pole out there.'

'Sure, he was fine to look at, but who's missing him at home tonight?'

Mystique nodded.

'Why do you stay if you're looking for something else in your life?' Jett asked a moment later.

Mystique grinned. 'The money, fool. It's brilliant. I've got myself terrific savings. I'm going to buy a house when I retire,' she said wistfully. 'Something posh in D2. Maybe then I'll find someone.'

'Sounds like a nice dream.' Jett smiled, knowing Mystique's expectations were lofty. D2 was the city center's affluent area. D2 meant big money.

'I think so, too.' Mystique paused, and then asked, 'Do you ever wonder what your guy will look like? What he'll do for a living?'

'Sometimes. What about you?'

'Yeah,' she sighed.

'So, go'wan. Tell me,' Jett encouraged.

A big smile crossed Mystique's face. 'He's a hunk, of course. Has money enough to support me. Treats me well. Has a nice car – the usual.'

Jett sighed to herself. Mystique had her own growing up to do. They'd never talked about age, but Mystique was decidedly younger.

'What about love? If he loved you, all that material stuff wouldn't matter, would it?'

Mystique looked disgusted. 'You're kidding, right?'

Jett was deadly serious and she knew it showed on her face as Mystique sat back in her chair to listen.

'The guy I spend the rest of my life with will be one who loves me. I don't care about how much money he has, or what material things he can give me. He'll forgive my past sins, accept me for the woman I am, and most importantly, he'll love me for me, not who he wants me to be or who he thinks I should be. Just me.'

'Wow, Jett. I never knew you were such a romantic.'

'I guess I am. I never realized it either until my ... someone told me about how he met his wife.'

Jett caught herself just in time before revealing more than she'd intended. Her heart beat anxiously at the near flub. When she'd taken this job, she didn't want to befriend anyone. Like all the other girls, she was only in it for the money. She had her own dreams, and the money she was tucking away would help her achieve them. But she'd found it difficult not to open up to Mystique as their friendship grew. How could she, though? She didn't even know her friend's real name.

'So tell me,' Mystique continued, grinning devilishly. 'If you found your Mr. Right, what would you do with him?'

Jett raised an eyebrow. 'What do you mean?'

'I mean, if Mr. Right came into your life, what would your first night be like? Would you insist he take you to Paris for a wild weekend? Or to Venice, and make him take you for a gondola ride on the Grand Canal? What would you do? I rather fancy the wild weekend in Paris.' Mystique wiggled her eyebrows.

Jett giggled. Her friend had touched on something she'd thought about quite a bit, that first time with Mr. Right.

'Hmmm...' Her lips turned up at one edge in a thoughtful grin. 'If I met Mr. Right, I would take him to a secluded cottage in the woods. We'd spend as much time as we could together, talking and getting to know each other. Evenings would be spent by firelight, afternoons walking in the woods.'

Mystique gave her a gentle shove. 'What about the s-e-x?' She wiggled her eyebrows again. 'You can't get him to a mountain hideaway and not do the nasty.'

Mystique was nothing if not blunt. Jett chuckled. 'I wouldn't call it that, but, if the timing was right...'

Mystique smirked. 'You're definitely a hopeless romantic, girl. I can see the hearts and flowers circling your head. Oh, wait, what's that I hear? Love birds chirping?' she teased, cupping her ear.

Jett laughed and batted her friend's hand away from her ear. 'Give over. It's my dream, not yours.'

'I know. I'm just having a go off you. So, I know where Paris is. Where's your cottage?'

Without thinking, Jett said, 'In the West Cork *gaeltacht*.' As soon as the words passed between her lips, she knew she'd said too much. She cast Mystique a side-glance, but she didn't seem fazed by the revelation as she started plaiting her hair. The costume for Mystique's next dance also included a pink plaid miniskirt and a lollipop.

'Sounds nice, actually,' she said, finally rising. 'Well, it's show time.'

She watched Mystique prance out of the dressing room, her plaits bouncing behind her.

Jett cast a look at her reflection in the dressing table mirror. The woman she saw wasn't the one she'd seen that morning in her bathroom mirror. She had spent the last year in Dublin trying to find herself. Was this who she really was all along, an exotic dancer? And if she were, would Mr. Right really want her?

24

Chapter Two

JD stood behind the bar at the Blues Tavern, drying a stack of pint glasses with a soft cloth. He watched Gráinne talk with a customer while she drew him a pint, smiling easily at the man. He knew he wasn't anyone special to her; she treated all the customers the same. She was friendly and sometimes flirtatious, but she never let it go any farther than that.

In the last six weeks since he'd been hired, he'd learned Gráinne was single and wondered why. She was certainly easy on the eyes.

He suppressed a groan when she leaned over the bar to hand her customer his pint and collect his money. She stood on her toes, making her shapely legs look longer. Her bottom strained against her jeans and he felt his groin tighten. Oh yes, she certainly was easy on the eyes, but hard on the body.

He raked her with his gaze, from the sensuous curve of her bottom to the swell of her breasts pressing firmly against her blouse. His attention fell on the riot of natural dark curls haloing her heart-shaped face. She was in profile, but he knew her every feature – he'd gawped at her like a schoolboy often enough.

She was a beautiful woman, no doubt, but it wasn't a traditional beauty. Overall, her eyes were set just a little too far apart, her mouth was just that bit too wide, and she had a healthy splash of freckles across her cheeks.

Even so, her eyes were a remarkable shade of green he'd only seen in the underside of sea waves – pale mossy green, yet with a hint of soft blue. Her freckles gave her a certain innocence belying her natural sensuality.

And her lips ... her lips had been made for kissing.

So had her breasts. He'd never forget the first time he'd seen them. They'd been made for kissing, too.

He'd noticed everything about Gráinne from the very first moment he'd seen her. He never expected to be so taken with her. If things were different, he would want to get to know her better. A lot better.

Just then she turned and caught him staring. Her lips twitched as she sauntered toward him. Her hips swayed with each step, her head tilted in such a way that he recalled the first time he'd seen her walking toward him.

His stomach knotted as she slid past him. She halted behind him and whispered against his cheek. Her breath on his skin was warm and as suggestive as her words. 'If you keep rubbing it like that, you'll wear it down to nothing.'

She continued past, the musky scent of her perfume lingering in her wake.

He knew she referred to the glass he was still drying, but her suggestion gave him a full erection. She made him feel like she'd caught him in the act of doing something naughty, and he was sure the flush rushing up his neck confirmed it. No doubt, her comment had the effect she desired.

Score a point for the lady's team.

He would have liked nothing better than to have a snappy comeback, but he couldn't think of anything. She had him tongue-tied, which was unusual for him.

Just then, Eilis motioned to him. He set the glass and towel on the bar and rushed over to see what his boss wanted, praying she wouldn't notice the prominent bulge in his trousers.

Kieran and Eilis had opened the Blues Tavern the previous year in one of Dublin's rejuvenated quarters – Temple Bar. From the information he'd gathered before he'd been hired, Kieran had been a blues guitarist and Eilis was a talent scout with Eireann Records who'd discovered him. JD didn't know the whole story, but they'd married just after they'd opened the pub. They still performed, but neither had the desire to perform professionally, despite repeated requests from producers who frequented the place.

As he approached the table, Eilis came to her feet in a rather ungainly fashion. Putting it delicately, she was with child. To say she was like the Titanic as she navigated the barroom wouldn't have been a lie, either. Regular patrons and staff alike were betting on twins, even though Eilis promised she was only carrying one child.

'Help me get him in the office, will ye? Then bring in a big plate of chips and a pot of tea.' JD nodded and reached over to help the man she'd been talking to get out of the snug.

'Easy, now. I can make it on my own,' the man said, who slid out of the snug and promptly hit the floor. 'You need to keep the floors a bit cleaner, Ei. A person could get hurt slipping like that.'

'Here, mate,' JD said. 'Let me help you up.' He curled an arm under the man's elbow and helped him to his feet.

Once he was safely stowed in the office, JD went to the kitchen to place Eilis's order, then headed back into the barroom. He looked around the room and spotted Gráinne coming toward him. She'd finished cleaning the table just vacated by Eilis and her friend, and was bringing the dirty glasses to the kitchen to be washed.

'Here, I'll take those.' His hand brushed hers, their eyes meeting when a tingle whispered between them. Again, he was lost for words. What was there to say? Her silvery-green eyes captivated him, leaving him speechless.

It was Gráinne who turned away, and he wondered at her sudden shyness when she'd practically mortified him with her comment a few minutes before.

JD wondered if Gráinne recognized him. She was the reason he'd fought so hard to get work in this particular pub. He wasn't a bartender by trade, though he'd worked in his fair share of them in his life. He figured if he could get close to Gráinne, get her to trust him, he'd be able to get the information he desperately needed. Women were chatty creatures and he hoped Gráinne's womanly nature would let some vital bit of information slip.

After nearly two months, though, he was still no closer to the truth than when he'd first started. The only thing he was getting close to was trouble with her and blowing his cover. He couldn't let this get personal, no matter how much he desired her.

Back behind the bar, he returned to the stack of glasses. An awkward silence fell between them. If he wanted the information he needed, he'd have to get her to talk, and to trust him.

'What's up with your man?' JD nodded in the direction of the office. He'd seen the man in the pub a few times before, but knew nothing beyond that.

She only glanced at him as she walked by. Finding a pile of clean bar towels, she started folding them.

'Mick? Who knows? He's a moody one.'

'Friend of Eilis's?'

'Yeah, they went to uni together.'

'He doesn't look like a performer.' He assumed since Eilis was a singer and Kieran a guitarist, it stood to reason their friends would be musicians as well.

Gráinne snorted. 'Mick? Hardly. He's an archivist, or something like that. He works at the museum.'

He felt Gráinne loosening up again. He had to keep her talking if he wanted to get anywhere with her.

'So, what's up with Mr. Museum?'

Shrugging, she said, 'Women trouble, I suppose.'

29

'Ah, that says a lot.' She flashed him a side-glance that said everything her lips didn't: *Watch your step*. 'I mean, isn't that why most men go on the piss alone?'

'I wouldn't know.'

'Wouldn't you?'

She turned to him then. 'What's that supposed to mean when it's at home?' She tossed the towel she'd been folding onto the bar, crossing her arms as she faced him. He felt the heat from her gaze.

Casually leaning against the bar, he said, 'You're a beautiful woman, Gráinne. No doubt you've a trail of broken hearts behind you.'

Even in the dimly-lit bar he saw her flush. She fidgeted nervously for a moment, looking everywhere except at him, then said, 'You thought wrong.'

Shoving past him, she grabbed up a tray and towel and strode onto the floor to wipe down tables that were already clean. Her body language was more animated than it had been a moment ago. He knew he'd hit a nerve.

She moved toward a couple who'd just walked through the door. Smiling brightly now, she showed them a table, chatted merrily and took their order, as if nothing had just happened behind the bar.

It wasn't so much her professionalism he admired as much as how it spoke of something within her. For all her blustering, he knew there was much more to her than she let on. The more she feigned aloofness and disinterest, the more he wanted to learn more about her.

30

Christmas music filtered through the room, and the pub's cheery decorations reminded him of another lonely holiday. This was just one reason why he'd asked for this assignment. It would give him something to do on Christmas Day besides sitting home on his own.

'Two pints of the black,' said Gráinne, drawing him from his thoughts. 'Better give them shamrocks.'

'Tourists?' She nodded, then she went to the kitchen to deliver the food order to Kieran, who was manning the cooker today.

JD grabbed a pair of pint glasses from his freshly dried stack and filled each three-quarters, then set them aside to settle. He watched Gráinne move behind the bar to collect cutlery, napkins and condiments on her tray.

'Gráinne,' he said, moving to stand beside her. 'I'm sorry if I said something to upset you.'

'I'm not upset,' she told him, sounding short.

'Sounded like you were the way you stomped off a minute ago.'

'Forget it,' she said, before returning to the tourists with their drinks.

Over the next couple hours, JD trod lightly around Gráinne and peace settled between them. He hadn't had the opportunity to talk to her again with the evening prep, but as he looked at his watch he knew her shift ended soon.

He'd tried almost every tactic he could think of to get her to reveal more about herself and he was getting anxious at her continued aloofness. He didn't want to have to resort to seducing her.

31

While the idea of getting her into bed was appealing, he just preferred to do it under other circumstances. He fancied her like hell, but he couldn't let his libido get in the way of his job. She was his best hope at getting the information he desperately needed. So he'd have to resort to another tactic if he was going to get her to talk. Blackmail was one he was loath to use, but at this stage in the game, he had little choice.

There was a lull in the pub now that the afternoon crowds were gone and the evening prep had been done. If he was going to confront her, he had to do it now.

Gráinne stood at the end of the bar, flipping through a magazine. The twinkling Christmas lights over the back bar shone on her dark hair. As she moved, the highlights reflected like electric current through the strands curling around her face. His heart thumped a little harder looking at her.

He reminded himself he wasn't here to bartend. He was here to gather information. His future depended on it. He couldn't afford another wasted day, so it was now or never.

His pounding heart made it suddenly hard to breathe. He hated having to do this to her.

'Gráinne, can we talk?'

'Talk?' She put her magazine aside. 'About what?'

'I think you know.' He locked gazes with her. He could tell she was nervous by the way she started fidgeting.

Then she turned away, refusing to look at him for longer than a millisecond. 'My love life is none of your concern,' she told him, reminding him unnecessarily of their previous discussion.

'That's not what I'm talking about.'

'Then I don't know what you mean.' She spun on her heel, intent on leaving the bar area.

He grasped her arm. To his surprise, she didn't struggle. But something odd happened as he loosened his grasp. He felt something powerful pass between them. His fingers tingled as he touched her. It radiated up his arm and shot through his body.

For the second time today, he felt himself stiffen, and wished that circumstances were different, that she was naked beneath him and gazing up at him with eyes he knew would undo him.

She glanced over her shoulder, but not directly at him. 'Let me go.' Her barely audible words shook him back to the moment. It wasn't a command, but he couldn't help noticing her words were tinged with pleading.

'Will you stay to talk with me? I think this is important.' His own voice was softer now. When she relaxed, he reluctantly released his hold. She kept her gaze averted, folded her arms protectively in front of her, and refused to look at him. He knew she was waiting for something, anything, to draw her away.

Reaching under the bar, he extracted the black plastic sack he'd brought in with him today. He knew the item inside would shatter any peace he hoped to make with her.

He looked at the sack for a moment, thinking about what could never be between them. There was a job to be done and it didn't include getting

33

emotionally involved. He hoped the more he reminded himself of this fact he'd eventually come to believe it.

Sighing, he extracted a black velvet bra and held it up for her inspection. She only cast it a side-glance.

'I take it you know where I got this.'

'Anne Summers?'

'No.'

'Well then, I have no idea.'

He saw her swallow hard then move over to the taps to pour herself a cola. She swallowed deeply from the glass.

'I think you do. Let's not ... dance ... around the subject, Gráinne. We both know where I got this, and I'd lay odds at Paddy Powers your brother doesn't know what you've been up to.'

His heart ached as he forced himself to goad her.

The look she shot him would have incinerated the average man, but he wasn't average. He was a man with a mission, and Gráinne was the only one who could help him.

'By that look, I'd say I've hit the nail on the head.'

'So, what of it?'

'Why haven't you told Kieran?' he asked, trying to keep his voice calm.

'I somehow doubt he'd understand why I'm ... moonlighting.'

JD chuckled lightly. 'Moonlighting? Is that what they're calling it these days?'

'Just stop. What do you want from me? Not that it's any of your business what I do on my own time.'

'I need your help.'

A single brow arched over her eye. 'With what? Wait, let me guess,' she seethed, throwing her hands on her hips. 'You want a private show. Or you want me to entertain some friends. And you're going to use this,' she fingered the bra he still held in his hand, 'as a bribe to get me to do it for free.'

'Not quite. While I wouldn't mind a private show, it's not entertainment I'm looking for.'

'What's this?' Kieran suddenly appeared behind the bar, startling them both. JD saw Gráinne's face go pale, and thought she would faint then and there.

Chapter Three

Kieran looked at the bra, then from JD to Gráinne and back again.

'It's a bra, boss,' said JD, winking at Gráinne. She was both angry and terrified and he well knew it, but he loved the way she flushed so easily.

'I can see that,' Kieran said. 'Is there a reason you're showing it to my sister?'

'As a matter of fact, there is.' Instincts told him to tread lightly with Gráinne's overprotective brother.

'It's nothing, Kier,' Gráinne interjected. She flashed JD a pleading look and he knew she thought he was going to rat her out.

'Actually, it is something, Kieran.' JD held the garment out for Kieran's inspection. Kieran took it and fingered the velvet.

'Aye, I'd say it is and all.' Kieran whistled. 'Where'd you get this? Eilis might like it.'

JD saw Gráinne swallow hard again. 'I thought so, too, when it landed in my lap.'

Kieran handed back the bra and turned to pour himself a cola. He apparently hadn't noticed his sister's discomfort.

'You see, Christmas is coming up soon and I need a gift for my sister. Her friend gave me this and said to find something like this for a present.'

Gráinne noticeably relaxed and mouthed the words 'thank you' under her breath, then turned away, busying herself.

Kieran flicked his head toward his sister. 'What does Gráinne have to do with it?'

'I think you've been married too long, mate.' He chuckled.

Kieran frowned. 'What's that supposed to mean?'

'It means I was getting Gráinne's opinion. I'm not sure giving my little sister a velvet bra is an appropriate gift for a brother to give,' he explained. 'Gráinne agreed, so now I have to try and find another gift for her.'

Kieran only grunted.

'It's true, Kieran,' Gráinne chimed in. 'I told him brothers just don't buy their sisters undergarments.'

'And what about those Superman–'

'That was a gag gift. Lord, Kieran. Don't tell me you're wearing them.' Gráinne gasped at the sudden silence, unspoken words flashed between brother and sister, leaving JD in the dark over an obvious family issue.

'Umm ... no. Are you kidding? I'm a grown man. What would I do with the likes of them?' Kieran muttered, stepping from behind the bar with his cola. He didn't so much as look over his shoulder as he disappeared through the kitchen door.

Gráinne spun to face JD. How dare he have a go at her like that? If he thought she was angry before, he hadn't seen anything yet.

She opened her mouth to give him what for, but before she could get the words out, he said,

'You're welcome.' The bastard had the nerve to smile at her.

'What?' she sputtered. Her heart pounded at the near-confrontation with Kieran and at JD's cheek. Her body shook uncontrollably.

'I said, you're welcome.'

'Of all the nerve–'

'You should be thanking me, love. I could have just spilled the beans on your little ... what did you call it? Oh, yes, moonlighting.'

She watched as he stuffed the bra back into the sack and stowed back it under the counter. She had it in mind to ask him to give the bra back but didn't want another confrontation.

Instead, she folded her arms across her chest and took deep breaths to calm down, counting backwards from ten. Before she reached one, she launched into him again. So much for anger management, she thought.

'You have no right telling him, or anyone else, what I do on my time off. I don't know who the hell you think you are, but I'll be thanking you to stay out of my life.'

'Or what?'

'Or I'll have you fired,' she warned.

She hated having to say that. She'd never use her position as the boss's sister to get her way, but this man threatened her privacy as well as stood in her way of achieving her dreams. If there was anything she'd learned in the last year, it was that nothing should stand in the way of achieving her goal, especially when it came to men.

To her way of thinking, it had been men keeping her from her dreams for years. She was tired of being their doormat, to be the recipient of their boot scrapes only to see the back of them once they'd had their fill of her.

'I will,' she promised. 'I'll have you out on your ear before you can blink.'

JD only laughed at her. 'I wonder if your brother would be interested in checking out the entertainment at The Klub!.'

Her blood pulsed so loudly in her ears she could barely hear herself think.

'You wouldn't dare! Who the hell do you think you are? Just stay out of my life and do the job you were hired to do.'

'Love, you have no idea what ends I'm prepared to go to, to do my job.'

'What do you want from me? I don't even know you.' She found it increasingly difficult to keep her voice down. Her arms were clasped so tightly against her chest she could barely breathe.

What she really wanted to do was follow Kieran into the kitchen and tell him to get rid of this guy. Failing that, she'd love to invite JD outside then lock the door as soon as he stepped over the threshold.

She knew she couldn't do either of those things, though. Not with the secret JD held over her. And, if asked, she couldn't very well deny she moonlighted at The Klub! as the dancer, Jett. All Kieran had to do was walk through the club's door and wait until she took the stage.

They both noticed the group of businessmen walk through the pub door and knew the time for talking was over.

'We'll talk later,' he told her, looking at his

39

watch. 'The suits are coming out of their offices for their evening gargle.'

Gráinne watched him turn away and moved out from behind the bar to see to the group's order. His easy dismissal of her and this issue angered her further.

She spun on her heel and stomped toward the kitchen, just missing Eilis waddling out of the door.

'You all right, Gráinne?' Eilis asked.

It was on the tip of her tongue to tell Eilis to mind her own business, but her sister-in-law didn't deserve being the end target of her anger.

'Yeah, I'm fine,' she finally said, taking a deep breath and forcing herself to look away from the object of her upset.

'You look rather flushed, love.' Eilis was nothing if not observant. 'You two not getting along?' She nodded to JD, who strode back toward the bar. He gave them both the thumbs up and an exaggerated wink as he passed by them.

Gráinne's anger peaked. 'No,' she fumed. 'Things are just fine.' She continued through the kitchen door and into the backroom, where her coat hung. She pushed her arms through it quickly and felt around the pockets for her car keys.

Kieran stepped into her line of vision as she turned to punch out. 'Where are you going?' he asked. His calmness accentuated how upset she was.

'I'm leaving. It's quitting time,' she told him.

'Siobhan isn't in yet and it's starting to get busy. Can you hang out until she gets here?' he asked.

She struggled out of her jacket and threw it on

the floor, along with her keys, and pushed passed Kieran.

From behind her, she heard Kieran ask Eilis, 'What's up with her?' She didn't wait around to hear what her sister-in-law had to say.

Stomping back into the bar, she made a point of staying as far away from JD as possible. Damn Siobhan for being late. She needed to get out of here. She needed some down time before heading to The Klub!. She needed to get JD out of her system.

She grabbed a towel off the back bar and moved quickly into the room. It was Friday, and offices traditionally started closing mid-afternoon. The room was quickly filling with office workers.

As she worked, her temper cooled, marginally. She tried thinking about anything but their confrontation, but her thoughts kept going back to JD.

She remembered the day Kieran had introduced her to the new bartender. Gráinne knew him instantly. She'd recognized him from The Klub!. He'd been one of the guys she'd danced for Halloween night, the one whose gaze seemed to penetrate through her disguise. He was hard to forget.

Then he'd turned up at the Blues Tavern.

Even now, as she thought about that dance, she felt the heat from his gaze returning to her. It lodged in the pit of her stomach, possibly lower. At the time, she had felt as though she were dancing just for him, as a woman might dance for her man. For a while, that's just what she'd pretended.

She'd seen the same gaze a number of times since he'd taken a job in the pub. When she caught him gaping at her this afternoon, she thought she'd have some fun with him, but she had no idea what he was hiding from her. When she'd dropped her bra on his lap that night, she assumed the stage hand had gone to retrieve it, like he always did. But as it was part of a Halloween costume she hadn't worn since, she'd forgotten all about it. Confronting her with the bra today was the last thing she'd expected.

What did JD want from her? He was willing to tell Kieran about her other job if she refused to help him, but with what? Her body shook with anger and fear.

She had to shake the feeling. She couldn't let JD get to her. He could spoil everything she'd been working so hard to achieve in the last year.

Thankfully, he maintained his distance while she worked, so she could loosen up a bit. She needed to be calm when she arrived at The Klub!. It was the only way she could psych herself up for what she had to do.

She had mixed feelings about dancing. On one level, she enjoyed it immensely. It gave her the chance to let go. She could unleash all of her pent-up frustrations and energy, and go wild. There was something exciting in pretending to be someone else.

On another level, dancing meant she had to hide – from her family, her employer, the other dancers, and most importantly, from herself. While there was a certain satisfaction in her anonymity, that anonymity also meant she wasn't free to be who she really was. Frankly, that was a journey she was still on. The dancing was the fastest way to earn the money to become who she wanted to be – the first college graduate in the Vaughan family. With that honor would come the recognition that she was a worthy person.

She wanted to be worthy.

She knew Kieran loved her, but she also knew he thought she was just skipping along in life without a care in the world. For a while, she had been. He'd been on the tail end of her bad relationships, knew how she'd managed to mess up even the easiest of jobs, and seen how she had failed to take anything in life seriously.

When Kieran first told Gráinne about Eilis, Gráinne thought, *Hey, sleep with the woman, do whatever it takes to get a recording contract.* When it turned out Kieran and Eilis had fallen in love – hard – Gráinne had decided it was time for her to grow up.

She remembered the day as clearly as if it was yesterday. Kieran and Eilis had disappeared to the Vaughan family cottage in West Cork. Kieran didn't say what he was up to but he'd been gone for quite a while. She wouldn't have been bothered if Eilis's friend, Megan, hadn't shown up, worried about her friend. That was when the two decided to drive down to the cottage to see for themselves what Kieran and Eilis were up to.

And, boy, had they been surprised.

It was painfully evident Kieran was in love with this woman, and Gráinne had instantly been jealous Eilis had stolen her brother.

She'd tried not to like Eilis, but the woman who

had since become her sister-in-law, couldn't have been any nicer. She realized in short order Kieran and Eilis were made for each other. They were two halves of the same whole, and any fool who looked at them could tell.

She wanted the same thing Kieran had found – love and joy. It was then Gráinne knew she needed to stop 'just surviving' and learn to live.

The first step was to stop letting men use her. Then she needed to get a job, and an education. She hoped it would all lead her to who she really was and then, just maybe, she could find some of what Kieran had found.

Plans set, she had packed everything – not that she had much – and moved back to Dublin. Almost instantly, things had started falling into place. Kieran and Eilis had offered to let her move in with them until she sorted herself out, but Gráinne really needed to do this on her own. And that's just what she was doing.

She didn't have many early memories from when their parents were alive, but the little house in Finglas had been their family home. After their parents' death, she and Keiran remained until she moved to Cork. She'd followed a boy, of course, and ended up living there, trying to make her way. Since Kieran and Eilis had bought a new house together, Kieran no longer needed the little house, so Gráinne moved back in. He told her the mortgage was paid for so she didn't need to pay rent, but she wanted to pay something so she didn't feel like she was taking advantage.

Then they found out Eilis was pregnant and Kieran put a halt on her driving around in 'the tin can,' as he called it. He bought her a proper mommy-daddy car and was going to sell the Mini, when Gráinne stepped up and said she'd buy it. She had gotten it for a song. Literally. Eilis wouldn't take any money from her, but she would accept music. Leave it to the musicians in the family to extort this kind of payment from her. But it really wasn't a hardship. She'd taken out her flute and played requests one evening, walking out the door with a set of keys to a car that would take her across town to her own house.

A job, a home, and transportation – what more did she need?

Money. And not the kind of money Kieran paid in the pub. Dancing might not be ideal, but it was the fastest way to earn money, legally. And she was quitting once she had enough for college tuition then she'd dedicate herself to classes. The kind of money she earned at The Klub! would be hard to give up, but her life was more important.

Gráinne was sorry she would miss this evening's performance in the pub. Kieran had told her about tonight's act and that he'd be playing guitar with them. She loved hearing him play. It reminded her of the times when they played together, him on his guitar and her on the flute.

The last time they'd played together was in her rented house in Cork City, more than a year ago. That was before the rebirth of the Blues Tavern, before she'd moved back to Dublin, before she realized how messed up her life had become.

The talk she'd had with Kieran the night he'd shown up on her doorstep in Cork had made her stop and think about where her life was heading.

Mistaking sex for love was a hard habit to break, but once she'd moved to Dublin she found it easier to start over. No one here knew her anymore; there was no reputation following her – only new beginnings.

Wiping away the rings of moisture from the tabletop, Gráinne wondered if the path she was following to achieve her dreams was the right one. Until a few months ago, she'd never fancied herself an exotic dancer. If it hadn't been for that article in Dublin City Magazine, the idea probably never would have occurred to her.

To some, her dream would sound pretty dumb, but for her it was everything.

College.

No other Vaughan in her family had attended. Not even Kieran. It wasn't until she really got to know Eilis that she decided she wanted to return to school. A college education was the key to her future, no matter what she decided to do afterward.

The article said there were a lot of girls paying their way through school by dancing. Why not her, too? So she interviewed at The Klub!. She'd always enjoyed the nightclub scene when she was younger, and found exotic dancing really wasn't all that different. The only hard part was taking her clothes off. Dancing was a doddle. Dancing with your clothes off was something different, altogether. It was too … intimate. Disguising herself as Jett made it easier.

She hadn't expected to be hired – certainly not right away – and with the encouragement of her new friend, Mystique, who was more than happy to show her the ropes, Gráinne found she was really good. So good, in fact, she had developed a following from the start. That scared and excited her all at the same time. If only she were as good at something as her real self, she might feel better about the adulation.

She jumped with a start at the hand on her shoulder.

'Geez, you startled years off me, girl,' she told Siobhan, using the familiar Cork endearment she'd picked up while living there.

'Sorry. I tried to get your attention, but you didn't hear me.'

Gráinne stood up straight and briefly looked around the room. How long had she been wiping the same table? It seemed the room was filling quickly. A group of women were waiting patiently for the table. She stepped away and watched them scramble for it before anyone else got there.

'You okay, Gráinne?' asked Siobhan.

'Yeah,' she said. 'Just tired, I guess.'

Siobhan took the tray of dirty glasses from Gráinne. 'Why don't you head off? I'm sorry I'm late, but I can take over now.'

'Thanks. I'll do that.'

Gráinne took the opportunity and went straight for the backroom to retrieve her jacket and keys. Someone had picked them up off the floor and hung up the coat. The keys were inside the pocket. She knew it couldn't have been Kieran. He'd just leave them. Eilis was too far gone with her pregnancy to bend over so far. That left one other person, because Siobhan had followed her to the backroom to hang up her own coat. JD.

47

Courtesy told her to thank him, but she wasn't going anywhere near him.

Looking at the wall clock as she passed back through the kitchen, she noticed she only had an hour before heading to The Klub!. She'd have to hurry if she were going to make it. She had to stop at her house first to get her gear and transform herself into Jett.

Chapter Four

'Jimmy's been looking for you,' Mystique said to Gráinne as soon as she entered the dressing room at The Klub!.

After a quick shower at home, Gráinne had become Jett. She had applied her make-up heavily before slipping into a hot pink bra and thong set. She coaxed her legs into a pair of matching tight pink jeans then slipped her arms into a silky pearl-colored blouse, which she left open low enough to reveal her bra. A wide black belt around her waist nearly completed her outfit. All that was left were her wig and shoes.

Her little detached garage had allowed her the privacy to walk through her back garden without her neighbors seeing, but she had thrown on a long black coat just the same. Once in her red Mini, she had concealed her own curly hair under the sleek black wig before pulling out and heading into town.

She parked well away from The Klub! And, just before she exited her car, she kicked off the flats she wore to drive and stepped into a pair of black stilettos.

'I wasn't due in until now. Do you know what he wants?'

'Uh-uh.' Mystique shook her head then went back to applying eyeliner.

Gráinne sat at her dressing table and slid out of

her long black jacket. She checked her make-up in the mirror before deciding what she was going to wear for her first act tonight. She made a mental note to speak with the house DJ about the new tune she wanted to end the night with. Mystique had been right about the Etta tune, and she wanted to try something new.

'I'll dress then go up to him.'

'He was pretty anxious to talk to you. You might want to head up first.'

A knot lodged in Gráinne's throat. What could Jimmy want to talk to her about so urgently? Certainly, she wasn't being fired. Though, oddly, the prospect didn't seem to bother her.

Upstairs, standing at Jimmy's office door, she paused with her shaking hand poised to knock, his reason for wanting to talk to her pecking at her. Had he discovered her true identity? Was she going to be fired? What else could it be? He'd barely spoken to her since he'd hired her.

She took a deep breath and knocked. *Better to get it over with now.*

The door opened the moment her knuckles touched the wood. Jimmy's bodyguard, Rusty – nicknamed for his rusty orange hair – greeted her with little more than a glare on his pale freckled face.

Rusty was a formidable man. Even though he was meant to protect the girls as much as Jimmy, Gráinne still didn't trust him. He looked Neanderthal with his deep-set, beady, ice-blue eyes, square jaw and lack of a neck. The fairness of his strawberry complexion belied his strength.

She took an involuntary step back when he

glared at her. 'Mr. Molloy wanted to see me,' she said, her heart racing.

Wordlessly, he stepped aside.

Jimmy sat behind his desk, which sat directly across from the door. Jasmine, one of the other dancers, stood behind him, rubbing his shoulders. She was dressed as if waiting to perform. Her two-piece bra and thong set was a pale shade of yellow-dyed rabbit fur, over which she wore a very sheer pale yellow wrap that came just to her bottom, the edges trimmed with matching yellow fur.

As Gráinne stepped up to the desk, she saw Jasmine's legs encased in sheer yellow thigh-high stockings, each held up by their lacy elasticated bands. Jasmine's wig was as noticeably false as her own, but was creamy yellow to her black. Gráinne wondered where the tail feathers were; the woman looked more like an Easter chick than an exotic dancer.

Gráinne had only cast Jasmine a glance – that's all it took to take in the woman's outfit. She didn't understand why, but ever since she'd started work at The Klub! Jasmine couldn't spare her a kind word. The more Gráinne tried being nice to the woman, the nastier she seemed to get, so she just avoided her as much as possible.

Jimmy silently waved Gráinne into a leather chair in front of his desk. Just as wordlessly, he waved Jasmine away, sending her and Rusty from the room. For some reason, her aloneness with her boss made her even more nervous. She clasped her hands in her lap to keep them from visibly shaking.

When they were alone, Jimmy steepled his fingers in front of his mouth, elbows on the chair arms, and stared at her.

She tried not to stare at him. It was hard not to with the way he was looking at her. He made it difficult for her to relax.

He was an average looking guy. Not overly tall or good-looking. His sandy-colored hair had been smartly trimmed around a ruddy complexion, his brown eyes lacking true emotion. If it weren't for his money, he would be nobody.

Worse, his sneaky demeanor would probably see him in prison one day. In a word, Jimmy was unsavory. If it weren't for her dream of college, she wouldn't be here. She had to keep reminding herself this job was only a means to an end, not her life. She could quit any time she liked.

'I've been watching you, Jett,' he finally said. Gráinne's heart leapt into her throat, forcing her to swallow hard. 'You've really come on since you started working for me. I'm impressed.'

'Thank you, Mr. Molloy,' she said, trying to keep her voice from cracking. She refused to let him see how nervous he made her.

'I'm so impressed that I'm going to make you an offer.' He spun his chair around to the table behind him and pulled a cigar from an ornately-carved humidor. Turning back, he went about the ritual of lighting up. He ran the length of the near-black stogie under his nose, sniffing it. He grinned lightly then snipped off the end.

She hadn't noticed until now, but a handgun lay on the table. Beads of perspiration suddenly covered her skin; droplets pooled and ran down the cleft of her breasts. Handguns were illegal in Ireland. She didn't want to know where Jimmy got this one.

Hadn't he just said she was his best dancer? Hadn't he just said he had an offer for her? Certainly, he wasn't going to kill her. What had she done?

Jimmy only glanced at her, completely unaware of her fear, as he lifted the handgun and fingered the trigger. To her horror, he aimed the gun and pressed the trigger.

Relief washed over her when a flame shot out from the muzzle, and not a bullet as she'd expected. She was sure he saw it, too, as he brought the flame to the tip of the cigar he now held between his thin lips. He rolled the cigar between his fingertips to make sure the whole tip burned evenly while he puffed. The smell of the cigar choked what little air she found left in the room.

Lord! She wished he had fired her instead of putting her through this.

As he tossed the handgun lighter on his desk, their gazes met again. He inhaled deeply then exhaled slowly, filling the space between them with smoke. Gráinne forced herself to breathe shallowly so as not to gag on the acrid smell. Obviously, the smoking ban didn't extend to The Klub!'s offices. If it did, Jimmy blatantly ignored it.

'What are you doing for New Year's?' he finally asked, sitting back in his chair, making it rock back and forth as he stared at her.

'Sir?'

'New Year's. Are you busy? Any plans? Cancel them. I've got a job for you.'

'I–I don't know...' she stuttered, shifting in the chair.

'Whatever you're doing, cancel it. This is big, and I want you there,' he told her in no uncertain terms.

Where was her choice? At what point would she be able to tell him she wasn't interested?

'What will I be doing?' she asked. She'd heard about dancers selling themselves to clients. Did Jimmy think she was the same?

'There's a private party in the penthouse on New Year's Eve and I want you there. Mr. Wade requested my best dancer.'

Me, his best dancer?

Wade! Gráinne came alert then. If Wade was going to be there, the party had to be serious. She'd never seen Taylor Wade before but she knew about him. If Jimmy scared her, the possibility of getting on Wade's bad side terrified her.

The media had dubbed him The Hunter. He'd earned the nickname because he liked to hunt. He was a sportsman of sorts. It was said around The Klub! that Wade only practiced on animals, but he made perfect on humans.

Wade had made the news a couple years back when he'd been accused of murdering his girl-friend, an exotic dancer who went by the name of Ayesha. He'd found her in bed with another man. Wade had taken them both into the mountains and set them free, naked and their hands bound. After a 30-minute head start, he set off after them then spent the afternoon toying with them before killing them.

Tourists had found their bodies. Ayesha had

54

lived just long enough to tell them what had happened, before dying. But no one could pin the murders on Wade. He bought an alibi from Jimmy. Ayesha's dying confession had been thrown out as hearsay.

This was just one of the stories going around The Klub!.

No, Gráinne didn't want this job. She didn't care what she would be doing.

'I – I'm sorry, Mr. Molloy. I can't do it. I already have plans. I – I'm going on holiday,' she rambled.

'Cancel,' he countered. 'I want you here.'

'Really, Mr. Molloy. I can't. They've been planned for a long time. My family–'

Sitting forward in his chair, he caught her gaze fully. 'I said, cancel it. Shake your arse, show him your tits, and collect a lot of money. There will be plenty of time for holidays later.'

Gráinne thought about what he said. If all she had to do was dance and the pay was good, could she do it? Even knowing for whom she was dancing? Was her dream important enough to put herself in possible danger?

'There's no choice here, Jett.' His voice was low and firm. 'Be here New Year's Eve at 10pm. You'll be out by 1am ... 2am at the latest.'

He pulled an envelope from his desk drawer and slid it across the desk to her. 'I'll pay you now. Cash.' He propped a foot on the open drawer and slunk back in his chair, weaving his fingers together over his stomach.

Gráinne gasped at the thick envelope. It was fat enough to hold enough money for two years' tuition. Her heart pounded at the possibility. Her dream of college was at her fingertips, staring at her, daring her to take it. Her heart pounded, knowing what she was looking at.

But Gráinne knew if she touched the envelope, just to see how much money was in it, she would automatically be agreeing to take the job.

She stared at the envelope for a long time, wondering what she should do. She knew she shouldn't. Not if Wade was the host. Looking at the fat envelope on the desk in front of her, her thoughts spun out of control.

'What if I quit?' she dared ask him. If she left the job altogether, he couldn't make her do this, could he?

'There's no choice here, Jett,' Jimmy repeated. 'Take it. You can quit after.' His voice insinuated an unspoken threat. She made the mistake of looking into his eyes. They were hard and determined. She knew by the look on his face he was right. He wouldn't give her a choice and it scared her even more. He was forcing her to sink deeper into the politics of The Klub!, whether she wanted to or not.

All she wanted to do was dance, earn some money, and get out. She was afraid of what he would do to her if she refused the job. By the look on his face, there was no walking away from this if she didn't agree. Stay or quit, she would be doing this job. Her only choice was to accept the money or not.

She was sure she'd stopped breathing when her shaking fingers finally reached for the envelope.

'Good girl,' Jimmy said, grinning around his stogie. 'Put the money in a safe place, then go shake that arse of yours like I know you can.' He pressed a button on the phone, calling for Jasmine on the intercom. The door opened almost instantly and the woman strode to Jimmy's side. He slipped his arm around her waist and hauled her into his lap, nuzzling her fluff-covered breasts before looking back to Gráinne. 'What are you waiting for?'

Gráinne clutched the envelope tightly in her hand and rose.

At the door, Gráinne jolted at the sound of Jimmy's voice. 'Jett,' he called. Her heart just about leapt from her chest. She'd thought he was done with her. Her first mistake was to believe everything he told her. 'You are my best dancer,' he stressed. 'It'll be okay. Promise.'

Her second mistake was to look back toward Jimmy. Instead of meeting his gaze, the only thing Gráinne saw was Jasmine, and the look on her face was pure hatred.

'Ten grand?' exclaimed Mystique. 'Are you shytin' me? Ten grand!'

Gráinne was as shocked as Mystique was. She'd never guessed the envelope contained so much money. A few hundred, maybe a grand; but thousands? She found it hard to breathe as Mystique went on.

'What kind of party are you agreeing to dance for, anyway?'

'New Year's Eve party in the Penthouse,' said Gráinne, unable to take her eyes off all the euro notes in the envelope. 'Jimmy said all I need to do is dance, but—'

Mystique snorted. 'That kind of money pays for a lot more than dancing, love. I'd say Jimmy isn't telling you the whole of it.'

Gráinne's head snapped up. 'What do you mean?'

'What I mean is, Jimmy will expect more than what he told you.'

Gráinne shook her head in denial. 'I'm not selling myself to him. I'm not like the others.'

'Maybe not, but Jimmy thinks you are. If he's paying this kind of money, he'll expect you to *perform*.' Mystique accentuated the last word.

Gráinne was speechless. She couldn't do what Mystique was implying. She wouldn't.

'There must be a lot of dosh floating around for Jimmy to be able to pay you so much,' Mystique continued, oblivious to Gráinne sudden silence. 'I wonder what's going on up there? No, I take that back. I don't want to know.'

Mystique rambled on, but Gráinne was oblivious as she thumbed through the envelope again. There were four bundles, each with twenty-five one-hundred euro notes. Certainly her dancing wasn't worth twenty-five hundred euro per hour. Mystique was right. This must be a huge party. She wondered just how much money Jimmy was making.

In the shock of opening the envelope, she'd completely forgotten this was The Hunter's party. She shot a look at Mystique.

'What?'

'I – I forgot who the party was for. I saw all this money, Myst, and it went right out of my head.'

'Who?' Mystique's brows drew together.

'Taylor Wade.' Gráinne knew those two words said everything she couldn't.

Mystique gasped. 'And you agreed to do this? Oh, Jett. I can't believe it.'

'I didn't agree.'

'You must have. You took Jimmy's money.' There was tension in Mystique's voice.

Gráinne tried to run her fingers through her hair, but was stopped by her wig. The shock of it against her fingers made her heart pump harder. It reminded her that anything she got herself into was her own fault. If she hadn't been so hard up to make her college dreams come true – to prove to Kieran she wasn't the kind of person he thought she was, to earn herself some independence ... to grow up for God sake – she wouldn't be in this predicament right now.

She looked back at Mystique, tearing her gaze from the envelope where everything she'd become in her life ended up as a few euro notes. Her voice was barely audible when she finally spoke again. 'He didn't give me a choice, Myst.'

'What do you mean he didn't give you a choice? We all have choices. Isn't that what you told me?'

Gráinne shook her head. 'He made it clear. He didn't actually come out and say it, but the only choice was to take the money or not. I'm still expected to be there.' She threw her face into her hands. The rough paper of the envelope grazed her tear-dampened cheek. 'Oh, sweet Jesus. What have I done?'

Mystique's arms were around her then, pulling her close. 'I don't know what to tell you, Jett. I wish I did.'

The sound of her stage name was a painful shock. She wasn't Jett. She wasn't a dancer. This whole mess was not what she wanted in her life. She just wanted to earn some quick money so she could go to school, but it seemed every day she was being pulled – no, pushed – deeper and deeper into the goings-on at The Klub!. Now it had come to this.

She had to get out. She knew she had to do this one last thing then she could leave. If Wade expected anything else but dancing, he was in for a shock. She'd dance as she'd agreed, then leave. And never return. As far as she was concerned, Jimmy could keep her last paycheck. The money in her hand was more than enough to make up for the loss of the pittance he paid. The real money was in the tips, anyway.

A long moment later, Gráinne pulled out of Mystique's arms, resolute. 'Thanks,' she said, gulping air to try to calm herself.

'So, what are you going to do?'

'Dance. I have no choice. Jimmy said it would be okay. He promised. It's only a couple hours and I'll be out of there. Right?' Gráinne hoped Jimmy was right.

'I hope so. But hey, I'm working that night so if you need anything, you come right down. Okay?'

Gráinne took Mystique's hand in hers briefly and squeezed it. 'Thanks. I appreciate that. I'm sure it'll be fine. I fully intend to avoid Wade. I'm going to just dance and get the hell out of there.' She looked Mystique square in the eye. 'Then I'm done.'

'Exactly. You can get back to dancing for the

boys out front.' Mystique winked and smiled lightly.

'No, I mean done.'

'Done? What do you mean?' she asked, panic etched across her face.

'Done, as in I'm quitting. I've got enough money now to move on. I don't want this kind of life. It's not for me. It was just a means to an end. It always has been,' she told her friend.

Mystique's eyes glistened with unshed tears, her voice softening. 'I know. It's just... I'd hoped you'd stay on. I kinda like having you around.' She smiled then.

Gráinne couldn't help but smile back. Yes, she'd made a friend in Mystique. Maybe when it was all said and done, they could find a way to strip off their club personas and meet each other under normal circumstances. Gráinne thought she'd like that very much.

'You never know,' Gráinne said. 'You could find your way out, too.' She threw her arms around her friend then decided where to hide the money until she could leave for the night.

Gráinne couldn't keep her mind on her dancing. All night her thoughts kept racing back to the money and what she'd sold herself into. When her final dance came up, she was thrilled with the knowledge she'd at last be going home. All she wanted to do was soak in a hot bath until her skin wrinkled then crawl into bed. If the Blues Tavern had still been open, she'd have stopped in for a while so she could get The Klub! off her mind. She knew Kieran and Eilis would have left early because of Eilis's advanced pregnancy. But Gráinne would appreciate a familiar face about now, even if it were only JD's.

As she slipped into her jacket, Gráinne remembered she'd intended to speak with the house DJ about the new music she wanted to try out. Sighing, she decided she could live with the music she was using now. She'd be gone soon, and new music wouldn't matter.

She waited until the dressing room was empty then pulled her newfound wealth out of its hiding place. She fingered through the notes just to be sure no one had touched the envelope, then stuffed it in the inside pocket of her jacket.

It was dirty money. She knew it had to be. Ten thousand euro in cash didn't just drop off trees or out of the sky. She didn't want to think about where the money had come from. She didn't want to think about what she had been forced to agree to do to get it.

Gráinne hoped over the next few weeks she'd get used to the idea she now had the money – dirty or otherwise – to make her dreams come true. And get used to the idea that before she could spend any of it, she'd have to meet her end of the bargain – dancing for the most dangerous man in Dublin City.

Chapter Five

As if Gráinne hadn't had enough excitement for one night, there was someone skulking on her darkened doorstep when she got home. She could tell by his size it was a man, but not who he was. He stood with his hands in his jacket pockets inside the narrow doorframe on her small porch, pressed as close to the house as possible to stay out of the pouring rain, but not doing a very good job of it.

His face was in the shadow of the tiny porch roof. The dim streetlight was little help. Shaking, she tried not to stare as she drove by as casually as she could.

Could Jimmy have followed her home? Good God, she hoped not. She had tried not to divulge who she really was. She didn't want Kieran knowing about The Klub!. She didn't want anyone to know. She just wanted to make some money and get out. She purposefully didn't make friends. Not even with Mystique, whom she actually liked. She didn't entertain, she didn't socialize with anyone from The Klub! outside of work, and she had certainly never told Jimmy where she lived. As far as they were concerned, Jett was an apparition who appeared when she was needed and disappeared when she wasn't.

So, if it wasn't Jimmy, who was it? She didn't

know and she certainly wasn't going to stop and ask.

Maybe she'd spend the night at the pub. She had the key and alarm code. She just needed a clean change of clothes. If she could slip through the back door and grab something off the stack she'd left on the kitchen table...

As she passed, the man stepped away from the door. Her dim porch light illuminated his face. JD! Instantly, Gráinne's frightened shakes ignited into shudders of anger. Damn him for scaring ten years off her life! It was after two o'clock in the morning, for feck sake.

Fuming, she drove past the house and around the corner to her little garage at the back of the row of houses. Once her Mini was safely parked, Gráinne made her way through the back door, locking it behind her, but not before the neighbor's wet marmalade cat, Milo, raced through.

Great! she fumed. On top of everything else that could possibly go wrong today, she now had a wet cat to chase out of the house before she could finally go to bed. And if JD thought he was getting in, too, he had another think coming. She may have been willing to settle for his familiar face at the pub earlier, but she was home now and he was the last person she wanted to see. Not after the heilish night she'd had.

As she flipped on the kitchen light, her mind raced back to the job she'd been forced to promise to do, and the money. She tossed her bag on the kitchen table beside her folded laundry and pulled out the envelope full of money. Just the sight of it sent shivers up her spine. She couldn't believe what she was going to do for this money. She felt no better than a prostitute by agreeing to do this job. Sure, it was only dancing, but she'd be dancing for The Hunter. The thought nauseated her.

The doorbell rang and she thought she heard pounding on the door. She knew he'd seen her drive by and must have seen the light go on to know she was now inside.

She picked up the envelope and looked around for a place to hide it. She moved a stool over to the counter and stepped onto it. She glanced along the top of her presses.

'Yuck!' she exclaimed. She was sure the grime dated back to the construction of the house. Obviously, no one looked up here. She stashed the envelope into one corner behind the decorative molding before stepping down and replacing the stool where she'd found it.

What she really wanted now was a hot shower, a hot toddy and a warm bed. In that order. She grabbed a fresh towel off the stack on the table and swung back through the extension where the bathroom was located.

The old terraced house had originally had two tiny bedrooms upstairs and the sitting room and kitchen downstairs. Kieran had had the brilliant idea of adding the small extension in the back to include the bathroom and a tiny laundry area. How they'd ever survived with the outside loo before their parents died, she'd never know.

The doorbell was still ringing by the time she'd showered and tossed her clothes in the washing machine. JD was nothing if not persistent. Well, let him stand out there all night for all she cared. Her priority now was to get Milo out of the house, get her hot toddy and get into bed. She tightened the belt of the silky green wrap and stepped back into the kitchen. She tried not to look up to where she'd hidden the money. She had to forget it was up there. At least for now.

She heard JD yelling at the door when she entered the sitting room.

'Come on, Gráinne. I know you're in there. Open the door.' There was no mistaking his frustration. How long had he been out there yelling, anyway? Her neighbors must have called the guards by now.

He pounded on the door between rings on her bell. 'Damn it, Gráinne. Open the door. For feck sake, this is important!' Gráinne decided to have the bell disconnected as soon as possible. The buzz of it grated on her. She'd never realized it until now.

Without turning on the living room light, Gráinne walked to the door. There was a barred window beside it. She pulled the curtain back and cracked open the window, knowing that he couldn't get through the bars.

'Will you not shut up?' she spat, flipping on the porch light. 'It's bad enough you skulking around in the middle of the night. I don't need you waking my neighbors, as well.'

'Jazuz, woman. Would you please open the door and let me in?' JD lowered his voice but he was no less calm. She knew he was cold by the way he pulled his jacket tighter around him, hunkering into the collar with his fists stuffed under his arms.

'It's the middle of the night and I'm tired. Can't whatever you have to say wait until tomorrow when I'm back to work at the pub?'

'No, this is important. You have to let me in.'

'I don't have to do anything.' She laughed to herself. That was a lie. 'And why would I do that? You're the last person I want to see right now.'

'We need to talk. I can't do this from out here.'

'Well, you have a problem then, because I'm not letting you in. Good night.' Gráinne tried to close the window but JD grasped the edge of it to hold it open.

'Let go or I call the gardaí,' she hissed. She hoped the look on her face made it clear that she was serious.

'Gráinne,' he uttered under his breath, his eyes boring into hers. 'I am the gardaí.'

JD, the police? That was rich. 'Good one, JD. You almost had me there,' she chuckled. 'Now, let go. Good night.'

She glared at him but he wouldn't release the window. She could only watch his free hand extract his wallet from his hip pocket and slide it through the window to her.

'Here, open it. My ID is inside.'

'Stop messing and let go of my window. I'm serious, JD. I'm tired and just want to go to sleep. I don't have the energy for this.'

He held her gaze for a long moment before simply saying, 'Take it.'

'Fine,' she huffed. 'If it will shut you up and get you off my porch.'

She took the wallet and flipped it open. His ID was exactly where he said it was. Her heart must have stopped because she wasn't breathing. She suddenly felt light-headed.

'Let me in.' JD's voice was just above a whisper when he spoke again. She slowly looked up and noticed his eyes were softer.

'I haven't done anything wrong,' she said. She hadn't. Well, except for taking ten thousand euro to dance for The Hunter. She couldn't keep her voice from trembling.

'No, you haven't, but your boss has. If you let me in, I'll tell you what I know.'

'How do I know this ID is real?' she asked, stalling. It was hard to think of JD as a guard. He was a bartender in the Blues Tavern. He irritated her beyond belief. And he was the only one who knew her secret. But a guard?

'You don't. You can only trust me,' he told her. 'You *can* trust me, Gráinne.'

'Can I?'

He nodded, never taking his gaze from her. He released the window and stepped back. The porch light shone fully on his face now. Gráinne saw what she thought looked like honesty and trust through the rain belting down on top of him. The longer she stared at him, the more she could picture him with the guards. He had the height and the build. And the look on his face could get him anything he wanted – from anyone. He'd given her a similar look Halloween Night when she'd danced for him in The Klub!.

Gráinne slowly pulled the window closed, latched it, and drew the curtain.

Her mind spun. The day really had been more than any person should have to bear. First the confrontation with JD in the pub, the fear he'd tell Kieran about her job at The Klub!, then another fight with JD afterward. And if that weren't enough, the meeting with Jimmy and the job he'd forced her to take. It all had her unnerved. Now JD was telling her he was a guard. What other surprises were in store for her today?

She glanced at the clock on the mantle. It was after half two in the morning. Surely, her day should be allowed to end without any more 'excitement.' Hell, she'd even let Milo stay in the house for the night just to avoid another unsavory confrontation.

Taking a deep breath, she unlatched the door and stepped back. She thought JD would fly through it after all his blustering on the porch, but his casual saunter added to her irritation as he stepped over the threshold.

Once the door was latched again, she stepped around him into the center of the small room. She crossed her arms protectively and prepared for whatever he wanted to tell her.

'Well?'

She watched JD move into the room and look around. His inspection of her things definitely screamed gardai. Now that she knew the truth, she was surprised she hadn't seen it before. He always seemed to be watching everything when he was working in the pub. Not just casual observance but really looking people up and down as they walked through the door, as if sizing them up. He knew where everyone was at all times.

What was he looking for now – evidence? He'd already admitted she hadn't done anything. If that was the case, why was he examining everything in the room?

'What do you want, JD? Or is that your real name?' she asked, not bothering trying to hide her irritation.

'You still have my ID. You tell me.' He turned to face her, stuffing his hands into his wet coat pockets while he waited.

Gráinne flipped open the wallet again and found his name. John Desmond. 'My friends call me JD.'

'I guess that means I'll call you John then. Or do you prefer Garda Desmond?'

'I'd prefer JD,' he said, winking.

She threw the wallet at him and turned toward the kitchen. She caught a side glimpse of JD's butt when he bent to retrieve his wallet from the floor. Gráinne muttered under her breath. Damn, but he did have a fine arse! His wet trousers clung to his legs so she made out the lean muscles of his thighs as well.

In the kitchen Gráinne thought, *A double hot toddy. That's what I need.*

'I'll have whatever you're having,' she heard JD say as he came through the kitchen door, shedding his wet jacket. Her anger stepped up a notch.

She spun on him. How was it he could make her blood boil with just a few words? 'How dare you?' she bit.

JD caught Gráinne's wrist as she swung around to slap him. The woman had spirit; he'd give her that. 'I could have you arrested for that.'

'Why don't you just tell me what you've come to say and leave? I've done nothing wrong. You said

70

so yourself. Instead, you waltz into my home, inspect my things then order me to cook for you?'

'If a cuppa's too much trouble then forget it.' He held her gaze a little longer than necessary. He couldn't seem to take his gaze off her. Her temper ignited something deep inside him he thought long extinguished. 'It was just a little cold standing out there waiting for you and I thought you'd help a guy out.'

'I'd like to help you out the door, but that's all I want to help you with,' she told him, yanking her wrist away from his grasp. He chuckled as he hung his wet jacket on the chair back then planted himself in it beside the table.

He watched Gráinne move around the kitchen as she filled the kettle and set it back on its base, clicking on the switch to get it going. He caught a glimpse of creamy thighs beneath her knee-length robe when she reached into the press for cups. He noted she took down two cups and smiled. No matter how angry she was she couldn't ignore her ingrained Irish hospitality.

He didn't need the sweet smelling clammy air to tell him Gráinne was fresh from a shower. Her damp curly hair told him that. And he didn't need anyone to tell him she was naked beneath her robe. The lack of panty lines was evidence enough. The robe's hem was just short enough that he almost got a glimpse of her finely shaped bottom when she bent to retrieve a bottle of Jameson from a lower shelf. His groin tightened as he watched, chanting to himself, *Just a little lower*.

JD resisted the urge to wrap his fingers around

her hips and haul her against him. He groaned and shifted to relieve the pressure in his rain-soaked trousers. Watching Gráinne wouldn't have been so hard on him except he knew exactly what that robe concealed.

He'd started going to The Klub! as part of his undercover investigation. It was amazing the kind of information one could gather just by sitting at a small shadowed table near the bar. From there, he was able to watch the stage and the rest of the room. No one bothered him. Hell, it was even hard to get his pint refilled. No one paid him any attention. Pints aside, being so out of the way meant he could observe freely without being observed himself.

When a new dancer called Jett started working, he started finding reasons to be at The Klub that didn't involve work. She was different from the other dancers. He saw it right off. She was cocky enough for the job but she lacked the passion the other dancers had. That didn't stop the patrons from falling over themselves to crowd around the stage at night, though.

JD had come to recognize her M.O. Each night she'd choose a lonely heart seated at the stage and dance just for him. She never chose anyone too eager for her dance. She continually turned down blokes shouting offers at her but still took their euro notes. She avoided obvious groups of men too eager for a private show. It was obvious she was dancing for the money and he wondered why, when she plainly didn't like the job.

The more he watched Jett, the more fascinated he became with her. Sure, he loved watching her dance. Her body was incredible. It was what she hid beneath her wig and caked-on make-up that intrigued him the most.

It was purely by mistake he'd discovered Jett's real identity. Mates from work had taken him into the Blues Tavern one night to hear one of their friends perform. That's when he spotted Gráinne behind the bar. His body instantly knew her, but it took his brain a few minutes to catch up. Then it hit him.

He'd spent most of the evening watching her instead of his friend on stage.

JD recalled the night he'd moved from the shadows of The Klub! to the front of the stage, and found himself the object of Jett's special dance. Did she think he, too, was a lonely heart needing her special attention? He hoped not.

OK, so maybe he was lonely. A cop's job was a lonely one. It couldn't be helped. Sure, some of the guys were married, but marriage wasn't for him. He'd never had trouble with the ladies. He always had company if he wanted it. Though lately, now he thought about it, he hadn't wanted it. It wasn't satisfying. He couldn't keep his thoughts off Gráinne.

That's when he started worrying about his motives for spending so much time at The Klub!. Was it for the job, or for the girl?

It wasn't long after that question he decided he needed to shift gears in his investigation. A job in the Blues Tavern would be perfect. Jimmy Molloy would get suspicious of a single patron spending so much time in his club, especially one developing a fixation on one of the dancers, and JD

73

could get closer to Gráinne in the pub to get the information he needed.

He thought he'd hit a snag when Kieran told him he didn't need any full time staff, but if he was interested in on-call work and maybe a night or two on the weekends JD would be welcome. JD had to control his elation as he left the pub. He'd scored a major move in the game with Molloy by getting a job where he could work beside the man's best dancer. At least, she was the best in his eyes.

When JD had proven himself a better than average bartender, Kieran decided to ask him to work more hours. Eilis's term was coming to an end and Kieran wanted to be available if she needed him. And it wasn't like Kieran couldn't afford to take the time off. Even though the pub had been open a year, it had done extremely well. That was down to his hands-on work ethic, which JD greatly admired.

He readily agreed to work more hours, but it was only to spend more time with Gráinne. By that time, he knew her schedule so was able to tell Kieran the shifts he'd be able to work. Ironically, they were similar hours to Gráinne's.

JD had hoped to spend as much time with her as possible in order to gather information on Jimmy Molloy and happenings at The Klub!. Only Gráinne hadn't proved very cooperative. In fact, she never said a word about The Klub!, not even in passing. Then it occurred to him she hadn't told her brother about her moonlighting. That truth put a different spin on things; as if they weren't complicated enough already.

The complication was that the more time JD worked with Gráinne, the more he got to know her. The more he got to know her, the more he wanted to get to know her a lot more.

Damn if he wasn't attracted to her. Every day had become increasingly difficult to get her to talk. It wasn't that she wasn't a chatterbox. He found she was actually quite pleasant to talk with. She just never talked about The Klub!. And it was becoming evident his heart was no longer up to the task. He'd only been forced to confront her with the velvet bra today after his commander pressed him for information, or said he'd find someone else for the job.

Working in the pub with Gráinne wasn't earning him anything except a constant erection. He stiffened whenever she was around, or when he thought about her, or if he caught a hint of her perfume, or thought he heard her voice, or...

'Earth to Garda Desmond,' he heard through his meanderings. He realized he was staring at Gráinne but not really seeing her. She must think him thick.

'Sorry. Daydreaming,' he said, shifting his gaze and his legs again. His erection was quite uncomfortable now.

'It's a little late for daydreaming, wouldn't you say?' He saw her lip twitch, fighting a grin.

'I guess I'm just a little tired.'

'I thought you cops never slept.'

'A myth. I love my bed. We have a very intimate relationship,' he said, grinning and wriggling his eyebrows. She blushed. He liked the effect he had on her.

'Typical male. Always thinking with your willie.'

'Yeah, I know. We're evil. Tell me what you wanted while I was so rudely ignoring your hospitality.'

She cast a glance over her shoulder as she poured ground coffee into the carafe.

'I said take off your clothes.'

Chapter Six

'What?' he croaked? Surely he must have fallen asleep and his fantasies were taking over. Had Gráinne just asked him to get naked?

'Take off your clothes and I'll throw then in the dryer. You're dripping all over my floor.' Her voice was gruff as she waved her hand at the evidence. She seemed calmer, if just a little. She grabbed a towel off a stack on the table and threw it at him. 'You can put this around you while you wait. The bathroom is through there,' she pointed then went back to making the coffee.

He left the bathroom door ajar while he stripped off. He hadn't realized it until now but he was soaked to the skin and freezing. Just watching Gráinne move about the kitchen had kept him warm.

'Sorry about the floor,' he called through the door, wrapping the soft towel around his waist. He heard her mutter something sounding like bastard but couldn't be sure.

He glanced at himself in her mirror. His ginger hair was a fright. He quickly ran his fingers through it before stepping from the bathroom. He held his wet clothes in front of him, trying to disguise his condition.

'What should I do with these?' he asked, padding into the kitchen.

Without looking at him, Gráinne took the

clothes. 'Put your shoes on the rad and I'll put your clothes in the dryer. That should sort you out.' When she returned to the kitchen, he'd reseated himself in his chair and crossed his legs.

Just then, a marmalade cat leapt into his lap and settled in the curve of his leg. He wasn't much of an animal person but he hoped the cat would help disguise the tent pole under the towel.

'Milo!' gasped Gráinne, coming toward him to remove the damp cat from his lap, but JD waved her off.

'It's okay. I like cats,' he quickly lied. He'd put up with the animal if it meant keeping Gráinne from knowing how much she turned him on.

'He's the neighbor's cat. He ran in as soon as I had the door open.'

'Thanks for drying the floor,' he said, shifting the conversation away from the cat. The longer Gráinne looked at the cat, the more nervous he became. 'I planned to do that when I came out.'

'No worries,' she said, turning back to the kettle when it switched off. She poured the boiled water into the carafe and gave the grounds a good stir before inserting the plunger then set the carafe on the table.

'Can I help with anything?'

'Everything's done.' While he'd been in the bathroom, Gráinne had moved her folded clothes off the table and replaced them with the coffee cups, milk, sugar, a plate of biscuits and the bottle of Jameson.

As if it were one fluid motion, she sat beside him at the table, pushed the plunger down in the carafe then poured coffee into both cups. Her long fingers moved between the carafe and cup; his eyes were transfixed with her gracefulness.

'Will you take whiskey in your coffee, or are you still on duty?'

'Sure, I'll have a sup,' he said, looking into her eyes. 'And no, I'm not on duty. Not technically.'

'Say when.' When he nodded, she tilted the bottle into her own cup before replacing the cap. 'Not really a proper Irish coffee, but it'll do.' They sat together in companionable silence for a moment. 'So, technically, what are you if not on duty?' He couldn't help but notice how she avoided looking at him.

For a split second, JD couldn't remember why he'd come here. His first thought was because he desired her. That fact was painfully obvious to him, and it would be obvious to her, too, if the cat decided to scamper off. The last thing he ever expected was finding himself sitting as good as naked at her kitchen table, sharing a cup of Irish coffee with her as if it was the most natural thing in the world. It felt natural, too, which kind of scared him.

Stalling, he took another sip of his coffee. The whiskey did nothing to cool the heat burning in his veins. The hot silk of the Jameson whiskey instantly hit his bloodstream, warming him to the core. Another sip and he sat back in his chair, relaxing a little.

'Well?' Gráinne asked, putting her own cup to her lips. JD watched as she sipped the dark liquid, and wondered if the whiskey would have the same effect on her.

He shifted, trying to find some comfort.

'A cop is never really off duty,' he finally said, stroking the cat. 'We're either just awake or asleep.'

'I suppose you sleep with a big gun under your pillow.'

JD glanced up at Gráinne through suddenly sleepy eyes. 'No, love,' he said softly, smirking. 'That's not where I keep my big gun.'

Gráinne regretted her comment as soon as she said it. Embarrassment instantly heated her face. She couldn't believe JD would dare make such a comment to her. No. Scratch that. She could believe it. As long as she'd been working with him at the pub, he'd always been cheeky with her but no cheekier than she was with him.

She had to admit, though, his comeback was a good one.

She fought to keep the smirk off her face by taking another sip of her coffee. It was hard to stay mad at him when she'd put her foot so firmly in her own mouth.

Gráinne couldn't deny she was attracted to JD in a big way. He was funny, interesting to talk with, and he could take as good a slagging as he gave. If she were still the same woman she had been in Cork, she would have tried it on with him.

But things were different now, and getting into anything with JD – or anyone else for that matter – would complicate her plans.

Not that her plans seemed to matter when JD was around. She couldn't think straight. His words said one thing but his eyes – his eyes told a completely different story. They smoldered, penetrated her, dared her to...

What? Dared her to what? Go against the promise she'd made to herself? She couldn't do that. Instead, she tried putting him off by throwing up her defenses. As much as she hated it, it meant being snarky with him even when the situation didn't call for it. She knew that's the way it had to be until she was able to save the money to get herself into school and quit The Klub!.

The money. She very nearly looked up to the press where she'd hidden it. She had to forget about it until after New Year's Eve, when she'd finally quit The Klub!. – when she'd be free to do as she liked. Until then, she'd have to go to Confession every Sunday and beg forgiveness for her sins.

The whiskey was beginning to smooth its way through her veins but barely touched the feelings rushing through her.

'Handguns are illegal in Ireland, Gráinne. The only time I carry one is on special assignment.'

'Right, I knew that.' Yep, fumbling fool. 'So are you going to tell me why you're here?' Maybe if she kept him talking it would keep her from further embarrassing herself.

JD shifted again. He was doing a lot of that. Was the topic that uncomfortable? Somehow she didn't think he was uncomfortable about anything.

'I need to talk to you about The Klub!.'

'I don't want to talk about that,' she said firmly.

'I wish I didn't have to make you. Gráinne, this is important. Jimmy Molloy is in over his head.

81

So are you.'

'I don't care what Jimmy does. I'm just there to earn some money.' Gráinne reached for the Jameson bottle and added a bit more to her coffee. She hoped the whiskey would help her get through this. Something in the back of her mind told her it wasn't going to end well.

'Under other circumstances, I'd be here to ask you to quit. You don't belong there.'

'I don't think that's any of your business. I'm a grown woman and can make my own choices.' She saw his gaze rake her up and down, and covered her discomfort with another sip of her coffee. She felt the flush begin again at his smoldering look.

'And well I know it, Gráinne, but your choice to work at The Klub! is a poor one. And unfortunately, because you work there I need to ask for your help.'

'What do you have to do with The Klub!?' Then it hit her. If JD was a cop, why was he working at the pub? Did Kieran know? She doubted it. If he did, he would have been on her porch right beside JD tonight.

Her intuition hit her hard in the stomach. If she thought her day couldn't get any worse, she had a feeling she hadn't seen anything yet.

'I'm working undercover. I've been casing The Klub! for some months now.'

'How long?'

'About a month before you started working there. I was hoping to glean something from club gossip. Sometimes the best information is gathered simply by observing.'

'Were you just observing when you decided to sit at the stage?' she boldly asked.

'I enjoy watching you dance.'

She blushed at his praise, but she wasn't sure it was the kind of praise she wanted from him.

'What's with the job at the pub?' she asked, trying to move him off the subject of her. 'Moonlighting? I heard the pay was poor with the guards, but–'

'I need information and you're the one I was hoping would help.'

'What do you mean?'

'That night you danced for me, I was there as a patron. I was just there to watch, like the rest of them. It was purely by chance I discovered who you were. Not long after that I approached Kieran for a job. My goal was to get close to you to see if you knew anything about the goings on at The Klub!. Women talk and I hoped you would, too.'

'I don't talk about The Klub!. Not to anyone.'

'Don't I know it.'

'Does Kieran know?'

'That I'm a guard? No. Just like you, I can't tell anyone. This operation is too important.'

'Then why are you telling me?' She had to admit she was curious about his job, but not curious enough if it involved her.

'Because I haven't been able to get the information I need. When we met the first time in the pub, I knew you recognized me but you never let on. After a couple weeks, I realized Kieran didn't know anything about your other job. I bided my time and tried to get you to talk about The Klub! or to mention Jimmy. Something – anything.'

83

Gráinne shook her head. 'So you were hoping to use me.'

'Something like that. We've been investigating The Klub! for a long time and have gotten nowhere.'

'Maybe there's nothing there.'

'Oh, there's something there alright. If Taylor Wade is involved, there's definitely something going on.'

She flinched at the name. By the look on his face, JD noticed. She didn't want to go there so she pressed on. 'What are you investigating?'

'The Klub! is being operated as a drugs and prostitution front. Jimmy's not the one at the top. He's just one of the players we'll take down on the way to number one – Wade.'

She squeezed her eyes shut, trying to keep the sudden tears at bay. Her heart pounded anxiously.

Weakly, she prodded. 'What do I have to do with this?'

JD sipped his coffee then looked down at Milo still in his lap and stroked him gently. Gráinne's heart twisted. JD was so gentle with the cat yet she felt like he was about to rip her heart out with his words. Then he squared his gaze with hers. She was sure she saw regret.

'Like I said, I need information. When I didn't get it at The Klub! or from you at the pub, I decided to confront you.'

'That's why you brought my top into the pub today?' He nodded. 'Why didn't you tell me then? Why wait until now?'

'Because Kieran interrupted me. Then it got busy and there wasn't time.'

'I still don't see what I have to do with it. I don't know what Jimmy or anyone else at The Klub! does. I keep my nose out of things. I go in to dance, and leave when I'm done. I don't hang around and I don't socialize with anyone. I don't talk about the pub when I'm there and I don't talk about The Klub! when I'm in the pub. I just don't want anyone to know anything about me. I'm only there for the money.'

'I understand that, Gráinne. Why in God's name you chose that kind of work, I'll never know, but–'

'Because it's quick and easy money,' she cut in. 'I wanted to earn money fast and get out. That was the only legal thing I could think of.'

'What gave you the idea it would be easy? Didn't you have any idea how seedy strip clubs are? We're investigating every one of them in the city right now. They're all doing something illegal. Most of them are tied to Wade. He uses these clubs to sell his drugs. Most of the dancers are his prostitutes.'

Gráinne began shaking, remembering Mystique's words. Jimmy was paying her handsomely because Wade expected Jett to perform, and not just dancing. He expected her to ... she couldn't bear thinking of it.

She wrapped her arms protectively around herself. 'I'm not like that.'

The timbre in JD's voice dropped just above a whisper, but his words echoed in the room. 'I know. That's why I want to protect you.'

She shot her gaze back to his and thought she saw truth there.

'Protect me? You don't even know me.'

85

'I think I do. But I can't help you unless you help me.'

'I don't know anything. I told you that.'

'I know, but you're working there and I'd like you to start keeping your ears and eyes open. I can't go where you can. You're on the inside. As far as they're concerned, I'm just a patron and I want to keep it that way.'

'What do you mean? You want me to be your snitch?' Her heart started pounding again.

'That's a harsh word, Gráinne, but effective.'

'I won't do it. If what you say is true, I'd be in danger.' Her voice rose as she spoke, her anger reigniting.

JD hung his head and shook it from side to side. 'I wish there was another way, Gráinne, but there isn't.'

'There's always another way,' she hissed, sitting forward in her chair. What she really wanted to do was get him out of her house, bury this whole day in the recesses of her memory and forget it ever happened.

'No, not always.'

'I'm not doing it,' she told him again. 'You can't make me.' She knew she sounded like a spoiled prat throwing a tantrum, but by God, she was just that.

'Gráinne, please, help me. If there was another way, believe me, I'd go that route. You're my best hope at bringing down Wade.' He didn't disguise the pleading in his voice.

'No.' One single word. That's all it should have taken. She should have said it to Jimmy earlier in the evening, regardless of his threat. By God, she'd tell JD now, though.

'Hear me out, Gráinne.' He sat forward as much as Milo would allow. 'I don't like this any better than you. Personally, if I had my way, I'd make you quit the job altogether. I don't like you working there.'

'You don't like me working there? I don't think you have a say in the matter.'

'I wish I did.'

Gráinne's heart flipped. Until earlier today, she'd fancied JD and hoped he might still be around by the time she got to college. Now, as much as she would have liked that he had a say in her life choices, she never wanted to see him again.

'Well, you don't,' she said, her voice barely audible, but her anger quite obvious.

JD sat up straight as if preparing himself for battle. He took a long, deep breath and released it slowly before raising his eyes to hers.

'I wish I didn't have to do this, Gráinne. You will do this for me. You don't have a choice.'

His words echoed Jimmy's. Chills raced up her spine.

'We all have choices, JD. My choice is to say no, I won't help. There's nothing you can say to change my mind.' She squared her shoulders and set her chin firmly forward, sure he would respect her decision.

'There's no other way to say this, Gráinne, so I'll say it straight. If you don't help me with this, I'll tell Kieran about your job at The Klub!.'

Chapter Seven

The silence hanging in the air was palpable.

Anything Gráinne could say to JD suddenly vanished. Her mind went blank. She stared at him, trying to gauge if he really would tell Kieran about her side job. When he held her gaze, unwavering, she knew he was telling her the truth.

'You wouldn't dare.' Even to her, her voice was barely audible.

'Yes. I would.'

She knew he was waiting for her reaction, and a reaction is what he got. She raised her hand to slap him across the face. As before, he reacted quickly and grabbed her wrist before she made contact.

His sudden movement startled the sleeping Milo, who swiped him angrily across the chest before bolting off his lap. JD instantly released her wrist and sprang back.

Gráinne gasped. 'Jazus! I'm sorry,' she said, her anger dampened. She leapt up and raced to the bathroom to get her first aid kit.

When she returned, JD was at the sink with a damp tea towel, dabbing at the wicked scratches across his chest.

'Here, give me that.' She took the tea towel from him, popped open the first aid kit and pulled out the alcohol and sanitary wipes.

'I'm so sorry. I never thought...' Guilt washed

over her. She should have put the cat out as soon as he came into the kitchen. She shouldn't have let JD talk her into leaving him on his lap. She couldn't tell him now, though. His eyes were distracting. 'I'm sorry.'

'Stop apologizing. It was an accident.' The moment the alcohol touched his skin, he flinched hard at the sting, sucking in his breath. 'Hey, watch it.'

'Don't be such a big girl's blouse. It's only a small cut.' She was startled by his chuckle. Even after their heated words, her attempted slap, and Milo's well-aimed strike, he still found the situation amusing. She probably would, too, if she thought about it long enough.

Silence pressed between them while she tended his wound. Gráinne became painfully aware of JD's nearness as she worked.

It wasn't a deep scratch, just jagged across his flesh, so she lingered over it to be sure it was cleaned properly. At least, that's what she told herself.

His skin radiated warmth and she felt his heart beating against her fingertips. She loved the smell of good whiskey on a handsome man's breath. He was so close she had to keep herself from leaning into him.

Was it her imagination, or was JD leaning into *her?* He was so close his own natural scent penetrated her senses. He didn't wear any artificial fragrance. His scent was purely male ... purely aroused male, if the bulge against her stomach was any indication.

His intrusion was stealth and she was sure it was

purposeful. Nothing about JD was done without forethought. As she thought about this, he leaned even closer. She was now trapped between him and the counter.

His nearness, the feel of his body pressing into hers, the scent of the whiskey on his breath, and the feel of his skin on her fingertips, all worked to steal her breath.

Breathe, girl, breathe, she silently chanted.

The wound was cleaned, but it had been a long time since she'd felt a man's arms around her, the comforting strength of a male embrace, how safe it made her feel.

She'd be lying if she said she'd never lain with a man before, but she'd never been loved by one. Not properly so.

Her desperation for love had always been ill-aimed, and she continually mistook sex for love.

She had a lot of growing up to do. She'd hoped to do that now she was living in Dublin again. New starts, finding herself, growing up. And, until she did, no men.

Gráinne's heart squeezed tight as her emotions ran circles through her mind. It would be so easy to pull JD into a kiss and hope, by giving herself to him, he would love her. Her head told her *no*, but her heart ached for her head to be wrong. JD felt so good against her, so natural. Her body cried out to be touched and cared for, even if just for the night.

No, this was wrong. She couldn't allow herself to break her promise. If she did, everything she'd worked toward, the humiliating job at The Klub!, lying to her brother, would all have been for nothing. It would only add up to failure, which she was all too familiar with.

JD shifted against her again. Something deep inside her groaned with need.

Oh, why did she torture herself like this? There was no future with this man. He didn't love her. He came here to tell her he'd been using her. She should hate him right now, not fighting to keep her hands to herself.

She had to keep her eyes on her future; money first, then education. Without money, there could be no education. She told herself this over and over again like a mantra, but as JD's heat seeped into her she felt her will collapsing.

He shifted again and Gráinne felt his erection pressing firmly against her. She didn't dare look up because he was so close; cheek-to-cheek but not touching. His breath caressed her skin at the opening of her robe.

She had to get away from him if she were to maintain some semblance of dignity. His unspoken intention was all too alluring.

Tossing the soiled pad aside, she said, 'That should keep you.' She was ashamed she couldn't raise her voice above a whisper.

'Thank you.' His own voice was barely a whisper, too.

She turned toward him slightly. It was in her mind to apologize again for Milo, but the moment she looked into his eyes, she couldn't think, couldn't move ... couldn't breathe. His eyes bore into hers, freezing her in place.

When he leaned even closer, she started panicking. Her heart pounded in her chest. What was he doing?

'I said I'm done.'

'I'm not,' he growled, then closed the gap between them.

The instant his lips touched hers, she was sure she'd melted into him. If he didn't have her pressed so firmly against the counter, her legs would have collapsed under her.

She'd often wondered what it would be like to kiss JD. Ever since the night she'd danced for him in The Klub! she'd let her mind run mazes through her fantasies about him. She'd permitted herself the fantasies, because that's all she'd allowed herself until school was done and she had the education she craved. But this was no fantasy. JD was nothing like anything her wild imagination could ever conjure. He was pure flesh, hardness and heat, and his kiss had her undone.

Instinct took over, and she wrapped her arms around his neck. Tilting her head, she parted her lips and welcomed his intruding tongue. The moment they touched, JD groaned deep in his throat and his arms hauled her against him, closer still. His hands were flat on her back, holding her, the pads of his fingers massaging her flesh.

Gráinne gasped when he pressed his hips against her again and again. No, not his hips. Something harder. He slid his hands around and grasped her bottom, squeezing it roughly, holding her as he slowly ground himself against her.

As his kiss deepened, Gráinne continued losing all sense of reality. She couldn't believe how easily JD made her drop her defenses. Was she so needy for a man's touch?

'JD,' she heard herself whisper, but he didn't seem to hear her. Or if he did, he ignored her. 'John.' He looked at her then. His eyes smoldered with desire. What she felt echoed in his gaze.

'You're so soft,' he murmured, as he stroked the backs of his fingers against her cheek, smoothing away an errant curl. His gaze followed his fingers as they traveled down her neck to her collarbone, and then dipped to the cleft between her breasts. He used both to part the collar of her wrap, easily pushing it off her shoulders. Too easily. She couldn't stop him. She followed his gaze to her breasts where he gently cupped them. Her nipples pebbled under his thumbs.

She felt his breath against her skin just before he claimed a nipple between his lips. The feel of his mouth on her was like lightning strike. It shot a bolt of fire through her body so intense she arched against him. She buried her fingers in his hair just to make sure he didn't stop.

Her body was on fire. Every nerve ending was alive with sensation.

He slipped his arms around her and the tiny hairs on his arms grazed her skin, sending tingles up her spine. The cool night air did nothing to tame the sensations racing through her. There was nothing she could to do stop him. Her will was gone.

He gazed up at her while he suckled her. Neither moved. His gaze was intense, questioning, as if asking for permission to continue.

Then he moved to her other breast.

'Jazus!' she cursed aloud.

She should have said no.

She should have said stop.

She should have said a lot of things. Later, when she had her senses back, she was sure she'd come up with several choice words. Right now, though, she found it hard just to breathe.

JD rose and reclaimed her mouth. His chest hairs on her sensitive breasts enticed her all the more. She was forced to grasp the counter to remain upright.

As if she wasn't having enough trouble standing on two legs, JD hauled one leg around his waist. It was by willpower alone she was able to stand at all.

The instant his lips touched hers again, it seemed her whole world stood still; his fire consumed her. It washed over her and drowned her in a pool of liquid passion the like she'd never felt before. No man had ever kissed her with as much feeling.

God, he would make her come if he kept rubbing against her like this. And God help her, she wanted him inside her. Now.

It was all too much. The realization of what she was doing hit her so suddenly, it left her shattered and weak. She had to remind herself sex was not love, no matter how good it felt. She craved approval. She wanted acceptance. She wanted to be loved, damn it! By God, JD's touch echoed something she fought hard to name.

'No,' she gasped, pushing him back.

Every inch of her flesh was alive with feeling. It had never been like this before. No man had ever made her feel this way. No man had ever touched her so lovingly. His touch was loving but it wasn't

94

love. She barely knew the man. No. It wasn't love, she told herself.

He shot his gaze up to hers, passion and confusion twisting as one across his face.

She was slow to come back to earth, but when she did, a wave of shame washed over her, drowning her contentment.

'I'm sorry. No.' She pushed JD away from her, but her legs refused to support her weight and she would have sunk to the floor had he not steadied her. She grasped the edges of her robe and pulled them back together.

Her eyes filled with tears. She bit her lip to keep them at bay. She would not let him see how this affected her. She couldn't look at him, but his fingers were on her chin and turning her toward him. His eyes were filled with passion and ... something. She couldn't read his expression.

'No,' she gasped through the tears suddenly spilling down her cheeks. 'Leave me alone.'

It had to be the stress of the day making her feel this way, making her so vulnerable, and not that she desired JD. But she did desire him. She had since Halloween night when he surreptitiously stepped into her life.

'Sshhh,' he whispered, and pulled her against him. 'It's okay.'

'Please, just ... don't.' He refused to listen to her. He wrapped his arms around her and pulled her against him. He cupped the back of her head in his hot palm and held her to his shoulder where she finally lost it.

Chapter Eight

JD stroked Gráinne's back as she cried against him. His heart pounded so hard against his ribs he found it difficult to breathe. It took every ounce of willpower he possessed just to hold her and let her cry when what he really wanted was to stroke her and tease her body into responding to his touch.

He loved the feeling of her against him. It felt so natural. She smelled good, too. The sweet soap she'd used in the shower mingled with her own natural scent of passion-warmed skin.

Her arousal enveloped them like a shroud. Its cloying scent in his nostrils was like flicking petrol onto a fire, a fire he was already having difficulty controlling.

He buried his face in her still damp hair and inhaled deeply as he held her. 'It's all right,' he whispered, stroking her back.

It wasn't long before she went still in his arms, but he continued holding her. Not tightly. She could have moved away at any time.

When she finally did, it was slow, as if she were on automatic pilot. She didn't look at him as her hands traveled down the length of his chest to the towel just barely clinging to his hips. There was no mistaking his arousal for either of them, but Gráinne still avoided looking at him as she slipped her hand through the folds of the towel to grasp him.

The feeling of her cool fingers on him ignited his pulsing need for her. He squeezed his eyes shut and summoned up his last shred of control.

'No, love,' he heard himself say, gently removing her hand.

Only then did she look up at him.

'Isn't that what you want?'

'Oh, aye. I want, all right.'

He brought both of her hands to his lips and kissed the backs of her fingers. If she touched him again, he knew he wouldn't be able to stop.

Was he crazy? She was willing, so why not?

This wasn't what he'd come for, that's why not. He'd dreamed of making love to Gráinne, but not on the floor of her kitchen, and certainly not under these circumstances.

'Then why–'

'Gráinne, love, I want you very much,' he said. 'But not here. Not now. You're tired. It's late. And we have unfinished business we need to sort out.'

He knew his last comment affected her when she suddenly pushed him away. Whoever came up with the saying *third time lucky* was very wise; much wiser than he. Gráinne's palm connected firmly with the side of his face. His head jerked back painfully at her strike. It stung. Boy, did it sting!

Moving slowly, he stepped away from her, giving her space, and looked at her. Her brows were drawn together. Her once passion-filled eyes were now shadowed with anger. Her kiss-swollen lips drew together in a fine line, her jaw clenching. He was sure she was looking for a few choice words to spit at him.

'Gráinne,' he started.

'Don't talk to me,' she bit. He watched her disappear into the back room. He heard the dryer switch off, and a heartbeat later she reappeared with an armload of damp clothing.

'Get dressed and get out.' She threw his clothes at him. There was no mistaking what she desired now. His absence.

'Gráinne, we have to talk about this.'

'I have nothing to say to you.'

He tossed his clothes on the table and removed the towel. He took pleasure in the flush that shot across her face when she saw his arousal.

'Bastard,' she spat, spinning away from him.

'We need to finish this business with Jimmy and The Klub!. I need your help.' His clothes had been in the dryer just long enough to heat the saturated fabric. His jeans clung to his legs as he squeezed into them.

'Right. And what was that,' she waved to where they'd stood just moments before, 'a bribe? Jazus! What kind of fool am I?'

It dawned on him then. She thought kissing her was a bribe to get her to help him. Now who was the fool?

'No, Gráinne. 'Twas no bribe. It just happened,' he said, shrugging into his damp shirt. He didn't bother buttoning it up, opting to tuck it into his waistband. He slipped his bare feet into his wet shoes. His toes squelched in the saturated insoles.

'I've wanted to kiss you since I first laid eyes on you.'

'You mean Jett.'

'No, woman, I mean Gráinne Vaughan.'

When he was dressed, he turned back to her. She fought him when he cupped her cheeks and turned her to face him, but she finally turned. He slid one hand around her shoulder and palmed her head, pulling her against him again. She struggled halfheartedly but finally settled stiffly against him. His eyes bore into hers.

'Listen to me, Gráinne. I know you're angry right now. You think what just happened was another attempt on my part to use you. I can't tell you how wrong you are.' She sniffled loudly but didn't say anything.

'Things are complicated. I have to finish this job and you're the only one who can help me. I wish things were different. I really do. But I can't let what I feel for you get in the way of this operation. I've been working on this case for too long to jeopardize it now.

'If things were different, I'd love the chance for us to get to know each other better. I really like you.'

Gráinne snorted and looked away.

JD took her chin gently between his fingers and turned her to face him again. 'Whatever you think, know one thing. I'll never lie to you, Gráinne. What I'm saying is the truth. If things were different, I'd have you upstairs in your bed showing you just how much I want you.'

'You've been using me all along. Why stop now?'

There was no mistaking the bitterness in her words. Her words stung much more than her slap had. 'I deserved that. I just wish you could understand how difficult this is for me. I never intended for things to get personal with us. I just needed some information. It was supposed to be easy.'

'It was supposed to be easy, or I was supposed to be easy? Isn't that the assumption, that all exotic dancers are easy? Or that you can pay for services ... maybe a little extra on the side for a private lap dance?'

'I've never made those assumptions about you. Get that through your head now,' he snapped, stepping away from her to pace the tiny kitchen. 'I never planned on getting involved with you. What happened here tonight...'

'Just happened.'

'I didn't come here planning to do this. Until now, I've done a damn fine job of keeping my hands to myself.'

'Yeah, you've made it clear what you're here to do. You want to use me to get to Jimmy. Everyone wants to use Gráinne. Well, I have news. I'm not doing it. I won't be used, ever again. I have nothing to do with Jimmy. I don't care what he's up to. I'm just there to earn some money.'

'I don't get it, Gráinne. What do you want that kind of money for, anyway? You had to realize the risks of taking a job like that.'

'What risks? I go in, dance, and leave. No risk.' She said it as if she believed it.

'Like putting yourself at personal risk if any of those yobs around the stage try taking you up on that private show you keep teasing them with? Like working for a guy fronting his business for a drug kingpin? Being in the middle of things when Molloy and Wade are taken down? And what about the risk of Kieran finding out?' he reminded her.

'Keep Kieran out of this,' she hissed. 'This is my life. I'm an adult and can make my own decisions. I don't need his approval, and I don't need yours.'

'Maybe not, but you need a brain in your head, woman,' he said, his voice rising alongside hers until they were shouting at each other.

Gráinne gasped. 'Do you seriously think I'd take a job like this without doing my research? This is the fastest legal way to earn money. A lot of money.'

'Are you daft? Taking your kit off for a bunch of losers is one of the most dangerous jobs you could have chosen. You're not just putting yourself in danger by working for Molloy. You're just asking for trouble on the streets if anyone recognizes you. What in the world could make you do such a thing?'

'I need the money for college,' she blurted.

JD knew by the look on her face and her sudden silence she hadn't intended to let that bit of information slip. He stared at her for a long moment, waiting to see if she'd try explaining away her confession.

She remained silent, standing stiffly with her arms crossed, her gaze unwavering.

His temper slowly evaporated. He didn't know what to say. He just slumped into his chair and stared at her.

'Gráinne,' he finally said, his voice lowered considerably. 'Sit down.'

'Get out,' she told him, her own voice low but

no less intense than when she was screaming at him.

'Please, sit. Now I know what you're on about, we can work through this.'

'I have nothing else to say to you.'

'Fine. You can listen to me talk.' When she didn't move, he continued. 'Okay, stand. I don't care. What I do care about is getting you out of The Klub!. Since you're unwilling to help me with this case, I want you out of there. You're in too much danger and I don't want you hurt.'

'It doesn't matter what you want.'

'Gráinne, open your eyes. Please, see some sense in what I'm asking,' he pleaded, sitting forward anxiously.

'Believe me. My eyes are open. When I have what I want out of The Klub! I'll leave, but not before.'

JD threw up his hands. 'You're impossible.'

'I know. It's one of my most endearing qualities.' She went into the living room. He heard the front door open. He knew he wasn't going to get Gráinne to agree to anything tonight. They were both tired, and he was sure his slip-up had caused him to lose Gráinne, both in helping him gather information on The Klub! and as a friend.

His jacket was still soaked when he threw it on and stuffed his wet socks into the pocket, but he paid his discomfort no mind. His attention was focused on Gráinne and how to keep her safe.

He stopped at the front door and looked into her eyes for a long moment. 'Gráinne,' he said, his voice just above a whisper. 'I'm sorry you doubt me, but I'm telling you the truth when I say I won't ever lie to you. I won't let anything or anyone hurt you.'

When she still didn't respond, he added, 'And I will tell Kieran if you and I can't come to a compromise.'

JD was barely over the threshold when Gráinne slammed the door so hard he was sure he'd felt it bite his backside. She didn't waste time in turning out the light on him. Moments later, he saw her lights go out and heard her move up the stairs.

He remained on her small porch, thinking about his next move. It was still dark but many of the windows along the terrace houses were on, and a car was idling up the road, warming up for a work commute, no doubt.

He looked at his watch. No wonder Gráinne's neighborhood was starting to come alive. It was after five am. At least the rain had stopped.

A door opened at the next house, and a woman stepped out. 'Morning,' he said to her.

She glanced at Gráinne's door and smiled. 'And to you. Everything all right?'

JD flipped his guard's ID open to show the woman. 'Aye.'

The woman scrutinized his ID then nodded. 'Grand, so.'

'Mind yourself,' he said, heading across the road to his car.

He certainly had his work cut out. He had to find a way to keep Gráinne safe. If she wasn't going to help him, he had to find a way to keep her from hindering his job.

When he'd come here tonight, he'd hoped to

get her help. If things weren't complicated enough already, he knew kissing her would keep his blood boiling. It wasn't as if he was already having a hard time concentrating on the case, he thought sarcastically.

He got into his car and slammed the door. It had only been sitting since two am, but the temperature was like ice. That was just one of the things he loved about Ireland in December, he snorted to himself sarcastically. He cranked the engine over and turned on the heater, letting the car – and himself – warm up before heading home. Yawning loudly, he pulled the car out of its parking space and headed into the city.

Chapter Nine

'What are you doing here?' Gráinne snapped.

'I'm clocking in. I do work here, you know.'

'No, you're a guard. Since your secret is out, there's no need to hang around here anymore.'

'Maybe so, but you're the only one who knows, so there's no reason to quit,' he countered. 'As far as Kieran knows, I'm just a bartender. How would it look if I just quit without notice?'

'I don't care how it looks—'

'Well, I do. Getting on your brother's bad side is not part of my plan.'

'Yeah? And what is your plan? I won't stand for you harassing me on the job. It's bad enough you're harassing me at home.'

The bastard grinned. Gráinne could have slapped that smug look off his face if she didn't think it would attract her brother's attention.

'Is that what you call what happened last night? You seem to have enjoyed it, if I remember correctly.' He stepped closer and whispered in her ear. His male scent went right to her head before lodging itself in her belly and awakening her desire for him. 'You still have the smell of me on your skin. I like that.' Then he stepped away and winked.

'Oh!' she gasped in exasperation. She pushed him roughly away and left the backroom. In the kitchen, she spun around on him. 'Stay away from me.' She shook her finger at him. 'Do your job, but leave me alone.'

She heard JD chuckling behind her as she stomped out of the kitchen and into the pub.

The nerve of him! She seethed, grinding her teeth. She felt the tightness in her jaw ache as her mind raced back to the previous night. No matter what she did to distract herself, thoughts of last night kept creeping back.

She still felt JD's hands on her body. Thinking of how he'd kissed her sent tingles through her body and squeezed something low in her belly. She had to keep reminding herself she was angry with him.

Once she had slammed the front door on him, she'd made sure Milo was out then took herself to bed. She had been too tired to bother cleaning up. It had been enough just to get up the stairs. Her body thrummed all night, keeping her from sleep.

He was right about one thing. His scent still clung to her. She hadn't showered again after he left. Truth, she had taken comfort in his scent last night. It made her somehow feel safe. For just a moment at daybreak, before she finally tipped over into unconsciousness, she let herself pretend his touches were because he loved her and not because he wanted anything more from her.

Now, in the light of day, the reality of it all slapped her across the face. JD was a guard, he was working in the pub to use her for his case, and he'd been lying to them all. Worse, he'd used her last night in hopes of bribing her to be his snitch.

'*I'll never lie to you, Gráinne.*' Isn't that what he'd said to her? But wasn't that what he'd been doing all along?

No. He hadn't.

JD just never talked about himself, and she'd never asked. He always seemed to be interested in her. She had to kick herself at her self-centeredness. If she could see beyond the superficial, she would have seen JD was just very private about his personal life.

'*If things were different, I'd have you upstairs in your bed, showing you just how much I want you.*'

The memory of his statement made her smile again, but it was short-lived. Men had wanted her before. Would JD just use her willingness to his advantage?

She couldn't afford to be so willing. Not when she was so close to achieving her dream of a college education. She had the money now. Once she got through New Year's Eve, it would all be over – the dancing, the lying to Kieran and, as JD had said, the risk of being in the middle of things when the police finally took down Jimmy Molloy and Taylor Wade.

As much as it galled her, JD was right about the risks she was taking dancing at The Klub!. Well, it was almost over. Another couple weeks and Jett would be a memory to them all.

Gráinne gasped sharply at the hand on her shoulder. She'd been so lost in thought she didn't realize she stood staring into the pints left waiting to be served.

'Jazus, Kieran! You took ten years off my life,' she gasped. She pulled a tray from under the bar and put the pints on it.

'Are you okay? I called you from the end of the bar and you just stood there.' Kieran stepped around her to ring some charges into the register.

'Yeah, I'm grand. Just tired, I guess.'

'Eilis and I haven't seen you around much lately.'

'I know. I'm sorry. I've just been busy.' She lifted the tray and stepped around the bar to deliver the pints. When she returned, Kieran was still behind the bar, as if waiting for her.

'Busy? Do you have a boyfriend?'

Bless him. Kieran was always so interested in her love life. She shouldn't be so surprised by it, though. Since their parents had died when she was very young, Kieran was more than a big brother. He was the only father she'd ever known.

'No, I don't have a boyfriend, as if it were any of your business,' she said, winking.

'Hey, I have a right to know who's keeping my sister out late, especially if she's going to drag him to Christmas dinner.'

Gráinne flinched. Christmas dinner. She stole a quick glance at the calendar beside the register. How could it have gone unnoticed? Tomorrow was Christmas Eve.

'I'm not dragging anyone to Christmas dinner, and there's no one keeping me out late,' she told him.

'Hmmm...' was all he said. 'You must be moon-lighting, then. I haven't seen you this tired since your disco days.'

'Geez, Kieran. Will you not give over? What do you want from me?' she snapped.

'Gráinne, what's wrong? You're obviously upset

108

about something.' Kieran stroked her upper arm. 'Talk to me.'

At any other time, Gráinne would have spilled her guts about her worries and woes. She couldn't now. How could she tell him she was taking her clothes off for men? How could she tell him she'd taken ten grand to dance in a private show for Dublin's most notorious drug kingpin? She certainly couldn't tell him anything about JD or his case.

Worse, how could she look him in the eye and lie to him? Just as she had to do now.

Then she saw JD. He winked as he sailed through the kitchen door into the pub with a tray of food for a couple patrons.

She looked away quickly, but she knew Kieran had seen hers and JD's unspoken signals, his wink a reminder of last night and her glare telling him to feck off.

'Hmm...' he muttered again.

Summoning as much courage as she could, Gráinne looked up into her brother's eyes. For a moment, just a moment, she contemplated telling him everything. Her nerves were at breaking point. She was in danger at The Klub!. She recognized that now, and she wished there was a way to get out of it sooner rather than later. But, she only had one more week to work there, one big dance left to give, then a life to get on with, which included school. She had to keep that at the front of her mind always. Without the education, she could be nothing ... she would be nothing. She wanted this degree so Kieran would be proud of her ... so she was proud of herself. She had to face facts. Right now, she was anything but proud.

She looked away from Kieran then. 'No, Kieran. I'm not moonlighting. I don't have a boyfriend and no one is keeping me up late at night. Maybe I'm just not feeling well.' She looked at him then. 'Women problems.'

'Uh-huh.' She knew by the sound of his exclamation he didn't believe her. She'd heard it often enough.

'Was there anything you wanted? You said you were calling me,' she said, shifting the subject.

She watched Kieran think for a moment, then he said, 'We're still expecting you for Christmas.'

'Of course, I'll be there. Wouldn't miss it.'

'Do you think you could spare some time in your busy schedule to drop by tomorrow? Eilis thinks she can do everything herself, but she's not in any condition to prepare everything on her own. She could really use some help. I'm busy here at the pub and...'

'OK, Kieran. Enough. I'll help. I should have offered. I'm sorry. I've just had a lot on my mind lately.'

'Great. I'll let Eilis know you'll be over. I'll give you the day off so you can go over early, okay?' She could tell he was relieved to not have to do the work himself. Eilis was in the final stages of her pregnancy and was prone to mood swings.

Gráinne chuckled lightly. 'Sure.'

Kieran kissed her cheek. 'Thanks.'

'No. Thank you. You're still paying me for the lost time.' She winked.

Kieran walked back toward the kitchen. 'Did you say something? I didn't hear anything.'

110

'Chancer!' Gráinne chuckled again.

When she turned, she gasped sharply. JD stood close behind her. Too close.

'I love hearing you laugh.'

She stepped back quickly and moved around him, ignoring his comment.

She had to keep busy. It was going to be a long day if she let him anywhere near her. It was obvious he would take every chance he got to remind her about last night, not that she needed reminding.

'Thanks, Mystique. I owe you one,' said Gráinne.

'G'wan. I'm happy to work for you tomorrow. I can use the money. Besides, it's not like I have anywhere to go.'

Gráinne felt sorry for Mystique. If things were different, she would invite Mystique to Christmas dinner.

That phrase seemed to echo through her. *If things were different.* That seemed to be JD's mantra.

Things would be different – soon. Once Gráinne was free of The Klub!, she could come back to Mystique and get to know her real self. She'd find a way for Mystique to get away from The Klub!, too.

'I'm sure that's not true, but I appreciate your taking my time slots. I've got myself into a bind and...'

'I know. If your family found out, there'd be murder,' said Mystique.

'How did you know I hadn't told anyone?'

'You come to work in disguise. I don't even

111

know your real name. I've seen other girls like you ... hiding from something, or someone.'

'If things were different...' She was beginning to hate that phrase, but it was true.

'Pish. We all gotta do what we gotta do, right?'

What more could she say without telling Mystique everything. Keeping all these secrets was very draining. If it weren't for that last dance on New Year's Eve, Gráinne would tell Mystique everything now and quit The Klub!. Tonight.

'So, let me live vicariously through you. What are you doing for the holidays?'

Gráinne really admired Mystique. No matter what was going on, she seemed to always have a smile on her face and always saw the good in everything. Gráinne really wished she could invite her to Christmas dinner.

Sighing, she said, 'I don't know really. The usual, I guess. Food, a few gifts, more food.'

'Sounds nice.'

Gráinne thought she heard a bit of regret in her friend's voice, but wasn't sure if she was putting it there herself. For all she knew, Mystique could really love dancing.

She looked quickly around the dressing room to be sure they were alone. When she was sure they were, she turned back to Mystique.

'I don't really talk about my personal life when I'm at work, Myst,' she started, her voice low.

'Hey, none of us do. That's the beauty of this job, Jett. You can be anyone you want to be,' said Mystique, smiling.

Gráinne couldn't help but smile too. 'I know. But ... when I'm gone ... I'd like for us to be friends.' She looked into Mystique's eyes to see if she could gauge the girl's reaction to the news.

It seemed to take Mystique a moment to register the statement.

'Friends? Aren't we friends now?'

'Sure, but I'm talking real friends. You know, we can do lunch and go shopping, and all the other girly things girlfriends are supposed to do together.' Gráinne took Mystique's hands in her own and drew Mystique's eyes with her own. 'I mean it, Myst.'

'I'd like that.' If Gráinne thought Mystique had been smiling before, she really put on a show now. It left Gráinne wondering if her friend's other smiles were just a cover for her own personal anguish.

'Myst, I'd like to ask you to do something for me.'

'Sure.'

'I want you to quit.' She knew she'd shocked Mystique because she just sat there staring. 'Do you understand what I'm asking you?'

'You want me to quit? Are you crazy? Give up all this money?' Mystique laughed. When Gráinne continued looking into her eyes, she could tell that what she'd said had finally sunk in. 'I can't quit, Jett.'

'Of course, you can. There are other jobs in the city. You can go back to being you and have a life. This is no life.'

Mystique sat back, sliding her hands out of Gráinne's and looked away.

'There's a life after dancing for you, but not for me.'

'Just quit, Myst.'

'I can't. Can we please drop this?' Mystique glanced back to Gráinne.

'What do you mean you can't quit? It's just a job. Of course you can quit.'

Mystique took a deep breath and looked Gráinne in the eye. 'Jimmy owns me.'

The silence suddenly filling the room was palpable. Mystique turned away from Gráinne, but she could only look at her friend, trying to decide if she was serious or not.

With her voice just above a whisper, Gráinne said, 'People don't own people.'

Mystique whipped around to face Gráinne once more and, for the first time since she'd known Mystique, she saw tears well in her friend's eyes.

'Sometimes they do,' said Mystique. 'And if you don't leave, Jimmy will own you, too.'

Chapter Ten

Gráinne had put herself on automatic and let Eilis order her around the kitchen just to get through Christmas Day preparations. She was so tired by the time she got home, she couldn't remember half of what she'd made. She remembered Eilis's orders to wash, chop, and blend, but as busy as she'd been, it did little to keep her mind off JD's kiss, nor his confession of being a guard.

By the time she got home, she realized she was exhausted. She should've accepted Eilis's suggestion to stay the night. She could have slept in a little – a Christmas gift to herself. Indeed, she'd tried having a lie-in this morning, but Kieran's frantic call asking when she was coming over had forced her out of bed. He had always been crazy for the holidays. He was the biggest kid she knew.

Now, at their front door, a large sack full of gifts in one hand, she took a deep breath and knocked.

Ever since Kieran met Eilis last year, it seemed as if her brother lived a charmed life. Together, he and Eilis had reopened the Blues Tavern, and with the money the pub instantly generated, they were able to afford this great house in Dun Laoghaire, overlooking Dublin Bay. And now they were expecting their first child.

Gráinne was torn between being envious of Kieran's new life and the reality of becoming an aunt. The more she thought about it, though, the more she liked the idea of having a niece or nephew to spoil. Oh, the bedevilment she could cause! The thought put a grin on her face.

If nothing else, becoming an aunt was reason enough to get her life on track. She wanted her brother's children to be proud of their auld Auntie Gráinne, even if she was doomed to be a spinster for the rest of her life. She sighed heavily.

It wasn't a moment after her knock that the big door swung open. Kieran wore a pair of very loud red trousers, a red sweater with Rudolph and snowflakes stitched on it, and a Santa hat. Gráinne giggled. His kids were going to love him!

'Good lord, Kieran. Halloween is over,' she teased, stepping over the threshold into the hall. The smells of Christmas hit her instantly; from the cinnamon in the apple tarts to the plump roasting goose, to the scent of hand-cut turf that only came from a lighted fire. Gráinne couldn't help but feel merry herself.

Kieran hauled her into a great bear hug. 'Happy Christmas, Grain,' he sang, and planted a sloppy kiss square on her lips.

'Cads, Kier, what are you drinking?' She tasted something sweet on his lips, perhaps honey. He must have had quite a bit of it by the state of him.

''Tis a drop of honeymooners' brew. Will you have some?'

'Mead, huh? Sure, I'm for it.'

'I'll take your coat, and you can put my pressies under the tree.' He grinned as he fingered the overflowing sack in her hand.

'You'll get nothing, if you don't behave.' She playfully slapped his hand away.

She set the sack on the floor, tossed her hand-bag onto the hall table, and pulled off her long black coat. Kieran shielded his eyes dramatically.

'Damn, Gráinne. Couldn't you find anything brighter to wear? You look like a snowball!'

Gráinne punched him playfully on the shoulder. 'Shut up and get my drink.'

As Kieran disappeared down the hall, Gráinne stole a glance at herself in the big hall mirror. There was nothing wrong with her cream-colored crushed velvet dress. She thought it was very festive, with its long sleeves, short skirt and beaded trim around her deep-cut neckline. She'd tied a red satin sash around her waist to match her pumps, and the cream-colored tights sparkled like moonlight on snow. She'd left her dark curly hair down around her shoulders and put on a pair of colorful earrings with little bells hanging from the dangles. And to finish off her festive appearance, she'd dared to sprinkle some of Jeff's glitter in her hair, much of which now clung to the velvet.

Gráinne thought she looked damn nice, if she did say so herself. Like a creamy popsicle maybe, but not a snowball.

Grabbing the sack of gifts, she let herself into the parlor where the Christmas tree stood in the big bay window, twinkling, winking, and blinking with holiday cheer. Holiday music played softly from hidden speakers around the room.

She loved this house. It was a Victorian terrace with huge and very proper rooms. The front parlor served as their living room, but it had originally been a receiving room. A giant of a fireplace sat against one wall, surrounded by the original intricately-carved marble mantle. It was now strung with garland, and big church candles flickered against the heavily ornate gilt mirror. Tiny reflective lights danced around the room with those echoing off the tree, reminding her of a kind of holiday disco.

As suspected, a turf fire had been laid. The turf sods glowed and sent off the kind of heat no wood fire could match. The scent reminded her of the old days when Kieran would bring home turf sods to the Finglas house. During the year they had coal fires, but the turf fire at Christmas was something special. It wouldn't have been a proper Christmas without one.

Gráinne stepped over to the tree. Crouching, she placed her gifts amongst the others. She sat back on her heels, folded her arms over her bent knees, and looked up at the tree. The warmth of the lights awakened the natural oils of the conifer and filled the room with the smell of the season. She closed her eyes and deeply inhaled the fragrant scent.

There hadn't been time yesterday to appreciate all the decorations. There had been too much work to do in the kitchen. But the sight and smell of the tree brought back memories – both sweet and bitter – of Christmases past.

This time of year was the hardest for her. It was a time for families, food and cheer, all of which she loved and had shared with Kieran. But it was also a time that reminded her of the parents she barely remembered – of a mother who should have woken her up to watch her father, dressed as

Santa, putting her presents under the tree. Of a time when she should have been helping her mother prepare the meal in the kitchen, instead of Eilis. Or, perhaps now, both women.

Kieran had done a tremendous job raising her on his own. He did all the things their father would've done. He tucked her in at night and kissed her forehead. He packed her lunches for school and helped her study. He let her have sleepovers and indulged them all with pizza, candy, and a night at the movies she knew they couldn't afford. He went without so she could live as normal a life as possible.

Every Christmas, he'd put on the Santa costume and make enough noise to raise the dead so she'd wake to see him at the tree, putting out the gifts he always seemed to come up with each year. The poor tree often reminded her of the twig Charlie Brown tried to convince his friends was a beautiful Christmas tree.

They had been beautiful trees, she thought wistfully.

She recalled when she and Kieran had made decorations. She'd been too young to understand what being poor was, but looking back she remembered nights she and Kieran sat up together making their own ornaments. He told her home-made ones were better than any store-bought ones.

Together they'd made cutouts of their hands and feet then decorated them with crayons, and glued on bits of anything they could find around the house. They'd made popcorn and pasta trimmings and paper chains. And when they ran out of traditional things to make ornaments with, they'd found things around the house to decorate the boughs – spoons and forks tied with shoe laces, bits of twine tied into bows, and some cut-up pieces of coat hanger they'd painted with the nail polish Kieran bought for her so her nails would be pretty on the day. He'd twisted the wire together and bent them to look like candy canes and hung them on the tree, too.

Kieran had praised Gráinne's ingenuity at her tree topper, but assured her that his socks would *not* replace the angel, no matter how poor they were. Together they created an angel out of a small soap bottle for the body, an old porcelain doll head she had no idea where it came from, and lace doilies their mother had left behind.

Gráinne smiled at all the memories.

They may have been poor but Kieran made her feel like a princess.

Slipping out of her memories, she looked up the tree. Tears welled in her eyes when she saw their angel staring down at her.

Glancing at the other ornaments, she spied one special cutout and reached up to grasp it gently in her fingers. It was of a pair of paper hands, hers and Kieran's. They were cut out together to look like the hands were joined. Both of their names were scrawled across the back with the date. On the front it simply said 'Family Forever.'

She loved Kieran for everything he'd done to make her life as normal as possible, but as she looked at some of their childhood decorations on this tree, she couldn't have loved him any more at this very moment if she tried.

As much as she appreciated him trying to make her life seem normal, it had all been an act. He'd pretended for her sake. In return, she grew up pretending everything was normal, even when things were falling apart.

Especially when things were falling apart.

Last year, when she and Eilis's friend, Megan, had found Kieran and Eilis in their West Cork cottage, Gráinne had been furious. She had already been feeling as though her life were going nowhere and now she was angry with Kieran for betraying her. He was all she had and now he was replacing her with another woman. How could she not be jealous? Even at her age, the hurt was deep.

It took a while, but she came to love Eilis as a sister. She realized Kieran wasn't replacing her. He never could. They were family. But he was a man with a man's needs. She understood that. After all, she had a woman's needs, and wasn't that the crux of her problems for so many years?

Seeing how well Kieran and Eilis settled in together, Gráinne had been forced to think about where her own life was going.

It took a lot of hard thinking, but she realized no one would love her until she could first learn to love herself. To do that, she had to face the reality of her situation and step out of her pretend world.

But wasn't The Klub! just another version of pretend?

While she pretended being someone else for a few hours a week was all fun and games, deep inside she was screaming at herself for allowing

121

things to so out of control again. If it hadn't been for her dream of college, she never would have taken the job.

Gráinne could pretend all she wanted, but the realization was still there. She'd danced her way straight to the notice of Dublin's most notorious drug kingpin, and he wanted her badly enough to pay ten grand for the privilege. That scared the hell out of her, as well it should.

For a brief moment, very brief, Gráinne wondered if it were possible to do what Wade expected. Then she could disappear forever. She'd had one night stands before. What was one more?

Who was she kidding? Sleeping with Wade was the worst possible thing she could do. She'd only dig herself deeper into his world. He'd eventually discover her true identity and then she'd have to leave Dublin to keep Kieran and Eilis safe. She knew Wade wouldn't stop at using her family against her to make her compliant.

Looking at those joined paper hands hanging from the tree, Gráinne decided she had to find a way out of the New Year's Eve job. She couldn't go back to The Klub!. Jett had to disappear. Now. She couldn't risk the lives of those she loved by letting things play out to their potential end.

Her gut twisted at the thought.

No, she couldn't go through with it. As of tonight, as of now, she was done. She'd get the money back to Jimmy somehow, but she wasn't stepping foot back in The Klub! ever again. She'd have to find her tuition another way, a way that didn't involve selling herself or selling out.

Just then, a hand bearing a flute of mead was

thrust before her, startling her.

'Geekers, Kier,' she gasped. 'You shouldn't sneak up on people like that.' She stood and took the flute.

'I didn't mean to scare you,' came the deep timbre of a familiar voice.

Gráinne turned slowly and looked into JD's whiskey-colored eyes. His dark brows accentuated the intense look he wore. It was the same look he wore Halloween night in The Klub! when she'd danced for him – as if he were stripping her bare with his gaze. She flushed at the thought and stepped away from him, her heart pounding, but not before her gaze swept over him.

JD was dressed in olive-colored cords, brown loafers, and a thick cream-colored Aran sweater. His ginger hair meticulously trimmed, he looked delicious. Her heart pounded in her chest, making her breath deeply.

She turned back to the tree again, hoping to calm herself.

'What are you doing here?' Her hand trembled nervously as she sipped the mead.

'I was invited.'

He stepped closer. She felt him at her back. He didn't touch her, but she felt his heat and smelled his male essence permeate her nostrils. Instantly, her body responded by sending tingles up her spine. The pit of her stomach tightened, pooling heat lower.

'I can't imagine why,' she snapped.

'Because I told Kieran I didn't have anywhere to go.'

'To Hell would have been a good start.'

JD laughed at her rebuke.

'Come on.' He cupped her elbow in his palm. 'Sit with me.' Gráinne jerked her arm away from him. 'All right, we can talk here. I don't mind.'

'Why are you really here, JD?' She spun around to face him.

'I told you. Kieran invited me.'

'What lie did you tell for him to make that offer?'

'It was no lie, Gráinne. He asked what my plans were and I told him I was sitting home alone, watching the match. He said I could watch the match here and join the family for dinner. How could I turn down an offer of food *and* footie?' he asked. 'And I knew you'd be here,' he added, grinning seductively.

Gráinne grumbled. 'Uh-huh. What about your sister?'

JD chuckled again. 'I don't have a sister.'

'But you told Kieran...'

'I told Kieran I did to cover for you. You didn't want me to tell him where I really got your bra, did you?'

'Of course not. I just thought...' She was surprised JD had lied to cover for her.

Not knowing what else to say, she stepped away and walked over to the fireplace. She sipped at her mead as she watched the embers glow among the sods.

The knowledge she'd have to spend the whole day with him both unnerved her and angered her. She didn't know what it was he did to her. She couldn't keep her mind off his kiss, his hands on her body, his mouth on her breasts. She wanted it all again, God help her.

Just then, she caught his reflection in the mirror. Their gazes locked as he crossed the room to stand behind her once more.

She couldn't seem to pull her gaze away. Those whiskey-colored eyes pulled her in and held her, caressed her. Held her hostage, damn it.

He leaned forward to place his flute of mead on the mantle. His body pressed into hers as he did. She felt his erection against her bottom and sucked in her breath sharply. He only grinned at her, knowing.

He raised his hand over her head. When she saw what he held in his grasp, her eyes squeezed shut in denial.

This wasn't happening. How could he do this to her? How could he taunt her this way? Why couldn't he just leave her alone?

'Gráinne,' he whispered. His breath was warm against her cheek. 'It's bad luck not to kiss under the mistletoe.'

Her eyes flew open the instant his hot tongue touched her earlobe, and again their gazes locked in the mirror. His tongue toyed with the dangling holiday earring she wore, before running down the length of her neck.

Damn her body, anyway. Uncontrolled fire shot through her, making her body tremble.

He slipped his arm around her waist and pulled her against him. His lips and tongue continued tasting her as he ground his groin against her bottom.

'Mmm,' he groaned deeply. 'You taste as good as you look.'

Gráinne swallowed hard. She broke his gaze long enough to scan the room quickly in the mirrors. The door was closed and the room empty, except for them. The realization anyone could enter the room unannounced made her heart pound.

'Please,' she managed, pleading. 'Don't do this to me. Not here.'

'Would you have me take you home to continue?'

She was speechless. She only managed to shake her head.

That was a lie. If what he'd done to her the last time was any indication of what it would be like to give into him fully, she could very well break down and let him into her bed.

'You're trembling, love. I think you'd like me to take you home,' he teased. 'By the look in your eyes, I see I'm right.'

'Please, stop,' she gasped. 'I can't ... I can't do this.'

'I'm not holding you against your will, love. You can step away anytime.'

She defied herself by pausing, before finally moving back to the tree where she stared into the colored lights.

She'd be lying if she said she didn't enjoy his touch. She'd done nothing but dream about it since she'd first seen him. Once he'd kissed her in her kitchen, she'd been fantasizing about what it would be like making love with him.

His offer of a little more of what he'd done to her was more than tempting, but she couldn't allow herself to go down that road. Not here. Not now. Not in her brother's house. Not ever. He was a guard and wanted her to snitch for him. All this … enticement … was his way of coercing her.

Well, it wasn't going to work. She wasn't going back to The Klub!, so getting her to snitch for him was a moot point. He could tease her all he wanted.

Wiping at her tears, she let her anger rise.

'You have some nerve.'

'What are you talking about? Is it a sin to kiss a beautiful woman on Christmas Day?'

Gráinne spun to face him. She felt the pinch between her eyes as her brows drew tightly together.

'How dare you come into my brother's home, on Christmas Day no less, to harass me? Have you no respect?'

JD's chuckle infuriated her more.

'You call nibbling your neck harassment? I suppose you'd call this full-out assault.'

Before she could blink, he threaded his hand through her hair. In one fluid motion, he grabbed her by the bottom and hauled her against him.

She fought him, but struggling was futile. The instant his lips touched hers, she was gone. Her anger dissipated like a puff of steam.

He ravaged her with his mouth, his tongue stealing itself between her lips. He tasted of honeyed wine and smelled of spicy cologne. The heady mixture pooled warmly in her stomach, and lower still.

She whimpered, instantly intoxicated.

Damn her body for reacting to him so easily.

In the back of her mind, she worried Kieran or

Eilis could walk through the door at any moment. For that reason alone, the kiss seemed to last forever, yet the risk of getting caught was all the more exciting. The revelation disturbed her about as much as how quickly her body reacted to JD's touch.

But the kiss ended all too soon and he was pulling away.

She reached out to grab him to keep from collapsing, but when she opened her eyes, he had moved away.

Gasping, she grinned to herself. It was hard to stand after a kiss like that.

Chapter Eleven

Gráinne was right. Kieran and Eilis's house was not the place to provoke her, not emotionally and certainly not sexually. If he hadn't stopped when he did, things would have gotten out of hand.

Retrieving his mead from the mantle, he gulped the remaining liquid until the flute was empty. He'd never admit it, but kissing Gráinne left him shaking.

He ran his fingers through his hair and, staring into the fire, wondered what compelled him to arouse her. Maybe it was she who aroused him and he was just returning the favor. Whatever it was, he had a difficult time keeping his hands off her now that he'd kissed her in her kitchen. When they weren't together, it was just as difficult not thinking about her.

He knew he'd gone too far with her a few nights ago, and now his testosterone was raging. He wanted to touch her, taste her, and hear her cry out as she came. Just remembering her hands on him and her offer that night was enough to get him riled.

A movement in the mirror caught his attention. In its reflection, he watched Gráinne flop into a chair beside the tree.

What was going through her mind? The look on her face was unreadable. He saw neither anger nor embarrassment. She only sat with her elbows on her knees, her hands steepled over her mouth as she stared at the tree.

With a deep sigh, he set his flute on back on the mantle and went to her side. He knelt before her. Taking her hands, he looked at her but she refused to meet his gaze. Though he tried to gently turn her face with his fingers, she wouldn't budge. He saw tears pooling in her eyes, ready to fall, yet she saw her fight them. Did she not want him to see her cry?

'I'm sorry, Gráinne. That was uncalled for.'

He raised her fingers to his lips and kissed the backs of them. 'I ... I don't know what it is about you, Gráinne. Every time I'm near you, it seems all I do is provoke you.'

'Why do you suppose that is?' she asked, still refusing to meet his gaze.

'Because you're a beautiful and exciting woman?'

She looked at him then. Her eyes glistened, her voice flat. 'It wouldn't have anything to do with the fact that I'm an exotic dancer, and you think you can use my brother against me to get me to sleep with you. Or maybe it's because of my job at The Klub! and you think I'm an automatic shoe-in to be your snitch.'

Her words stung.

'I can see how you'd think all of those things. I can't begin to tell you how wrong you are. Yes, in the beginning I hoped to glean something from you about Jimmy and what's going on over there. But...'

'But what, JD?' she asked, her words flippant.

Just then the door flew open and Kieran

130

entered waving a bottle of mead.

'Refills anyone?'

JD caught a questioning look on Kieran's face. JD was sure he wondered what his sister was upset about and why he was on his knees in front of her.

'Did I interrupt something?' Kieran asked, his cheer noticeably diminishing. JD stood, walked back to the mantle and grabbed his empty flute.

'Not at all, Kieran. Gráinne's just full of holiday cheer,' he said, retrieving his flute and holding it out for a refill.

Kieran chuckled as he poured. 'She always did like Ho Ho Day.'

Gráinne groaned as she rose. 'I'll see if Eilis needs some help.'

There was a long pause, as Kieran seemed to size up JD.

Then Kieran waved a hand in his direction. 'Are you sure there isn't something you want to tell me?'

'Nope.'

'I suppose all this glitter sort of just leapt on you.'

JD wasn't sure if Kieran was mad or just nosey. Most likely, a brother looking out for his sister.

He reached for the spring he'd dropped on the mantle. 'Mistletoe.'

'Ah!' was all Kieran said in response.

JD sipped his mead then said, 'Thanks for inviting me. This is really great.' Kieran exhaled and the tension was instantly gone. He sat down on the sofa, setting the bottle of mead on the coffee table.

'No worries, mate. To be honest, I was surprised you weren't spending it with your sister,'
he said, leaning back.

JD hated lying to Kieran. He really liked the
man. But he had to protect Gráinne, even from
her own brother.

'Yeah, well,' he sighed for effect. 'We're not as
close as you and Gráinne. She's doing her own
thing.'

'No girlfriend?'

JD chuckled as he glanced back toward the door
Gráinne had just disappeared through. 'Working
on it.'

'By the looks of things, seems to me you were
working on my sister.' Kieran tapped his lips with
the tip of his finger. JD wiped at his own with the
backs of his fingers. Lipstick!

Looking into Kieran's eyes, what could he say?

'Listen, mate,' Kieran continued. 'If you want
to see Gráinne, that's your business. She needs a
decent bloke in her life. But as her brother, you
know I have to tell you, if you hurt her I'll have
to break your legs.' Kieran's face was as serious as
a winter storm.

'I've heard that one before,' said Eilis, waddling
into the parlor.

Kieran laughed, his mood noticeably lighten-
ing. JD was clueless to the family joke so he just
sipped his mead and wiped his lips again to be
sure the rest of the lipstick was gone. Thank the
Lord for small favors. Gráinne hadn't worn the
garish colors she normally wore at The Klub!.
But then, that wasn't Gráinne's M.O. She didn't
normally wear a lot of make-up when she worked

132

in the pub. Her natural beauty was enough.

Eilis stood in front of the men where they sat on their respective ends of the sofa, which faced the tree. 'I don't know how much you know of how Kieran and I met, JD, but let's just say when Gráinne found out, she said the exact same thing to me.'

His lips twitched as he tried suppressing a grin.

'As you can see, I'm alive and well.' She, very carefully, lowered herself onto Kieran's lap where she wrapped her arms around his neck.

'But he's bigger than Gráinne,' JD joked.

'And I won't hesitate to follow through with my threat,' Kieran emphasized.

JD knew Eilis was laughing at them and not with them.

'You're a big bear with a fierce growl, love,' she said to Kieran. 'Let Gráinne win her own battles.' She leaned over and nipped Kieran on the ear, causing him to growl.

'Now, if you two are done posturing, dinner is done. Gráinne just finished setting the table and the goose needs carving.' She tried standing, then looked back to Kieran. 'Give us a push, love, will ya?'

Kieran grinned at the request and gave her a boost ... with both hands firmly on her behind.

'Ooh!' Eilis gasped. 'Chancer!'

'Just give me the chance, love. I'll give you a push you'll never forget.' He wiggled his eyebrows at her and her cheeks flamed. JD grinned at the couple's exchange.

'Kieran,' she giggled, 'we have company. Behave.'

Kieran looked back at JD, his head hung low and pain etched across his face. 'Never have kids. I can't remember when the last time we–'

'Kieran!' Eilis cut in as she disappeared through the door.

'Coming, love,' Kieran called over his shoulder.

JD laughed at their love play. He envied them. He'd never felt that kind of love for a woman, but he thought he could with Gráinne. All he wanted to do was tease her, tempt her, get her temper going, and arouse her until she was calling out his name as he made love to her.

Kieran drew JD out of his thoughts as he moved to a set of double doors and unlatched them. He rolled one into the wall, then the other.

JD's mouth fell open. It was as if someone had waved a wand and a fairytale Christmas came to life.

Stepping into the room, his gaze quickly swept the room to take it all in. Lush green garlands festooned the ceiling coving. Silver tinsel threaded through it and caught the soft light shining from the candles flickering around the room and the old gas chandelier hanging over the table.

The dining table was elegantly dressed. Hand-cut Waterford Crystal goblets winked in the shimmering light. Newbridge silverware, with its traditional Celtic design, lay beside bone china so delicate-looking it could have only come from Belleek.

Cream-colored Irish linen covered the antique oval table, in the center of which a cornucopia of bowls and dishes were filled with all manner of food. And on one end was the goose, fresh from

134

the oven and steaming on the carving platter.

In the background, soft bluesy Christmas music followed him in from the front parlor.

The room hung heavy with the scent of vanilla candles, pine garlands, and a collection of foods, ranging from earthy herb stuffing to rich goose and homemade gravy to fruity Christmas pudding.

The fireplace matched the one in the parlor and had been decorated the same, and a turf fire had been laid in the hearth.

Heavy burgundy drapes had been drawn over large windows at the back of the room where Gráinne stood watching him. The moment he saw her, everything around him faded into nothingness.

She took his breath away.

In that instance, he felt like he'd come home.

It hit him like a blow to the chest and left him breathless. He knew deep in his heart he wanted to make Gráinne part of his life. Nothing and no one had ever made him feel the way she did. His blood still crackled from their kiss.

Seeing her now, standing before him with her kiss-swollen lips and knowing gaze, he wanted to take her in his arms and love her – on the table, on the floor, against the wall – here in this room where it seemed magic existed.

In the back of his mind, he heard someone talking to him. He tried shutting it out, but there was no ignoring the shove he received from behind.

Spinning around, he saw the grin on Kieran's face. 'I haven't been allowed in this room all week. It looks great, doesn't it?'

'Amazing,' was all JD could manage as he turned back to Gráinne. Her cheeks flushed at his statement, her lips threatening to smile.

'Seat yourselves,' Eilis called over her shoulder. 'We'll be right back.' Eilis grabbed Gráinne's hand and they disappeared into the kitchen.

Kieran pulled out a chair for JD. 'Have a seat, mate,' he said, then moved to sit at the head of the table where he would carve the goose. JD slid into his seat and set his flute of mead on the table before he spilled it. His hands were shaking.

He didn't think he'd ever been as stunned as he was when he realized he was falling for Gráinne. He wanted to make her his, whatever it took.

'What was that all about?' Eilis asked, grinning like a cat.

Gráinne paced the kitchen, looking for any last minute things needing doing.

'I don't know what you mean,' she said, avoiding her sister-in-law's eyes.

'Girl, that man is in love with you.'

Gráinne nearly dropped the dish she'd picked up.

As usual, Gráinne covered her disbelief with sarcasm. 'Somehow, I doubt it.' Eilis took the dish out of her hands and spun her around. When their eyes met, she saw how serious Eilis was.

'It's written all over his face.'

'I only work with the man a couple days a week. We don't even get along.'

'You two get along fine.' Eilis grinned knowingly.

136

'Give over, Eilis.' Gráinne side-stepped her sister-in-law.

'So, how do you explain that bruise on your lip?'

Gráinne's hand flew to her mouth as she ran from the kitchen. At the hall mirror, Gráinne gasped in horror at the faint bruise on her lower lip. She gently ran her tongue over it, remembering how JD had assaulted her with his mouth. Butterflies warred in her stomach remembering the kiss.

He could kiss for Ireland, but love her?

Looking at her reflection in the mirror, she didn't think so. Men didn't love her. They used her. JD, too. She had to keep reminding herself of that.

Opening her handbag, which still lay on the hall table, she pulled out her lipstick and made sure to apply a thick enough coat to take her through dinner. With any luck, the bruise would be gone in a couple hours and she could forget the kiss ever happened.

As if!

She fingered her hair and returned to the kitchen where Eilis waited. She leaned against the countertop with her arms folded over her enormous stomach, a Cheshire cat grin on her face. Gráinne only glared at her sister-in-law.

'Well?' asked Eilis.

'Well, what?'

'What about that bruise? He either hit you or kissed you. Which was it?' Eilis pressed.

'So what if he kissed me? It's Christmas. He had mistletoe and you've been plying him with mead before I got here,' she snapped.

'Love, that ain't no mistletoe kiss.' Eilis snorted.

Without thinking, Gráinne bit, 'And how would you know?'

'I wonder.' Eilis cast a quick glance at her stomach and winked.

Silence as heavily pregnant as Eilis hung in the air.

Gráinne wanted to be angry. She wanted to tell Eilis to mind her own business. She also wanted to tell Eilis everything, but couldn't without telling her about The Klub! and the danger she'd gotten herself into.

With her voice lowered, she said, 'Eilis, let's not fight. It's Christmas.'

'You're the only one fighting, Gráinne. I'm just pointing out what I see.' Eilis stepped over and ran her hands up and down Gráinne's upper arms. 'I don't know what's going on between you two, but if he's got a loving look on his face and kissing you within an inch of your life, I'd say there's a lot to this story you're not telling.'

'Eilis–' Gráinne started.

Eilis cut her off. 'I'm not asking you to tell me what's going on. I'm only saying it wouldn't be such a bad thing to see where it goes.'

'I don't want a man in my life. I'm trying to get myself straightened out.' They'd had a few sisterly talks in the last year, so Eilis well knew why Gráinne had left Cork. She didn't know about college, but she knew about Gráinne's past with men.

'I know you are, but it doesn't mean you have to become a nun in the process. Just be more selective. I think JD is a good man. It wouldn't be wrong to take a chance with him.'

'Thanks for your advice, Eilis. I appreciate it. I really do. I'm just not ready for a relationship right now. I'm still trying to find out who I am.'

'Can't JD help you look?'

'No.' She wished things were different, but she knew JD's motivation.

She stepped out of Eilis's grasp and moved back to the counter then picked up the dish of cranberry sauce before heading for the dining room.

'Gráinne, are you still staying over for the night?'

She stopped at the door and smiled lightly over her shoulder. 'Yeah.'

'I should tell you Kieran asked JD to stay over as well. He thought JD might enjoy going out with us tomorrow, and he didn't want him driving home after drinking all day.'

'And he agreed?'

Eilis nodded. Gráinne's gut twisted. She couldn't seem to shake the man. 'Great,' she groaned.

Heading through the door, she now had to look forward to not just getting through a night with JD under the same roof as her, but also surviving St. Stephen's Day with him as he accompanied her family on a day at the races.

Chapter Twelve

'Are you sure you're OK with this?' asked JD. He sat on the sofa with a mug of steaming tea in his hand.

The house was quiet, save for the CD playing softly from the corners of the room.

Dinner had gone surprisingly well. He'd really enjoyed himself, almost feeling like one of the family.

Afterward, they'd retired to the parlor to open presents. He watched, with a grin on his face, as the Vaughans exchanged their gifts.

He was particularly interested in the gifts Kieran and Gráinne exchanged.

Gráinne's gifts to Kieran included a large box of Tunnocks Teacakes, a liter of milk, and a package of briefs with a Superman logo printed on them.

Kieran's gifts to Gráinne came in the form of a giant box of crayons, a Father Ted DVD, and a plastic tiara.

JD knew he'd missed some family joke between brother and sister as the wrappings flew about the room in their haste to see what the other had given them, but their enthusiasm was infectious. He couldn't help but laugh along with them.

He hadn't been expecting gifts, but as an invited guest he'd made sure to bring something for each of them – a big bottle of Hennessy for Kieran, flowers and chocolates for the ladies, and a stuffed bear for the baby.

To his surprise, Kieran and Eilis had given him a Christmas bonus. They said they were very happy with his work at the pub, and even though he'd only been there for a few short months, they felt he deserved it. JD had never been more touched, nor felt so guilty for accepting it. He decided to hold onto the money until the case was over, before returning it.

Sipping carefully at his tea, he watched Gráinne, waiting for her reply. She sat on the floor amidst the debris. The paper was in tatters but she carefully folded each piece neatly, as if she were savoring this last bit of Christmas.

He brought something special for her, but wanted to give it to her when they were alone. Soon, he said to himself with a sigh.

'It's not my house,' she said casually, keeping her gaze on her task. 'If Kieran asked you to stay over and invited you to go with us tomorrow, I can't do anything about it.'

'I don't want to upset you. If you want me to leave, just say the word and I'll slip out tonight and make my excuses at work the day after tomorrow.'

As much as it killed him to make the offer, he didn't want to push himself into her life. He had to find a way to regain her trust. If it meant giving her some space, he would do it.

Gráinne sighed, looking up at him. 'Nah, it's okay. I know you don't have anyone to spend the holidays with. I would feel worse if you were home alone.'

'I wouldn't be alone, love.' When her brow

lifted at his statement, he felt he should qualify it so she didn't get the wrong idea, though the spark of fire he saw in her eyes told him she must feel something for him.

'I have parents, but they're not in Ireland at the moment. They decided to spend the holidays in Lanzarote.'

'Oh? Oh!' she gasped, suddenly realizing her assumption was showing. 'I'm sorry, I thought... A sun holiday for Christmas? I'm for that.'

'Mum would move to a place with sun all year round, if she had the chance, but Dad will never leave Ireland. Instead, she makes him travel to the sun every chance she gets now he's retired.'

'What did your dad do?'

JD couldn't help but notice Gráinne shift her seat to face him. The mention of his parents and she lit up.

While working in the Blues Tavern, he'd learned Gráinne and Kieran's parents had passed away, leaving Kieran to raise her on his own. Beyond that, he knew nothing of their upbringing. Realizing Gráinne missed her parents made him want to love her all the more.

'Dad was on the Force until two years ago, when he had to take early retirement,' he said. Gráinne's questioning look made him continue. 'He was shot while trying to apprehend a suspect. If it hadn't been for Mum, he would have lost the leg. Doctors didn't expect him to walk again, let alone live, after losing so much blood, but now he's out playing golf.' JD thought back to that terrible time and his heart clenched.

'Wow,' Gráinne exclaimed. 'Your mum must

have been some nurse.'

Sighing, JD looked away from Gráinne. 'Life is ironic at the best of times. A kid illegally obtains a handgun to hold up a petrol station. Dad was off duty and filling up the car when it happened. He tried to apprehend the kid and got shot in the leg. The kid leaves him bleeding to death and gets away with less than two hundred euro. For two hundred lousy euro,' he repeated.

He felt Gráinne's hand on his thigh and looked into her eyes.

'I'm sorry, John. He was very lucky. You obviously love him very much. His loss would have been devastating.'

He chanced his arm by weaving his fingers with hers, holding her lightly. 'I do, and yes, it would have been.'

He gazed into her eyes for a long moment. He desperately wanted to kiss her. The lights danced off the natural highlights in her dark hair. Her skin glowed with rosy softness. And she'd reached out to him. As much as he wanted to pull her into his lap, he held back.

'How long have you been with the guards?' she finally asked, pulling her hand away and quickly scanned the room.

He had closed both the hall door and the sliding doors when he'd brought their tea in earlier. Kieran had taken an exhausted Eilis to bed, so it was just the two of them alone with the Christmas tree and their respective secrets.

'Almost fifteen years now. I made detective three years ago.'

'Did you join because your dad was a guard?'

JD chuckled lightly. 'Did you expect anything else? It's a family tradition. Granddad was on the Force, too. My great-grandfather stood side by side with Michael Collins and helped formulate the new Irish Police Force.'

'I'm impressed.'

'It's funny. Looking at it from this side, it's kinda cool to follow in the family tradition. But I can't help thinking I wouldn't want my child joining up.'

'That's the father in you talking. You'd probably be just as proud of your child as your father must be of you,' she told him, 'no matter what they decided to do.'

Her observation touched him.

'Maybe. But things are changing in Ireland. It's more dangerous than it was in my father's time. I can only imagine what it will be like in twenty years when my child would be old enough to join.' If he were lucky enough to have children, that is.

'Do you want children, Gráinne?' His gaze wavered, hoping the question sounded like he was curious for the sake of being curious, and not because he wanted to know what to expect when they were married. They would marry, he vowed.

'Sure I do. Don't you?'

He released a pent-up breath. 'You bet.' As long as it's with you, he heard his inner voice say.

Somewhere along the evening, the holiday music on the player had been replaced with Adele, which now played softly in the background. The woman's sultry voice sang about forever love.

JD couldn't help but find the moment ironic. If

things had been different between them, this moment would have been perfectly spent curled up together on the sofa, watching the lights twinkle on the tree, talking about their future together. Instead, he knew Gráinne thought he was using her to get to Molloy and Wade. She didn't trust him because he'd covered up his true identity until it suited him to reveal who he really was.

He would earn back her trust, though. He wanted Gráinne in his life.

They sat together in comfortable silence, listening to the music. Gráinne was the first to break the spell that had settled over them.

'I ... I suppose I should just come out and say this.'

JD turned his full attention to her. She wasn't looking at him as she spoke, but her body language told him how hard this was for her to say. He wondered what could be so difficult.

'I'm listening.' Yes, she had his full attention.

'I'm not going back to The Klub!.'

He waited for her to continue, but only silence followed as she focused on the tree.

'Go on.'

'What more is there to tell? I'm not going back. I quit.' She glanced at him briefly, before picking up another scrap of paper to fold, busy work for her nervous fingers. He saw her hands shake.

'Gráinne…'

She looked up, defiant. 'I've made up my mind.'

He was flummoxed. A weight lifted from his chest he hadn't realized was there. He'd been worried about her working at The Klub!. He wished she'd chosen any other side job besides

145

one where she took off her clothes for men. But he desperately needed to learn more about Molloy's and Wade's business and she was his only hope.

While he was relieved she wasn't returning to The Klub!, he was now left back at square one and three months' worth of work was down the drain.

JD decided it would be worth it to keep Gráinne safe.

'Well...' he said, looking for words.

'I mean it, John. I'm not going back.'

'It's okay, Gráinne.'

'Okay?' Her brows drew together, as if unsure she'd heard him correctly.

He nodded. 'Yeah. I'm glad, to be honest.'

'This means you can stop harassing me about snitching for you.'

He chuckled lightly. 'You weren't cooperating anyway, so I was going to have to find another way to get my information.'

He paused to watch her. She had started off prepared for battle, but now confusion, relief, dismay, and surprise played across her face as she tried to decide how she felt.

'How did Jimmy take it when you told him?' The look on her face told him what he was afraid of. 'You haven't told him.'

'Not yet.' Her eyes glistened. Something was going on and, whatever it was, it scared her.

'When did you decide you were quitting?' he asked, trying to stay calm.

'Tonight. I was thinking about some things and realized, as much as I hate to admit it, you were right. It's not safe there. The longer I stay, the deeper in I'll get. It's all getting out of control. I just want it to end.' Her words tumbled out one after the other.

'What's getting out of control?'

'Nothing.' His heart flipped. He knew she was hiding something.

'You think quitting will make it all go away?'

'Yes. No one knows me outside The Klub!. Jett will disappear forever. They'll never find me ... her.'

He was sure she believed what she was saying. He hoped she was right.

'When did you plan to tell Molloy?'

'I don't know. Sometime this week, I suppose.'

'I thought you said you weren't going back? Do you plan on calling him? I don't want to scare you more, but he can trace you from your caller ID if he has the right connections.'

'I–' she started, pausing to wipe away a tear. 'I was going to send him a letter in the post. I won't have to go into The Klub! or call him. He won't be able to reach me. That will be the end of it.'

'I hope to God you're right, Gráinne.'

He took a sip of his tea only to find that it had gone cold.

'Do you suppose Kieran would begrudge a man a drop of his whiskey?'

'I'll get it.' He watched as she disappeared through the sliding doors.

He groaned at the sight of her bottom and the way it made the back of her short skirt sway from side to side. He remembered the feel of her in his palms when he'd kissed her earlier. Despite

147

Gráinne's startling news, he'd still managed to get an erection. Hell, just being under the same roof with her did it to him.

He groaned, flinging his head against the sofa back, squeezing his eyes shut, willing his discomfort to abate.

'Down, boy. Down.'

'Who are you talking to?' Gráinne asked, walking back into the room. She carried a bottle of Jameson and a pair of Waterford cut crystal tumblers.

'No one. Here,' he said, quickly sitting up. 'Let me take those for you.'

'I forgot to ask if you took ice.'

'And ruin a good whiskey?'

She grinned and let him take the bottle and glasses, then went back to her place on the floor in front of the sofa. He lowered himself to sit beside her where she watched him uncap the bottle and pour a measure into each glass.

She sighed, watching him going about such a mundane task as pouring her a drink. The colored lights on the tree danced along the contours of the cut crystal, reflecting rainbows across his hands.

She focused on his fingers, remembering how they felt on her body and the feelings they had awakened in her. His touch made her feel a way no other man ever had.

If only things were different.

JD handed her a glass and she nearly dropped it.

'You're trembling,' he said, catching the glass just in time. 'You all right?'

148

She nodded quickly. 'Sure.' She'd never admit the memory of his kisses made her quake with desire.

To prove to him she was fine, she grasped the glass and took a sip. Her hand trembled again as she lifted the glass to her lips and ended up getting as much of the whiskey down her front as into her mouth.

He was on his knees before her immediately, taking the glass. He set it on the table and started to wipe the whiskey from her chin with the edge of his sleeve, having removed his jumper earlier in the evening.

She flushed with angry embarrassment. Why did things have to happen to her? Why couldn't the evening just pass quietly?

Why did his nearness make her act like a damn teenager?

Tears spilled down her cheeks before she could stop them.

'Please. Stop,' she snapped, halfheartedly batting at his hands.

When she met his gaze, her heart pounded by the way the tree lights danced in his dark golden eyes.

For a moment, neither said a word. Gráinne couldn't have spoken had she tried. Just looking at him took her breath away. And all thought.

'You know,' he whispered, just inches from her. He was so close. 'It's a sacrilege to waste good whiskey.'

The words were innocent enough, but his impassioned gaze, the feel of his thumb outlining her lips, and her own need, made her body tremble

149

even more. Slowly, he leaned into her. She didn't move, couldn't move, and let him come to her. Her breath caught in her throat.

His lips were warm when they touched hers, gentle yet cautious. It wasn't a possessive kiss, but it sent her head reeling just the same.

It was ... sweet ... protective ... loving. And her heart ached for more.

He demanded nothing of her. He wasn't even touching her with anything more than his lips. Yet...

He pulled away all too soon, but it was for the best. No matter how much she desired John Desmond, she had to keep her head about her and her priorities in line. He made it so damn tough, though.

He sat back on his heels and grinned at her. She saw something in his eyes she didn't recognize; yet her heart ached to pull him back to her.

'I got you a present,' she heard him say. She watched as he pulled a small package from his trouser pocket. Even as she took it from him, she wasn't sure why he was giving her anything.

'What is it?' she managed to ask.

He smiled softly. 'If I told you, it wouldn't be a surprise. Open it and find out.'

It was a small package, wrapped in wrinkled emerald paper and tied with a slightly crushed gold ribbon.

Any other woman might find the presentation of the gift insulting. Gráinne thought it was rather cute.

Still, she was leery of the gift as she fingered it. Something told her her relationship with him would change if she accepted the gift. But hadn't it already changed?

'Go on, love,' he prodded.

She looked into his eyes. 'I ... I didn't get you anything. I didn't know you would be here or I–'

'I already got my present.' She felt her brows draw together. She knew she hadn't given him anything. Then he said, 'You kissed me back.'

'John–' she started. She had kissed him back, but she didn't think he'd noticed.

'Now, would you not give over, woman, and just open it.' He chuckled. 'Jazus. Most women would be at the exchange counter by now.'

Gráinne suppressed a laugh. She picked at the ribbon until it came loose then she pulled off the paper.

In her hand was a small red velvet box.

For a moment, Gráinne imagined the box held an engagement ring, and her pounding heart was what any woman would have felt, anticipating a proposal.

In reality, she hadn't known JD long enough, nor would she get the chance. Not in her wildest dreams did she ever expect a proposal from any man. It didn't keep her from pretending ... for just a moment.

What she found inside the box was not what she expected or pretended. It wasn't a ring of any kind, nor was the box a fancy container for a gag gift. Nestled in the velvet folds was a delicate gold heart with a ruby center. It was suspended from a finely-spun gold chain.

She was speechless. It was lovely.

JD reached up and took the box from her and

151

set it on the table. Removing the necklace, he edged closer to place it around her neck. Her skin tingled where he touched her. Her heart pounded at his nearness and from the intimacy of what he was doing.

Sitting back again, he looked at her, smiling softly. 'It suits you.'

'John–' she started again.

'Shh. Just let me look at you.'

Her heart fluttered wildly as his gaze swept over her. He was doing it again – stripping her with just a look. She turned away, embarrassed.

'You have no idea how beautiful you are, do you?'

She'd never heard him sound so serious. Not even the night he came to her house to tell her he worked for the guards and wanted her to snitch for him.

'Don't–' she murmured.

'Gráinne, look at me.' With gentle fingers on her chin, he turned her to face him.

She'd felt like an emotional female earlier when she'd gone for the whiskey. She'd used the time in the kitchen to get herself together.

She thought she had.

Now, as she gazed into his eyes, hearing him speak to her so gently, her eyes welled up once more. She breathed deeply to calm herself.

'I can't begin to explain my feelings for you. All I know is somehow you've gotten inside of me and wrapped yourself around my heart,' he confessed. 'I know we haven't gotten off to the best start. I know you've lost trust in me. But I'd like the chance to get to know you better. Maybe when you get to know me, you'll realize you can trust me.'

Her heart flipped. How she wished she were the woman he thought she was.

She squeezed her eyes shut, trying to block the feelings he woke in her. When she opened them again, she had it in her mind to tell him there could be no future for them.

Then he touched her again.

He ran his finger over the gold heart at her throat then looked back into her eyes. Was it her own heightened emotions, or were his eyes glistening with more than tree lights?

His voice was thick as he continued. 'You've stolen my heart, Gráinne Vaughan.' He lifted the pendant in his fingers. 'This is it. It's yours.'

It was all so confusing. She had a dozen things in mind to say to him. She just couldn't seem to get her lips to work.

Instead, she buried her face in her hands and cried like a baby. Why did she turn into a blubbering idiot with him? She hadn't cried so much in all her life as she had since he kissed her in her kitchen. That didn't stop her from falling into his arms when she felt his arms go around her.

She kept wishing things were different. There might have been a chance if they had been.

But weren't they different now she had decided not to go back to The Klub!? He didn't need her to snitch for him anymore. That was a start, wasn't it?

What about school? When she gave the money back to Jimmy, she wouldn't be much better off than when she started. She had her tips and what she'd earned dancing. That might take her through a semester, but what about after that?

And what about her self-made promise of abstinence until graduation?

Her mind kept racing back to her talk with Eilis in the kitchen. Could she still go to college and see JD at the same time?

He'd mentioned trust. Did she trust him? She understood the reasons why he had to go undercover. She trusted the oath he'd taken as a guard at the academy. She trusted him as much as any other citizen who needed a guard. But could she trust him with her heart?

It was all too much to think about. She needed time to think.

When she finally pulled away, she looked into his eyes. They hadn't changed.

'I ... I need time,' she said, finding her voice.

'You've got it,' he answered instantly.

'There are things you don't know about me,' she continued. 'I need to sort through them.'

'I'll wait,' he countered.

'It might be a long time before I'm ready for this.'

'It's all right, Gráinne. I'm not going anywhere.' He smiled so lovingly she almost gave into him.

'What about your job at the pub? If I'm not going back to The Klub! there isn't any reason to remain undercover, is there?'

'I have to stay undercover until the case is closed. Besides, my bosses just told me I'm brilliant and gave me a great bonus to prove it.' She appreciated his attempt to lighten the subject. Then he added, 'And ... I'll be working with the woman who holds my heart in the palm of her hand.'

Gráinne snorted. 'Let's not romanticize things too much. I could crush that heart of yours.'

'I'll have to trust you won't.'

He stood and held his hand out to her. 'Indulge me, won't you?' She wasn't sure what he was on about, but she decided if she was going to learn to trust him she might as well start now. She placed her hand in his and stood.

He guided her over to the hearth where the turf glowed. He drew her down to the floor, saying, 'Lay with me for a little while.' Reluctantly, she stretched out in front of him. He slipped a bent arm beneath her head and held her against him with the other as they spooned.

Lying there in the warmth of the fire, and JD's embrace, Gráinne's absentmindedly fingered the pendant – JD's heart.

Could she trust JD with *her* heart?

Her heart squeezed remembering what he'd said. No other man had ever said such things to her. None had even given her gifts. They just took from her.

JD, on the other hand, was offering her his heart. Did that mean his love, too?

His arms pressed her closer as Adele sang of promised love, as if he was telling her the song was what he felt. Could he make her dreams come true? Would he go to the ends of the Earth for her? He said she had his heart, and he'd given her the pendant as proof. She'd never been touched so deeply before and it scared her.

Could she trust JD with her heart? How could she not? She was falling in love with him.

Chapter Thirteen

The Mini's wipers were working on full speed to swipe the downfall of rain from her windscreen. The gloom of the wintry night had no effect on her feelings of contentedness.

The days had flown by, Gráinne thought, as she drove home from the pub. St. Stephen's Day had been spent at the Leopardstown Races with Kieran, Eilis, and JD. Gráinne had a wonderful time, despite being so nervous, and had even won a few euro on a horse appropriately named Fresh Start. It wasn't a lot of money, but it would go into her college savings. At this point, every cent helped get her closer to her dream.

JD had been the perfect gentleman the entire day. He hadn't tried kissing her again, but the look in his eyes told her he wanted to. Instead, he had given her the space she needed, and for that, he endeared himself to her more.

No matter how she tried to rationalize her thoughts and work around her feelings, there was no denying she was falling headlong in love with the man. She probably had been since the first night she'd seen him nearly two months ago when she'd danced for him on Halloween night.

The more she thought about it, there was no reason not to trust him. He hadn't given her any reason not to. He had eventually told her his real job, so it wasn't like he had lied. He just hadn't told her everything until she needed to know.

Her trust issues were with men in general. It would take time to learn to trust JD wouldn't hurt her. If his behavior since Christmas were any indication, she was sure it wouldn't take long.

The day after St. Stephen's Day, Gráinne had sat down and written a resignation note to Jimmy. It was brief and self-explanatory. 'I quit.' She didn't sign it. Jimmy would know when he saw the money.

She'd stuffed the ten grand into a padded envelope with the note and had it delivered by courier. That was the only way she could get the money back to Jimmy.

Gráinne felt an incredible sense of liberation. That had been the day before yesterday. She still didn't have the money for college, she couldn't tell anyone about The Klub!, and couldn't contact Mystique. Not for a while yet.

She knew she owed Mystique an explanation. Myst had become a good friend at The Klub!, a true confidante, and Gráinne wanted to remain friends with her. She would have to wait, though, until things cooled down before contacting her friend.

No doubt, Jimmy was hopping mad right about now. She knew he was accountable to Taylor Wade for her disappearance, but she wasn't going to worry. It was his problem, not hers. Jimmy would have to get another, more willing, dancer. One who was willing to do the things she was sure were expected of her for that kind of money. She was sure Jasmine would jump at the chance, if the look she'd given her that day were any indication.

Gráinne shook thoughts of The Klub! and all its trappings from her mind as she drove.

It had been a good night.

She and JD were still working similar hours. He continued keeping his distance, but at the same time, the look in his eyes told her he wasn't giving up. True to his word, he was waiting for her to work through her personal issues.

She fingered the heart pendant at her throat as she drove, remembering Christmas night for the thousandth time, smiling at the feelings washing over her.

As she rounded the corner, Gráinne saw someone standing on her doorstep. She chuckled to herself. JD didn't have the good sense God gave him to stay out of the rain. She was going to have to give him a key.

Her thoughts snapped to attention at that thought. She'd never given a man a key to her place before. Hell, she'd never held onto a man long enough to make the offer. It tickled her to think JD would be the first. She hoped he'd be the last, too.

'One step at a time, girl,' she said aloud, as she rounded the corner to park her Mini in the garage at the back of her house.

As she raced through the back garden to the house, she had an overwhelming feeling of happiness. She was in love with a man who respected her like no other, and he was, at this moment, waiting on her doorstep.

She wondered how he beat her home. They'd left the pub at the same time. The thought left as quickly as it came in her excitement to get into the house.

Without stopping to dry her face or take off her raincoat, Gráinne raced through the house, rain water splashing off her, to the front door. She flipped on the outside light and fumbled with the locks.

'Girl, you got it bad,' she murmured under her breath. 'Calm down or you'll give yourself palpitations.'

She laughed at herself. Too late! Her heart was pounding so hard right now she couldn't breathe.

Finally, the temperamental lock gave and she flung open the door.

'John,' she gasped, looking up into his eyes as he turned toward her. 'Come in out of the rain, you daft man.'

The man who stepped over her threshold, however, wasn't JD.

Jimmy!

Jesus, Mary and Joseph, she cursed to herself. How had he found her?

She struggled to keep the shock off her face as she stared at him, reminding herself she wasn't in the guise as Jett. He wouldn't know her as Gráinne Vaughan. Breathing deeply, she tried to calm her racing heart.

'I ... I'm sorry. I thought you were someone else,' she said.

'Really. And who did you think I was?' Jimmy grinned.

'Can I help you with something? It's very late to be skulking on someone's doorstep,' she dared. Maybe if she were firm with him, pretend she didn't know him, he'd just leave.

Jimmy stepped closer, forcing her back into the house.

'Yes, you can help me … Jett,' he added. 'I must admit I never would have fingered you on the street. However, now I've seen you up close, I can't see how I couldn't have recognized you.'

He stepped closer. He was inside the door now.

'I … I don't know what you're talking about. You have the wrong house.' She tried to close the door, to make him step back onto the porch so she could lock the door on him, but he refused to budge.

Before she knew what was happening, Jimmy had his fingers wrapped around her throat and was forcing her into the living room. He kicked the door shut with his foot as he propelled her through the room. The edge of the fireplace mantel bit sharply into her back as he pushed her into it. Her breath lodged in her chest, his fingers pressing firmly against her windpipe.

Gráinne's struggle was futile. She clawed and kicked at him, but he had her pinned and she couldn't get free. She gagged for air as he pushed his body against hers to hold her still, his free hand grabbing her by the hair, forcing her to look up at him.

She was scared to death. Jimmy was furious. The fire of hatred and disgust flashed in his eyes. His lips curled to bare his teeth like a rabid dog.

She tried screaming, but she couldn't get air into her lungs to even breathe. His fingers pressed painfully into her larynx.

As she struggled, her vision started getting fuzzy around the edges. She knew she'd pass out if she

160

couldn't get Jimmy to let her go. She couldn't help herself if she were unconscious. If she could get loose long enough to get her breath back, to scream bloody murder, she might stand a chance. The walls of this house were like paper. If anyone was home and awake on either side of her, they were sure to phone the guards.

Struggle as she might, Jimmy would not loosen his grasp. And as she started to slip into unconsciousness, all she could think of was how the total sum of her life had amounted to nothing notable. She'd failed her brother, she'd never see her niece or nephew born, and she'd never had the chance to tell JD she loved him. Had Jimmy not been choking her already, her tears of this realization surely would have.

Gráinne felt her eyes roll back in their sockets. Her body slumped between Jimmy and the mantel.

'That's it,' Jimmy growled under his breath. 'Don't fight it.'

In the back of her mind she felt him loosen his hold, slightly. He let just enough air into her lungs to remain conscious. She could barely keep her eyes open.

'Now, what am I going to do with you, Jett? Of course, you're not Jett, are you? You're Gráinne Vaughan.'

He grinned evilly. If Gráinne weren't so close to losing consciousness, she would have wondered how he'd found her.

'You're the sister of Kieran Vaughan, the owner of Dublin's hottest blues pub. I should be impressed. Though why you're working at The

Klub! has confused me. Certainly, your brother wouldn't have allowed you to work for me. Unless he doesn't know,' he added.

Gráinne tried desperately to keep her eyes open, her mind focused. She blinked rapidly trying to clear the black fog hanging just at the edge of her mind, threatening to send her into its darkness.

She knew her lips were moving but no words came out. She tried to tell him he had the wrong person.

'There's no use denying it – Gráinne – I know everything about you. I know everything about all the girls who work for me,' he informed her.

If she couldn't grasp any other thought before she died but one, it would be she was born a fool.

'Let's get down to why I'm here, though I'm sure we both know why.'

Jimmy released his hold on her hair and a moment later he was waving money in her face. She squeezed her eyes shut at the sight of it.

He shook her roughly by the throat. 'Open your eyes, damn it,' he cursed roughly. She reluctantly did as he told her. 'Just so there's no mistake in what I'm saying, I want you to pay careful attention this time.

'You are going to perform as arranged. You will dance as if your life depends on it. Do you know why? I'll tell you. Because your life does depend on it. You will do whatever Wade tells you to. And if you try pulling another disappearing act, I will not hesitate to go to your brother. Will I tell him about our arrangement? You bet ... right before I kill him.'

Tears of fear and hatred streamed down

Gráinne's cheeks. She was completely helpless with her body on the edge of consciousness.

'And if I still can't find you, I'm going for your sister-in-law next. I'm sure I don't have to tell you what I'll do to her and that baby she's carrying. Yes, I can tell by the look in your eyes you understand me.' He chuckled so wickedly that a new kind of unnamable fright rose in her.

'Do we have an agreement then ... Gráinne?' he asked, emphasizing her real name.

What else could she do? She had to agree. She'd already put her family in danger. If she had to dance to save their lives, then by God she'd do it.

Gráinne nodded as best she could with Jimmy's fingers still around her throat.

'Good.'

Stepping away from her, Jimmy used the hand around her throat to toss her to the floor in front of the hearth. She was too weak to protect herself as she fell and banged her head off the floor. She was suddenly grateful for the small things in life, like carpeting.

As she lay there barely breathing, she heard Jimmy's movement. Then he was in her vision. She didn't have the strength to lift her head so she only saw his shoes. One foot rose and kicked her shoulder to roll her onto her back. She saw him then, towering menacingly over her. She tried blinking the tears from her eyes, but even that effort proved too exhausting.

'I want to hear you say it, Gráinne. Tell me you agree to perform and I'll walk out of here,' he told her.

163

She tried to get enough air into her lungs through her bruised throat. Her lips moved but nothing came out.

'Say it! Or so help me, I'll kill you where you lay,' he seethed.

The last made her gasp sharply. The effort forced air into her lungs.

'I...' she gagged. 'I'll do it.' Her body shook with the effort it took to get the words out, and from fear.

Jimmy only smiled before turning for the door. She heard the door click open.

'My ... my money,' she managed, stopping him at the door.

Jimmy came back into her line of vision and crouched down beside her. His eyes bore into hers angrily.

'Fuck your money. You just used it to buy your brother and sister-in-law's lives.'

Gráinne choked on a sob as Jimmy rose and left her house, slamming the door after him.

When she was sure she was alone again, she found the strength to roll onto her side and curl into a ball. She clutched at her throat and sobbed.

Somewhere in the back of his mind, JD heard ringing. He'd been dreaming. It was nothing significant, and the more awake he came, the quicker the memory of the dream left him.

Rolling over, he picked up his mobile to check the number on the caller ID.

Gráinne.

The bedside clock glowed two am. He'd only just gotten to sleep half an hour ago. What could she want at this hour? It didn't matter. She was ringing him. Clicking the receive button, he said, 'Hey, Gráinne.'

Silence.

'Gráinne,' he repeated, propping up on his elbows. His heart pounded a little harder in his chest at the silence on the other end of the phone.

Then there was something. Rustling. Rasping.

Something was wrong.

He swung his legs over the edge of the bed. Without disconnecting the call, he wedged the mobile between his ear and shoulder and grabbed his pants off the floor where he'd left them.

'Gráinne, love. Are you there? Are you okay?' He didn't know what he gained by talking to her, but it made him feel ... better?

No, not better. He was scared something was wrong and he could do nothing to help from here.

He raced through his flat, dressing on the way to his car. 'Hang on, love. I'm on my way to you. Don't hang up.'

As he drove across the city, he kept encouraging Gráinne to say something to him, to respond somehow, to let her know he was on his way to help, but he was met with silence. The rustling sound had stopped and he could no longer hear rasping over the roar of his car's engine as he raced though the city.

Then the signal died. Throwing the mobile onto the floor, he put the accelerator down. If any guards were out, they could damn well just follow him to Gráinne's.

He didn't bother finding a parking space as he screeched to a halt in front of her house. He switched off the engine, threw the transmission into neutral, and pulled up on the handbrake. The car was still rocking as he ran to the front door.

He banged on the door shouting her name, then tried the latch. Unlocked.

Carefully easing the door open, he stepped into the near darkness of the room. The dim porch light shone around him. There was something on the floor in front of the hearth.

He felt for switches by the door and tried each one until the overhead light switched on.

When he saw Gráinne laying unconscious on the floor, his heart lurched into his throat.

Without thinking, he raced to her side.

Her mobile lay in the palm of her hand. She was fully dressed, and her coat was still damp. She hadn't been home long.

'My God, what happened, Gráinne?'

He gently brushed her hair from her face and felt her throat for a pulse. That's when he saw the bruising.

She was alive. He crossed himself for that.

'What's happening here?' came a voice at the door. A man stood with a hurly in his hands, ready to do business. He wore nothing but his jocks and a 'don't mess with me' edge to his voice. *Where were you half an hour ago?* JD wanted to ask.

'Call an ambulance,' he said, turning back to Gráinne.

'Maybe I'll just call the guards. They'll sort you out,' the man told him, stepping into the house.

JD reached into his trouser pocket and, withdrawing his wallet, he threw it at the man. 'I am the guards, asshole. You can check my ID on the way to the phone. There's one in the kitchen.'

Instantly, the man stepped around them and went to find the phone. JD put the man out of his mind as he crouched closer to Gráinne so he could examine her further.

He ran his hands over her body under her coat, carefully checking for injuries. There didn't seem to be anything broken. He didn't dare move her, though, in case things were much worse than they looked.

With the bruising on her neck, it could be broken.

It seemed like forever until the ambulance arrived. The neighbor had disappeared. JD didn't know when and didn't care. His only concern was making sure Gráinne was going to live.

'John,' Gráinne rasped.

He lay by her side instantly.

'I'm here, love,' he said, his voice low. 'Don't move. The ambulance is on its way.'

'N ... no ambu–,' she managed. 'Pl-please, help me...'

JD held her down with a gentle hand. 'Don't move, love. Something might be broken.'

'Noth... ing broken,' she croaked. 'Help ... me ... up.'

Gráinne struggled to sit up, but it was clear she was weak. JD sat up and helped her climb into his lap. He wrapped his arms around her carefully. He really wanted to squeeze her to him, to envelop her in his embrace where nothing could hurt her again.

'Can you tell me what happened, love? Were you robbed?' he asked, kissing the top of her head.

167

Before she could answer, the ambulance arrived and an EMT came through the door to assess the situation.

JD recognized the man instantly as Mac. One didn't put in as many years on the Force as he had, without meeting people in other related services.

He told Mac how he'd found Gráinne. He didn't think anything was broken and she refused to go to hospital. Mac nodded as JD spoke.

'I'll have to examine you, Ms. Vaughan,' he said, speaking to her calmly. 'Is that all right?'

Gráinne glanced up at JD then nodded.

Over the next half an hour, Mac took the details Gráinne chose to give him and let him examine her.

As Mac and JD helped Gráinne remove her raincoat, she explained she'd interrupted a burglary. The man had choked her and left her for dead.

Since she refused to go to hospital, Mac could only advise her to see her doctor in the morning.

When they were alone again, JD helped her into her night clothes then wrapped a blanket around her. He left her for just a moment to fill the kettle in the kitchen.

When he returned with their steaming mugs, Gráinne rasped, 'Tea?'

He shook his head. 'Hot toddie. I thought you could use it more.' The honey and lemon would be good for her throat, and the whiskey would soothe her nerves and hopefully help her sleep tonight. But not before he got the real story out of her.

'You're ... very good,' she said. He cringed every

time she spoke. Her voice was stronger, but it was still weak and sounded like she'd smoked a pack of cigarettes a day for most of her life.

He noticed how her hands shook when he handed her the cup, so he scooted closer to help her drink.

As he held the mug to her lips, he asked, 'Care to tell me what really happened? Don't think for a moment that I believe it was a break-in.'

Gráinne's brows rose innocently.

'Don't look at me like that. You forget I'm a detective.' Even in her state, she still challenged him. 'Okay. There was no forced entry. That tells me you knew who it was and let them in. Nothing appears to be missing or even gone through. That tells me you didn't interrupt a robbery. The fact you're still alive tells me whoever was here wants you that way. Shall I go on?'

He stared at her for a long moment before she finally looked down, pushing the mug away with shaking hands. He put their mugs on the coffee table and drew her into his embrace. She came to him easily and buried her face in the folds of his jumper. He felt her fingers digging into the wool covering his chest.

'Ah, Gráinne,' he sighed, stroking her hair. 'Please tell me what happened. I'll keep it off the record. I swear it.'

A moment later, she looked into his eyes. His heart flipped at the sadness in her gaze.

Over the course of the next hour, she told him everything.

'He told me the ten grand was the pay-off to keep Kieran and Eilis safe. He told me he'd kill

169

them if I disappeared again.' Her voice remained raspy, and probably would for some time, but as she spoke, her efforts decreased with each breath.

He pulled her back into his embrace and held her firmly, burying his face in her hair. 'Ah, Jazus,' he sighed over and over.

'I messed up.' It was a simple statement, but the tone in her voice was unmistakable. His heart lurched. All he could do was hold her tighter.

A long moment later, Gráinne broke the silence. 'Will you stay with me tonight?' she asked, her voice barely audible.

'You couldn't make me leave.'

She looked up at him once more. Sadness still lurked behind her long lashes. He longed to kiss away all the hurt and fear he saw there.

'Thank you.'

'In the morning, you and I are going to have a serious discussion about this job. I want you to tell me everything you know about what happens in The Klub!. I don't care if it's just rumors, or anything you've seen with your own eyes. I want to know about it,' he told her.

Gráinne nodded. 'In the morning.'

Standing, he held out his hands to her. She rose and let him scoop her into his arms. Carrying her up the stairs to her room, he cursed Jimmy Molloy under his breath. JD should be carrying her to bed to cover her with his body, fill her with his love, and waken her desire. Instead, he'd lay with her until her fear subsided enough to allow her to sleep.

Once she was settled, he returned downstairs to

be sure the doors and windows were locked and all the lights were off.

He paused at the foot of the stairs and cast a glance at the spot where he'd found Gráinne. His breath caught in his chest, choking him with emotions.

Anger, fear, revenge, hatred.

He collapsed on the bottom step and buried his face in his folded arms. He refused to let Gráinne hear him, but there was nothing he could do to stem the raging feelings.

Above all else, the realization of what could have happened to her ripped through him.

Hopefully, the information she gave him in the morning would see she'd remain safe forever, once they took down Jimmy Molloy and Taylor Wade.

Drying his eyes, he took deep breaths and forced himself back up the stairs to his love's side. He would keep her safe however he could.

He vowed it.

Chapter Fourteen

New Year's Eve

Gráinne sat in the dressing room at The Klub!, as Jimmy had instructed her, waiting to be called to Taylor Wade's party in the penthouse. Earlier, Jimmy had presented her with a box – a gift from Wade. She remembered how the knot in her stomach had tightened when she was forced to open it. She'd gasped audibly at the new costume.

'I can't wear this, Jimmy,' she'd told him. Her voice was still hoarse, but at least she wasn't choking on her words any longer, even if the bruises still remained.

'You *can* wear it and you will.' Her skin crawled, as he looked her up and down. 'If I have to strip you down myself, you *will* wear it.'

Then he was gone, leaving her staring at the sheer fabric. Sighing heavily, she had to remember JD's plan.

He was in the main room for the evening. He'd be waiting for her and would be on hand if there was any trouble. If she couldn't come to him herself, she was to send Mystique to get him. They'd deal with the consequences afterward.

While she waited, she had the forethought to make some adjustments to the costume Wade had sent her.

The original costume was little more than a small midnight blue velvet thong and a matching blue sheer bolero-styled top, with long gothic sleeves. The fabric shimmered like a clear midnight sky.

It had taken her a few moments to figure out how the bits of the fabric fit, but with Mystique's help, she eventually got it. She slid her arms through the sleeves and drew the longer sections of fabric over her breasts, crossing between them until the overall effect looked like her breasts were in individual slings. There had been just enough fabric to tie the garment, if it could be called that, in the back.

Also in the box were a pair of equally sheer smoky blue stockings and a pair of spiked blue velvet pumps.

Once completely dressed, Gráinne gasped. She would have been more dressed if she only wore a bikini. Even though the top was midnight blue, her pale skin shone through bright as day, her nipples two rosy spots pushing at the fabric.

'No way, Myst, I'm not wearing this,' she gasped.

'You don't have a choice, Jett,' Mystique told her.

'Maybe not, but I'm not wearing it like this. Help me find some scarves or something to add a little ... I don't know ... something to this get-up. I feel naked. It's bad enough I had to shave ... down there ... just to wear the thong.'

'You've shaved before.'

'Not all of it!'

Mystique laughed at her. Had Gráinne not been so scared to go upstairs, she would have thought it funny, too.

Mystique dug into her box of accessories and pulled out some colorful scarves. Gráinne waded through them and picked out ones to match the blue costume – ruby red, emerald green, shimmering gold – and wove them through the top and thong. She folded the ends of two dark blue scarves and padded her breasts with them until her nipples no longer showed.

When she was done, she looked more like a gypsy, or a demented Morris dancer, with all the colorful scarves fluttering about her. But better that than a wanton strumpet looking for action.

Now, as Jett, Gráinne sat at her dressing table staring at her reflection in the mirror and wondering who the hell she was anymore.

'It's time.'

Jimmy was at the door.

When she met his gaze, she could tell he would have rather had her up to his office than send her to the penthouse. His lascivious gaze told her as much. JD's gaze made her hot and needy. Jimmy's only sickened her. So she looked away to see if she'd forgotten anything.

Before she could finish the survey of her table, Jimmy's hand was on her arm, pulling her through the room to the private penthouse lift. He pushed the button and the door instantly slid open. He shoved her in and punched the 'up' button.

'Aren't you coming up?' she asked.

'I'll be up after I check-in with Rusty.'

The doors slid shut and the tiny box shuddered as it ascended. She could barely stand in such spiky shoes, and the lift's jerky movement didn't make it any easier. She gripped the rail tightly, watching the up arrow on the display blink. She kept her gaze on the arrow because, if she'd looked anywhere else, she would have been met with crazy reflections of herself bouncing off the mirrored interior of the lift box. It was like strangers surrounded her, all dressed alike, staring at her, swallowing her in unspoken accusations.

Suddenly, the lift jolted to a stop. The bell dinged to announce her arrival. Before the doors even opened, she heard the distinct sounds of soft drums and what she knew from years of playing instruments was a *taghanimt* flute.

She'd never been to the penthouse before, so she wasn't sure what to expect. As the doors slid open, soft light spilled into the dim lift.

Gráinne was taken aback at the sight before her. As it was a New Year's Eve party, she expected the usual balloons and streamers. Seeing the room before her, she realized that a man like Wade would want more than cheesy party favors. Instead, the penthouse looked like the inside of a Bedouin-style tent. Or, at least one like she'd seen on telly.

Long swathes of creamy fabric had been strung across the ceiling to drape onto the floor. Tiny fairy lights had been strung along the ceiling panels, possibly to mimic stars. Beautiful Middle Eastern-style lanterns glowed around the room, with electric candles.

Several large red and gold carpets were laid out across the floor, and on top of them were strewn dozens of large colorful cushions and pads for sitting or leaning upon. Small tables were dotted

175

amongst the pillows for drinks. Even now, with the party really just starting, the room seemed filled with people who were standing, sitting, or lying around the room.

A pole had been mounted to the ceiling at the central peak of this tented room. Two women Gráinne only knew by sight, danced together at the pole to the sound of traditional Arabian Berber music. The seductive tempo filtered through the room as they swayed and undulated.

Directly across the room from her, a long divan had been set against the wall and had been covered with colorful fabric, the tasseled ends of which drifted onto the carpets. Several cushions were pushed up against the wall.

Guests filtered around the room, but she didn't recognize any of them. However, there was no mistaking who the man sitting in the center of the divan – Taylor Wade. He was dressed all in black, from the long Berber tunic and loose fitting trousers to the *babouche* slippers, and *dishdash* around his head.

The exotic setting and rhythmic music could easily have seduced her, but when her gaze settled upon Wade, she shivered with dread.

Wade was an attractive man and, with a deeper tan, he could have made her believe he belonged in this setting. If he were anyone else, she would have found the whole effect erotic and alluring. But the aura surrounding him radiated danger. Her gut instinct told her the people in this room feared him, too; no one seemed truly relaxed, even if they did appear to be enjoying themselves. No doubt, they were only associated with Wade for the money.

The thought of ill-gotten money stung her. She was now going through this exercise for nothing. Jimmy was keeping her money.

Correction. She'd bought the lives of her family with that money. Their lives were priceless, and she would do anything to keep them safe.

Gráinne realized her stalling had caught Wade's attention. He rose and strode, animal-like in his prowl, toward her. She still clutched the lift's interior railings but tried to appear casual. In reality, she couldn't move for the fear rippling through her.

'You've got brass, Jett.' She lifted one brow at the comment. He laughed at her. 'People come to me, not the other way around.'

She was sure Wade's gravelly voice was meant to sound sexy. It only grated on her.

His gaze roamed over her body. She didn't want him seeing her fear, so she remained still as he examined her like merchandise.

When he met her eyes again, his gaze had changed. He was irked.

'This isn't the costume I sent you,' he grumbled.

She cleared her throat to speak, her voice still hoarse. JD's hot lemon and honey teas had helped, but she wasn't healed yet. He said her voice sounded rather sultry, but she'd trade all of her voice if she could just go back three months in her life to rethink her decision to work at The Klub!.

'It's your costume. I just embellished it,' she told him. 'You didn't want to spoil things by seeing the goods too soon out of the box, did you? Some things must be left to imagination.'

He thought for a moment then extended a hand, grinning, and said, 'Dance for me.'

Gráinne willed her body into moving. She let him take her hand and guide her to the pole, waving away the two women already there.

She looked around the room and found the DJ in the corner. Wade waved to him and music came up again, something slow and rhythmic. It was more erotic sounding than what the two other women had been dancing to, and much different from the traditional rock and roll or disco she preferred.

When she didn't move, Wade asked, 'What are you waiting for?'

'Are you going to stand there, or sit down and let me dance?' She regretted the tone of her voice the instant the words left her mouth.

Wade's dark brows drew together. 'You should be careful how you talk to me.'

Gráinne put herself in check. 'I don't mean any disrespect, Mr. Wade, but you paid to see me dance. I can't do that with you standing so close ... to the pole.'

He looked her up and down once more, then grunted before returning to the divan. He flicked his wrist and everyone instantly sat. Wade took his seat again, leaned back against the divan pillows, and motioned for the two dancers to settle against him.

Gráinne stepped up to the pole, reached up with one hand to grasp it and squeezed her eyes shut. 'Okay, here we go, girl,' she said under her breath. 'It's just dancing.'

She gave herself a moment to get into the

rhythm of the music, letting her hips sway, then her shoulders. With her hand firmly grasping the pole, she spun a slow lazy circuit around it to start her dance.

She was no belly dancer – the music would have been perfect for that – but she let the rhythm inside her and moved her body to the cadence of the sultry music. The only way she could get through this was to pretend she was dancing for JD again.

She had only danced for him that one time – Halloween night. He'd been too much the gentleman to ask her to dance for him privately. In her mind, though, whenever she worked, it was him she imagined rather than the usual lonely souls at stage-side.

It seemed like hours before Jimmy finally made his appearance. He strode across her field of vision as she worked the pole. His destination was Wade, but Wade waved him off with a flick of his hand. She knew his gaze hadn't wavered from her since she'd begun. She made the mistake of looking at him and stumbled at the impassioned look in his eyes, but quickly recovered. The dancers he had under each arm had started pleasuring him while he watched her dance – one nuzzling his neck, while the other had her hand under his tunic. Gráinne's stomach squeezed into her throat in a dry heave.

When the song ended and there was a purposeful pause in the music, she asked, 'May I take a break, Mr. Wade?' He gazed at her for a moment then nodded, pushing his girls away and straightening his clothes. Jimmy rushed forward as she left the center of the room.

While dancing, Gráinne had noticed openings in the fabric as people came and went. She now ducked out of the room, hoping to find something to drink.

To her surprise, the rest of the penthouse looked like a regular apartment. As she entered the kitchen, she scanned the counters through the throng of revelers for bottled water or colas. Her gaze came to an immediate halt. Beside trays of finger foods, a woman leaned against the counter. A man knelt before her. He'd pushed up her short skirt around her hips and was pleasuring her in a room full of people.

The woman smiled widely when she saw Gráinne gaping at her. 'Come on in, honey. Join the party.'

'No thanks. I just came in to get something to drink.'

The woman flicked a finger at the fridge on the other side of the room. Gráinne had to step over the kneeling man to reach the fridge. She grabbed a bottle without looking to see what it was, then wove her way through the people and out of the kitchen.

'Sure you won't join us? He'll be at this for hours, and frankly I'm getting tired.' Gráinne wondered how the woman could remain so lucid during ... that. She just shook her head and went looking for the loo.

She knocked on the first door, once leaving the kitchen. No one answered so she opened the door and came to an abrupt halt.

'Sorry, sorry,' she chanted as she backed out.

'It's okay, baby. Three's company, too,' said the man sitting on the toilet. He pulled the door open for her to enter but she backed out. A scantily-clad woman knelt on a bathmat in front of the man, her head bobbing, and her hair thankfully obscuring what she was doing to him.

'Jazus,' Gráinne swore aloud. 'Why don't you use the bedroom for that so I can use the toilet?' What the hell had she gotten herself into? She was beginning to feel like she was in some perverse nightmare.

'In ... use,' the man grunted. He slapped the side of the woman's head. 'No teeth, bitch.'

Gráinne left them to it and closed the door behind her. She stood in the hall wondering where to go next. She realized then she really needed to go.

A woman passed her in the hall. She'd come from what Gráinne suspected was the bedroom.

'Is there an ensuite loo in there?' she asked the woman, who nodded as she passed. 'Is it free?' The woman only shrugged without looking back.

Gráinne heard noise coming from behind the closed door and knew there was no sanctuary in this room, either, but she had to see whether or not the loo was occupied. She wished her bladder wasn't so small. When she was scared, she locked up, but as soon as she started relaxing a little, it was all go.

What Gráinne found in the bedroom was beyond her wildest dreams, or nightmares.

In the center of the room was a very large round bed, and it was covered with bodies, all writhing together like a pit of vipers hissing and

181

slithering to and fro. The room smelled of alcohol, marijuana, and sex.

Gráinne stood frozen in place, her hand still on the door latch, as she stared at the incredible scene before her. She tried counting the bodies but they seemed to melt together. It was difficult to tell where one ended and another began. Bodies undulated like ocean waves, legs and arms flagged in the air, and the room echoed with moans and gasps of pleasure.

At once she was both horrified, yet fascinated.

A push from behind pulled Gráinne out of her shock. Another couple wandered into the room. She watched them strip and join the others on the huge mattress. Their bodies seemed to get swallowed by the original mass.

She shivered and pulled her gaze away from the writhing group. She saw a door across the room and quickly strode to it. Without knocking, she took a deep breath and pushed open the door. She flipped on the light and was thankful to see it empty. Once inside, she latched the door and checked it to be sure it couldn't be pushed in.

She took care of the business at hand. Once dressed, if she could call herself that, she flipped the lid down on the toilet and sat to drink whatever it was she'd pulled from the fridge. Fortunately, it was just sparkling water with apple flavor, but at this point, she would have taken anything.

She groaned audibly. She's been here for less than ninety minutes, but it seemed like the night would go on forever. The next two-and-a-half hours were sure to feel like an eternity.

Gráinne didn't know how long she'd sat there, but she figured she'd better get back to the dance floor or Wade would surely send one of his henchmen looking for her, or worse, come looking for her himself. She couldn't risk upsetting him, so she rose. Before opening the door to leave, she took a quick and disappointing look at herself in the mirror. As before, a complete stranger looked back at her.

Taking a deep breath, she flipped off the light then cracked open the door. She didn't want to disturb the people on the bed and certainly didn't want to get another invitation. She intended to slip through the room unnoticed, as she had earlier.

As the door opened, Gráinne almost missed the silence in the room until she heard Jimmy's voice. She peered through the crack in the door and saw the bed was now empty and Jimmy stood in the room with Wade. Wade had his back to the room as he looked out the big penthouse window at the Dublin skyline. From where Gráinne stood, she only saw blackness shining through the window and an almost perfect reflection of the bright room. And Wade's reflection. He watched Jimmy through the glass, and not the skyline as it was meant to appear.

Gráinne noticed two things just then – Wade had removed his tunic and now just wore a thin black top with the loose-fitting trousers, and he had a gun tucked into the front waistband. The black butt was just visible against his black clothes. He turned slightly as if surveying the skyline, and Gráinne caught the length of what first appeared to be an erection but was an extended length barrel concealed inside the trousers.

The look Wade wore was one of disappointment and anger. He said nothing as Jimmy spoke to him. Gráinne would have liked to just slip through the room unnoticed and return to the party, but she knew that was impossible. She only hoped neither man would want to use the loo before leaving the bedroom.

She moved to close the door when Wade's voice stopped her. Until now, she hadn't understood anything Jimmy was saying. His voice had been too low. There was no mistaking what Wade had to say to him, though. Her skin crawled as she listened.

'I don't want anymore of your excuses, Molloy,' Wade growled. 'I gave you very clear instructions. Were they not clear enough for you?'

When Jimmy failed to answer, Wade spun around, his hand on his hips now. 'Were my instructions not clear, Molloy?' Wade bellowed. Gráinne's heart leapt in her chest at his bark.

'Very clear,' Jimmy croaked, pulling at his collar. She'd never seen Jimmy afraid before, and almost felt sorry for him. Almost.

'Then why did you not follow my instructions to the letter? Tell me.' Wade waited for Jimmy's answer. It was obvious he was looking for something to tell Wade to deflect the man's anger. 'Tell me!'

Jimmy jumped noticeably. 'I-I–' he stuttered.

'You what?'

'I did follow your instructions,' Jimmy finally said.

'Then why am I still left with product? It's New

Year's Eve. My stock should be well gone by now. Partiers all over the city should have their noses full of snow. This is my busiest time of year. I should be looking to my supplier for more product, but instead, I have a container down on the docks full of shit,' he told Jimmy, his voice still threatening in its tone.

'Mr. Wade, I have all my best people out there, but no one's buying. We can't force them to buy,' Jimmy explained.

'Sure you can.' Wade lowered his voice and spoke simply so Jimmy could understand him. 'They already want the shit. You just tell them how much they're going to pay for it. Don't break up the weights because some yob only has a few euro on him. If the buyer wants it badly enough, he'll cough up the rest of the money. If he doesn't, you break his legs. Easy.'

'You can't go around breaking people's legs because they don't have the money, Mr. Wade,' Jimmy told him.

'Why the hell not?' he snapped.

There was a pregnant pause between the two men.

Jimmy broke the silence. 'They're just not buying blow like they used to. Kids today want cheaper stuff with a bigger bang.'

'Since you're the expert now, Molloy, tell me what the "kids of today" are looking for.' Wade crossed his arms over his chest and took on a waiting stance, annoyance creasing his face.

Jimmy swallowed hard. Gráinne saw him from where she stood. It must have been some lump in his throat, she thought.

'Kids want roofies and X, shit they can slip into their date's drink without notice, or take themselves to get an instant high.'

'You're telling me that there's no instant high with smack?'

'Of course there is, but it doesn't last. It's an expensive habit with too many side-effects ... nose bleeds, violent episodes, people throwing themselves off rooftops and bridges, thinking they can fly.'

'That,' Wade barked, 'is what coke does to you, Molloy. It makes you feel like you can fly. It's an instant high. There are bound to be adverse reactions. No drug is safe, but safety is not my responsibility. Getting people high is. Your responsibility is to make me money by finding buyers.'

'But they're not there anymore. What am I supposed to do, corner people on street corners and rob them?' Jimmy chuckled nervously.

Wade stared at him for a long minute, then calmly said, 'Yes. If that's what it takes.'

'Jazus, we can't do that,' Jimmy told him. Wade only stared at him.

Silence fell between the men again for a long moment. Gráinne held her breath to see who would break the silence first, to see what result this argument would have.

The door opened then and a giggling couple entered the room, practically falling over themselves with drink.

'Get out!' Wade shouted.

Both she and Jimmy jerked with a start. Gráinne thought her heart lodged in her throat. The couple snapped to attention instantly and backed out of the room, closing the door behind them.

When the men were once again alone in the room, Wade's gaze never leaving Jimmy, Gráinne had to force herself to breathe again. She took slow, deep breaths to calm the shaking in her body. She wasn't just cold from the lack of clothes in this tile-covered room; she was scared cold. Icy perspiration trickled down her spine.

When Wade finally spoke again, his voice was the perfect example of controlled calm at the peak of extreme anger.

'I'm done with your excuses, Molloy. I'm done with your taking advantage of my generosity. I'm done with you.'

'Please, Mr. Wade, I'll make it up to you,' Jimmy promised. 'I'll double the sales to make up for the loss of holiday business. We'll be back on top inside six months.'

'Really? How do you expect to do that?' asked Wade. 'Didn't you just tell me kids today aren't buying what I'm selling because they want a cheaper high?'

'Yes, but we can use that to our advantage.'

Wade said nothing as he waited to hear what Jimmy had to tell him.

'Yeah, all we do is start supplying what sells. Who's to say we can't sell Rohypnol and X?' Jimmy smiled and nodded as he spoke, his hands flying about as if they helped to shape his idea. 'Yeah, yeah, that's what we do. We'll be rich.'

'I'm already rich,' Wade reminded him.

That took a little wind out of Jimmy's sails. Gráinne gave him credit, though. He fought admirably for his job. She was sure Wade was going to fire him.

Instead, Wade pulled the gun from his waistband and fired a shot dead center through Jimmy's forehead. The silencer on the gun muffled the loud pop she expected, but the impact of what had just happened had the same effect on her. As Jimmy fell forward onto the bed, she heard someone scream. It was when Wade spotted her glaring through the crack in the bathroom door that she realized she was the one who had screamed.

And now he stomped toward her, gun still in hand.

Chapter Fifteen

Wade threw open the door, grabbed her by the hair, and pulled her out of the bathroom. Gráinne stumbled on her spiked heels and fell to the floor at his feet.

'Where the hell did you come from?'

Gráinne gasped for breath as she sobbed. Her world had spun out of control.

Wade kicked her, his foot landing firmly against her thigh. She yelped in pain. He was going to kill her, too. She was sure of it.

'Answer me!'

'I was using ... using...' she broke down in a fit of hiccupping sobs.

'You were just using the jax, was it?' She nodded. 'And when you came out, you saw us and decided to hang around to see what you could learn?'

'Yes, I mean no. I mean...' she stuttered, fear ripping through her.

Wade's angry glare bore into her.

'Yes, I was using the loo. When I came in there were people ... here ... before,' she stuttered. 'When I came out, they were gone and I saw Jimmy. Heard him talking to you. I didn't want to interrupt. I didn't know ... know that...' She couldn't finish as fear choked the breath from her. Tears spilled down her cheeks.

Wade grabbed her by the hair. Her wig came loose in his hand. He gasped audibly then tossed it aside and dug his fingers into the pins holding her own hair in place. He pulled her to her feet. She tried getting her footing, faltering again on the heels. He continued pulling her up, ripping her hair from her scalp as she struggled to kick off the heels.

When she finally stood, he spun her to face him, crushing her against him. She gasped as she slammed into this chest.

'So you're the innocent bystander,' he prodded. She could only nod. 'Well, now. What am I going to do with you? I can't very well let you walk out of here, can I?'

'Please,' she begged, her voice barely audible, her eyes wide with the horror of what he would do. 'I won't tell anyone. I swear it. I'll do anything you want. Just let me go. Please, just let me go. I swear it. I swear it.'

Wade chuckled. 'Anything? Well now, that's quite an offer, isn't it?'

She nodded quickly. 'Just let me go. I swear I won't tell a soul. I'll leave the city. I'll leave Ireland. Just let me go,' she pleaded.

Wade continued to chuckle. 'That's not what I'd have you do, Jett.' His gaze swept over her breasts and continued, 'No, not what I'd have you do at all.'

Gráinne realized what he was on about and struggled against him. He grabbed her back to him, holding her by the back of the head with his fingers digging into her scalp. More pins flew, giving him a better grasp of her real hair.

'You said anything.'

Gráinne knew then if she were going to survive

this, she would have to do exactly as he told her. She stopped struggling at that moment and put her body on automatic. She'd let men use her before, so this should be no different.

But it was different. She'd been looking for love with the others. There was no love in what Wade would do to her.

'Good girl,' he said, grinning.

She was forced to walk backwards as he guided her to the bed. He tossed the gun away as he pulled his shirt from the waistband. His gaze never left her as he untied his trousers and pulled out his...

She turned her gaze away, refusing to look at him. This couldn't be happening.

She gasped audibly when he suddenly pushed her down on the bed. Just then she saw Jimmy's vacant eyes staring at her, and a scream lodged in her throat. She tried pushing away, but Wade was between her legs, pulling the scarves out of her thong straps.

Gráinne panicked. She fought him as best she could as she tried to scoot up the bed away from Jimmy's corpse. Wade followed her, grappling for her with both hands now.

'Hold still, bitch,' he warned, but she had to get away.

She couldn't do this. She couldn't do this.

Her gaze spun around the room, heart pounding, looking for something to defend herself with. There was nothing. She was in trouble. The realization hit her like a physical blow. There was nothing she could do to get out of this.

She should just let him do this thing to her.

She'd close her eyes and let him have his way. Once he was done maybe ... maybe she'd have a chance.

Just then the door opened and slammed against the wall, startling them both. They both looked up to see who'd come through the door.

A small group of people stood in the doorway, their mouths agape. She knew they'd intended to either join the previous fun and games, or start some of their own. They had no idea they were walking into a room with a dead body and a woman about to be raped. Everything showed on their faces.

'Get out,' Wade bellowed, but they just stood there. Gráinne realized this was her chance. God was looking down on her tonight, after all.

She took a deep breath and propelled herself off the other side of the round bed and ran for the door. As she pushed through the growing group of people and raced down the hall, she heard Wade screaming behind her, 'Catch her, damn it. Don't let her get away.'

Then she heard a thump and she realized he must have fallen as he tried coming after her. He hadn't stopped to remove his shoes or trousers in his attempt to get between her legs.

When she entered the tented lounge, she spun around looking for an escape. The lift doors opened and a couple stepped into the room. She raced to the lift and leapt inside just as the doors were shutting. She saw Wade in the lift mirrors, pulling up his trousers as he ran for her, screaming for someone to stop her.

She spun, pushed the down button repeatedly,

hoping the lift would start its descent before he could reach it and push the open button. She squeezed her eyes shut, praying.

The lift seemed to take forever to get going, but it did. It jerked to a start as it began to descend and she crossed herself again.

Her eyes snapped open and she caught sight of herself in the mirror closest to her and jerked back. She was a fright, with her hair half-pinned to her head. A clump of hair hung on a few pins where Wade had pulled it loose.

She ripped at the pins as the lift continued to the ground floor, five floors below the penthouse. She was thankful it was a one-way journey. To her knowledge, there weren't any stairs, though she knew there must be to comply with fire regulations. But she hadn't seen any other doors in the lounge upstairs or near the lift as she stepped out.

Without the spiked heels, she moved much faster down the hall to the dressing room. Her handbag was still under her dressing table. She snapped it up and retraced her steps past the lift, which was on the way up again, and ran down the hall to the main room.

The stage was the quickest exit out of the building so Gráinne slipped between the curtains and raced onto the dance floor.

Mystique whirled to a stop at the pole at Gráinne's intrusion. Her eyes snapped open at the state of her friend's appearance.

Gráinne swept her eyes around the room looking for JD. She didn't see him. 'Oh, God, where is he?' she whimpered aloud.

She went to Mystique, grabbing her by the hand. 'We've got to get out of here. Wade just killed Jimmy.' Gráinne tried to pull Mystique with her as she ran, her face expressionless.

'What?' Mystique wobbled on her heels, protesting, trying to understand what Gráinne was trying to tell her.

'Please, Myst. There's no time to explain. Trust me. You have to get out of here. Jimmy's dead. Wade's coming for me. I have to go. Get yourself out of here. This is your only chance. Please!' she pleaded.

Then JD was there. He spun her around in his grasp, his brows drawn together. She fell into his arms instantly.

'What's this?' he asked. 'Wade killed your boss?'

Just then, two thugs came through the curtains at the end of the stage and spotted her.

She tried getting free of JD's grasp, but he held her tightly.

Out of the corner of her eye, she saw JD pull a handgun from inside his jacket and fire a shot toward the ceiling over the thugs. She knew he could have killed them if he'd wanted to, but she also knew he was protecting confused patrons. That was a warning shot.

It gave them enough time to get to the front door, where JD turned and fired another warning shot.

People suddenly started screaming and running for the door. In the scuffle, Gráinne was pulled out of JD's grasp, but she kept moving out the door with the crowd.

Once on the sidewalk, JD was beside her im-

mediately, pulling her to a gap between the buildings where he guided her down the side alley. He
kept turning to look behind them to see if the
thugs followed. When they reached the end of the
alley, JD fired another shot as the thugs appeared.

She dug into her handbag as she ran to find her
car keys. Just a few more meters and they'd reach
her car.

She found the keys and fumbled for the one
that unlocked the door. JD fired another shot
when the thugs started forward again. She raced
for the driver's side and tried sticking the key in
the lock, but it wouldn't go. It was upside down.

'Damn it, damn it,' she cursed. Flipping the key,
she tried again. Her hand trembled, but eventually
the key slid home and she twisted it in the lock.
The door opened and she slid in. JD fired again
before racing to the passenger side. She flipped the
lock open on his side then slid the ignition key into
the slot.

JD slammed the door while she tried starting
the car.

She pumped the accelerator but it wouldn't
start. 'Damn it,' she cursed again, panic ripping
through her, continuing to flip the ignition key,
the car just sputtering.

She made the mistake of looking in the
rearview mirror and saw the thugs standing at
the top of the alley. They heard her attempts to
start the car and stalked toward them.

'It helps if you pull the choke,' said JD, pulling
the lever for her. Instantly, the car started up. He
watched as she pushed down on the clutch, put
the car in first, and gunned the engine. The wheels

spun, sending up a cloud of debris. When she released the handbrake, the Mini peeled out of the parking space, whiplashing back and forth as it tried to find traction on the damp pavement. JD holstered his handgun then held on for dear life as they sped down the road.

He was thankful it was late and the backstreets were sparsely populated. By now, New Year's Eve revelers would be ensconced in their respective places of celebration waiting for the midnight countdown.

He spun in his seat at the end of the street and looked behind them to see if they were being followed. The thugs fired a couple shots at them, but they were too far away. Or so he thought, until a bullet crashed through her back window and continued through the front windscreen between them. His heart leapt into his throat.

She shifted gears and the car lurched forward as it accelerated.

Gráinne wove through the city. He wasn't sure where she was going, only wanting to get as far away from The Klub! as possible.

When they were several streets away, she slowed the car, but kept her concentration on the road.

'Put on your belt,' she told him. She didn't look at him as she drove, but pulled her own belt around her with trembling hands and snapped it into place. He did the same.

'Care to tell me what that was all about?' He looked behind them again and saw nothing, but it didn't put his mind at ease.

She told him everything as she drove. When she was done, he wasn't quite sure where they were, but knew they had to ditch the car. Wade's henchmen would be looking for the little red Mini.

JD snapped to attention when she pulled off the road into an open petrol station. She quickly glanced at him. 'I need petrol.'

When she started to get out of the car, he put a gentle hand on her arm.

'Get out of the car dressed like that, love, and we'll have more trouble.'

Gráinne's face paled. She must have just realized the state she was in.

JD got out and pumped the petrol for her. The small tank didn't take much. He went to the night window and paid, asking the attendant for a couple bottles of water at the same time. He didn't know about Gráinne, but his throat was as dry as cotton.

Waiting for the attendant, he thought about Gráinne's story. It was amazing she was still alive. He squeezed his eyes shut and thanked whoever was watching over her tonight for her safety. He was a lapsed Catholic. He'd never really believed in that whole business with the Father, Son, and Holy Ghost, but after tonight he was giving serious thought to attending church as soon as he could.

Back in the car, he said, 'Pull around back for a minute. We need to talk.'

Thankfully, she did as he asked. She found a dark corner and backed in, shutting off the motor and lights. He handed her a bottle of water.

'Thanks. I didn't realize how thirsty I was.'

'Just looking after you, love,' he said with a grin. Gráinne took a long drink then recapped the

197

bottle. Her gaze never wavered from the side of the garage. He knew what she looked for. He did, too. But they hadn't been followed. He was sure of it. And they were well hidden back here in the dark. For the moment, they were safe.

He took a minute to call in the incident at The Klub! on his mobile phone. No doubt one of the patrons already had, or maybe a club employee. But since he had been on the scene and had a vital witness with him – not to mention being the lead detective on the case – he was obligated to check in.

When the call ended, he tossed the mobile onto the shelf under the dash. He took a deep breath, running his fingers through his hair. Silence enveloped them in the dark car.

By the time Gráinne spoke, a thousand thoughts had been whirling through his mind, trying to put the puzzle pieces together.

'What am I going to do?' she asked, her voice barely a whisper. It was rougher than when he'd taken her to The Klub! just a couple hours ago, yet he thought he heard a change in her mood.

'I've been thinking about that, too, love,' he said, turning in his seat to face her. She kept her eyes on the side of the garage.

He leaned forward and pulled her into his embrace. He put his arms around her as much as the tiny space would allow, and held her tightly. She trembled uncontrollably, but didn't cry. Her skin was covered in goosebumps. He stroked her briskly to get some heat back into her.

'Do you have a change of clothes in the car?'

She shook her head. Without looking up, she

said, 'All my clothes are back in the dressing room. I go in disguised as Jett and get into costume there.'

Shrugging out of his jacket he helped her into it.

'We need to get you some clothes, but first we need to ditch this car. They'll be looking for it.' He leaned back to look into her eyes. He stroked his fingers over her temple and along the curve of her cheek. 'It'll be all right, Gráinne. I promise.' He sealed his promise with a gentle kiss then pulled her back into his arms. While still holding her, he said, 'Gráinne, I think we need to talk to Kieran.'

She shot out of his embrace and sat away from him, her eyes wide. 'I can't do that,' she croaked.

'I'm afraid we don't have any choice. Wade will be looking for you. He won't stop until you're ... no longer a witness.' He hated reminding her of the fact.

'There has to be another way.' Her brows drew together. He knew her mind had to be spinning, searching for other alternatives.

'I've been thinking about this, and I don't think there is. After what Jimmy said, Kieran is going to have to protect Eilis until this is over. Just as I'm going to have to protect you,' he added.

The sadness in her eyes broke his heart.

'I can't face him. Please, don't make me do this.'

He stroked her cheek with the backs of his fingers, saying, 'I wish to God there was another way. We need his help and he needs to know what he's up against.'

'He'll murder me.'

'He'll be angry with you. We can work around it. Our first priority is to get you into a safe house. We'll deal with Kieran's temper when this is all over,' he told her. Then added, 'My guess is he'll be happy you weren't killed tonight.'

Gráinne snorted, rolling her eyes. 'Right.'

JD turned her to look at him again. His eyes bore into hers. 'You were very brave tonight. I've never known a woman as strong as you. I'm very proud of you.'

She twisted out of his grasp, looking away. 'I'm not brave. I only did it to save Kieran and Eilis. What I've been doing these past few months is nothing to be proud of. I've been a fool.'

He saw she wore his heart pendant and smiled. Reaching up, he touched the heart with his fingertip. Gráinne glanced at him.

'I don't give my heart foolishly, nor to fools,' he told her.

A moment later, she took a long, deep breath and turned back to him. Now, determination had replaced hopelessness.

'OK, so we tell Kieran. You'll stand in front of me so he can't strangle me. Then what?'

JD grinned. Yes, she was a very brave woman. All or nothing – that was his girl.

'Then we get you into a safe house until we can catch Wade.'

'What if he disappears?'

'You witnessed him kill your boss. He won't stop until you're found. If there's nothing else I've learned about this man while I've been on this case, is that he lives up to his reputation in spades. The stories I've heard would straighten your beautiful curly hair.'

'Like the one about the couple in the Dublin Mountains who were found by tourists?' she asked. 'Yeah, I've heard a few stories myself. You don't work in a place like The Klub! without hearing things.'

'I'm sorry, Gráinne.'

'About what?'

'That you have to go through this.'

Gráinne snorted. 'It's not your fault. I'm the one who got myself into this mess.'

'And I'm going to help you get out of it.' She looked into his eyes again. 'I promise.'

She had a lazy grin on her face. 'You're full of promises tonight, aren't you?'

'You have no idea what I'm prepared to promise you.'

Her eyes narrowed. JD wondered what was going through her mind.

Grinning, he said, 'So, let's get this over with. We need to get you dressed, get this car off the road, talk to Kieran, and get you into the safe house.'

She nodded. 'Clothes would be good right about now.'

'Switch seats with me. I'll drive you home. You can grab some clothes and whatever else you need, we'll leave the Mini in your garage and take a taxi to the Blues Tavern to talk to Kieran.'

'I'll drive,' she said.

'Are you sure? I don't mind.'

'No, I'm alright.'

JD nodded and she started the car. They both put on their safety belts then she pulled out from behind the garage.

Chapter Sixteen

They hadn't driven half a mile when JD heard screeching behind them.

He spun in his seat to see a black Range Rover with tinted windows speeding to catch up with them.

'Ah, feck!' he cursed.

'What?' Panic filled Gráinne's voice, her gaze snapping between the rear view and side view mirrors. 'Ah, feck!'

Pulling the handgun from his shoulder holster, he slid out the magazine. He'd shot four warning shots on their way to the Mini. One in the chamber meant he still had five in the magazine.

He reached into a pocket of the jacket Gráinne still wore and pulled out a full magazine. Triggering the release, the half-filled magazine fell into his lap and he slid in the full one. He tossed the half-filled magazine onto the dash shelf in case he needed it. Better to have a full magazine now if things got really ugly.

'What do I do?' she asked, glancing between him and the road.

'You drive as if the Devil is on your tail.'

'He is.'

She dropped the car down a gear, put the accelerator to the floor, and the little car shot forward. The Range Rover was a much larger and heavier vehicle than the Mini, but it managed to catch up with them. While the SUV had a more powerful engine, the main benefit to the Mini was agility – it could take corners at higher speeds and negotiate tighter turns. JD just hoped Gráinne was up to the challenge.

'Where do I go?' Her voice was filled with panic.

JD thought for a moment. They couldn't go to her house or the pub. They didn't dare go anywhere near anyone Gráinne knew. Why didn't he think of that before? He wasn't sure if only Jimmy knew where she lived, but he couldn't take the chance. Just as they couldn't take the chance of drawing the thugs to Kieran and Eilis.

There was only one place the thugs wouldn't dare try anything.

'Pearse Street Garda Station,' he said. 'Turn left here.' Gráinne slowed and took the corner smoothly. The Range Rover kept up.

'You're going to have to take those corners a little faster, love. And don't signal next time.' He almost laughed at the look she shot him.

'Sorry. Habit.'

Just then, the rear window shattered and fell into the back seat. The bullet passed through the car and lodged in the dashboard. Gráinne yelped. The car swerved, but she quickly got it under control. More shots were fired, but they ricocheted off the roof and corners of the car.

'To hell with this,' she cursed.

JD glanced at Gráinne. He'd only seen that angry look one other time – that night in her house when he'd confronted her with snitching for him. Whatever was going on in her head now, he knew she was serious about it.

He had just enough time to double-check his safety belt was firmly in place before the car lurched forward as she changed gears again.

Gráinne mumbled angrily under her breath, but he couldn't tell what she said over the car's screaming engine and squealing tires. She took the first corner sharply, then the next and the next after that, as she wove through the city. There was nothing to hang onto in the car except the narrow dash. If the interior light had been on, he was sure he would've seen white knuckles glaring at him.

They sped down narrow alleys and backstreets, and wove through pedestrian districts. In a matter of minutes, the Mini gained some distance over the Range Rover with Gráinne's expert driving. But they weren't out of the woods yet.

He looked over his shoulder for the thousandth time. The Range Rover was easy to see through the missing rear window.

'They're still following us.'

'Ye think?' Gráinne shook her head at him.

JD sat forward in his seat once more. He looked around for landmarks to see where they were and saw the entrance to Dublin Castle on his left, as they sped up Lord Edward Street toward Christ Church Cathedral.

In the blink of an eye the Cathedral was in front of them. Gráinne whipped the car to the right onto Fishamble Street and drove for the river.

Just before the river, Gráinne did a handbrake turn and spun the car 180 degrees. Driving back up the road, she passed the Range Rover coming at her. As she past the SUV, she turned the car left onto West Essex Street. JD heard screeching as the SUV spun around to come after them.

The Mini fishtailed as it turned onto West Essex but didn't flip as it caught traction and continued up the road.

When Gráinne whipped the car to the left, JD caught a glimpse of the Range Rover just turning onto West Essex. So intent was he on watching the SUV that when he faced forward again he saw the front of a building coming at him. He could only squeeze his eyes shut and brace for impact.

When it didn't come, he opened his eyes and saw Gráinne had maneuvered the Mini through the narrow gap between office buildings. They raced through a small courtyard toward the quay once more.

JD spun in his seat again and saw the thugs crash out in the Range Rover. They'd found out too late the gap was too narrow, and smashed into the corner of the office building. Flames shot out all around the SUV, then it exploded. He felt the blast reverberate through the Mini as it rocketed across the courtyard and out to Essex Quay.

They flew down a set of steps, veered left onto the quay and kept going.

'Jazus, woman!' he exclaimed. 'Where did you learn how to drive like that?' He was breathless when he looked over at her. Her gaze was intently focused on the road.

Without looking at him, she simply said, 'Nintendo Wii.'

JD didn't know whether to laugh or cry. He chose to laugh. He laughed so hard his stomach hurt and he had to double over to catch his breath.

'What's so funny?' she asked, glancing quickly at him.

Sitting up, he wiped tears from his eyes. 'That was some *Italian Job.*'

His laughter ebbed to heavy chuckles, remembering how he thought she'd lost control of the car, only to find she'd saved their lives after learning to drive on a video game.

'Very funny.'

'Ah, baby. Don't be upset with me. I think I love you,' he chuckled, wiping the tears from his eyes.

Gráinne stuck out her tongue at him and turned her attention back to her driving.

'You can probably slow down now, love,' he mentioned, noticing her foot was still firmly planted on the floorboard, the accelerator under it.

She eased up on the accelerator and the car slowed. 'Now, where do I go?' she asked, stopping behind several cars at the next traffic light, catching her breath.

'You're not going to like it, but...'

'But what?'

'I think we need to go straight to the pub.'

'You're right. I don't like it,' she said, but flipped on her turn signal once she reached Heuston Train Station and turned right to cross over to Wolfe Tone Quay.

It was just after midnight when they arrived at

the Blues Tavern. After parking, JD helped her rearrange her remaining scarves so they looked like a crazy skirt. At least they concealed her thong, which was the main purpose.

She still wore his jacket to disguise the fact her top was more than a little see-through.

The only thing she could do about her hair was to put it up in a ponytail to disguise the patch that had been ripped out.

As they'd walked up the street to the pub, JD held her close. Considering everything that had happened tonight, she felt safe with him on the open street.

They'd passed through the pub easily enough. No one gave them a second glance, except Siobhan. Her eyes had gone wide – not at Gráinne's costume, she guessed, but that she was in JD's arms on New Year's Eve. Siobhan knew she and JD didn't get along at work and probably wondered how they'd ended up together on such a night. The girl's mouth hung open as they walked through the room to the back office.

Getting from her car to the office door took no more than a couple minutes. As they looked at the door, the knot in Gráinne's stomach tightened to the point she felt physically ill. She couldn't remember a time feeling this nauseated without truly being sick.

'I ... I can't do this, John.' She tried taking a step backward, but he held her firmly.

'We're here now. Let's just get it over with. I know it's easier to just forget what happened, but you can't. Wade will follow you until he finds you.' His voice was calm and reassuring, or at least she knew it was meant to be reassuring. She felt anything but.

'I know, I know. I'm just afraid.' Afraid of what Kieran would do to her, how disappointed he'd be with her. That was the worst part – his disappointment.

JD gave her a quick squeeze and an equally quick kiss before lifting his hand to knock on the door for her. 'I promised it would be okay, and it will be.'

She trusted JD. She knew she could, heart and soul. She just wished this whole night had never happened. She was sure if she had five minutes of peace, the reality of what she'd been through would have driven her to madness. If that didn't do it, she was sure her brother's disappointment would. Everything she wanted to be and had tried to be was for nothing, and she might have lost her brother's love in the process.

Just before JD rapped on the door, it swung open. Eilis rubbed her eyes and yawned. 'Time to go home, love?' she asked, not seeing them yet.

'Hey, Eilis,' said JD. 'Just us. Can we come in?' Eilis blinked and stepped back.

He kicked the door closed as soon as they were in. Gráinne was afraid to look into Eilis's eyes. When she did, she wasn't sure what Eilis was thinking. Her brows drew together but there was a look of confusion on her face.

'I'm not sure I should be thrilled you two got it together, or worry why you're not wearing shoes but are wearing what must be the ugliest dress I've ever seen,' said Eilis.

Before Gráinne could say anything, JD spoke

up. 'Where's Kieran?'

'At the bar, I expect. Why? What's happened?'

'Gráinne's in trouble.'

Gráinne flinched at that comment. She was sure Eilis thought she was pregnant. She almost wished that's all it was.

'Watch her while I go find Kieran.' JD slipped back through the door.

'Well–' Eilis started.

Gráinne spun away from her and threw herself onto the sofa against a wall near the desk. The room wasn't very big, but it served its purpose.

The desk faced the door, a filing cabinet stood in the corner to the right, and the sofa was on the left wall. A couple chairs faced her on the opposite wall.

The sofa had been brought in for Eilis, who often took naps during the day with her advanced pregnancy. By the dozy look on her sister-in-law's face, it was probably where she'd been resting before they'd knocked on the door.

Gráinne flung her feet up on the small table in front of the sofa, folded her arms in front of her and looked away from Eilis's scrutinous gaze.

'Is there anything you want to tell me before your brother comes in?' she asked. Gráinne saw her waddle toward the sofa from the corner of her eye and watched her sit down beside her.

'No, you'll hear it soon enough.' Gráinne let out a deep sigh and looked into Eilis's eyes. 'I'm not pregnant, but I wish I were.'

'Two months ago, I would have agreed being preggers was pretty okay. Now I'm now so sure.' Eilis smirked. Gráinne knew she was trying to lighten the mood. How she wished a few jokes would do that.

'Things okay with you and JD?' she pressed.

What could she tell Eilis about herself and JD? Things were complicated.

'We're friends,' Gráinne blurted.

'Friends? That's it?' Eilis chuckled. 'I'd have put money at Paddy Powers there was more than friendship there.'

'We're taking things one step at a time.'

'I'm getting the feeling you really don't want to talk. Are you all right?' Eilis looked genuinely concerned. Gráinne knew she was and loved her sister-in-law's sincerity and frankness.

Sitting up, Gráinne tucked her legs under her and turned to Eilis. 'I'm sorry, Eilis. It's been a rough night. You'll hear all about it when John gets back. I just hope you don't shock too easily.'

Eilis's brow lifted questioningly. 'Oh? And it's John, is it?'

'Yeah, yeah, you were right. He's pretty special. I'm not sure I deserve him, though.' Gráinne looked into her lap and started fidgeting with the corner of one of the scarves, rolling and unrolling it at the corner. 'I'm not sure I deserve anything right now.'

Eilis's hand came to rest on hers, and Gráinne looked up into her eyes. 'Whatever it is, Gráinne, we'll get through this as a family. You're not alone. Whatever it is isn't just your problem. It's ours.'

'You may come to regret saying that,' Gráinne said, 'but I do appreciate your support.' She leaned forward and gave Eilis a hug, praying to herself Kieran would be just as supportive.

Then the door opened and Kieran strode into the room before JD. When he saw her, his brows drew together with as much curiosity etched across his face as Eilis's had moments before.

'Hey, Grá,' he said, standing in the center of the room, hands on his hips. JD quietly shut the door behind them then came to sit on the edge of the sofa beside her. He put his arm around her shoulder and rubbed it lightly, reassuringly.

Kieran just looked at her. His eyes raked over her as he tried figuring out what was going on. She saw it all over his face.

'So, what's this about? JD said something had happened, and you were in the office and needed me. You look okay,' he said, then added, 'except for that hideous dress.'

Gráinne wasn't sure if she was grateful JD hadn't said anything to Kieran or not. She had hoped he would have told her brother so she wouldn't have to. Yet, it was her responsibility. She'd gotten herself into this mess.

She took a deep breath and said the first thing that came into her head.

'I love you, Kieran.'

Kieran was obviously taken aback, but didn't move. 'I love you, too, Gráinne. That doesn't explain what you're doing here dressed like a demented lampshade. And what's wrong with your voice?'

JD snickered. She elbowed him in the side. 'Sorry, love.'

At the endearment, Kieran looked to JD, brows raised. 'Something you need to tell me?'

JD cleared his throat. 'You and I can talk about that later. Right now, I think you need to listen to what Gráinne has to say. I mean *really* listen.'

Kieran scowled. 'Sounds like something I need to sit down for.' He pulled one of the chairs from against the wall to the table, sat and leaned forward, his elbows on his knees, his gaze boring into Gráinne's.

She swallowed hard. Where to begin?

'I ... I'm really sorry, Kieran,' she said. Her mind drew a blank after that.

'Sorry about what, Grá?' Kieran's voice was low and calm, but she could hear his confused concern.

'I don't know where to begin.' She looked up to JD. Tears stung her eyes. 'Help me,' she whispered. 'I don't know how to do this.' She buried her face against JD's side and cried. His arm instantly tightened around her.

'I think someone needs to tell me what's happening right now,' Kieran suggested. The tone of his voice left nothing to guess what he was thinking.

'Kieran, this is really Gráinne's responsibility to tell you, but she's afraid you won't love her anymore,' said JD.

Gráinne pinched his side. 'Ow! It's true, Gráinne.'

She looked into his eyes, his features blurry through tear-filled eyes. 'You didn't have to tell him, though.'

'Gráinne,' said Kieran. She looked into her brother's confused eyes. 'No matter what you've done, I'm not going to stop loving you. Tell me what this is about.'

She placed her hand on JD's thigh. Just touching him made her feel safe. He gave her strength.

'I really screwed up, Kieran,' she sniffled heavily. 'Everything I've done was so you'd be proud of me, and I screwed up.'

'Are you pregnant?' Kieran growled, shooting daggers at JD.

'No, I'm not pregnant, but I wish it was just that.'

'Then you better tell me what this is about.'

Taking a deep breath she asked, 'Remember that black velvet bra John showed you a while back?' Her brother blushed at the memory.

'What bra?' asked Eilis.

She turned to her sister-in-law. 'A few weeks ago, Kieran caught John and me talking about a black velvet bra. At the time, John told Kieran he was looking for a present for his sister and showed it to me for my opinion.'

Eilis looked over to Kieran. A wrinkle developed between her brows. 'I wondered where you got the idea for that get-up you bought me.'

'Eilis,' Kieran muttered, shaking his head and switching the subject quickly. 'So, what about the bra?'

'Well, it wasn't for his sister. John doesn't have a sister. It was mine.' The room fell quiet.

Then Kieran prompted her. 'And?'

The story spilled out. Gráinne wasn't sure if it made sense, but she tried making sure she mentioned every detail she could remember, from her earliest decision in Cork to get her life straightened out, to trying to save for college, to taking the job at The Klub!. She told him everything leading up to Christmas and her decision not to go back to The Klub!, Jimmy's attack in her house, the agreement she'd made with JD so she could go through with the job, and everything else leading her to the back office in the Blues Tavern tonight.

In the telling, she had to reveal JD's true identity, but she was sure that was part of the deal. The only part of the story she kept to herself revolved around JD and herself. The last thing she wanted to tell her brother was the intimate detail of her love life.

By the time she'd finished, her voice was almost gone and the room had fallen silent. The only interruption to her confession had been when Patrick came back to tell Kieran the pub was shut and locked up. He and Siobhan were headed home.

The four of them in this room were the pub's only occupants, and the room was as quiet as a tomb.

Gráinne tried reading Kieran's thoughts, but he just sat there scowling at her.

She didn't know what else to say, so she said nothing.

Then Kieran stood and left the room.

Chapter Seventeen

Gráinne's back stiffened instantly. Fresh tears stung her eyes.

Kieran had said he would love her no matter what, but he'd just walked out on her.

She fell against JD's side and clutched his shirt, trying to draw some of his warmth into her. She didn't know what she'd do if Kieran refused to ever talk to her again.

She felt a hand on her shoulder. 'Give him some time, Gráinne. This has been a big shock for all of us,' said Eilis.

Gráinne spun on her sister-in-law. 'You're still here. He left,' she croaked, waving her hand from chair to door as she spoke. 'He just got up and walked out.'

'What did you expect him to do, Gráinne?' Eilis asked.

'I don't know. Just not that.'

'I'll bet he doesn't know what to do about this anymore than you do. You've been going through this for three months. He's had an hour,' Eilis reminded her.

She was right.

Gráinne shouldn't be expecting Kieran to have any answers to this problem. Not that she should be relying on him to come up with any. It was her problem, though she was sure Kieran was trying to think of a way out of this. Why wouldn't he?

He'd baled her out of every other scrape in her life.

She couldn't expect him to bale her out of this one, though. She'd put him in a difficult position. She'd put them all in a difficult, and very dangerous, position. It was her responsibility to get them out of it.

'I'm sure you're right, Eilis. I've screwed up pretty bad. The best I can hope for is that he'll talk to me again ... eventually.'

Gráinne pulled one of the scarves free and used it to wipe her eyes.

'What will you do now?'

Gráinne saw Eilis's question was directed at JD.

'I'm going to put Gráinne in a safe house until we can capture Taylor Wade. She won't be safe until he's in prison.'

JD rubbed the back of Gráinne's neck with his thumb. Even through all of this, she marveled at the feelings a mere innocent touch could elicit within her. He made her feel safe and loved as she'd never felt before, and she wished he'd never stop touching her.

She was getting too used to the feel of JD's hands on her, though. She wondered if he'd still be around when this was all over. And if he left, she knew it would be her ruin.

'I'm sure you're right,' said Eilis.

'I'll also arrange round-the-clock protection for you and Kieran.'

'Do you think that's really necessary?'

'Taylor Wade is the most dangerous man in Dublin right now. He won't hesitate to use you or Kieran to get to Gráinne. In your condition, you

216

can't afford to get mixed up in this.' Eilis nodded at his observation.

'I'm really sorry, Eilis,' said Gráinne, her voice barely audible. She was sure she was going to have a good case of laryngitis by tomorrow.

'If I'd known how out of control things would get, I never would have taken that job.'

'We can't predict the future,' Eilis told her.

'No, but I should have known.'

'That dream of college must be a pretty strong one. Kieran would have helped you. I would have helped. Kieran would never have had to know where your tuition came from. You only had to ask.'

Gráinne leaned over and hugged her sister-in-law. 'Thank you, Eilis.' Pulling away, she continued, 'I wanted to do this on my own. I didn't want to rely on anyone else. Kieran has always covered for me and cleaned up my messes. I wanted to prove to him I could save for tuition on my own. The only thing I proved is what an eejit I am.'

'We all make mistakes, Gráinne,' Eilis told her.

Gráinne lifted a brow and smirked. 'And when was the last time you put those you love the most in mortal danger?'

'Well, I can't say it was my fault, but I seem to remember your brother doing a very good job of saving my life not too long ago.'

Gráinne groaned. Yes, she was an Eejit, with the capital E.

Just then, the door swung open and Kieran appeared with a tray full of cups. Gráinne's heart stopped beating as she watched him walk back

217

into the room. He sat the tray on the table and handed her a mug. He avoided looking at her. Gráinne saw his blue eyes were rimmed with redness that hadn't been there when he left the room.

'I thought you could use this for your throat,' he told her, his voice hinting at emotions he fought to suppress.

Her hands trembled as she took the mug from him and sniffed it. 'Hot arsenic toddie?' she asked, trying to lighten the mood a little.

'Tempting, but no. Just hot lemon and honey with cognac. Much better for bad throats than arsenic.' He passed a mug of coffee to JD and one of tea to Eilis, before sitting down with his own cup of coffee.

Her heart soared. Kieran had only left to make her something for her throat. He hadn't really walked out on her.

'JD has just been telling us his plans,' said Eilis, breaking the silence. Kieran sipped at his mug, focusing his attention on JD.

JD repeated what he'd told her and Eilis just moments ago. Gráinne thought it was a good plan, but Kieran just shook his head.

'I don't agree, mate. There's not a safe enough safe house in Dublin.'

JD shifted his seat on the arm of the sofa beside her and cleared his throat. 'Kieran, they wouldn't be safe houses if they weren't safe,' he assured her brother.

'Correct me if I'm wrong, but safe houses are supposed to be secret locations, right?' JD nodded. 'Then why do I know about the one on

Upper Abbey Street, the one on Ship Street, the one on Copper Alley, the one on...'

'Okay, okay,' sighed JD. 'I get your point.'

'Kieran, how do you know about those places?' Gráinne asked her brother.

His eyes settled on hers, serious. 'I have friends on the Force, and they ... talk.'

She felt JD stiffen beside her. Then Kieran chuckled. 'You looked familiar, mate. I just couldn't place your face. Then I remembered you'd come in with a group a couple months ago. A few days later, you asked for a job.

'At first I was surprised that a cop was looking to moonlight as a bartender. I saw the way you were looking at Gráinne that night, and thought you just wanted to get to know her. While I wasn't keen on the idea, I needed a part time bartender and your references checked out.'

JD shifted nervously in his seat.

'Then I found out you were a detective.' Kieran continued. 'Detectives don't moonlight unless they're on a case or need money, and you don't look like you need the money. By then, I was curious and let things play out. If it involved the pub, I was sure you would come to me as soon as you could. Since you didn't, I figured you just wanted something to do in your off-time, so I treated you just like everyone else. I had no idea about any of this or that Gráinne was involved.'

Kieran locked gazes with her for a moment. She saw his love for her in his eyes. He was her brother, surrogate father, and best friend. She should have trusted he would never abandon her. Even over something like this. Yes, he was probably very angry with her right now, but his love for her surpassed all other feelings that might be spinning inside him.

All she could think of to say was, 'I'm really sorry, Kieran. I wanted you to be proud of me. I messed up.'

Kieran put his cup down, pushed the table aside, and knelt before her. He set her mug on the table and took her hands in his own.

'Gráinne, I don't know why you think I'm not proud of you. You don't have to prove anything to me.'

'I wanted to go to college. I wanted to do something with my music. After all my protesting, I wanted to go for it. You've been telling me how good I am and I wanted to see if you were right,' she explained. 'I know I could have asked you for the money, but you've been picking up the pieces my whole life. I wanted to do just one thing on my own, without your help. I wanted to succeed at it so well you'd be proud of me.'

'Gráinne, you're not hearing what I'm telling you.' He put his palm against her cheek. His heat seeped into her. 'I am proud of you ... every single day, I'm proud of you.'

The tears stinging her eyes earlier now fell down her cheeks unchecked. 'I've never given you any reason to be, Kieran.'

'You exist, Grá. That's the only reason I need.' Then he took her in his arms and held her. 'I love you. Nothing you could do would change that. Not even this,' he said, referring to the danger she'd put them in.

She leaned away and looked into his eyes.

'You're not angry with me?'

'Bloody hell right, I'm angry with you. Taking that job was the dumbest thing you've ever done,' he told her, 'but I still love you, regardless. How you ever lasted so long in a job like that I'll never know, nor do I want to know, but it took guts to even step into the place.'

Everyone turned at the sniffles coming from the opposite end of the sofa. Eilis was mopping up her own tears, watching Gráinne with her brother. Kieran put his hand on her thigh and squeezed. The love in his eyes for his wife was evident. Gráinne thought she'd seen something similar in JD's eyes a time or two, but couldn't be certain if it was real or her imagination.

When JD spoke, there was an edge to his voice. She looked up and saw how tired he looked. She wondered if she looked as tired. She certainly felt it.

'So, where does this leave us? You won't let me take her to a safe house, and she can't stay in her own house or in yours.'

'You said you were putting round-the-clock security on Kieran and me. Couldn't you do the same for Gráinne?' asked Eilis, wiping away the last of her tears.

'That's what I intended to do at a safe house. If she stayed with you then you'd all be in much more danger than if she was housed safely on her own.'

'Geez, JD. You make me sound like a piece of merchandise.'

He rubbed her shoulder. 'Sorry, love.'

'Then where will you take her?' Eilis pressed.

'If I can't take her to a safe house here, I'll have to get her out of the city. I just don't know where yet.' JD ran his hand through his hair. He threw back the last of his coffee and set the mug on the desk beside him.

In the silence of the room, Gráinne could have sworn she heard gears and cogs squealing as everyone worked hard thinking of a solution, herself included.

It was Kieran who spoke first.

'Why don't you take her to the cottage?'

JD's brows drew together. 'What cottage?'

'We have a little cottage in West Cork,' Gráinne told him. 'It's very remote.'

'It's more than remote,' Kieran said. 'It's at the top of a mountain in one of the more isolated parts of the county, with only one road in. There are no other houses for miles, and this one is tucked away so far no one would ever find it unless they knew where to look. And, right now, there are five people on the planet who know it exists.'

Everyone waited for Kieran to explain. 'Myself and Gráinne, obviously. Eilis and her friend, Megan.'

'Who's the fifth person?' Gráinne knew that if they went there, JD would want to know everything he could.

'A friend who works for Coillte, the forestry service. The cottage is buried in the woods. The land was leased to them years ago to grow their trees. That money paid to restore the cottage and provide us a fun little place to get away,' Kieran explained.

'I can't go there, Kieran,' she said.

'Why the hell not?' he asked, his brows twitching in confusion.

She didn't want to embarrass him, but...

'That's yours and Eilis's place now. I couldn't go there. Good lord, Kieran. Anytime I think about the place, I see you standing there–' She shuddered at the thought. She couldn't finish the sentence. Kieran wouldn't let her.

'Gráinne!' he cut in. She met his gaze. JD had no business knowing Gráinne had caught her brother rampant, ready-to-go and on the hunt for Eilis, when she and Megan had gone to the cottage looking for them last year. She was sure Kieran and Eilis would prefer the episode slip into the Vaughan family history. 'It's the only place, unless you want to leave Ireland altogether.'

'Kieran's right.' She spun to meet JD's gaze. 'If the cottage is that remote and virtually no one knows about it, it's our best hope.'

Gráinne flung herself against the back of the sofa and crossed her arms in front of her. The room seemed to chill suddenly. It caused goosebumps to rise on her skin.

'Great. You just dump me down there and leave me alone and hope this maniac will be caught ... eventually?' she grunted. 'Bloody fabulous.'

'You won't be alone, Gráinne. I'll stay with you.' All eyes were on JD now. Gráinne's heart thumped in her chest. Alone with JD?

The prospect of staying alone at the cottage with him was both terrifying and exciting. He'd made it clear he wanted her, and being alone in such a remote place put her at a distinct disadvantage. Okay, so she'd rather like the opportunity to wrap her legs around him, but she wanted to do it on her terms.

'You can't stay there with me,' she gasped. She turned to Kieran. 'He can't stay there with me.'

'Why not?' asked Kieran.

'There's only one bedroom,' she purposefully whispered.

'He'll sleep on the sofa like I did,' Kieran told her.

Gráinne sputtered sarcastically. 'There didn't seem to be much sofa sleeping by the state of you when–'

'Gráinne' Kieran cut her off again. 'He'll sleep on the sofa. This is the only way.'

'I'm afraid he's right, Gráinne,' said JD. 'This is only temporary. Wade will be caught, then you can return to Dublin.'

'When?' She knew there was no definite answer, but the idea of being secreted away in a remote mountaintop cottage with a man who'd been trying to get her into bed since before Christmas, was more than a little nerve-racking. Having nowhere to go, it was the perfect set-up for JD's antics. 'When?' she repeated.

'I can't answer that,' JD confessed. 'But he'll be actively looking for you. This is the best chance we've had in months to capture him. This has become personal. He won't hesitate to do what it takes to find you.'

Gráinne swallowed hard.

'Do it, Gráinne,' said Eilis. 'Just get it over with. Right now, it might seem like a week or even a month is too long. But once they catch this guy, you'll have the rest of your life in front of you.' She smiled and stroked Gráinne's shoulder reassuringly.

Gráinne looked at the faces of the people surrounding her. They were the faces of the people she loved most in her life. Yes, including JD. While she didn't like how they were being forced together, getting out of the city for a while was a good idea. Even though she'd grown up in the city, she really loved the quiet of the country.

They were right. This was the only way. Since only a handful of people knew about the cottage, they would be safer there than anywhere else on the island. Safer than the wrong handful of people who may know where the safe houses were in Dublin.

'OK,' she finally said, acquiescing. 'I'll go.'

Everyone sighed with relief. They'd all been holding their breaths waiting for her to decide. She cast them an amused glare.

'And you will sleep on the sofa, JD,' Kieran stressed, his gaze settling on him.

'Wouldn't think of any other place, Kieran,' JD promised.

Kieran grunted and stood. He held out his hand to Eilis and helped her to her feet. 'You alright, Ei?' he asked.

'As alright as I'm going to get in my condition,' she said, smiling sleepily.

JD held a hand out for Gráinne, and she untangled herself from the scarves to stand.

Kieran flinched at the state of her. 'I sure hope the rest of that dress isn't as ugly as the part I can see,' he said.

She laughed as much as her throat would let her. 'This isn't a dress, Kieran.' She pulled several of the scarves loose to prove her point. 'This was my attempt to cover up before going to the penthouse.'

'Well, you can't go out like that.' He moved around the desk and pulled out a drawer, removed something and closed the drawer again. He tossed the bundle at her. 'Put these on. I'll get you a pub shirt from storage.'

Gráinne was thankful for the track pants, dingy gray as they were. Kieran wore them on stock days, so they were far from clean, but she was cold now and knew she'd freeze once she left the pub.

As Kieran disappeared through the door, Gráinne slid off JD's jacket and started removing the scarves. Kieran returned just as she was rolling down the iridescent stockings. His shock was audible. She quickly pulled on the pants then covered her breasts with her arm, reaching for the shirt with her other hand.

Turning away from her gawpers, she slid the shirt over her head, saying, 'Now you know what it was like for me when you walked out of the bedroom at the cottage.'

Before she slipped her arms through the shirt, she reached behind her and unfastened the top's tie and pulled the fabric off. Once her arms were through the sleeves, she pulled the dance top free and dropped it to the floor beside the scarves.

'You don't happen to have a spare pair of socks laying around do you?' she asked.

Kieran's jaw still hung open with stunned distress.

226

'I thought all guys liked scantily-clad women,' she said, looking at Eilis.

Eilis leaned closer and whispered, 'Oh, he does, alright, but you're his sister.'

Gráinne chuckled, then bent to retrieve the top off the floor and handed it to her sister-in-law. 'Then you might enjoy this. It's actually kind of sexy.'

Kieran sputtered, coughing dramatically to cover up his discomfort. He grabbed the garment from Eilis and tossed it back on the floor. 'You will not wear this,' he told her.

Then, to her surprise, he plunked himself down on a chair, flipped his shoes off and slipped out of his socks. 'Put these on,' he instructed, as he slipped his bare feet back into his shoes. She didn't like the idea of wearing her brother's smelly socks, but she disliked the idea of freezing even more.

'So...' she said, looking into JD's eyes as she put on the socks. 'I guess we drive to West Cork.' When no one said anything, she stepped around them. 'Let's get going. I want to get this over.'

'We'll take my car,' said JD. 'We need to get your Mini off the road first, though.'

'I'll take care of it,' Kieran said. 'Just tell me where you parked it.' Gráinne handed him the keys and gave him the car's location.

As they walked through the pub, JD said, 'If you give me a minute, I'll phone the station and arrange for a guard to come here immediately to escort you home.' Kieran nodded and JD stepped away to use his mobile phone.

Gráinne shivered at the thought of stepping through the pub doors onto the street. She'd be exposed again. What if someone waited for her out there? If Jimmy knew who she was, did that mean Wade did, too? Could he be outside waiting for her?

'I'm really sorry about all this,' she said for the hundredth time.

'Stop apologizing, Gráinne,' said Eilis. She was leaning against Kieran now, her eyes drooping. She rubbed her stomach with one hand; the other was wrapped around Kieran's waist. 'It'll be OK. JD's a good man. He'll take care of you.'

'I'm more worried about the two of you,' she told them.

Kieran reached over and pulled her against his other side. He didn't say anything. He didn't have to. She heard his heart thudding in her ear and felt his hand squeeze her shoulder. He placed a kiss on her forehead, as he'd always done when she was a child.

'It's all set,' JD said, stepping back to them. 'Your escort has been pulled off the scene at The Klub! so they'll be here in a couple minutes.'

'Thanks, JD.' Kieran pulled a chair off a nearby table and sat it on the floor for Eilis, who slid into it gratefully.

'I got a preliminary report from the group on the scene,' he added. All eyes spun to him. 'They found Jimmy's body in the penthouse, but otherwise the place was clean.'

'Have they finished going over the apartment? There has to be something there. Some clue where to find Wade,' said Kieran.

'They're using the fine-toothed comb, as the man says, but so far nothing more than a few

228

remnants of coke cutting, and a lot of condoms in the bedroom where Jimmy was found. There was an orgy going on in there.' JD ran his fingers through his hair and yawned.

Gráinne gasped, and all eyes swung her direction. 'I just remembered something.' How could she have forgotten? 'When Wade was yelling at Jimmy, he said he was left sitting on a lot of product Jimmy should have sold.'

'You told us that already, love,' said JD.

'But I forgot he mentioned where it is. It's down at the docks. Maybe you can catch him down there when he goes to get it,' she suggested.

JD grasped her cheeks gently in both hands, pulled her in for a rough kiss and came up grinning like a cat that got the cream. 'Has anyone ever told you how brilliant you are?'

'I have, but she doesn't believe me,' Kieran remarked.

Gráinne gave JD the details. He rushed to make another call into the station.

A few minutes later, a knock sounded at the front door of the pub. Just one loud thump.

JD held up his hand to stay back and drew his handgun from the shoulder holster. He stepped up to the door and cautiously listened for the next rap to sound. The person on the other side of the door sounded out the prearranged code, and JD unlatched the door to admit a pair of officers.

Once the pub was secure, the officers escorted Kieran and Eilis to their car, with the intention of following them home. They would remain with the couple until the next shift took over, and so

229

on until Wade was captured.

As Kieran and Eilis disappeared with the officers, JD slipped his arm around Gráinne.

'Hey,' she snapped. 'You're sleeping on the couch. Don't forget that.'

'Of course I am,' he agreed.

'Then leave off with this getting fresh business.'

'You're wearing my coat, love. It's a bit nippy out here. I'm just trying to get warm.' His grin would have been charming had his teeth not been chattering.

'Then we better get to your car and get you warm. Where is it?'

Flagging down a passing taxi, he said, 'At work. I went to The Klub! with you in your Mini, if you recall.' He gave the driver the address.

They weren't in the car for two minutes when the driver let out a slow whistle. 'Der was a big shootin' tonigh',' he told them in a thick north-side accent. Typical of Dublin taxi drivers, he was trying to create some small talk to pass the time.

Curious, JD asked, 'What happened?'

'One a dem sexy dancers a' Da Cloob! sho' da owner, is wha' I heard.'

'Brutal,' JD exclaimed.

Chapter Eighteen

'Did someone break in while you were at work, or do you live like this?' she asked, delicately lifting a pair of dirty jocks off the corner of a chair with one long nail. He would have laughed if mortification hadn't choked the breath out of him.

JD was a true bachelor. His 'pad' was littered with pizza boxes and Chinese takeaway packages, beer cans, old newspapers, and a collection of dirty clothes. He'd never bothered with tidiness in the past. No one ever came over.

Now, as Gráinne stood in the middle of his living room spinning a tight circle amongst the debris, embarrassment flooded through him.

He lived like a pig.

He quickly grabbed the jocks from her and tossed them to the floor with a scowl. 'I gave the housekeeper the week off.'

He cleared a place for her to sit on the sofa. 'Have a seat. I'll be ready in a minute.'

'There are some things I'd like to get from my place, too,' she called to him, as he rushed around collecting the things he'd need for a week or more away – clean clothes, the few that were clean; his mobile charger; the e-reader off his bedside table, and whatever else he thought might come in handy. He tossed everything into a large canvas duffle bag and dropped it on the floor beside the door on his way into the kitchen.

'No can do. If Jimmy found you, I'm going to assume Wade knows where you live, too.'

'But–'

'Right now, we can't afford to go anywhere near your place.'

'John,' she pleaded.

He stopped at her side on his way back upstairs and touched his palm to her cheek. 'Is there really anything in your place that can't be replaced?' When she shook her head, he smiled lightly. 'Tomorrow, I'll take you to the nearest shop and give you my credit card. Whatever you need. Okay?'

She gave him an understanding nod. 'I was just hoping to take a quick shower and put on some clean clothes, that's all.'

JD looked at his watch. 'If you're fast, you can grab a shower here. I'll find you something clean to wear.' The look she gave him echoed the doubt he had about the freshness of the garments. 'It's through there. Hurry.'

He watched Gráinne disappear through the kitchen door, dropping garments as she moved. A moment later, he heard the shower turn on. It took all of his strength to turn and go back upstairs.

As much as he'd like nothing better than to help her bathe, then take her into his arms and carry her up to his bed, he knew he needed to get her out of the city as soon as possible. It was risky just bringing her here.

Upstairs, he pulled the down-filled duvet and a pillow off his bed. It was a long drive to West Cork from Dublin. If she wanted to stretch out and get some sleep, at least she'd be comfortable.

Back in the living room, he found Grainne dozing on the sofa. Either she was very fast, or he'd spent too much time thinking about what he wanted to do with her instead of finishing packing.

He went to her side and let his gaze admire her. She was wrapped in a towel, with her head resting on the crook of her arm where it rested on the arm of the sofa. Her damp hair curled in a riot around her. The garish make-up was gone now, but there was no mistaking the dark circles under her eyes, or the bruises on her throat. Even still, she took his breath away.

He went to his knees before her and stroked her temple with his fingertips. Her eyes fluttered open and gazed at him sleepily.

'I must have nodded off.'

'It's okay, love. You've got to be tired after all that's happened. We have to leave now. I've got what I need. You can sleep in the car.' He rose and held out his hand to her. She accepted the offer and stood. 'Here are a few things you can wear until we get you into the shops.'

She took a pair of clean jeans and sweatshirt from him, and the cleanest pair of socks he could find. He turned around while she put them on.

A moment later, after a stop at his CD collection, they were on the road. Gráinne flipped through the assortment she'd pulled from the shelves.

'Can we listen to this one?'

'Sure.' He switched on the car stereo and she slipped the disc into the slot.

'I can't believe you listen to Adele,' she said.

'This one has a special place in my heart.' JD had never given this particular singer much notice, but after the time he'd shared with Gráinne at Christmas, he'd rushed right out and bought the CD. Every time he listened to it reminded him of that special night. What a sap he was, he thought, fighting a grin.

Gráinne gratefully accepted the duvet and wrapped herself in it, before securing her seat belt. Once the CD began playing, she levered the seat back and tucked the pillow under her head. JD grinned in the dark at her little cocoon. She looked so comfortable, he longed to join her.

Adele's soulful voice filled the car as JD negotiated through the quiet city streets and onto the motorway.

It was a new year already. New Year's Eve celebrations had passed them by without so much as a whisper of recognition.

Some way to start a new year. He grunted softly.

'Something wrong?' Gráinne asked.

'I thought you were sleeping.' He reached over and stroked her hair quickly before returning his attention to the road.

'Listening to the music. It's hard to sleep when so many things are going through my head.'

He understood. It had been a horrific night for them both. 'Anything you want to talk about?'

She didn't say anything for a long moment. He wasn't sure she wasn't dozing, despite her protest. He knew he'd try catching some shuteye had he not been driving.

He could only imagine what must be going

through her mind. It was bad enough, for the time being, she'd lost her home, car, and contact with her family. He shivered at the thought she'd very nearly lost her life in the process.

His thoughts whipped back to their escape from The Klub!. That was some driving she'd done. He wasn't convinced she'd learned it all from Wii. Something told him she spent some free time at Mondello Park, too.

He smiled at the thought of her behind the wheel of a racing buggy. He saw it in her eyes. She had a wild streak. He knew some of it came out as Jett.

He'd have to teach her how to channel her wildness into something more constructive, such as focusing her dancing on just him.

The thought made him stiffen. He squirmed in his seat, trying to get comfortable, focusing his gaze more intently on the road in front of him. They were well past Kildare now and heading for the Portlaoise bypass to catch the Cork road.

He had to focus on driving. If he couldn't, he'd either get them into an accident or he'd have to stop and have his wicked way with her on the roadside.

The latter sounded quite appealing, actually. There was no one on the road this late at night. It would be easy enough to pull onto a side road and slip the seat belt off her.

Would she protest?

'I was just thinking about how Kieran took it all. I thought he'd yell and scream for hours.'

Her voice pulled his lascivious thoughts out of the gutter that was his mind.

'He loves you, Gráinne. He is angry, but I'm sure you still being alive outweighs anything else he might feel,' he told her.

'Do you think they'll be safe?'

He could lie to her and tell her they would be, but he knew how The Hunter worked. If harming Kieran and Eilis could get Gráinne to come forward, Wade would do it.

Instead of answering her questions, he asked one of his own. 'Did Kieran really save Eilis's life?'

'Yeah, he did,' she sighed. He heard admiration in what voice she had left.

'Tell me about it?'

'Do you want the long version, or the short version?' she asked, humor in her voice this time.

'We have about three hours until we hit West Cork,' he reminded her.

As it turned out, the long version was so gripping it kept JD wide-awake while he drove. If he didn't know her well enough, he would have thought she was giving him the plot of the latest action adventure romance movie.

He recalled the story going around the station about some head honcho at Eireann Records who'd been accused of raping a staff member. As it turned out, he'd been using Rohypnol on more than just the one woman.

Rohypnol was called the date rape drug because the perpetrator would slip it in his date's drink. The drug caused the victim to pass out, giving the offender the opportunity to have his way with her, or him. Most victims would suffer complete unconsciousness and partial memory loss. An unfortunate few would lose the use of their limbs, suffering the rape with a fuzzy awareness yet not able to defend themselves.

The guards had thought the E.R. executive had left Ireland, but in fact, it turned out he was hiding in the home of one of his employees who'd been out of town. On her return, she'd been attacked. Her boyfriend found them. Somehow, the executive ended up with an iron railing through his back after being thrown out of an upstairs window.

The woman who'd been attacked turned out to be Eilis Kennedy, and her savior, Kieran Vaughan. JD grinned as he remembered the headlines when they'd married.

Damsel in distress marries Knight in Shining Armor

By the time Gráinne finished her story, they'd reached Macroom. The main road snaked through the sleepy market town. Even in winter, the town had the feeling of freshness about it. Colorful homes and shop fronts in every color of the rainbow lined the road. Old-fashioned lamps were draped with holiday garlands and lights.

In the old market square, the gatehouse to the ruined castle stood proud in mock defense, with dual cannons mounted at the gates. Crenellations were lined with strings of white lights and the figure of St. Nick had been placed atop one of the small towers, his wave frozen in plastic.

The road dipped past the castle to cross over the old arched stone bridge as they continued out of town.

JD couldn't help but notice a few cars appearing on the road now. He checked the car clock and noticed it was nearly seven am.

A few miles west of town, Gráinne said, 'Turn left at the next junction.' He did, and continued to follow her directions into the countryside until he thought they were lost.

'Turn here,' she directed.

JD slowed the car to a stop at the entrance to what looked like a donkey trail.

'Are you sure, Gráinne?' She nodded. 'I'm not taking my car up that road. It's barely wide enough to walk up. We'll never get down again,' he groused.

Gráinne just laughed at him. 'I drove my Mini up here on a few occasions, Kieran's taken his Harley up here more times than I can count. Just take it handy and you'll be grand,' she assured him.

'Are you sure it's this road? It's dark. What if it's the wrong one?'

'Stop being a big girl's blouse. Will you not just give over and get on with it? Or do you want me to drive?'

Groaning, he made the turn and drove slowly up the rutted path. By the time they reached the first plateau, JD had a good idea where Gráinne had learned her driving skills, and it wasn't Wii or Mondello Park.

JD suffered two miles of this road before the road curved around some thick hedging and a small white cottage appeared. A light clicked on and he stopped the car instantly.

'What's wrong?'

'Someone's here.' He quickly looked around to check for movement.

'It's automatic lighting.'

Relief washed over him as he pulled the car into a carport beside the house and got out.

He stepped to the back of the car and stretched his muscles, surveying the area. The cottage may have been surrounded by forest, but Coillte had been up recently and cut away a small clearing.

When the automatic light switched off, JD saw there was a fantastic southern view of the countryside. In the distance was the sea.

Movement behind him clicked the light back on and Gráinne appeared at his side. He slipped his arm around her shoulders. She was still bundled in his duvet, looking like a sleepy child. His body warmed with desire for her as they stood watching the clouds pinken over the far hills.

He was going to really enjoy this time alone with Gráinne.

But first things first. They had to get into the cottage and see what waited for them. Before he could relax, he had to make sure they were truly safe, and that included taking a quick walk around the cottage – inside and out – and checking the immediate perimeter of the property.

'Let's unpack the car and get settled inside,' he said.

Gráinne produced a key. He took it and opened the door.

He stepped in first and looked around the darkened room. Instant warmth sent alarm bells off in his head.

'The heating is on a timer. You know how these old places can be. Leave them for five minutes and the damp rises.' Gráinne stepped around him, flipping on a light as she past him.

'Great. We have electricity.'

She spun around with a sly grin on her face. 'Oh, yes. We have all the mod-cons here, including hot and cold running water. You'll have to step out the back to the shed to do your business, though.' With that, she spun and went toward a door on the far side of the room.

'What do you mean, I have to go outside to use the loo?' he asked, following her. No one told him he'd have to use a bucket while he was up here.

She'd tossed the duvet on the sofa and flipped on the light as she entered the kitchen. He watched her bend over at the sink and groaned. When she stood, she had a fresh sponge – still wrapped in factory plastic – in one hand, and a bottle of dishwashing soap in the other.

'Gráinne, answer me. What do you mean I have to go out to the shed? I thought you said this place had all the mod-cons?' He didn't like this at all, at all.

She unwrapped the sponge and turned the tap. 'Damn,' she cursed. He watched as she spun to the back door. She found a hidden key on an upper cupboard shelf and unlocked the door.

'I'll be right back. I have to turn on the water.' She was back within a minute, but it was a minute too long. It was a minute full of thoughts of rainy nights and being forced to race through the muck to an outhouse.

He caught her coming through the door again. 'Gráinne!' he pleaded.

She laughed at him. 'I was kidding.'

Relief flooded through him.

When his heart rate slowed, he laughed at himself. He must be really tired. Gráinne had a go off him and he'd fallen for it hook, line, and sinker.

She went back to the tap and the water sputtered on. She let it run until the water came clear, then washed out a kettle, filled it with water then switched it on.

'That wasn't very nice, you know,' he told her, leaning against the door jamb with his arms crossed over his chest.

'I know,' she said, wiggling her brows at him as she passed to a press. She opened the door and withdrew mugs and tea.

'Is this what the next week or two will be like?'

Gráinne nodded quickly. 'Probably.'

JD groaned audibly.

By the time they'd bedded down, it had been going on nine am. As promised, JD had slept on the sofa, but by the looks of him, not very well. He had dark circles under his whiskey-colored eyes and his mood was sour.

She, on the other hand, had slept like a baby. She was surprised she'd lasted as long as she had. But now they were both awake, Gráinne wasn't sure whose stomach was protesting the loudest at its empty state.

'What did you expect?' She waved a frozen loaf of bread and equally frozen pack of sausages she'd pulled out of the freezer, and a tin of baked beans she'd found on a nearly empty shelf beside the box of stale teabags. Other than that, they were poor in food assets.

241

'But I'm a vegetarian.'

She was sure her face looked as shocked as she felt. 'You eat bunny food?'

'You have a problem with that?'

'No. You just look like a meat-and-two-meat-man to me, is all.'

'Don't you mean meat and two veg? And just what does a meat-eater look like?'

'I'm just saying, I would've never guessed. Anyway, we'll just have to go into town for what we need. You're taking me shopping anyway, right?'

JD moaned audibly. 'You're telling me I have to take that damn road again? Twice, no less?'

'Yes, that's what I'm telling you. We could always resort to hunter-gathering, though this time of year it'll be more like just hunting.'

There was no mistaking what JD thought when he looked at her then.

'Okay, poor choice of words.' The last person they needed to be reminded of was Taylor 'The Hunter' Wade. When she spoke again, she said, 'I'm sorry, but this is all we have. We'll have to go shopping or you'll have to live on beans on toast.' She looked at her watch. 'If we're going shopping, it means we better hurry because it's getting late and country folk tend to close much earlier than city folk.'

JD groaned again, relenting. 'Okay, okay.'

She watched him disappear through the kitchen door and laughed. This was going to be an interesting stay. She had no idea he was vegetarian, the very fit man he was. Come to think of it, she'd never seen him eat meat while in the pub. Sure, he ate, but it was usually salads or one of the other non-meat options. Quite often it was just a toasted sandwich ... sans the ham.

Come to think of it, he hadn't eaten the Christmas goose, either.

She laughed again. She'd never make a good detective. She missed the slightest clues.

They headed back into Macroom to do their shopping. The village shop nearest the cottage would have had the basics, but nothing like tofu or natural yogurt. She was doubtful of finding those in Macroom, either.

Well, he'd just have to get what was available. Like he kept telling her, they weren't going to be at the cottage forever. It was temporary. They could both put up with some discomforts for a few days. Couldn't they?

Chapter Nineteen

That had been a week ago, and the situation in the cottage hadn't improved. JD was as cranky as ever.

Gráinne felt sorry for him sleeping on the sofa, but not sorry enough to let him into the bedroom with her; not that she was sleeping much better. She had enough room, but after the first night, thoughts of JD's hands on her body and the promises he'd made over the holidays had kept her eyes wide open. Knowing he was under the same roof, and knowing how easily he would come to her if she asked him to, set her nerves on edge.

She knew it was more than just his sleeping on the sofa irritating him. It was the daily trips into town for food and having to suffer the road to the cottage. He didn't say anything, but just mentioning town changed the tone of his voice.

And today was no different.

She waited at the door while he gathered his things.

Boredom had set in on the second day. The cottage didn't have a TV, and radio reception was dodgy at best. There were books to read – he even had his e-reader – CDs to listen to, and endless trails through the forest to hike when it wasn't raining. But without a TV, even just to watch DVDs on, JD was going spare.

He told her he felt disconnected. He couldn't get

the news so he had no idea what was happening in Dublin or with the case. He had his mobile, but reception at the cottage was as unreliable as the radio. He had tried to phone the station yesterday when they'd stopped in the village, but the battery was flat. He'd forgotten to recharge it the night before.

The only thing keeping him busy was writing up his report on what had happened on New Year's Eve at The Klub!. Now that was finished, he would post it today while they were in town.

The drive into Macroom passed in silence. She watched him from the corner of her eye as he drove.

He was cute with his face squished up like that. His scowl darkened his eyes, making them more intense. The tightness around his lips gave his face a more chiseled look. He really was quite handsome, even if he was grouchy.

'I'm really sorry about this,' she said, breaking the silence. She tried to sound sincere. She really was sorry.

She saw him relax a little. 'Stop apologizing. It's not your fault. I'm sorry if I'm taking it out on you.' He glanced quickly at her as he drove.

'I just realized this must be hard for you.'

'What do you mean?'

'You're a city boy whose been forced into the country. You're a true bachelor, who'd like nothing better than sports on the telly all day and a box of pizza on your lap.' She grinned knowingly at him.

He slowed the car as they entered town. Traffic was heavier the closer they drove. He cast her another side glance and added, 'I'd much rather have you on my lap.'

Her heart fluttered. She had wondered when the innuendos would start up again. She knew he loved teasing her, but since they'd been at the cottage he'd done everything except. He'd promised Kieran he'd behave, and he had, but she was beginning to miss his teasing and was hoping it would come back soon; she had some witty repartee waiting for him.

Ignoring his comment, she turned her attention back to the road.

As they came into the old town square, tent-covered stalls and street vendors' tables erupted in a riot of color.

Today was market day.

Gráinne had forgotten about the tradition. She was surprised to see them in the middle of winter, but the day was clear and dry, albeit crisp.

To her surprise, they had a brilliant time over the next couple hours. They strolled from table to table, stall to stall, tent to tent, buying bits and pieces from most of them.

One stall sold home-baked cakes and breads, another local cheese, and another dozens of different flavored olives and bean salads. There were stalls selling organic fruit and vegetables, eggs, cream and buttermilk, one sold herbs and plants and flowers. There was even a fishmonger with his stainless steel tray layered with crushed ice, fish, and other sea creatures.

Other stalls sold handcrafts, hand-knitted garments, traditional music, books, and even pet supplies.

At one point, JD disappeared. He wouldn't tell her where he'd gone or what he'd bought, only that she'd know soon enough. She laughed off his secretiveness, but in reality, she was curious to know what he was up to.

Over the course of the day, Gráinne told JD about the town and the people who'd lived there over the centuries, including William Penn, who eventually gave his name to the American state of Pennsylvania, and Lady Ardilaun who married Sir Arthur Guinness. Both had once lived in the castle, which now sat in ruin beyond the old gatehouse on the square.

She also told him how the market used to be in her grandparents' day, and many decades before.

'It's flourished for more than 800 years,' she told him.

'That's incredible.'

'Even more so when you consider that before the town was founded, the area was a center for Druidic learning. And the mighty Brian Boru gained the kingdom of Munster on the eastern side of town at the Meeting of the Waters.'

JD's eyes widened. 'We Dubs think we've cornered the market in history and culture.'

By the time they left for home, the car was laden down with sacks of food, some potted herbs for the kitchen sill, and a few bottles of wine from the off license. With all they'd bought, they wouldn't have to suffer the cottage road for a few days.

Gráinne couldn't help but feel today had been a turning point in their stay at the cottage. Once JD was loaded down with vegetarian delicacies, his mood had lightened considerably. He teased her relentlessly, and up until they'd had too many purchases to carry, he'd held her hand as they strolled through the market.

She'd really enjoyed the day out with him, and for a while she allowed herself to pretend they were a couple. If today was any example of a life together with him, Gráinne envied the woman he would marry.

'I've got her, Mr. Wade,' said the man.

At the news, Taylor Wade's heart quickened. 'Brilliant!' he exclaimed. 'Bring her back to Dublin. I'll deal with her here.'

The man cleared his throat. 'What I mean, Mr. Wade, is I've found her. I don't actually ... have her in hand.'

Wade's joy quickly turned to anger. There were no in-between emotions for him. When he spoke, his words were chosen with care and spoken with deliberation. 'Then what are you doing bothering me? Your instructions were clear. I expect them followed to the T.'

'B-boss, I am. You said to find the woman and let you know when I had her,' the man said.

Wade rubbed the bridge between his eyes with his finger and thumb, squeezing his eyes shut. The incompetence of Molloy's staff amazed him. They were a shower of twits. That didn't speak well for Molloy. He'd enjoyed removing Molloy's DNA from the gene pool. And if this particular twit didn't shape up, he'd find himself in similar circumstances when he returned to Dublin.

Taking a deep breath, Wade opened his eyes and pictured the guy standing before him. When this was over, he needed a fall guy for when he sent Jett to the Big Sleep.

'Fine. Now you've found her, pick her up and bring her to me. Is that clear enough?' he said, jaw clenched.

'Aye, boss. Only it might be a while,' the man told him.

Wade growled audibly. 'What now?'

'I-I followed her out of town, to see where she's staying.'

'And,' Wade prodded when the man paused too long.

'I lost her.'

'You lost her.' The pressure behind his eyes returned and he squeezed them shut again trying to block the pain.

'Aye, boss. You see, she turned off the road. By the time I caught up, she'd disappeared,' the man explained.

'Did you follow her?'

'Aye, boss,' the man replied. 'She was gone. It was like she just disappeared.'

'What do you mean disappeared? You'll be disappeared if you don't start making sense,' Wade warned.

'When I got to the place she turned off at, there was no sign of a car or nothin'.'

'She couldn't have just disappeared. Describe the area and be quick about it.' The man cleared his throat nervously and continued. 'She pulled through a cattle gate at a Coillite site. There's no road, no car park. Nothin'.'

'Well, she couldn't have disappeared into thin air. Was there a path of any kind she could have taken? Anything wide enough for a car?' Wade prodded.

The man thought for a moment. 'The only path through the place is too rough for a car. I tried driving up it, but I turned around when the exhaust fell off. It's too rough. There's no way she could have driven it without wrecking her car. There would have been bits of her car all over that path. That road's meant for logging trucks. There's no way a car could make it up there.'

Wade thought for a moment. He would get no satisfaction out of this man. He should have sent one of his own men to find Jett.

Taking a deep breath, he thought for a moment while he tried to calm himself.

'All right, Dusty,' he started.

'Rusty, boss. Not Dusty,' the man corrected.

'Whatever.' Wade took a deep and exasperated breath. 'This is what you're going to do. Stay where you are for a few more days. See if she goes back to town. If you can't capture her there, then ride her tail all the way back to where she's staying. And call me when you have her in your hands or you've found where she's staying. Can you do that?'

'Sure, boss,' said Rusty.

'What are you waiting for, Dusty? Find that bitch,' he spat.

'Rusty, boss. It's Rusty.'

'Whatever,' he said, slamming down the phone.

He really didn't have time for this kind of incompetence. It was becoming obvious to him he would have to see to this job himself.

The more he thought about it, the more he

liked that idea. It had been a while since his last sporting venture.

A smile creased his face. Yes, yes! That's what he'd do.

He picked up the phone and dialed his pilot. 'Dermuid, prepare the chopper. Yes, we'll be heading to West Cork. I'll need the gear. I'm going stalking. Be ready. We may need to leave on a moment's notice.'

On their arrival back at the cottage, JD sent Gráinne to have a nap. Or a bath. Or whatever, as long as she stayed in the bedroom and let him 'work.' He needed an hour, and would come for her when he was ready.

True to his word, he knocked on her door an hour after he'd closed it behind her.

'Can I come out now?' she asked. 'I promise I'll be good.' She pouted for effect. At first, she felt like she was being treated like a naughty child who'd been sent to her room for misbehaving. Except, her curiosity won out and kept her pacing while she was waiting.

She earned a kiss on the forehead for her trouble. 'And here I was hoping you'd be bad.'

He wove his fingers through hers and guided her through the cottage to the front garden. Amazing smells drifted through the house. Her stomach growled loudly, protesting at being pulled outside into the chilly air instead of the kitchen, where she wanted to find something to eat.

JD guided her to a table and chairs he'd set out at the edge of the property, overlooking the rolling hills to the south where the trees had been

251

clear cut.

Gráinne stood with her mouth agape at the sight before her.

The garden table and chairs had been brought around from the back. The table had been covered in a cloth he'd found in the kitchen. He'd spared nothing decorating it – dishes, flatware, glasses, candles – and one of the little potted flowers she'd bought earlier was in the center of the table.

He'd built a makeshift hearth he'd constructed with spare bricks he must have found out back, and a fire was ablaze in it.

'It's lovely,' she sighed.

JD pulled a chair out for her. She sent him a string of silent questions in her gaze. *What are you up to? What is this all about? What do you want?* Questions rolled through her mind as she took her seat. JD only said, 'Wait here.'

She watched him disappear into the cottage. It wasn't a moment before he returned, his arms laden with foil-covered plates and a baguette stuck under his arm. 'Take this, will ya, love?' She caught the bread and watched him set the dishes on the table. 'No peeking. One more thing and we're set.'

Gráinne shook her head. What fool thing was he up to? It was too bloody cold to be eating outside, though the fire was quite warm, she had to admit. Maybe it wouldn't be so bad.

'I know it's early,' JD said, as he placed the last dish on the table and sat. She heard music coming from the cottage now, too. Crooners! JD was full of surprises. 'But I thought if we're going to catch the sunset, we'd better eat now.'

'The sunset—'

'Yeah. You know. That big yellow thing that sometimes appears in the Irish sky? It comes up in the morning and goes down in the evening?' His whiskey-colored eyes sparkled as he teased her.

She narrowed her eyes and played along. 'Ah, right. I think I recall seeing it a time or two, alright.'

JD chuckled then removed the foil covering the dishes.

Incredible scents wafted to her nostrils and she inhaled deeply. 'Mmm, smells delicious.'

'I hope you like it.' He served them from each of the serving dishes, then a bit more from another just for Gráinne.

'What's this?' she asked, referring to the last portion.

'Remember that bit of smoked cod you bought today at the market? I cooked some of it for you. It's sort of a cross between a fish pie and a pasta thingy.'

'A pasta thingy, eh?' She couldn't help but smirk at his culinary vocabulary. He just winked. 'Well, it smells wonderful. Everything does. I can't believe you whipped this up in an hour.' She ripped a piece off the baguette and dug into her meal.

'To be honest, most of it's just bits and pieces from the market. I just fixed them up a little,' he told her, settling into his own meal.

'You know, I never would have taken you for a chef,' she said, shaking her head at the amazing flavors. Gráinne didn't think she'd ever eaten anything so tasty, and wondered if the flavor was

253

purely from the food or made all the better because JD had prepared it for her. She couldn't remember a man, except for Kieran, ever cooking for her, let alone doing anything else on her behalf.

He nearly choked at her comment. 'A chef? Hardly. I like to dabble. Being a vegetarian, I'm forced to be a bit more creative with my meals. I can't just flip a steak under the grill anymore. Unless I want to live on nothing but steamed vegetables, I have to be creative to make things interesting and flavorful.'

'How long have you been a vegetarian?'

She watched as he poured them each a glass of red wine. 'About ten years now, I guess.'

'Did you have a big epiphany, or just decide it seemed like a good thing to do at the time?'

'I don't think it was either. I just eat what I like the most. As it turns out – much to my mother's astonishment – it happens to be vegetables. It wasn't a conscious decision to stop eating meat. It just–'

'Happened?' she finished for him.

He chuckled. 'Something like that.'

A moment later, he lifted his glass toward her and waited while she did the same. He touched his glass to hers while he gazed deeply into her eyes. For a moment, he said nothing, his gaze gentle and thoughtful.

Nervous, she asked, 'Were you going to make a toast?'

'I was just looking for the right words, but when I look at you, they escape me.' His eyes darkened.

A breath lodged in her throat and refused to budge. She knew the look. It was bad enough her voice still hadn't completely returned, but now she could barely speak at all.

'You should have been a fertilizer salesmen. You'd be wealthy,' she said, setting her glass down. She looked back to her dish but wasn't sure she was still hungry.

JD took her hand in his. 'Gráinne.' His voice was deep and smooth. 'Don't turn away.'

'You're making me nervous. I don't handle compliments well,' she admitted, glancing at him.

'Get used to it, because I intend to bathe you in them.'

Where was her witty repartee when she needed it? She'd prepared a handful of comebacks for his smart remarks, but she wasn't prepared for this.

He smoothed an errant curl from her cheek. His fingers caressed her skin, tingling where he touched.

'I love the way the sun catches your hair. When you move, fire dances along the curls and shimmers with red and copper through the black.'

'Please,' she whispered, discomfort warring with desire.

'Your eyes sparkle with golden flecks when you're aroused. Did you know that?'

So much for his being speechless.

Her heart skittered along her ribs as his hand slipped across her shoulder and down her arm. His touch left a blaze of fire in its wake. He took her hand in his and wove his fingers with hers.

'I love the glow on your cheeks when you blush, as you are now.' He had the gall to smile at her then. And he was teasing her, too, tickling her emotionally and touching her in places she'd

255

never been touched before. All that, and he only held her hand and spoke a few pretty words.

She needed to get a hold of herself. He knew what his compliments did to her. They made her unstable. She'd fallen for his caresses before. She couldn't let it happen again. If they ever got out of this mess she'd put them all in, she still intended to go to school, and she couldn't afford to get emotionally involved until she graduated. A man would be too distracting.

She took a deep breath and dug into her store of witty comebacks to see which ones would work best with him.

'It's not the glow you're seeing, John Desmond,' she said, using his full Christian name. ''Tis only the cold. That's hardly a fire you've built. A body could freeze to death.'

JD chuckled, glancing at the flames dancing over a pile of very warm turf sods. 'Then come into my arms, love, and I'll warm you myself.'

'And have my food go cold? Not on your life,' she retorted, guiding a forkful into her mouth. The flavors of the warm beans and vegetables, and a seasoning she couldn't place but knew was familiar, melted on her tongue.

'Hmm,' he muttered. 'Am I going to have competition with my cooking?'

'Keep cooking for me like this and you will.'

'Love, give me the chance and I'll cook for you every night.' His voice practically dripped honey.

Gráinne looked into his eyes. She understood his insinuation, but she wasn't going to acknowledge it. She'd take him literally, though, and see how it went over.

'You're hired. As long as we're on this mountaintop, you're the chef.' She grinned, flicking her
brows up and down mischievously.

JD chuckled and sat back in his chair with his
glass of wine. 'I accept. No better time to begin a
lifetime of servitude than immediately. No sense
in putting off the inevitable, right?'

She glared at him. Was he playing her own
game with her?

'At least you know your place.' That earned her
another chuckle, but he didn't reply. They finished their food in companionable silence.

Once the meal was done, JD took their plates to
the kitchen and cleared the table. On his return,
he brought another bottle of wine.

'Trying to get me drunk?' she asked, holding
her glass up for a refill.

'And if I did, would you let me take advantage
of you?' he dared.

'You do that easily enough without alcohol.'

For a moment he just stared at her, as if trying
to decipher her meaning. She turned her gaze
toward the setting sun and tried blocking out the
image of him in her kitchen back in Finglas, kissing her as no man had ever kissed her. And again
at Christmas, before he'd given her the pendant.
The very pendant she idly fingered now.

Letting it fall from her fingers, she hoped the
firelight disguised the flush she felt heating her
neck and cheeks.

The winter sunset wasn't as vivid as the summer's, nevertheless it was spectacular just the
same.

The icy winter blue sky gave way to a thick

blanket of fog coming in off the sea miles away. The darkness of it told Gráinne a storm was coming. She wondered if it was something within herself portending warning, or simply that they would have a hard rain tonight.

As the sun dipped, its glow radiated peach, apricot and orange against the underside of the dark fogbank, turning it a deep slate. Far-off trees were shadowed in taupe, fading to black as night fell around them.

The sky was on fire then, just that part beneath the clouds. The icy blue of the sky overhead was soft lavender. Behind them, the lavender darkened to steel blue that heralded the night.

This was a fitting end to a lovely day. It was made even more so by the effort JD had put into preparing this meal for her. It had been luxurious compared to the last few nights.

She stole glances at JD as he gazed across the mountains. He'd scooted his chair around for a better view, but it also put him closer to her. She said nothing.

She said nothing, too, when he reached over and took her hand in his. It was warm and strong. Smiling to herself at how natural it felt to sit beside JD like this, she focused her attention once more on the horizon and the changing colors as the sun disappeared.

It amazed Gráinne how quickly the sun sank behind the mountains. It took the sun hours to traverse the sky, but the most spectacular part of the day ended within minutes. Along with, she was sure, this seemingly perfect moment with a man she loved but couldn't have.

Chapter Twenty

JD stroked Gráinne's fingers as he watched the sun go down. He'd been pleasantly surprised she hadn't pull away from him when he'd taken her hand. He loved touching her. She was hard to resist. He didn't want to push, though. He wanted things between them to happen naturally.

It was said you never really knew someone until you had to live with them. To JD, this forced time at the cottage was the perfect opportunity to learn as much as possible about the woman he loved, especially if he thought he wanted to spend the rest of his life with her.

He never thought he'd ever want to settle down. He'd been slagged for years by his mates that he'd die a bachelor.

Women loved a man in uniform and he'd played up on it the entire time he was on the beat. Since he'd made detective, his dating prospects had seriously diminished. He tried not to think it was because he was no longer in uniform. He blamed it on the hours. Though, he was pretty sure it was the uniform thing.

If he wanted Gráinne, he'd have to rely solely on his personality. Judging by her kisses, he thought he was going all right.

Once the sun had set, JD was hard-pressed to break the spell settling over them, but either the fire needed stoking or they needed to move indoors. The drops landing on his nose decided for him.

'We better head in. It looks like it's going to rain,' he said.

'I think you're right. The wind seems to be picking up, too. By the looks of those black clouds,' she nodded to an approaching thick blanket of fog to the southwest, 'it looks like there could be a proper storm brewing.'

Once they'd secured the table and chairs in the carport and outed the fire, they headed indoors. 'I'll get a fire going then we can have dessert.'

A single brow lifted over her emerald green eyes. 'Dessert, too? This should be interesting.' She gave him one of her sexy smiles as she walked over to the old stereo. At least *he* found it sexy. He doubted she even realized what a simple grin did to his insides.

He placed some dry moss on the grate, then kindling on top, and turf sods on top of that. He kept glancing over his shoulder at Gráinne while he worked. He knew what the collection contained and saw she was having trouble making up her mind what to play next. He knew she loved music. She was constantly putting something different into the pub CD player instead of letting one CD run all day. He often found her moving along with the music and mouthing the words when she thought no one else was looking. No one else probably was, except him. Keeping his gaze from her was difficult. He could look at her forever and not get bored.

Striking a match and setting it to the moss, he asked, 'What are you planning to study in college?'

She didn't answer him immediately. He wondered if she heard the question. Once the fire was going, he sat back on his heels and turned to look at her. She had a couple CDs in her hands she was considering. She chose one and replaced the CD that had ended just before they came inside. The electric sound of Goldfrapp assaulted the room.

JD chuckled. He'd assumed – incorrectly – that Gráinne would be a fan of blues, like Kieran. Her CD choices continually seemed to be something other than blues, except for those in the pub. She seemed to prefer mind-assaulting electronics to soul-searching ballads.

'Music,' she finally replied, turning toward him as he stood.

'Music in general, or do you play an instrument?'

'I play the flute, but I'd like to learn as much as possible about the whole industry,' she said.

'I would have never guessed the flute,' he remarked.

'Really? What did you think I played?'

He moved to stand before her and picked up the jewel case for Goldfrapp. 'Synthesizers, or maybe a guitar like Kieran, but not a flute. Somehow, I just can't imagine you playing the flute and listening to this.' He waved the case at her teasingly.

'I'm full of surprises,' she said, teasing him back.

He chuckled at her admissions. 'Of that, love, I have no doubt.' She scowled at him. He could tell she was trying to think of a smarmy retort, but couldn't come up with just the right one. Before she could, he continued. 'So, maybe you'll play

261

for me. I noticed there's a flute on the bookshelf. I'd love to hear you.'

'Hmm, maybe.' She smiled thoughtfully. 'We'll see how good your surprise dessert is.' She winked then disappeared through the bedroom door.

He chuckled, shaking his head disbelievingly. She was certainly something, alright.

When she emerged from the bedroom, she'd slipped on an oversized flannel shirt with matching baggie bottoms. Fuzzy pink slippers adorned her feet.

When he'd first seen her dressed like this two nights ago, he'd thought she was on her way to bed early. He soon learned this was just her evening routine and, if he said so himself, he quite enjoyed it. She looked like a big kid in her oversized pajamas and slippers that looked too big for her feet. He knew she was all woman, though, and he longed to cuddle her in his arms.

He discovered the Vaughans kept a few changes of clothes in the cottage. He was sure Gráinne was thankful, though he would have happily suffered through her nakedness while she washed the single change of clothes he'd given her at his place.

His lip wasn't the only thing twitching at the thought of Gráinne naked. He would like nothing more than to have her writhing beneath him. If he had anything to say about it, he would get rid of all the clothing in the cottage. He had nothing to hide from her, including his body, and wanted nothing more than to share it, and his life, with her.

'So where's that dessert you promised me?'

Gráinne asked, curling up on the sofa.

'Demanding wench, aren't you?'

'When it comes to sweets, you betcha.' Her smile was disarming.

'Far be it from me to withhold anything from you.'

At the kitchen door, he turned back. His breath caught in his throat at the sight of her. The glow from the fire danced across her hair as she swayed to the music. He wanted to climb into her warmth, and very nearly went to her. Instead, he asked, 'Tea or coffee?'

She spun her gaze on him and he couldn't help notice how her eyes flashed with the firelight. She bit her lip, considering his offer. 'I'd fancy a coffee with a drop of Bailey's, if you're of the mind.'

'I'm of the mind for more than you know,' he muttered under his breath.

While the kettle boiled, he poured some of the ground coffee they'd bought earlier in the day into a cafetière. He knew where the Bailey's was. He'd found it earlier when he was searching for sherry.

He didn't know how he was going to survive the rest of their stay in the cottage. They'd only been here a week and already he was having a hard time keeping himself in check. What he wanted was to strip her naked and take her where she sat, or stood, or leaned over, or wherever.

Whenever he looked at her, he stiffened so quickly it was almost painful. He knew the only thing to help ease his pain was to bury himself deep inside her. Or a cold shower. And he'd had plenty of those over the last few days. He was thankful there was a sizable stack of turf behind the cottage, because their nightly fire was the second best thing to getting him warm again. Second to burying himself deep inside Gráinne, that is.

He groaned to himself at the paradox of that.

True to his promise to Kieran, JD had slept on the sofa; if that's what it could be called. It was little more than a loveseat. While it was perfect for getting close to Gráinne in, it wasn't an adequate bed. He knew his mood was suffering from the lack of sleep. He knew his back was. He certainly didn't want Gráinne thinking he was a bear all the time. Something would have to change. The wine had helped relax him, as had their day out, but if his good mood was going to continue, he'd have to get off that sofa.

Once the coffee was made, he found a tray and put the cafetière, bottle of Bailey's, cups, bowls, spoons and his dessert onto it. Taking a deep breath, he lifted the tray and went back into the sitting room, hoping Gráinne wouldn't notice his erection.

'I didn't know how much Bailey's you wanted in your coffee, so I brought the bottle.' He sat the tray on a table beside the sofa.

'You're a smart man, John. I love that in a man,' she said, smiling up at him.

Her smile beguiled him. 'Is that all you love about me?' he dared ask. His heart quickened, waiting for her answer.

'Certainly not,' she replied, her voice smooth and seductive. 'I love your cooking as well.'

He groaned. 'You shouldn't tease a man like

that, love. Especially one who's already having a difficult time keeping his hands to himself.'

Her reply was a single lifted brow. Good. He'd gotten his message across.

'So, where is this surprise dessert you promised?'

'Are you sure you wouldn't rather have me instead?'

'The deal was your concoction in exchange for a tune,' she reminded him. He said nothing as he went about serving up his dessert. 'You made this?' she asked, taking the bowl with its colorful contents.

'I did.'

JD's groin tightened as he watched her sample his creation. As soon as the spoon touched her tongue, her eyes fluttered closed. She tilted her back, moaning her approval. He longed to stroke the long curve of her throat with his tongue, to nibble at her neck, to drive his tongue inside her mouth to taste what she tasted.

When she opened her eyes again, they gleamed with contentment. 'This is delicious. I haven't had trifle in ages.'

His voice was hoarse when he spoke. His arousal unsettled him. 'I take it you approve then.'

'Oh, yes,' she moaned, spooning more of the luscious dessert into her mouth. 'What did you put into this? I don't think I've ever had trifle that tasted this good.'

'It's my mother's recipe. It's just fruit, jelly, sherry, custard. And a couple family secrets,' he added, winking.

She cast him a sexy side-glance. 'Family secrets, eh?'

'Yep. But I'd be willing to share them with you.' JD smiled. 'I'll trade you something for each secret.'

'Trade me?' Her eyes widened in surprise. 'I've already bargained away a tune on my flute. I have nothing else to offer.'

'You have more to offer than you think, but I'll settle for a kiss.'

'A kiss?' She swallowed hard.

'Yes, a kiss. One for each secret.'

He knew he'd stunned her by the way her mouth kept opening to say something, but no words came out. Finally, she asked, 'And what if I say no?'

He slung his arm over the back of the sofa and leaned toward her. 'What if I said I'd take it anyway?' he whispered.

Her eyes widened as he drew closer. She tried tucking herself into the sofa cushions but had no success. Instead, she asked with her voice trembling, 'Do you always take what you want?'

'Only from the willing.' He closed the gap between them.

Gráinne's lips were warm and pliant beneath his. He kissed her gently as not to scare her. Pleased she didn't turn away, he intensified his kiss. He only touched her with his lips, sucking and pulling, covering her over and over again, until she was panting.

When he pulled away, he watched her eyes flutter open. They shimmered with desire. Her gaze never wavered from his.

'Madeira cake,' he whispered.

For a moment, she just stared at him. When her

brows furrowed, he knew he had her attention again. 'Wh-what?'

'Madeira cake. That's one of the secrets,' he said. He leaned toward her again and poked at the sponge in the bowl he still held in his hands. 'Mum used Madeira cake, instead of white bread or those little sponge fingers. It makes the trifle denser and gives it a richer flavor.'

He took a spoonful and held it to her lips. Her gaze never left his, but her lips parted automatically and took his offering. As her lips slid over the spoon, JD's erection pressed painfully against his fly. He imagined what her lips would feel like sliding over him.

Dazed, her voice barely audible, she said, 'I see what you mean.'

'You've a bit of cream,' he whispered, 'here.' He used his tongue to lick the cream from the corner of her mouth. As if he'd begun where he left off with the first kiss, he covered her lips and drew her back. She tasted of sherry, cream and fruit.

He pulled away to set his bowl of trifle on the armrest then slid his arm across the sofa back to brace himself. With his free hand, he ran his fingers through her curls, stroked her inflamed cheek, cupped her face, pulling her back to him.

Gráinne slid her arms around him and kneaded his muscles like a contented cat. She arched into him as his kiss deepened, pressing her breasts against his chest.

He growled under his breath, pulling back to look at her. Her lips were kiss-swollen, parted, and silently asking for his return. Her lids were mere slits, her long, dark lashes curled giving him a sexy, come hither look. Oh, yes! He would come to her alright.

'Freshly whipped cream,' he said in short, clipped words.

'Mmmm,' she sighed. 'Cream.'

'Yeah,' his voice low, 'freshly whipped cream, not that premade muck, with a dash of pure bourbon vanilla and a touch of sugar just to sweeten.' He couldn't take his eyes off her.

Her passion-filled eyes fluttered open. 'Wh-what?'

'That was the second secret to make the world's best trifle.' He smirked then as she became more coherent.

He lowered his lips to hers once more, but stopped at the sound of her voice. He was so close to her mouth that her lips brushed his as she spoke.

'There's another secret?' she squeaked.

'Aye, love. I'm full of secrets I want to share with you.' He closed the gap once more, this time burying his tongue in her sweet warmth.

She made him feel whole. Her kisses and touches made him feel alive. His heart pounded in his chest at how much he wanted to share his body with her. He wanted to make her feel as alive as he felt.

Her fingers stroked the back of his neck, sending electricity racing along his spine, lodging in his groin. He pressed into her and met the firm curve of her hip. Groaning, he dug both hands into her hair, rubbing the soft curls between his fingers.

The position he'd gotten into, leaning into

Gráinne, was becoming increasingly uncomfortable. His erection was painfully pinched in a fold in his trousers. Without breaking his kiss with her, JD lifted himself onto one knee and pulled Gráinne between his legs.

As he lowered himself onto her, their kiss was instantly broken by a loud crash. He remained as still as possible, listening.

Taylor Wade couldn't have found them, could he?

His heart pounded in his chest with a new rhythm – panic.

He forced himself to breathe deeply to calm his racing heart. He listened intently but couldn't hear anything except the pounding of the blood in his veins and the snapping of the fire.

'It was only your bowl.' Humor filled her words and he saw the curve in her lips.

He looked back to where he'd left his bowl and saw the contents splashed across the floor, the bowl in pieces.

Releasing a pent up breath, he collapsed against Gráinne. He would have laughed if he hadn't been so suddenly terrified.

Gráinne's heart raced. She reveled in JD's kisses. He kissed her as no other man had kissed her. As he hovered over her, breathing deeply to catch his breath and her arms still wound around him, she couldn't push aside the new feelings racing through her.

She loved the way he felt, the way he touched her, the emotions he sparked in her. Everything about him screamed familiarity, safety, and – if she recognized the true emotion correctly – love.

Could JD really love her? He hadn't said he did, but his body told her he at least desired her. Or was it her own desperate need for love making her think he did?

She laughed to herself. Maybe she should take psychology instead of music once she made it to school. That way she could analyze herself and discover why she was such a hopeless case.

While JD had been kissing her, Eilis's words kept niggling at her.

'Girl, that man is in love with you. It's written all over his face.'

If Eilis thought he did, could it be true?

Eilis's last words as they'd left the pub a week ago also came back. *'You can trust him.'*

Gráinne glanced beside her as JD lifted himself away from her. Could she trust him? Trust him with everything she held dear?

Even with the fire beside them, Gráinne chilled the instant he sat up. It was as if he'd stolen all the warmth they'd generated together. She wanted it back. She wanted *him* back.

The realization stunned her. She wanted to be back in his arms. She wanted him to kiss her again as he just had. She wanted to feel his body against hers. God help her. She wanted to make love to him. She would worry about his love later.

She sat up and reached for him, but he slipped away without noticing her.

'I better get this mess cleaned up before it stains the rug.'

Pulling herself back into a sitting position, she tried maintaining some composure while her heart split. She just nodded, swinging her legs onto the floor and narrowly missing putting her foot in her own bowl.

When he had the mess cleaned up, the soiled paper towels tossed into the remainder of the fire, he stretched.

'I-I suppose I better get to bed so you can get some sleep. You look tired,' she managed.

He jerked his head in agreement. 'I'll shut down the house.'

'Goodnight, then.'

With great reluctance, she forced her feet to take her into the bedroom. At the door, she stopped and turned back to him. 'Do you need to use the...?'

'I'm grand. Goodnight,' he said, picking up their dessert tray and returned it to the kitchen.

She slipped through the door, closed it behind her then leaned back against it. The room was as dark and empty as she felt. It wasn't an evil darkness, but a consuming darkness that swallows a lonely person whole.

Something in her chest squeezed so tightly it almost choked her.

She was lonely.

She wanted college so desperately she'd pushed everything and everyone aside. She had refused to allow herself even the smallest of life's luxuries. It was all about work so she could save enough money for school. Every penny of every tip went into her special school account. She purposefully hadn't made any friends in Dublin so she could concentrate on saving her money. Having friends meant going out, and going out meant spending money she could ill-afford to spend.

Even after everything that had happened at The Klub!, she still was no closer to paying for tuition and she'd managed to put her family in danger. And the more she pushed JD away, the worse she felt because what she really wanted was to love and be loved. She wanted what Kieran and Eilis had.

She looked at the bed and remembered the time her brother and his wife had spent in the cottage last year. So much had changed for them in the short time they were here. Was JD just a tease who enjoyed kissing her senseless, or was there something more to it?

Pushing herself off the door, she went to wash her face. As she toweled her skin dry, she looked at her reflection. Her lips were swollen and her hair was tussled. JD had kissed the life out of her. Or had he kissed it into her?

Then her reflection disappeared and was replaced by JD's passion-filled expression, his lips parting as he lowered himself onto her. She still felt his erection pressing her against hip.

She didn't remember climbing into bed. She'd put herself on automatic as she relived the time on the sofa. She tossed and turned and couldn't get comfortable. The cottage was quiet now. The only sound was of the rain pelting the tiny window in the room and of the wind rushing through the roof thatching. The storm outside mimicked her own spinning emotions, chilling her to the bone until she shivered uncontrollably.

She thought of JD on the sofa, of the warmth of

his arms, the heat of his touches and kisses. Her mind spun circles, remembering each time he'd kissed her, his every touch, his insinuations hinting at promise.

Gráinne tossed in her lonely bed for an hour before she found her bare feet on the cool flagstone floor, her eyes staring at the door. On the other side was a man who'd given her his heart at Christmas. Absentmindedly, she stroked the heart pendant at her throat. He was the same man who'd risked his own life to save hers, the same man who'd vowed to stay with her until The Hunter could be found. She could never repay him.

Or could she?

Chapter Twenty-One

The embers cast a dim glow over JD. He'd pushed back the sofa and pulled the cushions onto the floor in front of the hearth. Her heart twisted at the sight of his feet dangling off the end of his makeshift bed. The sofa was really too small for him. She'd tried taking it, offering him the more accommodating bed, but he wouldn't hear of it.

He surprised her when he sat up. Couldn't he sleep, either?

'You okay?'

The blanket fell to his lap, the smoldering embers casting shadows off his lean muscles. Sitting here before the glowing hearth, his hair the color of Hennessy brandy, he was the sexiest man she'd ever met.

Take a chance, rang through her mind.

Taking a deep breath, she untied the ribbon at the top of her pajama bottoms and let them fall down over her hips. She pulled down her panties and kicked them both away, all the while watching the expressions playing across his face. His eyes widened, but he didn't move. Not even when she unbuttoned her top and let it, too, fall away from her body. The only thing she wore was the heart pendant.

She stood for a moment, letting him look at her. He raked her with his gaze, but still didn't move to touch her. Doubt started creeping in and she wondered, *Does he think I'm too thin? Are my breasts too small? Is it me he wants, or is it Jett?*

She was about to retrieve her clothes when he finally spoke. His voice was so low she barely heard him.

'My God.'

Take a chance.

Slowly, she lowered herself onto the cushions beside him, leaning on her elbow. 'Gráinne,' he choked through a hard swallow.

She was sure he felt her fingers tremble as she wove them around his neck.

'Kiss me again, John.'

Her body reacted to the memory of when he traded kisses for culinary secrets, and she wanted his mouth on her again.

But he held back.

'What's wrong? Don't you want me?' she asked through the lump forming in her throat.

'Oh, I want you alright.'

'Then–'

'Gráinne, why are you doing this?'

She felt the moment slipping away, embarrassment dampening her desire. Pulling away, she turned to look for her discarded top.

'Wait.' His voice was tender, his grasp gentle as he stilled her. 'Just tell me why you're doing this.'

She breathed deeply to steady her racing heart. She couldn't tell him she loved him. What would he think? They really didn't know each other, though it must have been long enough because she'd fallen for him – hard.

She couldn't tell him the whole truth, so instead she gave him a half of it. 'You saved my life and–'

'And you think you owe me sex in exchange?'

'I wanted to say thank you.'

'You don't have to do this.' His gaze skimmed her again.

'You put yourself in danger to save me, to help my family. There's no way to repay something like that. I thought–'

'You thought giving yourself to me was the way?'

She swallowed hard. 'You've made it clear you want me. Why else would you kiss me they way you do? I ... I thought, because of all you've done...'

'There's nothing more?'

Yes, damn it, there's a lot more. But she wasn't going to admit it. Telling a man she loved him only sent him scurrying.

'Gráinne, sex is the last thing I want from you.'

Her lungs burned as she strained to breathe. Humiliation ripped through her. He was just like the rest, except he'd skipped the sex part and gone right to the rejection.

She forced herself to move away from him. 'I see.' Her body shook so badly she barely managed to sit up.

'Gráinne.'

His voice was unnervingly gentle. His grasp even more so.

'Gráinne, will you please let me finish? You need–'

'What? What do I need, John Desmond?' she snapped, finally finding her voice. 'You seem to know what I need more than I do, so tell me, damn you.'

Anything she had felt when she laid down beside him was gone now and replaced with hurt. She disguised it with anger and a few cheeky comebacks. If it weren't for those, she never would have gotten through all the pain in her life. Her motto had always been 'swallow the hurt and never let them see you cry.'

'This.' JD pushed her down on the cushions. Her body ignited the instant his lips met hers. The tense anger enveloping her body gave way. A long minute later, he said, 'That's what you need, and plenty of it.'

She forced herself to breathe deeply to re-capture some of the breath he'd stolen. Her brows pulled together so tightly her eyes hurt.

'I thought you didn't want sex,' she bit sarcastically.

His voice was smooth and sexy. 'I said sex was the last thing. If you let me finish, I'll tell you what I do want.'

'Are you going to let me up?'

'Not on your life. Will you listen?'

'I don't suppose I have a choice, do I?'

'Sure you do. If you don't want the truth, I'll let you up now and you can run away. Or, you can stay and listen.'

When his grip lightened, she relaxed a little, capitulating.

'You are the most exasperating woman I know,' he told her, his eyes laughing at her, humor in the timber of his voice.

'If I'm so exasperating, let me go.'

'Would you not shut up for two minutes, woman?' he chuckled. It wasn't so much a question but a statement. The shock of it left her speechless. 'You're so afraid if you let anyone in that everything will fall apart.' He spoke softly and the laughter in his eyes softened. 'I don't just want sex with you. I want more.

'I want to know when you're giving me your body, it's not because you think you owe anything to JD the cop.' When he cupped her cheek in his palm, her heart pumped a little faster. Then he told her in no uncertain terms, 'I want you to want me, John Desmond, the man who loves you so much it hurts.'

He loved her? Her heart raced, pumping blood so fast through her veins it made her dizzy. Wasn't this what she wanted, his love?

Still, she heard herself say, 'You don't even know me.'

'I told you before. I don't give my heart foolishly or to fools. I know it hasn't been very long, but in the time I've worked at the pub I've come to know a woman who's passionate and strong-willed. You're also hardheaded, stubborn, and argumentative,' accentuated with a smile, 'but I know it's passion driving you, and enthusiasm for things you love. When you want something, you go for it. And, sure, isn't that why you came to me tonight?'

'I came to say thank you,' she weakly reminded him.

'Ah, Gráinne,' he sighed, pulling her against him. She heard the rapid beat of his heart and knew it matched her own. 'I want more than thank you.'

Of course he did.

Take a chance.

'I ... I want more, too.' There, that wasn't so hard, Gráinne, she said to herself. *Tell him how you really feel, damn it.* But the words got stuck in her throat. 'I'm not good at expressing my feelings. I've never been in love before. Not truly. But you...'

Damn! How could she tell him without sounding like one of those romance heroines?

'Do you love me, Gráinne?'

'Why else would I offer you the one thing I've denied myself until after school?'

His lips curved up slightly as he said, 'Then just say it. You don't have to find flowery words to tell me how you feel.'

She turned away from him. How could she say those three simple words? On their own, each was anonymous and harmless. Together, they had the power to change her world.

His fingers on her chin turned her gaze to his again. His kiss was gentle and sweet, but it was enough to ignite the fire within her. That, and his bulge pressing firmly against her thigh.

'Say it. I. Love. You.'

Change your world, Gráinne, she said to herself. *He's a good man,* Eilis had told her. And JD had told her he loved her so much it hurt. She hurt, too. She wanted this. She wanted *him*. She wanted what Kieran and Eilis had, and wanted JD to be the one to give it to her. All she had to say were three little words.

'Take a chance, love.' This time it was JD saying the words and not the voice in her head.

'I–I love you. God, help me, I do love you.'

All of her pent-up emotions rushed to the surface. She did love JD and she would take a chance with him. She'd trusted him with her life and he'd saved it. Now she trusted him with her heart and he'd saved that, too.

She threw her arms around him and let her tears fall down her cheeks. She heard his light laugh but chose to ignore it. She didn't know what would happen once they left the cottage; it was impossible to say if Taylor Wade would ever be captured, or what he'd do to them if he found them. But right here, right now, she loved JD and appreciated every moment they had together.

'Let's get something straight before this goes any further,' JD said, leaning back once her sniffles had subsided. 'I didn't save your life. You got yourself out of the penthouse. You're the one who did that ... fantastic driving.'

'I was scared. I just wanted to get us out of there.'

'And you did, brilliantly.' Pride filled his voice. 'There was nothing Wii about your driving, love. I'd say you spend a bit of time at Mondellow Park.'

'I'm saying nothing,' she replied innocently, looking away from him.

JD just chuckled.

Then he pulled her under him, propping himself on an elbow. As he moved over her, his chest hair tickled her breasts. His heat seeped into her. Yet, as he slid his hand up the curve of her waist to the side of her breast, icy tingles shot through her body, the kind of ice only the most intense fire gives off. She sucked in her breath at the sensation.

Inside the cottage, stillness settled around them.

The once-smoldering turf embers had banked themselves and cast the room into near darkness, and quietness enveloped them as JD held her. The only sound was his beating heart in her ear and the storm raging outside.

Then the room lit up. Just a flash as if a car's headlight shone through. They both spun toward the window. Gráinne thought her heart had stopped. The clap of thunder following rumbled through the cottage. The storm she'd seen approaching at dinner was drawing closer.

They were both on edge. First the broken bowl, and now the lightning, reminding them both how precious their time was together.

Gráinne let JD pull her back into his arms. Feeling his strength reassured her of their safety. His purely male scent and the feel of his skin on hers reassured her she was with the man she loved.

In the darkness, she felt his hands all over her body – stroking her stomach, her hip, the side of her breast, her shoulder. He seemed content touching her this way, and she was content to let him. Goosebumps rose everywhere he touched, the roots of which seemed to stem from somewhere deep in the hollow of her womb.

Then he slid his hand to her nape and used his thumb to tilt her chin, before lightly kissing the bruises she knew still lingered. Her pulse quickened and she let her eyelids flutter closed at his tenderness.

She kneaded her fingers into his back like a contented cat and fought not to dig her nails into him.

He moved down her throat to her shoulder, and as he leaned away, he kissed a hot trail along her inner arm to her wrists, lingering there before grasping her hand and kissing each fingertip. He turned his mouth into her palm, his tongue tracing her heart line. When he found her lifeline, he ran his tongue along it and retraced the line up her inner arm and back to her throat. Her stomach quivered at the erotic sensation. He used his mouth and hands to kiss and stroke her body until that place deep in her womb vibrated with need.

Sounds of heavy rain on the thatch above them filtered through her mind's haze. Knowing there was a raging storm outside only enhanced the raging storm within her. JD's hands and mouth electrified her skin wherever they touched, his tongue leaving fire trails in its wake. Her heart thundered from his kisses and at the anticipation of what was to come. No one had ever made her feel like JD did, and she didn't want it to ever stop. She sighed and felt her eyes roll back in their sockets. He left her breathless.

'John,' she sighed throatily, her head lolling on the cushion.

Lightning flashed again. Her eyes shot open just in time to see JD's mouth settled on her breast. He drew in her nipple, making her shiver from the suddenly intense sensation. Thunder rolled outside as her back arched off the cushions, the static charge racing right to her core.

He stroked the flat of his hand along her ribs and down her stomach, and lower still until he cupped her mound. She arched again, crying out as he slipped a finger along her cleft.

Gráinne had never thought about it until this moment. She'd been forced to wax so she could get away with wearing such a skimpy thong on New Year's Eve. Now, with JD's fingers playing across her bare flesh, she noticed her sensitivity was compounded a hundred times. She nearly came right then and there.

She panted hard, trying to control her body's reaction to his onslaught. Liquid heat pooled in her womb. Her whole body tingled as if charged with electricity.

'John,' she sighed again, feeling his short stubble brushing her stomach. 'Kiss me. Please,' she pleaded.

He rose instantly and captured her mouth with his. She parted her lips and welcomed him inside her, letting her body flame up. His slick fingers expertly found what pleased her and had her panting in his mouth.

She didn't think she could take anymore. 'John, please. I want you inside me.'

JD leant away just enough to speak. 'What, love?'

'Kiss me. Make love to me. I want you inside me.'

JD rolled over and pulled her on top of him, then sat up. He cradled her in his arms, wrapping her legs around his hips. Using both hands now, he caressed her body. Lightning flashed again outside and she saw the amber flash of his eyes against the darkness, the carnal expression on his face, his lips part as he closed the distance with hers. He drove his tongue into her mouth and she held onto him with fists in his hair.

She felt him hard between her thighs and rubbed her bare flesh against his shaft. The movement sent pulse waves of pleasure rippling through her.

Gráinne felt JD move away from her then heard rustling. A flash of lightning illuminated the room and she saw him rummaging through his things. Then she heard the familiar sound of an opening box and instantly knew what he was about. When he came back to her, she took the tiny packet from his fingers.

'I'll do it.'

She tore open the packet and withdrew the condom. The task of putting it on was usually so perfunctory – something required, and usually taking away from the intimacy of sex. But performing the task for JD brought Gráinne closer to him. She stroked his warm penis for a moment as she leaned in to kiss him. She let her fingers work in the darkness, let her mouth angle over his and her tongue search his mouth's inner warmth.

Once the slick barrier was in place, she lifted and settled herself upon him, sheathing him to the hilt. She moaned into his mouth from the sudden and intense feeling of being so completely filled. Her inner muscles tightened as she tried gaining some control of her body's reaction.

Not yet, not yet, she chanted to herself.

Pulling her closer, he used his hands on her bottom and his body to gently rock her. He slid in and out of her as purposefully as a tender caress.

She'd thought she wanted him to throw her back on the cushions, drive himself into her and they would have wild, sweaty sex. But now she realized this was the most perfect thing they could share together – this closeness, the tenderness ... their love. This was exactly how their first time together was meant to be, and God help her, she wanted to remain just like this for the rest of her life – safe and secure and very much loved in JD's arms.

His hands played along her spine, making her arch into him. Her peaked nipples grazed his chest hairs and sent more tingles through her. She raked his shoulders with her nails and felt his breathy gasps on her cheeks between kisses.

And his mouth. His mouth consumed her as the storm consumed the mountaintop.

Lightning flashed and was almost immediately followed by rolling thunder, telling her the storm was almost right over them, just as her own storm was peaking.

She panted into JD's mouth, not wanting to release him completely, yet finding it difficult to breathe. Her body tensed with each thunderous crack and felt inner muscles clenching around JD's shaft.

Not yet, not yet.

He must have felt it, too, for he swelled within her with each stroke. And into her mouth, his words came on deep moans, 'Don't hold back, love. Come for me.'

She didn't need any more encouragement. No longer fighting her release, she let the sensations pool at her core. Her inner muscles tightened and blood rushed to the spot where they were joined. She felt like her body was soaring, higher and higher to the ceiling, and out through the thatched roof. Her body prickled with feeling, as if the storm splashed fiery droplets all over her.

Suddenly, thunder cracked right over head, lightning right on top of it and lighting up the room. The sound was so loud it made her body jerk with surprise. Adrenaline instantly shot through her, releasing molten heat to envelop her. She bucked against JD again and again as she cried out, her spine arcing. She felt whipped around by the storm's heavy winds, the power of them taking her higher into the sky.

JD firmly grasped her bottom and rocked her faster against him. She heard him cry out as his own release took him over the edge.

And when she finally floated back and collapsed into JD's arms, she was gasping for air.

Gráinne held JD for long minutes while they both caught their breaths.

Still joined, she felt fresh tears filling her eyes. Now they were tears of joy and of complete contentedness she'd never felt before. She'd fallen in love with JD long before now, but making love with him brought home just how much she loved him. Making love in such an intimate way proved how much he loved her, too.

As they sat before the hearth with him still firm inside her, rocking gently and her body warming once more, everything thing else outside the tiny cottage ceased to exist. The storm battering the cottage was moving away now, and all she heard was the sound of their own labored breathing and thunder in the distance.

Her body was alive as it had never been before.

She felt every sensation around her, from the chill of the room to the warmth of JD's hands and his hot breath whispering over her skin. And that place where he nestled within her was awakened and hot with need.

Disagreements and petty arguments of the last few days, as they'd settled into the cottage, were forgotten. As was the reason they were in the cottage in the first place – the Klub!, Jimmy's murder, and Taylor Wade – all pushed into the dark recesses of her memory. The only things existing at this very moment were JD's arms around her while he held her, and all the love they had to share.

Gráinne had a lifetime to catch up on now she'd found a man who overlooked her past indiscretions and loved her for who she was.

Joy so profound rose up in her she had to swallow hard to keep from sobbing. Her chest tightened with emotion and her womb tingled once more. For once in her life, things were perfect.

Chapter Twenty-Two

'I'm sorry!' Gráinne snapped.

She and JD were beginning a new relationship together. She wanted this morning to be perfect, especially after such an amazing night. By the time they'd finally succumbed to sleep, they'd made love so many times she'd lost count. They'd spent the night making love, talking and laughing like teenagers.

But she wasn't laughing now.

Gráinne had risen before JD so she could shower and dress. When she came out of the bedroom, he was still nude and stood folding the blankets. She'd watched the way his muscles flexed and how his hands moved over the fabric. She'd shivered, remembering his hands on her body. She loved the way he touched her, loved the way he made her feel.

Hell, she loved *him*.

Things had changed between them – her entire world had changed. There were no more secrets between them, no more hidden glances, no more wondering, no more pretending, no more hiding. With a man like JD at her side, she thought maybe she could balance school and a relationship. She'd never know until she tried.

Then, seeing her in the doorway, JD had dropped what he was doing and come to her. His stride was panther-like – predatory – his gaze unwavering. He flattened her into the door jamb with his hard body and kissed her senseless. Maybe that's why she was in her current predicament.

She was amazed how every one of JD's kisses held the same intensity. There was nothing slight or insignificant about any of them. Even a light peck on her forehead managed to stir the embers at her core. Every touch reminded her how much he loved her – how much she loved him, damn it. And even though her lips were bruised and swollen, and her body had been pleasured to the point of tenderness, the instant JD touched her all she wanted was to lay with him again. And again and again.

It had taken all her strength to push him away and send him to the shower.

And as she'd walked into the kitchen with so many new feelings whirring inside her, she thought this must be what Kieran and Eilis felt for each other, because right then she felt just like what she saw when Kieran and Eilis looked at each other.

But now she'd blown it.

When JD rushed into the kitchen, she'd been standing at the counter staring out the window, watching the winter birds pecking the ground, last night's storm long gone and her thoughts lost in memories of the previous night's love making.

Last night had been perfect and she'd wanted to start the day off flawlessly in an effort to keep last night alive.

And she'd gone and burned their damned breakfast.

JD had run in, pulled her away from the cooker,

and put out the fire flashing up in the frying pan. She'd been so out of it, she didn't smell the smoke or feel the heat right beside her. She was so stupid.

It should have been simple – toast a little bread, poach a couple eggs, fry up some tomatoes and mushrooms, make the coffee. However, while she'd been staring out of the kitchen window, everything had gone haywire.

The toaster was turned up too high and the bread was literally toast. She nearly choked on a sudden and absurd thought; in about a million years, the carbon would transform and make someone very happy. Insanely, she wondered what toast diamonds looked like.

Their poached eggs were well beyond poached and looked like white conkers, and the sliced tomatoes and mushrooms were now cousins with the toast.

The coffee had been the only survivor in her breakfast apocalypse. Even though she'd started it way too early and it was cold now, at least it could be reheated on the cooker.

Now, JD stood behind her in the cottage's tiny sitting room. Embarrassment had sent her running out here while he put out the pan fire. He'd found her staring at the little table she'd planned to set up for the meal, but hadn't gotten around to yet. She couldn't look at him so she continued staring at the tabletop but not seeing it. She couldn't contain her embarrassment so she buried it in anger.

'It's all right, Gráinne.' She felt his hand on her shoulder. 'It's not that bad. Really,' he assured her, even as she detected a hint of humor in his voice.

God love him. He tried to sound like it was no big deal, but she was sure she had disappointed him. Feeling she had made things worse, she tried pulling away from him. He wrapped an arm around her shoulder and cupped her face, drawing her head back to his shoulder and held her. She wanted to turn into his comforting embrace, but how could she when she couldn't look him in the eye?

As if sensing her embarrassment, he started kissing her throat while his free hand slid under her woolly sweater; his palm flat on her stomach radiated his heat into her and she felt her anger slipping away. Then his fingers dipped under the elastic band of her leggings. When his nimble fingers found what they were looking for, she couldn't suppress a deep sigh and she melted into him.

She didn't know what to do with her hands, so she grasped his upper thighs and kneaded him through his ... towel?

Her eyes snapped open, realizing he must have been in the shower when he smelled the smoke and came running.

Reluctant to move away from his intimate touch, she turned in the circle of his arms and gazed up at him. While she may have heard suppressed laughter in his words a moment before, there was no humor in his eyes now. Written across his face she saw only love. When his head dipped and their lips met, he left no doubt that he wanted her. She pressed her hips forward against the hard ridge

291

beneath the towel, giving a signal of her own. She wanted him, too.

Slipping a finger under the corner of the towel, she pulled it loose and let it drop to the floor. And when she palmed him, he gasped into her mouth. He was hard and hot in her hand. Just the memory of him inside her made her womb vibrate with need.

As if sensing her thoughts, JD used both hands to pull off her sweater and let it fall to the floor beside his damp towel. Then, hooking his fingers into her leggings' elastic waistband, he pulled them off her in one sharp tug and threw them aside, too.

JD locked his gaze with hers as his hands roamed over her. He cupped her breasts and rolled her nipples with his thumbs while he watched her. Her body arched into him as tingles raced through her.

Then his hands slid down her ribcage to her hips as he went onto his knees before her.

Oh, God! Was he going to propose? Her body started shaking uncontrollably. Thoughts spun out of control. What would she say? They hadn't known each other long enough. She knew they loved each other but this was way too soon. Even she recognized that.

Then he did something no other man had done. He put his mouth on her. The feeling of it nearly rocketed her through the ceiling.

Gráinne grasped the edge of the table behind her and held on while her legs went weak. When they did, JD slid her bottom onto the table edge and hooked her legs over his shoulders. The feel of his tongue on her was hot, slick, and demanding. And he was going to make her come faster than she ever had in her life. If she thought his touching her with his fingers was a hundred times more sensitive because she'd been forced to wax, this sensation was a million times more intense. She couldn't suppress a cry when he entered her with his tongue.

'Mmm,' he moaned into her, his breath hot on her bare flesh. 'You taste so good.' His words caressed her soul. He liked the way she tasted. And when he added, 'Much better than blackened tomatoes,' she could have boxed his ears.

Instead, she said, 'No talking. Just do ... that.' The last was said as JD sucked her clitoris between his lips. He chuckled when her hips came off the table.

His hands were hot on her thighs, stroking them to her hips as he buried his face in her. He nipped and sucked her bare skin, tonguing every part of her. Her heart pounded in her chest, choking off her gasps as she tried to stay aware of what he was doing to her. To her dismay, he was sending her over the precipice of ecstasy one lick and one stroke at a time.

She came suddenly and violently. She gripped the table edges as her body spasmed hard. When the first contraction hit her, her breath caught in her throat, making it impossible to breathe while the aurora danced behind her lids. She was only superficially aware of JD kissing a line up her stomach to her breasts. It was when he entered her that her eyes snapped open.

Then he was kissing her again, refusing to let her come down from her orgasmic high. She clutched him to her, fingers in his hair, his tongue anchoring itself in her mouth. Coiling her tongue with his, they sparred together until she was moaning once more. She wrapped her legs around his waist as he drove into her.

This was the kind of hot and sweaty sex she thought they would have had last night, but he had treated her tenderly and with love through the night. This other side of JD also appealed to her. Now she knew he wasn't just a gentle lover, but he could also handle hot and sweaty.

JD broke off his kiss and concentrated on lifting Gráinne against him. He felt engorged inside her. She did things to his body he didn't understand, and probably didn't need to, but it never seemed enough just to be in her. He wanted to devour her. So he had. He loved watching her come, and loved knowing he did it to her. Watching her now, with her breasts bobbing with each thrust and the look in her eyes, her love for him written all over her face, brought him to the brink of orgasm quicker than he could remember since he was a teenage boy.

Perspiration broke out over his body in an effort to keep his orgasm at bay. He didn't want this to end yet. But Gráinne's inner muscles clamped around him as she came again and he couldn't hold back. He cried out as tremors rocked his body. For a moment there was only blackness as intense pleasure ripped through him, his eyes squeezing shut at the sensation.

When the stars dancing in his head abated, he pulled Gráinne into his arms and held her, both of them panting hard.

'Jazus, I'm out of shape for this kind of carry-on,' he said, chuckling. To her credit, she laughed, too.

'Don't tell me I'm wearing you out already.' Humor lit in her eyes when he looked into them.

'Not a hope. Just promise me one thing.'

'Anything.'

'Promise you'll never cook for me.'

That earned him a pinch on his side. 'Ouch!' He rubbed at the spot.

'Serves you right.' Before she could move away from him, he pulled her back into his arms.

Taking her face in his hands, he held her gaze for a long moment. 'I love you, Gráinne. I don't know how I've lived until I found you.'

'I love you, too, John,' she whispered against his neck when she pulled him against her. Then she added, 'Probably wise not to let me cook for you. You'll probably live a lot longer.'

JD laughed at the same time his heart clenched at Gráinne's words of love. She was the most incredible woman he'd ever known. She did things to his insides he could never explain. He knew all this was new for both of them, and wanting to make love with her as much as she could bear was natural, but he hoped they'd still be at it long into their old age. Lord, help him; it seemed all he wanted was to make love with her as often as possible. He just didn't think he had it in him right now. The mind was willing, and all that.

As he relaxed and his heartbeat returned to normal, he slid out of her. Then it hit him and he groaned aloud.

'Ah, feck it anyway,' he cursed, squeezing his eyes shut at what he'd done. Talk about making a balls of something perfect. Gráinne's burnt offerings held no comparison.

'John?' Worry tinged her voice. He noticed she'd started calling him by his Christian name the night he'd told her he was a guard. He liked that. But he didn't like what he'd done to her.

'I think it's my turn to apologize, love,' he said, raising his gaze to hers. Her confusion was obvious. 'I didn't use a condom.'

Unspoken words hung between them. Every other time they'd come together he'd made sure to slide on a skin. His heart pounded anxiously. Her burnt breakfast had nothing on this cock-up.

'Well,' was all she seemed capable of saying. What was there to say? He'd messed up and could only hope she didn't get pregnant because of his mistake.

Of course, she could rail at him, carry on, wave her arms in the air, tell him what a son-of-a-bitch he was for being so careless. But she said nothing and left him wondering if that was worse.

He moved to step away from her. He thought he might be feeling some of what Gráinne felt earlier when she'd burnt their breakfast, and it was all self-inflicted.

Gráinne's touch stopped him in his tracks. Her fingers were light on his arm, but it hit him like a bolt of lightning going straight up to his shoulder and right into his belly.

'It's all right,' she said, echoing his earlier words. But this wasn't a burnt breakfast. They were talking about a child here. For all they knew, his little divers could be swimming their way to Baby Babylon this very moment.

He loved Gráinne. With all his heart, he loved her. He wanted to marry her, and loved the idea of having a family with her. In fact, he counted on it. But their relationship was new. And while he knew last night the moment he saw her standing over him that he would propose to her, he did not want to marry her knowing Kieran held a weapon to his groin. But, of course, if he had gotten her pregnant with this one monumental cock-up, he would make it right with her, too soon or not.

When he met her gaze, she was the one laughing this time. 'It's okay. I'm protected.'

JD stared at her as if she were speaking Chinese. He had no idea what she said until she repeated her words.

'Protected?' he wheezed, his breath still stuck in his chest. She nodded. 'How long? I mean, when... I mean, what...?' He was lost for words. Protected? What did she mean by that?

'After that night in my kitchen,' she told him, 'I went to my doctor.'

'But–'

'I guess, great minds think alike,' she interrupted. 'You said you knew you'd never get out of the cottage without making love to me. I think I knew back then after you'd kissed me the way you did,' she said, blushing, 'I was eventually going to cave in to the rest.

'Eilis was right. At Christmas, she said she knew you were in love with me. I denied it because I was so focused on school. But I thought if she could see it, then I knew I was in for trouble with you and it was just as well I'd prepared myself.'

He shook his head. He couldn't remember her taking the pill since they'd been in the cottage. Of course, that was a personal woman thing, but still, he might have seen something.

'Gráinne, I don't think you've been on the pill long enough. I haven't seen you take it since you've been here, or have you?

She just laughed again. 'You live in the stone ages, Desmond,' she teased. 'I have those under-the-skin things. It lasts for a few months. I don't take anything. It's always there protecting me. Us.'

JD sank against her with relief. Then he re-membered the condoms and looked back at her again. 'You could have said something last night, love,' he said, a smirk twitching at the corner of his mouth.

'Yes, I could have, but I needed to know you appreciated me enough to protect me yourself, without having to ask. Now I know you do.'

She was absolutely right for letting things go the way they had last night.

'Ah, love.' Even he could tell his voice was full of mischief. 'You may regret telling me this. Here I was thinking we were down to our last few condoms and I'd have to suffer that horrendous drive back to town. Though you're worth it, don't get me wrong. But now ... now we don't have to go anywhere.'

'Why would I regret telling you?'

'Because I'll want to make love to you every chance I get, no matter where we are or what you're doing. I already have a hard time keeping my hands to myself. Now you've let me inside, it's the only place I want to be.'

Her lips parted as she smiled and he took advantage. He kissed her until she was panting against his cheek. Breakfast remained long forgotten.

Chapter Twenty-Three

The last few days flew by. How could it not when they were in the middle of one mind-bending lovemaking session after another. It had begun that night before the hearth and hadn't ended until he cried cease after their shower this morning, three days later. But lord help him, as he watched Gráinne prepare food for their hike into the woods, all he wanted to do was bend her over where she stood and take her then and there. She was wearing those black leggings again, which made her legs look ultra long and shapely.

In his heart and soul he wanted her again, to drive himself deep within her heat and lose himself. In reality, he felt if he tried, his penis just might fall off. He chuckled at the thought, though that was not really a laughing matter.

'What are you looking at?' she asked sweetly, turning at his muffled laughter. Her smile was relaxed but her gaze shone with joy. He hoped to keep that look on her face for the rest of his life.

He reached out to her, murmuring sensually, 'I'm looking at you, love.' She backed out of his grasp. His brows furrowed instantly. She only laughed.

'Enough of that. I need to get out of this cottage now it's stopped raining. As much as I'd love to make love for the three hundred and ninety-third time, I think we both could use the walk.'

JD chuckled. She couldn't be far off her estimated figure, he was sure.

He grabbed up his jacket and slid into it. He wore a pair of blue jeans with a chunky cream-colored Aran sweater. He hadn't thought about shoes when he was packing so he only had the ones he'd been wearing that night in The Klub!. But Kieran had a pair of Wellies in the shed that just about fit.

Gráinne also wore a heavy jumper in black to match her leggings, and had slipped into her own Wellies. She'd found them both knitted caps and gloves, as well. While it had stopped raining, they'd gotten a flurry of snow when the temperature dropped. By the looks of the dark clouds hanging miles away on the coast, it was possible they could get much more by this evening. But for now, the sky was mostly clear – the perfect opportunity for a walk.

He picked up the pack containing the food and held the door open for his love.

His love.

He grinned looking at her. She was, too – the love of his life.

The moment she stepped outside, she was thankful for all the woolens they'd found tucked away in the house. The day was so crisp it felt like shards of ice in her sinuses. The feeling dissipated after a few minutes, but it still made her eyes water. She wasn't surprised; not after spending the last few days holed up in the cottage. Between the rain and all their lovemaking, and the heat spread through the cottage by the fire, she needed to reacclimatize to the Irish weather.

JD closed the door behind them, not bothering to lock it. Why? They were the only ones on the mountain, and as far as she knew, the deer hadn't learned how to use the latch.

As they walked hand-in-hand toward the back gate, Gráinne had the feeling again something wasn't quite right. She'd woken with the feeling but couldn't place it. She was sure she was just imagining things. Everything seemed so perfect with JD, but in the back of her mind something kept niggling at her. She couldn't put her finger on it. It was just ... something ... that wasn't quite right.

Or maybe she'd forgotten something important, like a birthday or anniversary, or some task she was meant to do today that slipped her mind. She couldn't do anything about it up here, though, so she shook off her worry and smiled up at JD, squeezing his hand. Things were perfect. Nothing could ruin this time they had together. God willing, the guards were bearing down on Taylor Wade even now and they could return to Dublin. Once there, they could have their first fight over whose house they'd live in.

She sighed at the thought of something so mundane as deciding where to live. She knew her place was too far from the station where JD worked, and his place was too small for the two of them. Maybe one day they could afford to buy a house together.

That idea tickled her. Would they buy a place in the city or suburbs? Would it be a house or an apartment? Would they choose a place near schools for their kids?

Kids! Gráinne's heart lodged in her throat. That was something they'd have to talk about. Of course, assuming JD wanted to marry her.

She cast him a side glance as they strolled through the trees. He'd promised forever love but hadn't come out and asked her to marry him. Promises were easy to keep, and break, but marriage was a completely other thing altogether.

It was too soon to talk about those kinds of things, anyway. They were still just getting to know each other.

Not far from the cottage, they crossed a small stream and were met by woodland.

The forestry service, Coillte, had planted trees here years ago which were now nearly full-grown. They'd eventually be cut down and sent for processing. The land would be cleared then re-planted once more, the process repeating itself decade after decade.

She suspected this was what had happened at the front of the cottage and why they had such a spectacular view now. Fortunately, the service rarely cut down a whole area, but only sections of it, so as not to strip the land of the soil. Because of that, the cottage would always have the ideal location and be sheltered from most of the weather.

As they wended their way through the trees, Gráinne was mesmerized, as always, at the forest's enchanting effect. The pines were straight and tall, their branches graceful as they swayed in the breeze. Bright green moss grew in large patches and traveled up the tree trunks and over some surrounding rocks and fallen debris. She knew in late summer, all sorts and colors of mushrooms grew in the moss, but in the winter the moss was undisturbed except for a few fallen twigs and patches where birds and other wildlife had been digging for worms and other ground dwelling creatures.

The stream they'd crossed at the back of the cottage originated from deep within the woods at the top of the mountain, where there was a small pool. She remembered hiking up there years ago with Kieran. It had been during one of their first stays once the cottage reconstruction had been completed. The trees had been saplings, not much taller than herself at the time. Gráinne smiled to herself at how they'd both done a lot of growing since then.

The mountain wasn't very tall, but was rocky and had a few cliffy areas. The top was called a bald, sometimes a scalp – a mainly flat and barren plateau of weather-smoothed limestone but for the natural pool of water. She wondered what it looked like today. It was early enough in the day. Maybe they could make it.

'You're quiet,' said JD, lifting her hand to kiss the backs of her gloved fingers.

Gráinne looked beside her, marveling at the way the filtered light danced through his hair. He looked as contented as she felt.

'Just thinking.'

'Ooh, dangerous thing, that.' He was such a tease. She loved him all the more because, and in spite, of it. 'Are you going to tell me what you're thinking about?'

Oh, the grief she could give him with that question. But she decided to be nice. It was a beautiful day. They'd just shared several days making love. And everything seemed right in the world. Well, everything but that little thing niggling at the back of her mind.

'I was just remembering the pool at the top of the mountain. It's early yet, if you're interested in the walk. It's not far, maybe a mile. Kieran and I used to go up there years ago.'

'I'm for it.'

Gráinne guided him through the trees, remembering the path well, though some of it was overgrown. They reached the bald quickly in the good weather.

The pool was exactly as Gráinne had remembered, though now it seemed smaller. The mountaintop was virtually flat, except for the impression filled with rainwater. It wasn't a big pool, but substantial enough that she and Kieran would swim it in if the weather was warm. They'd laughed how they were probably the only family in Ireland with their own private mountaintop swimming pool. The water had chilled them to the bone and turned them blue in the process, but it was their very own and unlike anything else in the country.

Today, the water was calm and reflected the clouds in the sky as if a giant mirror had been placed on the ground. There were few plants growing in the crevices and any loose stones had long since rolled down the mountain, but there were a few larger boulders not even the strongest Irish winds could budge. It would be the rain's constant drumming on the stones, slowly wearing them down before they could be shifted from their ancient positions.

There was a very prominent ancient tomb beside the pool and Gráinne guided JD over to it. The tomb consisted of three upright loadstones with a massive capstone.

'Wow!' he exclaimed, stepping over to the tomb. 'Do you know anything about this?'

'It's supposed to date back to the third millennium BC,' Gráinne explained.

'What a great place to have yourself buried. The view is incredible.'

'It was excavated just before Coillte planted these trees.'

'Did they find anything?' His curiosity was obvious.

'The archaeologist expected to find just a few bodies, like they had at the Poulnabrone Dolmen. Tombs like this were usually used as clan gravesites, but this one surprised them.'

'How so?' JD asked, resting his palm against the rough, cool stones as he listened to her.

She, too, stroked the ancient stones, the rough limestone grazing her sensitive fingertips. Laying her palm flat against the capstone, she swore she could hear the voices of the people who'd set the stones, felt the power of the man they'd buried here.

She hadn't realized she'd shut her eyes at the visions swirling through her mind, until JD spoke.

'What did they find here?'

'A warrior.'

'Do they know anything about him?'

'Only what they found with him.' She guided him to the western end of the tomb and showed him the entrance under the wide end of the capstone. 'He was buried with his shield, spear and sword...'

'Anything else?'

Gráinne rolled her eyes at his interruption. 'Yes. They found his personal effects – some coins, crockery, and such. He must have been wealthy, because he was wearing a lot of gold, which also probably explains why this site was chosen.'

'Were you and Kieran here when they were excavating?'

'Yes.' She nodded. 'It's our land. They didn't take very long but they allowed us to be on site, and even let us help a little.' She smiled wistfully, remembering the day.

'How so?'

'When they had the tomb open and let it air, they discovered the space was too tight for any of their crew. I was just the right size.'

'Wow!' JD's eyes widened.

She laughed at him. 'Don't you know any other exclamation?'

'Yeah, but I'm watching my language.'

Smiling, she continued. 'It was one of the most amazing experiences of my life.'

'One of them?' JD grasped her around the waist and pulled her to him, grinding his hips against her.

'Do you walk around with that all the time?' she asked, giggling.

'I kind of have to. I was born with it.' He placed a quick kiss on her lips and, without releasing her, said, 'Go on. Tell me the rest of your story.'

'They gave me strict instructions on care. Not

only handling the artifacts and the man's remains, but of my own. If at any time I felt the tomb would cave in, I was to get out of there immediately. Then they gave me a torch and sent me in.'

JD shivered for effect. 'This is like a movie. I'm on the edge of my seat here. What happened next?'

Gráinne laughed lightly. He was so easily amused, she thought to herself.

'At first, it wasn't very impressive. I told them exactly what I was doing and what I saw as I moved around the space. It was open, but dirt and dust covered everything. They gave me a special brush to use gently to expose things. I started closest to the entrance and worked my way forward.'

As she spoke, she pulled out of JD's arms, but grasped him by the hand and guided him to a few large stones beside the pool and sat facing the tomb.

'It was disturbing to be in a man's burial site. I was crawling over him, and all. I mean, burial is sacred, right? It's supposed to be your eternal resting place. But once I got into it, I realized how much history was buried with the man, and how old his remains were, and they still existed for someone to find. He was over three thousand years old,' she said, accentuating the years. 'Everything in the tomb seemed to be talking to me and trying to tell me about the man and his life. Then I really got into it.

'He was fully dressed for a man of his time – boots, crude leggings and a tunic of sorts. He was wrapped in his cape. The brooch holding it together was the most remarkable thing I've ever seen. It was pure gold with colored stones in it. The lead archaeologist later told me the stones weren't ones found in Ireland, so the man had either traveled or had come by them by some other means.'

'You mean like stealing them?'

'More like winning them in battle. Or possibly buying them from a trader. Thievery wouldn't have been a warrior's style.'

Realization dawned on JD's face. 'No, I suppose it wouldn't have been, would it?'

As the afternoon passed, Gráinne regaled JD with all of the finds in the tomb and how exciting it had all been. All the while, JD just stared at her, asking the required questions to keep her talking. The enthrallment in her eyes told him she really loved what she'd done, and the more detail she gave him, the more he wondered if her calling wasn't really in archaeology and not music. After all, if she'd been a true musician, she would have been playing every day and he hadn't yet received that promised tune on her flute.

As she spoke, JD tried imagining Gráinne as a young girl of about thirteen, being given the chance of a lifetime to participate in such a remarkable discovery. She described everything in such great detail he had no trouble seeing her memories.

Pride welled in his chest at his remarkable woman. Gráinne was his woman. As soon as they got down from this mountain and back to Dublin, she'd agree to marry him. He'd make sure of it.

Toward the end of her story, he asked, 'Did

they ever discover who the man was?'

'That's the incredible thing. They did, but one of the things they found in the tomb...'

'You mean, that *you* found in the tomb,' he corrected.

Gráinne giggled lightly. 'Yes, that I found. It was a piece of decorated vellum, loosely rolled in leather. No one knew what it was until they got it back to their labs. They did some treatment on it to flatten it out then had it translated. It was in ancient Irish.'

'What did it say? Did you ever find out?'

Nodding, she continued. 'If I can remember the exact words, it said, 'Here lieth the remains of Eireann's greatest warrior, Desmumhnach.'

Something in that sounded familiar to JD. His brows drew together in thought as he gazed over to the tomb. He couldn't place it.

'I keep thinking the name sounds familiar, but I can't place it,' he told her.

'Have you ever heard the legend of Deasún?' she asked, grinning.

'Yes,' he drew out, feeling that Gráinne had something to tell him.

'Well...' She paused for dramatic effect, laughter in her eyes.

'Well, what, woman?' he asked, chuckling lightly. 'I'm on the edge of my seat here.'

She leaned in and kissed him quickly, then continued. 'Well, the legend goes that Desmond ruled this part of Ireland. Deasún literally means man of Munster.'

'Hey,' JD gasped at the sound of his own name. 'That's me.'

''Tis, and wait until you hear the story.'

'Okay, get on with it then.'

'Desmond was the mightiest warrior in Munster. It was said no man could beat him in battle. He was taller than any man, more powerful, and the fiercest. Men were said to tremble in his presence; some simply fainted on the battlefield at the prospect of having to draw a sword against him.

'There came a time of peace, and Desmond laid down his weapons. He wanted to settle down with his ladylove. He was also said to have been the handsomest of men and women fell over themselves trying to get into his bed, but he turned them all away. All but one.'

'Gráinne,' JD said, remembering the story.

'Aye, that was her name. But he couldn't have her. She'd shamed the family by sleeping with Desmond before their marriage ceremony could be performed, and she became pregnant. She was sent away, banished from the settlement forever. Desmond took up his weapons once more and went in search of her.

'Neither were ever seen or heard from again, but tales of Desmond's battles for the truth were legends in their own time, as they are in ours.'

'He never found his ladylove?'

Gráinne grinned knowingly. 'It was years later. He was an old man by then. He found her in the far north of Ireland. She was found living in a cave guarded by the Grey Man.'

JD knew the legend of the Grey Man. As the legend went, he was said to creep in from the sea on the fog and take his victims at random, creeping back out to sea just as furtively.

311

'Desmond made a deal with the Grey Man in order to be let into the cave, so he could look for Gráinne. Desmond's lifeless body was found outside the cave. No one knows if he ever found his Gráinne, or if the Grey Man made a pact to take Desmond to Gráinne in the spirit world.'

JD shivered once more, but not for dramatic effect. The tale was chilling. How ironic was it that a Desmond and Gráinne could reunite three thousand years later? And at the man's tomb.

'Desmond's body was brought back to his native land and given the burial befitting a warrior of his stature. It's said he was buried on the tallest mountain on his land, so his spirit could keep watch for Gráinne's return.'

Neither spoke for a long time once Gráinne finished her story. Thoughts rolled through JD's mind as he remembered the story. The legend seemed to parallel his own life.

In modern terms, his role as a police officer then a detective mirrored that of the ancient day warrior. Okay, so he wasn't very tall, but he was very good at his job.

He considered himself fair looking, and must have been so if he'd attracted so much feminine attention when he was younger. He had thought it had been the uniform. He thought now maybe it was him the women were attracted to. Since he'd made detective, he hadn't really had time to date. But when he first laid eyes on Gráinne dancing at The Klub!, something had triggered in him – he thought perhaps he recognized her from somewhere. She'd been in disguise so his inner feelings were confused. Then, when he'd seen her in the pub, he knew without a shadow of a doubt she would turn his world upside down. And she had.

He watched Gráinne gazing past the tomb to the sun, low in the sky. The light danced upon her face and for a split second he thought he saw something else – someone else. It was not impossible to imagine she was Deasún's Gráinne.

She turned then and smiled at him. She stole his breath and made him dizzy with desire. The fire in his chest liquefied and oozed into his stomach where it pooled around his groin. He looked down to his hand resting on his thigh, and for a moment – just a moment – he thought he saw the hand of Deasún the warrior, powerfully thick-fingered, callused and bruised, yet JD knew he'd held his Gráinne so tenderly.

In a flash, the image was gone as quickly as it had come. He turned to Gráinne then and pulled her into his lap, burying his tongue between her lips as she gasped. JD held her tightly and kissed her. He had three thousand years to make up for.

Chapter Twenty-Four

A long while later, JD leaned away from Gráinne and held her while they gazed over the landscape. When he heard her sigh, he asked, 'What's on your mind, love?'

'I was just thinking how much I love it up here. If I had my way, I'd build a house beside the pool and move here permanently.'

'And how would we survive?'

Gráinne turned to face him. 'We?'

'Sure. A restraining order couldn't keep me away. Where you go, I go,' he said, winking.

'You'd give up the gardai to move here.' It wasn't so much a question but an incredulous statement.

'Sure. I'll become a ranger instead. My new job will be to protect the forest and keep down the crime level in the animal kingdom.'

Gráinne laughed, playfully pushing him with her hand. JD grasped her hand in his and pulled her against him. Sighing, he said with all seriousness, 'Gráinne, I'd follow you anywhere.'

Her face lit up at his declaration, but there was still mirth in her voice when she said, 'Then you'll be following the blind, because I have no idea where I'm going.' JD only chuckled again.

Then she was off his lap and he wondered what she was about. He watched her extract something from her pack and smiled when she opened the box and fitted her flute together.

She moved to stand beside the warrior's tomb, and putting the flute to her lips, she tested the notes.

When she was happy the instrument was working correctly, she took a breath, closed her eyes, and put the instrument back to her lips.

JD recognized the tune immediately as *Brian Boru's March*. While she played, the music made him think of times long gone, great warriors, and the stories following them through time.

When the tune came to an end, JD clapped lightly so as not to disturb the peace around them.

'That was amazing. You're some talent.'

Without saying anything, she began another tune. This time, he recognized the *Lonesome Boatman*, a sorrowful tune normally reserved for sailors. It reminded JD of Vikings on the high seas, returning home after months away from home.

She played a couple more short tunes, then said, 'One more. I'll dedicate this one to you.'

JD laughed when she started up the lively tune, *Wild Rover*. He was sure Gráinne thought the title was quite poignant, imagining him as the wild partier now forced to settle into a domestic life.

JD came to his feet, clapping and whistling. She curtsied ladylike and blew him a kiss. Then he pulled her into his arms.

'You play brilliantly. Now I can see why you're so interested in studying music.'

She stepped away from him to return the instrument to its case. 'Funny you should mention that.' She glanced up at him while she went about her task. 'After telling you Desmond's story, I got to thinking about how much I loved that time when the tomb was excavated. I've had a few chats with Mick Spillane about the goings on at the museum where he works, too. After telling you the story, I'm wondering ... should I study archaeology instead?'

'Have you had a change of heart, then?'

'I'm not sure, but I'm giving both subjects serious thought.'

'Whichever you chose, I'll fully support you.'

'Thanks, John. I appreciate that.'

He took her back into his arms then. 'I like it when you call me that.'

'Call you what?'

'John.'

'Do I?' Her brow lifted as she appeared to think about it.

'You do. You started the night I told you I'm a guard.'

'I didn't realize. It just sounds natural. JD sounds so ... juvenile, I guess.' She flicked her gaze over him. 'Nothing juvenile about you. Immature, maybe, but not juvenile.'

JD's mouth fell open and her remark. 'Well, you cheeky little–'

Gráinne shot out of his arms and raced to the other side of the pond with him quick on her heels. 'I'll show you immature,' he threatened.

She just laughed and spun out of his grasp, but he caught her quickly enough. Or did she let him catch her? He had it in his mind to take her right here on this mountaintop. The cold be damned. He pulled her into his arms, parted his lips and lowered his mouth to hers.

Just then, the near silence of the mountaintop was broken by a dull fluttering in the distance. They looked skyward in the direction of the sound and saw a helicopter coming slowly toward them.

'Looks like a Search and Rescue chopper,' said JD. 'We're not far from the coast, are we?'

'Not too far. Usually S.A.R. sticks to the coastline for a sea rescue. This one is probably rescuing hikers somewhere. That happens a lot in Kerry on MacGillycuddy's Reeks. That's just a couple ranges over from here near Killarney. We're probably in the flight path.'

As the chopper neared, JD saw it wasn't an S.A.R. chopper at all but a private one. It was painted black, except for its white identifying numbers. The sound of the blades grew louder as the aircraft neared, slowing as it reached the mountaintop.

Instinctively, they waved to the occupants of the chopper as it hovered over them. The gust created by the blades sent dirt and dust swirling around them, the once glass-like surface of the pool now a torrent of waves. It was when the chopper spun around that they saw the side door open and a man lean out.

JD's heart stopped.

Everything around him seemed to move in slow motion. The sound of the blades slowed to a whomp-whomp-whomp overhead. The swirling debris moved like snowflakes caught on the gust.

Gráinne moved slowly in view. Her lips moved but he didn't hear what she said. His mind spun as he fought to shield his eyes from flying debris

317

and focus on her words. Then her eyes rolled back and she was falling.

JD caught her as she fainted. As he knelt on the ground cradling her head, the man in the chopper expertly descended from a line and landed on the ground in a crouch. The line reeled away as the chopper moved off the mountaintop. And they were left alone and vulnerable.

He'd never seen the man before, but based on Gráinne's reaction, this had to be Taylor Wade.

JD cursed himself for allowing them to remain in the open for so long. How was he to know anyone could possibly find them buried so deeply in West Cork on a mountaintop in the middle of nowhere?

Reaching into his pocket, he felt the keypad on his mobile phone, dialing 999 for emergency. He prayed to God he got some kind of reception up here. He'd intended to call into the station to get an update on Wade's capture, but had decided to wait until after Gráinne's recital. He'd tried a couple times on the way up the mountain. The best he could manage was the weakest signal available as he registered onto the network, but it wasn't a strong enough signal to make a connection. He'd hoped to do that up here.

Wade strode slowly over to them, having to move around the pool. JD couldn't help but notice he was loaded down with weapons. He wore a black flak jacket with bulging pockets, as were his black combat pants which were tucked into black calf height combat boots. The only other garments Wade wore were heavy black hiking boots and a black beret, which he pulled out of a pocket and donned as he moved toward where JD sat with Gráinne. The cocky bastard had the gall to tip the beret over to one side, military-style.

JD recognized Wade's assortment of weaponry, from the small grenades hanging off vest hooks to the handgun and long blade knife sheathed on opposite hips, and the semiautomatic rifle slung over his shoulder. All were illegal, of course.

JD's heart raced, praying for that connection. When he heard the recording, 'We're sorry but we cannot connect your call at this time,' his heart lurched and he pressed redial. He pulled Gráinne into his lap and held her tightly. His gaze never once left Wade's.

'Well, well,' said Wade, stopping a few feet away. He relaxed, shifting most of his weight onto one foot as he looked down at them. One hand rested on the semiautomatic rifle. The other perched on his hip.

'Who are you?' asked JD, trying to stall for time.

'I should be asking you that very question,' replied Wade. JD couldn't miss curiosity in the man's voice.

'I asked first.'

Wade chuckled, glancing skyward before meeting JD's gaze once more. This time, the man was dead serious. 'I'm Taylor Wade, and I've come to kill you.'

'Do you always drop out of the sky to scare anyone you fancy?'

'Oh, I choose my victims carefully. I've been tracking this particular bitch for several days now.' JD followed Wade's glance down at Gráinne, who began stirring in his arms.

319

'What has she done to deserve death?' he dared ask.

'That's between her and me.'

'I'd say threatening anyone's life would be my business. You see, I'm with the gardaí and I don't take too kindly having to clean up your messes,' JD informed him.

'A guard.' Wade exhaled with a whistle, obviously surprised. His eyes lit up. 'I haven't killed one of your kind – yet. This will truly be a pleasure.'

'So, what ... you're just going to gun us down where we sit?' JD had no idea if he'd provoked Wade, but if it kept them alive a while longer, he'd do whatever it took.

'That's hardly sporting now, is it? They don't call me The Hunter for nothing.' Wade grinned wickedly. 'I see by the look on your face you've heard of me. I'd be surprised if you hadn't, if you really are with the gardaí.' JD made no reply. He'd let Wade draw his own conclusions. 'So, are you the boyfriend? I know she's not married.'

Ignoring Wade's question, he asked, 'You gonna tell me what she's done?'

'Since you're both going to die, I suppose you should know. After all, you're just the innocent bystander, right?'

'Bystander? Maybe. Innocent? Never.'

Wade cocked a brow at JD's statement. 'She witnessed something she shouldn't have, and I need her to disappear.'

'So, pay her off. Buy her silence and let her get on with her life.'

Wade shook his head quickly. 'I can't take the

chance. And if she's involved with you, then I'll have to worry about your Dudley Do Right conscience. You're a cop. You can't let me go. It's not in your nature.'

'Maybe I'm a bad cop.'

'Somehow, I doubt it.'

Gráinne stirred again. She moaned aloud, masking another failed connection on his mobile phone. JD shifted her on his lap, disguising his motion to press the redial button through the pocket fabric.

'Easy, love,' he said.

'Wh-what's happened?' she asked weakly, coming around.

'You fainted, *love*,' called Wade, accentuating JD's endearment. JD cast him a deadly glare. Gráinne's eyes shot open, flashing a panicked glance between the two men. She blinked repeatedly to clear the fog. When she saw Wade, she clutched at JD's sweater, panic flashing across her face.

'Ohmigod, ohmigod ohmigod,' she chanted, her eyes quickly looking around for escape.

'Hush now, love. It'll be alright,' JD told her, stroking her hair and holding her to him.

'Listen to your man, Jett, or should I say, Gráinne. Soon you'll be dead and then you'll be perfectly alright.'

Wade sounded happy about the prospect. JD's stomach tightened. He'd heard how much Wade enjoyed 'the hunt.' By the look on the man's face, his cocky attitude, and his over-confidence, JD was afraid they were going to learn more about Wade first hand than he ever wanted to know.

Gráinne's body shook violently. Or was that his?

'There's no need for that, Wade. If you're going to kill us, just do it and get it over with. There's no need to torture us,' JD snapped. Maybe Gráinne wasn't the only one who disguised emotions with bravado.

Wade laughed. 'Of course there's a reason to torture you. You see,' he said, kneeling down so he was eye-to-eye with them, 'it's more fun that way.'

'How did you find us?' Gráinne asked, her voice barely a whisper.

Wade looked at down at her, his gaze serious. 'Your friend, Mystique, told me.'

JD saw Gráinne's eyes widen. 'But she didn't know about this place.'

'That's where you're wrong. Jasmine overheard you talking to Mystique ... about the perfect man.' Wade raked his gaze over JD, as if sizing him up. 'And I must say, I expected more from you, Gráinne.'

JD's gaze followed Wade's back to Gráinne, who had squeezed her eyes shut, remembering the discussion.

'I thought only five people know about this place.' JD remembered what Kieran had told them New Year's Eve in his back office.

'I forgot. It just slipped out. I thought Mystique and I were the only ones in the dressing room.' She looked back to Wade once more. 'But she didn't know the exact location, and she would've never told.'

'It's amazing what you can get out of a person with a little ... convincing.' He had the gall to wink at them. 'All I needed was the location. I sent scouts out to the surrounding towns and villages. It was only a matter of time before you were spotted.'

JD's heart skipped a beat remembering every trip they'd made into Macroom for fresh produce.

He gazed down to Gráinne. He knew she had to be thinking about Mystique, and if she was alright after Wade had finished with her. Knowing Wade's reputation, JD doubted she was alive. He didn't want to ask that question, afraid of how it would affect Gráinne. Right now, he had more important things to do. Like save their lives.

'So, now that we're all up to speed, this is how we play the game. I'll give you a head start. Eventually you'll believe you can escape. Then when I find you, you'll realize there is no escape. There's no hope. Then I'll kill you first,' Wade pointed at JD, 'so she can watch you die.'

'You're a sick, sad bastard. You know that, right?' JD spat.

'Yeah, I know. It's one of my more endearing qualities.'

Wade rose and spun a circle to admire the view. 'This is a terrific spot. I can see for miles.' He glanced over his shoulder quickly and said, 'I just might build a house here. Of course, I'll have to knock that pile of stones over there,' he added, waving to Desmond's tomb.

'Don't you dare touch it,' Gráinne warned.

'What are you going to do about it, my helpless little bird? You'll be dead and in no position to do

323

anything about what I do on this mountaintop.' He spun back to the scenery. 'I'll have to fill in this pool as well, level the whole site. That's the job,' he sighed, as if he had a sense of accomplishment.

Before JD knew what happened, Gráinne launched herself out of his lap and flew at Wade. The impact sent them both flying into the pool. JD went after her but didn't catch her in time. When she surfaced, she came up kicking and clawing at Wade. He was weighed down by his heavy gear and was getting tangled in the strap of his rifle. He sputtered and cursed, trying to fight off Gráinne's attack.

JD waded into the pool just in time to catch Gráinne as Wade threw her off him. He took a swing at her with the rifle butt, only missing when the strap caught on a grenade. The grenade broke free of his vest and dropped into the pool at his feet.

'Shit!' Wade exclaimed. He struggled to pull himself out of the water, but his waterlogged clothes and heavy weaponry dragged him down.

JD put himself on automatic and pulled Gráinne away from the pool. Half-dragging her, they raced for the forest without looking back.

They'd run only a few dozen steps when the grenade went off. JD threw Gráinne against a large tree trunk and covered her with his body to protect her from flying debris. The sound of the explosion echoed through the forest, shaking the ground and sending tremors up through their legs and the tree they stood against.

When the forest went silent, JD sagged against

Gráinne, breathing heavily.

'Good God, that was close,' he said.

'My flute,' she whispered.

'You're alive. I'll buy you another flute,' he said, kissing her forehead.

'It was my mother's.'

'I'm sorry, love.' He held her while she wept. But they were safe. He couldn't ask for more than that.

Chapter Twenty-Five

'Goddamn it to hell and back again,' swore a seriously pissed-off voice from behind them.

JD whipped around to see the dripping wet Wade standing at the edge of the forest, and cursed under his breath. Wade must have gotten out of the pool before the grenade detonated.

'Feck it, anyway,' JD grunted, spinning Gráinne around to the back of the tree where they stood. He wasn't sure Wade had seen them or not, but he wasn't taking any chances.

'Gráinne, you have to listen to me carefully,' he whispered, cupping her face in his palms. Her gaze met his but he wasn't sure she was seeing him. 'You're going into shock, love. You have to stay focused if we're going to get out of this. Do you understand me?' She nodded weakly.

He pulled the mobile from his pocket and tried 999 once more. This time it rang. The connection was very weak so the ringing sputtered in his ear, but he was connecting. He just needed another moment in this spot for the emergency operator to answer.

'Gráinne!' Wade shouted into the forest. Gráinne jumped with a start at Wade's voice and started shaking anew. JD wrapped his free arm around her and held her close. He put a finger to his lips, indicating she had to remain quiet, then hazarded a peek around the tree to keep an eye on Wade.

'Goddamn it, you conniving bitch. I'm going to find you. Mark my words. And when I do, you'll pay,' Wade railed.

Gráinne whimpered but didn't say a word.

Just then, the emergency operator answered.

'999, what's your emergency?' the officer answered. Static on the line was her only answer. 'Hello? Is there anyone there?'

'Crank call?' asked another operator.

'I don't know. There's only static. Damn mobile phones,' she muttered. 'Hello? This is the emergency operator here. Is anybody there?'

The operator listened carefully. A moment later she heard a voice. It was faint. 'Mary, plug into this call and help me figure out what he's saying.'

Mary plugged into the line and listened along. 'I don't hear anything, Mag,' Mary whispered. 'Oh wait, I hear something.'

Static filled the women's ears. They heard something but the transmission was broken. '...guard Jo ... esmond ... Warri ... Hill ... Taylor Wade ... kill us ... Vaughan ... ues Tav ... send help ... he knows...'

'Was that gunfire?' Mary asked.

'Jazus,' exclaimed Mag. 'Keep listening. Try telling him you're getting help. Keep them on the line while I contact the phone company and get this call triangulated.'

The bullet shattered the bark on the tree just past where JD and Gráinne hid. She wanted to bolt but JD held her fast to the tree. She felt his heart pounding as he pressed her back against the trunk.

Another shot rang out in another direction. 'I don't think he knows where we are. He's firing randomly to see if he can flush us. We have to stay calm, love.' She nodded.

Sweat poured down JD's face, but he didn't move to wipe it away. Gráinne felt the trickle of her own perspiration run down her temple. It tickled desperately, but she knew if she moved, it could be just the movement Wade needed to find them, so she stood as still as Desmond's tomb.

JD had the mobile up to his ear. He whispered the same thing into it over and over hoping someone on the other end was hearing him.

'This is garda John Desmond. I'm on Warrior's Hill near Macroom. Taylor Wade has found us and is trying to kill us. I'm with Gráinne Vaughan. She's the sister of Kieran Vaughan of the Blues Tavern in Dublin. If you can't find us to send help, contact him. He knows our location.'

Gráinne couldn't believe reception was so bad, especially on the mountaintop. If anywhere, this should be the place where he had the best reception.

'You can't hide from me forever. I'm going to find you,' Wade called out.

JD peeked around the tree quickly. 'Feck! He's starting this way.' JD murmured.

A drop of perspiration slid down her cheek as Gráinne looked at JD. She saw by the look in his eyes he was trying to figure out what to do next.

Her heart filled with such love for him. He'd saved her life once before, had vowed to always protect her, and here he was trying to find a way out of this situation to save her again. It seemed then she'd swapped champions – Kieran for JD.

How could her life have gotten so out of control?

Her whole life seemed to be a series of dashed hopes and mistakes. Just when she thought she was finally getting somewhere, something always happened to send her hopes crashing down around her. Just like Taylor Wade had told them – let the prey get a head start so they could build some hope they could get away, then at the last moment sneak up on them to remind them there had been no hope to begin with; just a cruel game of cat and mouse. And in the end, the mouse always lost.

She had to do something. JD was innocent. He shouldn't have to lose his life because she'd screwed up. Again. If she'd done nothing else worthwhile in her whole life, she would do this right. She would save JD.

'I-If I run, he'll chase me. You can get away.'

'No.' He kept his attention trained on Wade's footsteps.

'It's the only way, John. I don't want you dying because of me. It's me he wants. Not you.'

'I said no, Gráinne.'

'If I can draw his attention, you can get to a place where you can get reception and call for help. It's the only way,' she pleaded.

Finally, he fastened his gaze with hers. His eyes were full of fear, worry and anger. Mostly anger, and she had a feeling it was mainly directed at her. Well, fine. Let him be angry with her. At least he'd live.

'Gráinne, be quiet. Let me think.'

'I'm right and you know it.'

'Stop. Just stop. I'm not letting you do this. We'll both get out of this. I promise you.'

'Kiss me, John.'

'We don't have time for that.'

'In case we don't make it out, I want to know your kiss one more time.'

JD didn't protest. He took only a moment to peek around the tree to check on Wade's location. He was still well away from them, so JD lowered his lips to hers.

Her lips parted the instant he touched her and welcomed him into her mouth. It was the kiss of a desperate man. He drove himself into her repeatedly to rub his tongue with hers. His lips tugged and sucked at hers. She met him in every instance, as she was a desperate woman. She had to touch him and taste him one last time.

Gunfire sounded off in the distance but Wade was getting closer. At the sound, JD hesitated before dragging his lips from hers. She tried pulling him back, but he pulled her into his embrace instead.

'I love you so much, Gráinne. I'm sorry I let this happen.'

'It's not your fault, John. It's mine. It's always been mine. I'm sorry you got dragged into it.'

'I don't get dragged into anything, Gráinne. I'm with you because I want to be.'

She gazed into his eyes, memorizing the whiskey color of them. She searched his face, trying to memorize every contour, every whisker from his missed shave this morning, his windswept hair.

Would he remember her in the afterlife?

If she were bold enough to imagine they were the reincarnations of Desmond and Gráinne from days of old, would they meet again in a future time? Would they know each other?

She couldn't let her mind go there. She had to concentrate on the here and now. She had to concentrate on getting JD safe.

'I love you, too, John Desmond. I don't ever want you to forget it.'

'No, love, I'll never forget you love me.'

'Eilis was right when she told me to give you a chance. I'm glad I did. This has been the most incredible week of my life. I never thought I'd know a love like ours. Even if it only lasted for a week, I'm glad we had at least that.' Her chest tightened with every word. Her mind flashed suddenly with every touch and kiss.

'Don't talk like we aren't getting out of this, love. We will.'

'I know. I'm just saying.'

It was when JD peeked around the tree to check on Wade's location that Gráinne took the opportunity to slip out of his arms. She inhaled deeply and took off at a full run across the woods.

Everything went crazy as JD watched Gráinne spin out of his arms and race through the forest. Out of the corner of his eye, he saw Wade turn in her direction. He lifted the rifle and fired without aiming. JD could have sworn he saw the bullet rocketing through the air. His heart stopped beating as he waited to see where the bullet would connect. It exploded when it hit a tree Gráinne had just passed. She leapt behind the next tree at the sound of the crack, seeking shelter.

'Damn it, Gráinne. I told you to stay put,' he whispered loudly between clenched teeth.

Gráinne glanced in his direction and mouthed the words 'I love you' before setting off again.

His feet were rooted in place as he watched her disappear through the trees – Wade hot on her trail.

JD looked down at the mobile in his hands. It still seemed to be connected to the emergency number but he couldn't rouse anyone on the other end.

'Screw this,' he muttered coarsely, shoving the phone into his pocket. He found Wade easily and took off. He darted between trees, following him.

If he were lucky, Wade would be so intent on getting to Gráinne, he'd forget JD was missing. By the time he remembered, JD would be on top of him – literally.

He only hoped Gráinne had enough sense to stay out of the open.

JD kept a close eye on Wade as they all raced through the forest. Occasionally, Wade stopped to fire a shot, and once to reload, but so far, Gráinne remained unharmed. JD knew their luck was running out so he had to think of something quickly if they were going to get out of this.

A flash of movement caught his attention. Gráinne bolted between trees again. This time she ran across a small stony clearing. She stumbled a few times, but caught herself. When he thought she'd reached the edge of the clearing safely, Wade fired another shot. The bullet hit the ground near Gráinne, scaring her. She stumbled and this time fell. JD could tell she landed hard. She lay on the ground, scanning the surrounding trees trying to find Wade.

JD looked back to Wade, but he was gone. JD spun around, trying to find the bastard, but he was nowhere to be seen. JD's heart pounded from the run and from panic he'd lost sight of the bastard.

Mentally kicking himself, he cursed under his breath. How could he protect Gráinne if he couldn't see the man chasing her?

The forest remained silent. Not so much as a birdsong. The wind stilled through the trees. Time froze.

Well, time could freeze all it wanted. JD had to get to Gráinne.

Carefully, after scanning the forest, he moved from tree to tree and circled the small clearing. Gráinne remained where she was. He saw the dread on her face, her eyes wide with fear, her face pale though her cheeks were flushed from her run. Had she given up hope?

No. He wouldn't let Wade take that away from her.

Slowly, JD moved between the trees until he was standing close to Gráinne. When she caught a glimpse of him, her gaze shot up. He put a finger to his lips to quiet her.

'When we get off this mountain, Gráinne,' he whispered angrily, 'we're going to have a talk about communication.' JD glanced around carefully as he sank to his knees then settled his gaze back on Gráinne. 'Are you hurt?'

'I think I twisted my ankle.'

'We need to get you out of there. Can you scoot

closer? I don't know where Wade's gone, so we'll have to move quickly.'

'I'll try.' Gráinne tried to stand on her foot but it wouldn't support her weight.

'Stay down, love, and scoot toward me.'

The moment Gráinne moved, gunfire cracked and a bullet ricocheted off a stone between them. Then the forest went deadly quiet once more.

Gráinne shivered noticeably from where JD stood.

'You're going to have to move quickly, love. I'm going to reach out and I want you to leap forward. Take my hand and I'll pull you to safety. Can you do that?' Gráinne nodded, her eyes wild with fear. 'Okay. On my mark, I want you to put all of your energy into this. Push off with your good foot.' She nodded again. 'Now!'

Gráinne shot forward, reaching out with her hands toward his. She landed just shy of his grasp. Another shot shattered the silence of the forest and hit a rock near Gráinne's foot. Her leg jerked away instinctively as the rock shattered, pieces of it scattering like shrapnel. Another shot followed, closer this time, and Gráinne scrambled forward. JD leaned forward, took her hand in his, and hauled her to safety behind the tree with him.

He wrapped his arms around Gráinne and hugged her to him. 'You foolish, stupid woman. Don't you ever do that again,' he cursed, kissing her forehead. She collapsed against him.

'I-I'm sorry. I was trying to distract him so you could get to safety.'

'I know what you were trying to do, and I love you for it. But don't ever do that again. Do you hear me?' he commanded, shaking her in front of him. When she finally nodded, he pulled her back against him.

Good lord, she was going to be the death of him, but he'd be damned if it would be on this mountain and at the hands of Taylor Wade.

He peered around the tree to check on Wade's position, but the forest was quiet and his adversary remained aloof.

'Can you put any weight on your foot at all?'

Gráinne tried to stand on her injured foot but fell into JD. 'I don't think so.'

JD crouched to examine her foot. The skin was already turning purple.

Back on his feet, he met Gráinne's gaze once more. 'Your ankle isn't broken. That's the good news. The bad news is it's going to slow us up, but we'll have to move quickly. It's going to hurt. A lot. But we're sitting ducks. I don't know where Wade has disappeared to but we can't stay here.' Gráinne nodded again.

JD thought about his options for a moment. 'Do you know where we are?'

'No. I don't remember ever walking this direction before. Kieran and I always just walked from the house to the mountaintop and back. We've never really explored the back of the mountain.'

'Well, we'll have to make our way around the mountain to get back to the cottage. Once we're there, we can get in my car and get you off this mountain. If we can get to the garda station in Macroom, we'll be safe.'

'I'm for that,' said Gráinne. 'Let's do it.'

JD kissed her forehead again then peered around

the tree. Still clear. 'Okay. It's now or never.'

JD slung one of Gráinne's arms over his shoulder to support her, and motioned to the next big tree. He took a deep breath, hauled Gráinne against him, and bolted.

Gráinne stumbled along beside him but they were moving. A shot shattered the bark of a young tree as they passed it, but clearly missed them. Once they reached the next tree, JD thought about the shots. Each had been close but none had been directly at them. Yet.

Wade was playing with them.

If that was so, then there was hope they could get to the cottage and to his car. He'd left the keys in the ignition. What was the use of removing them in such a remote place? He was glad he hadn't now. They couldn't waste any time.

That's exactly what they were doing now. They had to keep moving. The more shots Wade fired as he played with them, the more he'd have to reload. They had a chance of escape, even if it was a small one.

JD took a deep breath once more, settled Gráinne against him, and set off for the next tree. He didn't stop as he flew past it for the next, and the next. Bullet fire continued to follow in their wake, splintering tree bark and rattling needles off their limbs.

Gráinne stumbled as they neared the next big tree. JD stopped long enough to see if she was all right.

'It hurts, JD.'

'I know, love. Can you go on?'

'It hurts like hell, but what am I going to do?'

JD fished in his pocket for his handkerchief. He shook it out and bent quickly. He lifted her foot onto his bent knee and tied the kerchief around it tightly. Rising, he said, 'That should help to keep it from swelling too much and will restrict movement a little. But we have to keep moving, even if it means I have to put you over my shoulder and carry you. Do you understand me?' He hoped the look he gave her told her how serious he was. It had taken him a lifetime to find her. He wasn't about to lose her now.

To his astonishment, Gráinne managed a grin. 'As long as I don't have to carry you, I think we'll be okay.' He shook his head at her comment, smiling. God, how he loved this woman.

Hauling her against him, he set off at a slow run to the next tree. Like clockwork, bullet fire followed behind them.

JD looked around once they'd stopped again. Nothing looked familiar yet, but at least they were moving down the hill. They'd eventually either come to the cottage, or another house where they could get help.

Scratch that. They were on their own. They couldn't risk getting anyone else killed. They had to pray they reached the cottage. He didn't think Wade knew where the cottage was. If they could just reach it first...

Bullets rang out in front of them this time. Wade was trying to cut them off. JD refused to let the man dictate their direction, but it became obvious they either turn around and find another direction, or take a bullet.

JD headed straight down the hill this time.

When they came to a steep slope, he sat down, tugging Gráinne next to him, and slid down carefully as not to cause further damage to her foot. He hoped taking this route had momentarily confused Wade when he lost sight of his prey.

He got Gráinne to her feet and pulled her against him, then set off in their original direction. Silence followed them, except for the crunching of the forest floor beneath their feet.

Had they lost Wade? JD knew they hadn't, so they couldn't risk slowing down.

His heart pounded in rhythm with his feet as they moved. He would run forever if it meant getting Gráinne to safety.

'J … D, can we … stop?' Gráinne stuttered between breaths. 'I-I need to … rest.'

'Not now, love. We're so close,' he told her, pressing on.

Gráinne spun out of his grasp and collapsed to the damp forest floor, breathing hard. 'I said, I need a break.'

JD quickly glanced around them for any sign of Wade. Maybe they had lost him. JD doubted it, though.

Doubling over, he placed his hands on his knees trying to catch his breath. 'Okay. One minute. But that's it. We can't afford to waste much time. I don't think we've lost him, just confused him a little.'

'I'm starting to doubt he's the great hunter of all those stories I've heard,' said Gráinne. 'He can't aim worth shite.'

'Don't doubt his skill for a minute. He's only been playing with us. He could have killed us at

338

any moment back there,' he told her. Realization must have dawned on her then, as she started to rise. 'Ready to go?'

'Oh, aye,' she replied, reaching for him.

He glanced around once again before setting off.

They stuck to the curve of the mountain and tried keeping a downward path as they moved.

Things were too quiet. Something was wrong. Wade should have found them by now. But JD refused to slow their pace as he pondered what Wade was up to.

A moment later they came to a rugged cliff face; a dead end in the mountain path.

'Damn it!' he cursed, spinning a tight circle and seeing only the rocky cliff in front of him. They seemed to have found an impassible crevice in the mountain, stretching out on both sides of the path-end. Prickly gorse grew thickly amongst the rocks.

'What's wrong?' asked Gráinne, setting herself onto a large stone to rest.

'We'll have to turn around. We've reached a dead-end.'

'What?' Gráinne gasped.

'If we backtrack a little, we'll find another path out of here, but we can't go any further from here,' he told her.

'Can't we climb?'

'Not with your sprained ankle. The only option is to go back.'

'We'd better hurry then,' she suggested.

'How's the ankle holding up?'

'Well, it's a toss-up. I either keep going and bite

my lip at the intense pain that's making me want to black out, or I sit down to rest and possibly get killed in the process.'

'Right. We keep moving.' Bracing her against his side once more, they turned to retrace their steps along the path.

That's when Taylor Wade stepped out from behind a tree.

Chapter Twenty-Six

The instant JD saw Wade, he knew they'd gone as far as they could. Wade had toyed with them, given them the promised hope of escape. And they had had hope. Now, also true to Wade's promise, that hope was being dashed into the dirt as if it never existed.

Then it started raining.

It was a light rain. The tree cover helped to shelter them, but once the boughs and needles filled with water, the excess found its way to the forest floor. And JD was sure he was standing under the worst of it.

'So, we've come to the end of the game,' said Wade, in his annoyingly relaxed way.

'Fuck you, Wade,' spat JD, pushing Gráinne behind him.

Wade chuckled, a wide smile stretching across the man's face, the laughter shining in his eyes.

When Wade's gaze settled back on theirs again, he said, 'I haven't had this much fun in months. I think the last great hunt was with that bitch Ayesha and her ... lover,' he spat. The humor left his eyes then and a maniacal grin replaced his jovial one. 'Yes, that was particularly satisfying for me, I must say.

'You remind me of Ayesha, Gráinne. She deceived me, too.'

'I did not deceive you,' Gráinne hissed over

JD's shoulder.

'Not yet, but you would have. You saw too much, heard too much. I can't risk it. Unfortunately, your boy scout here is going down, too.' Wade looked at JD when he said, 'Sorry, garda. Can't be helped.'

'Wrong place, wrong time? Is that it?' JD asked.

'Something like that. For both of you.' Wade brought the rifle to his shoulder and aimed.

Gráinne stepped out from behind JD. 'Wait,' she said, holding up her hand.

'Gráinne, get back here,' called JD. His heart pounded in his chest like never before. She was going to get herself killed before he could come up with another plan to get them out of this.

Gráinne ignored him as she hobbled forward. 'Wait,' she said again, then stopped just a few yards in front of Wade, between the rifle and JD. JD's breath caught in his chest. If Wade fired now, Gráinne would take the bullet and die instantly.

'Gráinne,' he whispered frantically. He would have shouted, but he couldn't get enough air in his lungs to make the words come louder.

'Are you sure there's nothing I can do to change your mind, Mr. Wade?' he heard her ask. 'You did want something more from me before ... didn't you? After the dance, I mean.'

'Aye, I did. I may just take it before I kill you, anyway. What do you think about that?' Wade asked, cocking his head, brows drawn together in anger.

'B-but wouldn't it be a shame to waste what could be a good thing?' she continued. JD saw confusion stretch across Wade's face as she spoke.

'You know, I am attracted to you,' she said, stepping closer. 'I was only scared the other night. I shouldn't have run. I should have ... trusted you.'

'Gráinne,' JD cursed. What in the hell was she up to?

'If you let Garda Desmond go, I'll go with you and do whatever you want. I promise. Just don't hurt him.' Gráinne glanced over her shoulder quickly then back to Wade. 'He's only protecting me. It's his job. Do you think I want to be locked away like a prisoner up here on this godforsaken mountain? Take me out of here and I'll do whatever you want.'

She stepped up until the rifle was pressing into her breast. JD watched with horror as she lifted her fingers to the barrel and slowly pushed it away from her. She moved close enough to Wade to touch him. 'I'll do ... anything ... if you just get me off this mountain.'

JD's stomach roiled as Gráinne reached up and curled her fingers around Wade's neck and drew him down to her. She kissed him, showing him she meant business.

She was so convincing JD almost fell for her act, too. But he knew she loved him with every part of her being. She would never betray him. And hadn't she tried to draw Wade's fire when she ran away before? She'd tried saving him then, just as she was trying now.

When Gráinne pulled away from the kiss, JD saw Wade's eyes blink repeatedly, trying to focus.

'You're very convincing,' he said, his voice hoarse.

'I can convince you of a lot more,' she said,

343

stroking her fingers over his flak jacket and down the arm that held the rifle, pushing it down gently, 'if you let him go and take me home with you.'

'You backstabbing, self-serving, greedy bitch,' cried JD.

Gráinne glanced over her shoulder, her eyes full of sadness and love. Then they changed. The look of malice matched the timber of her voice. 'Be nice, garda, or I might let him kill you, anyway.' She turned back to Wade once more and looked into his eyes. For a moment, Wade broke his gaze with JD and looked down at Gráinne's as she rubbed her body against his.

JD's stomach threatened to erupt watching the woman he love prostituting herself this way. What would it accomplish, anyway? Even if Wade let him go, he'd take her with him. Then what? JD would lose her forever, and Gráinne would be subjecting herself to all manner of punishment from Wade. JD couldn't stand to think about what she'd suffer in order to save his life. He'd rather be dead than know she was going through that so he could live.

He took Wade's moment of distraction to leap into action, and raced forward. He could only hope to push Gráinne out of the way before he threw himself on Wade.

Wade caught his movement and quickly looked up, drawing the rifle around Gráinne, and fired.

JD felt fire race through him. It hit him like a brick as he ran, spinning him in a half circle. He stumbled but stayed to his feet and continued on. The next shot hit him in the shoulder on his other side, spinning him the other direction. This time, it stopped him in his tracks.

The power of the two shots pierced his body like hot branding irons. The pain was so intense it made him dizzy.

Looking down, he frowned at the amount of blood soaking his sweater. The dark stains stood out against the cream of the Aran wool.

When he looked up again, JD's vision swam. Everything around him skewed horizontally. He listed in the opposite direction to try and compensate but it only made things worse.

He saw Gráinne's fists at her mouth, heard her scream, but it sounded far off. She seemed to be spinning off into the distance. His vision darkened and blinking quickly did nothing to restore his sight.

The forest spun before him. He felt something impact him, hard, but he didn't see what it was. He only knew he was on his back, staring into the treetops, and rain was pelting him in the face.

Gráinne screamed again and struggled against Wade's grip. She wanted to go to JD's side and tell him she loved him, and that she was sorry for all of this. She wanted Wade to let JD go, not kill him.

Tears streamed down her face as she continued pulling herself out of Wade's grasp. When she was finally free, she stumbled back suddenly and nearly fell on top of JD. Scrambling on her bad ankle, she crawled to his side and threw her arms around him. His eyes were still open but unseeing.

'John!' she cried, clutching to his sweater. 'John!' Tears streamed down her cheek unchecked, loss ripping through her so painfully her body ached with the strain of her sobbing. She cried out his name over and over, apologizing at the same time. But he didn't hear her. He was dead.

Dead!

The reality of it was too much to bear. She threw her face against his blood-soaked jumper and hugged him to her.

Their time together had gone too fast. Just this morning, they'd made sweet love together. Neither had wanted to get out of bed, but it was only due to her own insistence that they get out of the cottage for a while and take a walk. If she'd only known how close Wade was, she never would have left the cottage. She much preferred the romance of being gunned down in bed, wrapped in her lover's arms, to being chased through the forest like a wild animal.

She spun around to face Wade. He stood cock-sure of himself. 'Damn you!' she spat violently. 'Damn you to hell!'

Wade just laughed as he strode over to her. He grasped her by the arm and hauled her against him. 'Now, tell me more about doing whatever I wanted to save your life.'

'It was to save his life you scumbag.' She spat in his face. He wiped it away with his sleeve before backhanding her away from him with a loud smack. She fell to the ground beside JD, her shoulder slamming into his side. She heard a whoosh of air escape his lungs, but he still didn't move.

She couldn't look at him anymore. His eyes

were closed. He couldn't see her. There was no love left in his whiskey-colored gaze and it tore at her heart.

As much as she hated to admit it, if she were going to survive this, she'd have to leave JD's body behind and run for her life. Damn the pain in her ankle. Her chest hurt worse, negating any other pain in her body.

Rising quickly, she rushed Wade and knocked him off balance. He was reloading his weapon. The spare clip went flying into the prickly gorse. He landed hard on his back.

Gráinne righted herself and took off at a full run down the path JD had led her up just minutes before. She didn't know where she was going, just that she had to make her way down the hill as fast as possible, to find anyone who could help her.

She didn't dare look back as she ran. It would only slow her up. Pain shot up her leg from her ankle, but she struggled to ignore it. Her ankle would heal eventually. She couldn't get her life back.

Before she could reach a point in the hillside where she could descend, Wade was upon her. He threw his body into her, slamming them both to the ground. She struggled to throw him off but he was too heavy, too strong. He had her on her back in seconds.

In her struggle, she managed to catch her knee in his groin. He doubled up with pain and she took the opportunity to roll out from under him. She crawled on her knees, clawing at the earth in her effort to get away, but he grabbed her bad ankle and pulled her back to him. She cried out in pain and fear.

He was on top of her again. This time, he drew his dagger and held it to her throat.

'Kill me!' she shouted. 'Get it over with.'

'All things in their good time, bitch, but first we're going to talk about all those pretty things you promised me.' His voice was coarse and full of venom, his mouth spitting as he spoke. Sweat dripped off his brow.

With the thick blade held to her jugular, Wade drove his fist under her sweater and roughly grasped her breast. She cried out in pain.

'Ah, that's it,' he crooned.

Gráinne's stomach turned over. 'I'm going to be sick,' she told him.

'No, you won't,' he ordered. 'You'll do exactly as I say, and your death will be a quick one. Struggle, and I'll make you suffer for hours until you're begging me to take your life.'

'I'm begging now. Kill me, damn you. I'm going to die either way, so just get it over with.' Sobs tore through her, hoping the end would come quickly. She wouldn't be able to live without JD, and knowing she'd caused his death.

Wade laughed heartily. 'Oh, no, my little bird. We can't have that. I want you alive when I take you. I'm going to slit your throat as I fill your dying body.'

A terrified gasp choked the breath from her. How she wished she could turn back the hands of time to the day she'd decided to take the job at The Klub!. She knew her life would have turned out differently. She never would have met JD, but at least he'd be alive.

With the realization of what was going to happen to her and knowing she couldn't escape, Gráinne's body relaxed as she slipped into shock.

She was only vaguely aware of Wade's sloppy kisses up her neck, that he'd used his knife to rip her sweater up the front, and how he ground his groin against her womb. Just let him get it over with so she could get on with dying.

Far off in the distance there was a muffled whomp-whomp-whomp, and in the back of her clouded mind she wondered if his chopper was returning to pick him up. The forest around her spun like water down a drain as darkness threatened to close in on her.

Wade's heavy body on her struggled a bit then was gone, and everything went still. She thought she heard crunching beside her but couldn't turn to see what it was. Everything was muffled so she couldn't be sure of anything she heard, as the last of her vision faded.

'I-I thought I killed you.'

'I thought you did, too,' slurred JD. 'Now it's my turn to put you out of commission.' With that, he lifted the rifle and slammed the butt of it against Wade's temple again.

JD heard something overhead and looked up to see what it was. Bad mistake. His head swam, causing him to fall back. He landed on his arse in the dirt. He blinked hard to stay conscious. He had to get to Gráinne.

He dropped the rifle and crawled over to her.

'Gráinne, love,' he whispered. She stared unseeing. He checked for a pulse. It was there but weak. She was in shock and unresponsive, but she was alive. Thank God!

A quick look back to Wade confirmed the man wasn't going anywhere. JD collapsed beside Gráinne and pressed his body against hers to keep her warm. He threw his arm around her.

'I've got you, love. I've got you,' he said, before he passed out again.

When Gráinne woke, she was in the cottage. She was in bed with the blankets pulled up to her chin. Bright light spilled through the tiny window.

Had it all been a bad dream?

Wiggling her ankle confirmed her worst nightmares. It hadn't been a dream. It was all too real. But how did she get back to the cottage? And, lifting the blankets, she wondered how she had been put to bed naked.

Laughter spilled from the other room. JD's laughter. He was alive! She had to go to him.

Rising carefully from the bed, she hobbled to the door. Her heart filled to overflowing, tears of joy bubbled uncontrollably through her aching body and choked on her sobs. He was alive. Alive!

She flung the door open and stepped into the living room. She stopped in her tracks at what was before her.

JD sat at the small table at the back of the room. He wore a pair of dark trousers and was bare-chested, except for the thick bandages on his shoulder and side. He looked up suddenly, his eyes wide. She smiled brightly and started toward him.

'Damn, you're skinny,' came a deep voice off to her left. A familiar deep voice. Without looking, she squeezed her eyes closed and lowered her head.

Then there was a pair of cool hands on her bare shoulders, turning her around.

'Leave the poor girl alone, Kieran. She's had a hard enough time without you teasing her. Come love, let's get you back to bed,' said Eilis.

Gráinne glanced up and saw laughter dancing in her sister-in-law's eyes. Her brother's face, when she shifted her gaze, twitched but he held his tongue. She could tell he wanted to say something about her naked state, remind her it hadn't been so long ago he'd been standing where she was now, but he held his tongue. He'd be all the better for it as long as he did.

The instant the bedroom door closed behind her and Eilis, the men burst out laughing, followed by JD's hollering in pain. 'Oh, ow, that hurts,' he cried.

Gráinne grunted through the headache pressing at the back of her head. Serves him right.

'Come, pet, let's get you back to bed.' Eilis started turning her toward the bed, but she put her hand up to stop when she heard Kieran speak again. She pressed her ear to the crack in the old door to hear them better.

'Well, by the looks of her, you know I have to ask. Did you sleep on the sofa?' Kieran asked.

'Yes,' JD replied. Gráinne grinned. Well, he had. They'd made love everywhere in the cottage, including the bed, but he'd never slept in it.

'Did you sleep with my sister?' Gráinne's

cheeks flamed with embarrassment. Her brother didn't need to know the intimate details of her life. But he'd also raised her like a father, so she supposed the question was a valid one.

'Yes.'

'You going to marry her?'

'Yeah.'

'Have you asked her yet?'

'No.'

'Are you going to?'

'Yeah.'

'When?'

'Soon.'

'How soon?

'Soon.'

'Okay.'

'Okay?'

'Yeah. More coffee?'

Gráinne would have laughed if her head wasn't pounding. She let Eilis steer her back to bed and put her under the covers.

When she was tucked in again, Eilis sat on the bedside and looked down at her.

'I suppose you're going to have a go off me now about what just happened,' she said. Gráinne couldn't meet Eilis's gaze.

'Why would I?' replied Eilis.

Yes, why would she? After all, Eilis was the one who'd encouraged Gráinne to give JD a chance.

She looked at her sister-in-law. 'What happened ... out there?' She referred to the mountainside.

'I think that's something JD should tell you.' Gráinne just nodded. 'Is there anything you want to talk about? Seems like a lot has changed since

I saw you last.'

'Aye, it has,' replied Gráinne, her thoughts going back to the last few days she'd spent at the cottage with JD. 'Do you suppose this place is magical?' she asked Eilis, looking into her kind eyes.

'Why do you ask?'

'Well, Kieran brought you here pretty much against your will, and by the time you left you were head over heels with each other,' remarked Gráinne.

'Can I assume you're head over heels with JD then?' Eilis asked, grinning.

'Aye,' Gráinne sighed. 'Oh, aye.'

Chapter Twenty-Seven

One month later, February

Gráinne had left JD sitting on the sofa in the living room, on the pretense of going to make them both tea.

While she changed in the tiny bathroom in the extension off the kitchen, memories of the last month flitted through her mind.

Things had moved quickly after their rescue. JD told her he had come to not long after she'd run from Wade. Evidently, Wade had tried shooting her while she ran but, since he'd been in the process of reloading when she knocked the clip out of his hand, the rifle was empty. He'd thrown it down to chase after her. JD had picked it up. Bullets or not, it was a great weapon. He'd used it to knock Wade unconscious before he collapsed at her side.

The whomp noise she'd heard before she blacked out had been a rescue chopper. JD had convinced them she'd only fainted, which she had, and his wounds were only superficial. The first bullet had grazed his shoulder. The other grazed his side. The pain was so intense he'd blacked out, but only for a few minutes.

Paramedics bandaged him up and helped them back to the cottage, where Kieran and Eilis were waiting. They'd taken another chopper down from Dublin and the guards had picked them up to take them to the cottage.

It was miraculous the emergency operator had heard anything JD said to her, with such bad reception, but she was a frequent visitor of the Blues Tavern and all she had to hear was 'Vaughan' and 'Tavern' and she knew who to call for accurate directions. JD had seen both Mag and Mary commended for their speedy work.

JD had received a promotion at work, too. Capturing the infamous Taylor Wade was big news. He'd become a celebrity in his own right, though the fame was fading now that time was going by and Wade was incarcerated. He would be kept behind bars without bail until his hearing. No doubt, he would spend the rest of his life in prison.

JD's promotion came in the form of a captain's badge. He was asked to head the department's task force on drugs. To Gráinne's amazement, he turned down the offer. He told her he refused the job because he didn't want to run the risk of getting himself killed. He had a life with her to look forward to. If it meant taking a desk job, he'd do it. Instead, she'd convinced him to stay on the Force with his old job and the higher pay of captain. JD said he could live with that.

While JD still hadn't asked her to marry him, Gráinne knew he would eventually. Hadn't he told Kieran as much back in the cottage? He'd asked her to move in with him, and that was good enough for now. They had agreed to live in her place, as it was bigger and had been the house she'd grown up in, the place where Kieran had cared for her when their parents died. It was where she wanted to raise her own children, even if it was farther away from school than she would have liked.

John owned the house he'd lived in. Once he'd moved out, Mystique moved in. Or rather, Michele. By some miracle, she had survived Wade's beating, and after everything that happened at The Klub! she had decided to get out. Gráinne found a wonderful friend in Michele and couldn't wait to spend more time with her now they'd both shed their disguises.

Michele told Gráinne she'd been doing some thinking of her own and had decided going back to school was a great idea. With all the money she'd made at The Klub! she'd need to learn how to manage it, especially now she was working a regular job, so she'd enrolled in a business class.

Gráinne had convinced Kieran to give Michele a job at the pub. Since Gráinne was going to start classes soon, they'd split the shift. On top of that, Eilis had given birth to their first child, a boy they'd named Kieran James, and was taking a leave from work. So he'd practically need a new staff to cover all the sudden vacancies.

Those vacancies included the need of a new bartender as well, since JD had only been there undercover. Kieran hired a nice guy named Russell who just happened to be sweet on Michele.

Kieran had groaned loudly when he found out. 'Just what I need. Another barroom romance.' Gráinne just laughed. She was thrilled for her friend.

And herself? After long hard thought, and some discussions with JD, Gráinne decided to look into archaeology courses. She'd take music classes for recreation, but she rather fancied being what JD termed 'the dirt doctor.'

She didn't know if she could stick out so many years of school in order to get her doctorate, but she sure as hell was going to give it a try. Whether or not she actually got it, at least she would give it her best. That's all she could do.

Gráinne didn't think her life could be anymore perfect. She was going to school, she and Michele were becoming fast friends, she had a nephew to spoil, and she was starting a new life with a man she never thought to love so much in her wildest dreams. Just the thought of him was enough to squeeze her insides.

She glanced toward the kitchen through the bathroom door, as she fluffed her hair. She'd told JD she was making tea. She'd even gone through the motions of filling the kettle and getting cups down from the press. Then she'd escaped to the bathroom to change.

Her life was perfect. And she wanted tonight to be perfect, too.

She stepped from the bathroom and switched off the light.

'Switch on the CD, will you, John?' she called through the door.

'Yeah, okay,' he called back. 'Bring me a biscuit when you come in.'

'Sure thing,' she replied, grinning and grabbing a biscuit from the press.

When the music started, violins filled the living room. Gráinne had chosen Etta James' *At Last*, as it spoke what was in her heart.

Now, stepping through the door, she saw JD sitting where she'd left him on the sofa. He was leaning back against the cushions, his long legs parted at the knees, his nose buried in the sports section of an old newspaper.

'Here's your biscuit,' she said softly, tossing it at him. It hit the newspaper and dropped to the floor. When he bent to pick it up, he saw her and the paper fell away.

Gráinne swayed her body to the violins as she moved toward him. Earlier, she'd moved the coffee table to the side of the room so she had all the space she needed for this private dance. She had no need of a pole or a long runway as she danced for the man she loved. Gone was her disguise. She danced for him as herself, Gráinne Vaughan. She left her hair down, wore only the simplest of make-up, and had put on the new teddy she'd bought earlier in the day.

When she'd seen it, she knew it would be perfect. It was a short little number made of sheer flesh-colored material, edged with delicate matching lace.

The teddy had come with a thong, but Gráinne refused to wear it. She didn't think she ever wanted to see another thong as long as she lived. Instead, she'd found a sexy pair of bikini panties in the same shade as the teddy. They were high cut over her hip and made her legs look longer. There was a small pink bow embellishment in the center back. She liked how they were held up, not with elastic but by string ties at her hips.

While she'd stood at the register waiting to pay, she'd spotted the rack of hosiery. The shop assistant helped her choose a pair that fitted just right and were in the same color as the teddy. The stockings were held up by a snug lacy band around her thigh and made her legs look even sexier.

She felt very girly in the ensemble, but more importantly, she knew JD would love it on her. Not that she expected to stay in it very long.

The flowing material of the teddy floated around her as she swayed to the music before him. She ran her fingers through her hair then continued to stroke a path down over her breasts and down her hips. She gazed deeply into JD's eyes. Desire rippled through her body as she moved closer to him. She mouthed the words of the song as she swayed closer to him.

At last, my love has come along

In front of him now, she bent, unfastened his jeans and slid them, and his briefs, off.

Rising slowly, she swayed as she spun around, slowly gyrating her bottom in his direction before pulling the teddy's hem up over one hip. She glanced over one shoulder to JD, who sat with his mouth open. With just her finger and thumb, she pulled the bow loose and the side of the panties came apart. Then turning, she repeated the motion until the garment was lying on the floor.

Slowly, so slowly, she ran her hands down the length of one leg and back up again to give him a glimpse of her bare bottom. When she rose, she turned to face him once more, pleased to see his erection. It stood away from him, long and hard, ready and waiting.

Etta's voice faded and James Brown's voice

picked up, singing It's a Man's World.

It wouldn't be nothing without a woman or a girl

She swayed gently to this new music as she moved closer to JD. When she reached him, she didn't stop dancing until she was straddling his hips, his erection bobbing against her heated center.

She arched her body onto his and roughly pulled his shirt apart, the buttons flying every which way. The soft sheer teddy was the only barrier between them as she rubbed her breasts against his chest. His fine chest hairs poked through the fabric and tickled her. Her nipples peaked instantly at the sensation.

Leaning forward, she grasped him in her hand as she closed the gap between them and kissed him. She nipped and sucked his lips softly until they parted then slipped her tongue into his warmth.

His erection pulsed in her hand as she stroked him. She felt the moisture on the tip and knew he was ready. Without breaking their kiss, she rose slightly and positioned him under her. Then, ever so slowly, she slid onto him. He groaned deeply into her mouth when she finally had him buried to the hilt. She felt him swell even more as she rose and fell against him.

His arms went around her. His hands found their way under the material and flattened against the length of her back, holding her to him.

When his hands came around to her breasts, she leaned away to give him better access. He pinched and rolled her nipples between a finger and thumb.

He pulled the teddy away from her breasts and

replaced his fingers with his mouth and suckled her. His fingers pressed into the flesh of her hips and guided her movements. The feeling of him inside made her tingle, until all sensation seemed to culminate in her womb. She'd already been hot and wet for him; the moment he entered her, his shaft was instantly slick with her moisture, heightening both of their passion.

As the song neared the end, Gráinne felt JD pulsing hard inside her and quickened her hips.

They came together, both crying out until they collapsed against the sofa, breathless.

JD hugged Gráinne to him as he blinked back the moisture in his eyes. His orgasm had been so intense it brought him to tears. He buried his face in her breasts and held her close. Her arms went around his shoulders; her fingers buried in his hair. He heard her heart pounding in time with this own.

His love for Gráinne knew no bounds. He thought he'd lost her up on that mountain last month. He had thought he was dying from the bullet wounds he'd taken for her. He didn't know where he found the strength, but something had driven him to get up, to pick up that rifle, and find Gráinne. He hadn't been himself when he pummeled Wade into the dirt.

He hadn't said anything to anyone, but he didn't remember hitting Wade. One minute the man was kneeling before Gráinne, fumbling with his fly, the next moment he was sprawled across the forest floor. But something within JD had a satisfied feeling at what he'd done. The shock of it made him drop the rifle. Then he'd seen Gráinne on the ground and everything else around him had disappeared.

Looking up now, he stroked the hair away from Gráinne's face and gazed into her sea-washed eyes. They shimmered from her orgasm. Her cheeks were lightly flushed and her lips kiss-swollen. He loved how he put that impassioned look on her face. He would again, over and over until they were old and gray.

'Marry me, Gráinne,' he said softly.

Gráinne looked at him. Her gaze darted back and forth, her lips twitching, probably wondering if he were daft or not.

'Marry me. Be my wife. Have my children. Make love to me every night,' he prattled on. 'I want you in my life forever. I don't want to live another day without you.'

'Oh, John,' she sighed, falling against him. She hugged him tightly, rocking him in her arms. He was still deeply imbedded within her, his emotions stirring his flesh again.

He pulled her away from him and met her gaze. 'Say yes, love. Say you'll be with me, just like this, as we are now, forever. Be my wife.' He rose up and kissed her softly. 'Say yes,' he whispered into her mouth.

'Yes,' she sighed against him. 'Yes.'

Joy overflowed in his heart just as his erection swelled inside her. He had to make love to her again. It was an instant, raging need, as if to seal her promise.

He wrapped his arms around her and was about to lift her in his arms and carry her upstairs where he'd make love to her properly in bed – their bed – when the phone rang.

'Don't answer it,' she said into his mouth as she kissed him, arching her hips over him, stroking him.

The phone continued ringing.

'I have to, love. It could be work,' he told her through clenched teeth. She felt so good. She was so hot and slick, but he had to hold back until she was ready, too.

'Please, John, make love to me.'

JD buried his tongue in her mouth and deepened her kiss, yet the phone kept calling to him, drawing his attention.

'Damn it,' he cursed. 'I have to get it. They won't leave us alone until I do.'

Gráinne sat back but didn't move away from him. He leaned over, picked up the phone, and pressed the answer button. 'What?' JD made no pretense at hiding his irritation.

Kieran chuckled on the other end of the line. 'Is that any way to greet your soon-to-be brother-in-law?'

'What do you want?'

'I just called to see if you asked her yet.'

Damn Kieran and his ill-timed nosiness.

'Well?' he pressed.

'Well, what?'

'Did you ask her?'

'Yes.'

'What did she say?'

'Yes.' JD pushed the phone into the cushion beside him as he tossed his head back, trying to catch his breath. Gráinne rose up against him so sweetly. He wanted nothing more than to throw her onto the floor and drive himself into her until they were both sated.

When he brought the phone back to his ear, he heard Kieran telling Eilis Gráinne had accepted his proposal.

'So, when's the big day?' Kieran continued.

'We haven't talked about that yet.' JD wondered if there was a way to tell Kieran to bugger off and leave him alone without jeopardizing their relationship.

'Let us know when you pick a date. Eilis said she'd love to help Gráinne plan the shower. We can hold the reception at the pub.'

'Fine.' The words came out on a carefully controlled exhale.

There was brief silence on the other end of the phone, then Kieran asked, 'Did I call at a bad time?'

'Just a little.' It was hard to concentrate with Gráinne riding him. She rose and fell against him agonizingly slowly, her inner muscles tightening as she rose. Her eyes were filled with desire. The way she licked her lips like that made him groan aloud.

'You – you two aren't ... you're not having sex while I'm talking to you on the phone, are you?' Kieran exclaimed.

'As a matter of fact,' JD started, but was cut off when he heard Kieran call to Eilis.

'Hey, Ei, JD and Gráinne are having sex while I'm on the phone with him!'

JD heard a loud feminine gasp on Kieran's end. 'My God, Kieran. Hang up, then.'

'Damn, JD. Must be really hard to concentrate on the conversation,' Kieran laughed.

'A ... little,' gasped JD. If he didn't concentrate a little better, Gráinne was going to make him come before he was ready. 'Do you mind if we finish this a little later?'

'Sure, no problem. Oh, by the way,' Kieran continued anyway. 'Are you coming to the christening tomorrow?'

JD cursed under his breath. Damn the man. He knew he and Gráinne wouldn't miss the christening. Kieran was enjoying tormenting JD like this.

'Don't know, Kier. Ask Gráinne,' he suggested.

'Sure, put her on.'

JD handed Gráinne the phone. 'It's Kieran. He wants to know if we're going to the christening tomorrow. I told him to ask you.'

Gráinne grabbed the phone from him, said yes into the receiver then disconnected the call before slamming the mobile down on the table.

'God, I love you,' he groaned, pulling her to him. Gráinne drove her tongue between his lips to tangle with his.

'Prove it,' she challenged him between kisses. 'Throw me on the floor and prove it.'

JD chuckled heartily and did just that.

The publishers hope that this book has given you enjoyable reading. Large Print Books are especially designed to be as easy to see and hold as possible. If you wish a complete list of our books please ask at your local library or write directly to:

Magna Large Print Books
Magna House, Long Preston,
Skipton, North Yorkshire.
BD23 4ND

This Large Print Book for the partially
sighted, who cannot read normal print, is
published under the auspices of

THE ULVERSCROFT FOUNDATION